D0169527

THE
SILENT
SISTER

diane
chamberlain

St. Martin's Paperbacks

This is a work of fiction. All of the characters, organizations, and events portrayed in this novel are either products of the author's imagination or are used fictitiously.

THE SILENT SISTER

Copyright © 2014 by Diane Chamberlain.
Excerpt from *The Dream Daughter* © 2017 by Diane Chamberlain.

All rights reserved.

For information address St. Martin's Press, 175 Fifth Avenue, New York, NY 10010.

ISBN: 978-1-250-13065-5

Printed in the United States of America

St. Martin's Press hardcover edition / October 2014
St. Martin's Paperbacks edition / July 2018

St. Martin's Paperbacks are published by St. Martin's Press, 175 Fifth Avenue, New York, NY 10010.

10 9 8 7 6 5 4 3 2 1

Praise for
THE SILENT SISTER

"Chamberlain's powerful story is a page-turner to the very end." —*Library Journal*

"A story of redemption, paranoia, and the power of shared bonds, *The Silent Sister* is a powerful and thrilling novel. Chamberlain has a flair for the dramatic, immersing the reader in the frustrating, foundation-shaking process of Riley's discovery. This tautly paced and emotionally driven novel will engross Chamberlain's many fans as well as those who read Sandra Brown and Carla Buckley." —*Booklist*

"Hard to put down." —*Better Homes & Gardens*

"The readers of this tale will be surprised and shocked by the unveiling of a truth that they will never guess up front. Chamberlain has written an excellent novel with well-thought-out plotlines that never lose the suspense lover's interest for one solitary second." —*Suspense Magazine*

"A tense story with plenty of twists . . . Riley's world gets rocked and the readers' will be too." —*The Parkersburg News and Sentinel*

"This story had so many amazing twists and turns that I felt like I was right alongside Riley on her adventure to find her sister. And the way everything unraveled and came back together had me turning pages late into the night." —Tara Hans in *First for Women*

JANUARY 1990

PROLOGUE

Alexandria, Virginia

All day long, people stopped along the path that ran through the woods by the Potomac River. Bundled in their parkas and wool scarves, they stood close to one another for warmth and clutched the mittened hands of their children or the leashes of their dogs as they stared at the one splash of color in the winter-gray landscape. The yellow kayak sat in the middle of the river, surrounded by ice. The water had been rough the night before, buffeted by snowy winds, rising into swirling whitecaps as the temperature plummeted and the waves froze in jagged crests, trapping the kayak many yards from shore.

The walkers had seen the kayak on the morning news, but they still needed to see it in person. It marked the end of a saga that had gripped them for months. They'd looked forward to the trial that would never happen now, because the seventeen-year-old girl—the seventeen-year-old murderer, *most were sure—now rested somewhere beneath that rocky expanse of ice.*

She took the easy way out, *some of them whispered to one another.*

But what a terrible way to die, *others said.*

They looked at the rocky bank of the river and wondered if she'd put some of those rocks in her pockets to make herself sink. They wondered if she'd cried as she paddled the kayak into the water, knowing the end was near. She'd cried on TV, for certain. Faking it, *some of them said now as they moved on down the path. It was too cold to stand in one spot for very long.*

But there was one woman, bundled warm, gloved hands in her pockets, who stood at the side of the path for hours. She watched as the news chopper collected fresh aerial images, its blades a deafening dark blur against the gray sky. She watched as the police milled along the banks of the river, pointing in one direction and then the other as they considered how they'd retrieve the kayak from the ice . . . and how they would search for the girl's body beneath it.

The woman looked at the police again. They stood with their hands on their hips now, as though they were giving up. This case was closed. She pulled her jacket more tightly around herself. Let them give up, *she thought, pleased, as she watched a police officer shrug his shoulders in what looked like defeat.* Let them wrest that kayak from the river and call it a day.

Although a yellow kayak stranded in ice proved nothing.

They were fools if they thought it did.

PART ONE

JUNE 2013

1.

Riley

I'd never expected to lose nearly everyone I loved by the time I was twenty-five.

I felt the grief rise again as I parked in front of the small, nondescript post office in Pollocksville. The three-hour drive from my apartment in Durham had seemed more like six as I made a mental list of all the things I needed to do once I reached New Bern, and that list segued into thinking of how alone I felt. But I didn't have time to dwell on my sadness.

The first thing I had to do was stop at this post office, ten miles outside of New Bern. I'd get that out of the way and cross one thing off my list. Digging the flimsy white postcard from my purse, I went inside the building. I was the only customer, and my tennis shoes squeaked on the floor as I walked up to the counter where a clerk waited for me. With her dark skin and perfect cornrows, she reminded me of my friend Sherise, so I liked her instantly.

"How can I help you?" she asked.

I handed her the postcard. "I'm confused about this card," I said. "My father died a month ago. I've been getting his mail at my address in Durham and this card came and—"

"We send these out when someone hasn't paid their bill for their post office box," she said, looking at the card. "It's a warning. They don't pay it in two months, we close the box and change the lock."

"Well, I understand that, but see"—I turned the card over—"this isn't my father's name. I don't know who Fred Marcus is. My father was Frank MacPherson, so I think this came to me by mistake. I don't even think my father *had* a post office box. I don't know why he would. Especially not in Pollocksville when he lives—*lived*—in New Bern." It would take me a long time to learn to speak about my father in the past tense.

"Let me check." She disappeared into the rear of the building and came back a moment later holding a thin purple envelope and a white index-type card. "This is the only thing in the box," she said, handing the envelope to me. "Addressed to Fred Marcus. I checked the records and the box is assigned to that name at this street address." She held the index card out to me. The signature did look like my father's handwriting, but his handwriting was hardly unique. And besides, it wasn't his name.

"That's the right street address, but whoever this guy is, he must have written his address down wrong," I said, slipping the purple envelope into my purse.

"You want me to close the box or you want to pay to keep it open?" the clerk asked.

"I don't feel like it's mine to close, but I'm not going to pay for it, so . . ." I shrugged.

"I'll close it, then," she said.

"All right." I was glad she'd made the decision for me. I smiled. "I hope Fred Marcus doesn't mind, whoever he is." I turned toward the door.

"Sorry about your daddy," she said.

"Thanks," I said over my shoulder, and my eyes stung by the time I got to my car.

Driving into New Bern, I passed through the historic district. Old houses were packed close together on the tree-lined streets and gigantic painted bears, the town's iconic symbol, stood here and there among the shops. A pair of bicycle cops pedaled down the street in front of me, lightening my mood ever so slightly. Although I hadn't lived in New Bern since I went away to college, it still had a hometown pull on me. It was such a unique little place.

I turned onto Craven Street and pulled into our driveway. Daddy's car was in the garage. I could see its roof through the glass windows—one of them broken—of the garage door. I hadn't thought about his car. Was it better to sell it or donate it? I had an appointment with his attorney in the morning and I'd add that question to my ever-growing list. The car should really go to my brother, Danny, to replace his ancient junker, but I had the feeling he'd turn it down.

My old house was a two-story pastel yellow Victorian in need of fresh paint, with a broad front porch adorned with delicate white railings and pillars. It was the only house I could remember living in, and I loved it. Once I sold it, I'd have no reason to come to New Bern again. I'd taken those visits home to see my father for granted. After Daddy's sudden death, I came back for two days to arrange for his cremation and attend to other details that were now a blur in my memory. Had he wanted to be cremated? We'd never talked about that sort of thing and I'd been in such a state of shock and confusion that I couldn't think straight. Bryan had been with me then, a calming, loving presence. He'd pointed out that my mother'd been cremated, so that would most likely be my father's wish as well. I hoped he was right.

Sitting in my car in the driveway, I wondered if I'd been too hasty in ending it with Bryan. I could have used his support right now. With Daddy gone and Sherise doing mission work in Haiti for the summer, the timing couldn't have been worse. There was no good time, though, for ending a two-year-old relationship.

The loneliness weighed on my shoulders as I got out of my car and looked up at the house. My plan had been to take two weeks to clean it out and then put it—and the nearby RV park my father owned—on the market. Suddenly, as I looked at all the windows and remembered how many things were in need of repair and how little my father liked to throw things away, I knew my time frame was unrealistic. Daddy hadn't been a hoarder, exactly, but he was a collector. He had cases full of vintage lighters and pipes and old musical instruments, among zillions of other things I would have to get rid of. Bryan said our house was more like a dusty old museum than a home, and he'd been right. I tried not to panic as I pulled my duffel bag from the backseat of my car. I had no one waiting for me in Durham and the summer off. I could take as much time as I needed to get the house ready to sell. I wondered if there was any chance of getting Danny to help me.

I climbed the broad front steps to the porch and unlocked the door. It squeaked open with a sound as familiar to me as my father's voice. I'd pulled the living room shades before I'd left back in May and I could barely see across the living room to the kitchen beyond. I breathed in the hot musty smell of a house closed up too long as I raised the shades to let in the midday light. Turning the thermostat to seventy-two, I heard the welcome sound of the old air conditioner kicking to life. Then I stood in the middle of the room, hands on my hips, as I examined the space from the perspective of someone tasked with cleaning it out.

Daddy had used the spacious living room as something of an office, even though he had a good-sized office upstairs as well. He loved desks and cubbies and display cases. The desk in the living room was a beautiful old rolltop. Against the far wall, custom-built shelves surrounding the door to the kitchen held his classical music collection, nearly all of it vinyl, and a turntable sat in a special cabinet he'd had built into the wall. On the north side of the room, a wide glass-fronted display case contained his pipe collection. The room always had a faint smell of tobacco to me, even though he'd told me that was my imagination. Against the opposite wall, there was a couch at least as old as I was along with an upholstered armchair. The rest of the space was taken up by the baby grand piano I'd never learned to play. Danny and I had both taken lessons, but neither of us had any interest and our parents let us quit. People would say, *They're Lisa's siblings. Surely they have talent. Why don't you push them?* But they never did and I was grateful.

Walking into the dining room, I was struck by how neat and orderly it appeared to be compared to the rest of the house. My father had no need for that room and I was sure he rarely set foot in it. The dining room had been my mother's territory. The wide curio cabinet was full of china and vases and cut-glass bowls that had been handed down through her family for generations. Things she'd treasured that I was going to have to figure out how to get rid of. I ran my fingers over the dusty sideboard. Everywhere I turned in the house, I'd be confronted by memories I would need to dismantle.

I carried my duffel bag upstairs, where a wide hallway opened to four rooms. The first was my father's bedroom with its quilt-covered queen-sized bed. The second room had been Danny's, and although he hadn't slept in our house since leaving at eighteen—*escaping,* he would call it—it would always be "Danny's room" to me. The third room was mine, though in the years since I'd lived in the house, the room had developed an austere air about it. I'd cleaned out my personal possessions bit by bit after college. The memorabilia from my high school and college years—pictures of old boyfriends, yearbooks, CDs, that sort of thing—were in a box in the storage unit of my Durham apartment waiting for the day I got around to sorting through them.

I dropped my duffel bag on my bed, then walked into the fourth room—my father's office. Daddy's bulky old computer monitor rested on a small desk by the window, and glass-fronted curio cabinets filled with Zippo lighters and antique compasses lined two of the walls. My grandfather had been a collector, too, so Daddy'd inherited many of the items, then added to them by searching through Craigslist and eBay and flea markets. The collections had been his obsession. I knew the sliding glass doors to the cabinets were locked and hoped I'd be able to find where my father had squirreled away the keys.

Propped against the fourth wall of the room were five violin cases. Daddy hadn't played, but he'd collected stringed instruments for as long as I could remember. One of the cases had an ID tag hanging from the handle, and I knelt next to it, lifting the tag in my hand.

It had been a long time since I'd looked at that tag, but I knew what was on it: a drawing of a violet on one side and on the other side, my sister's name—*Lisa MacPherson*—and our old Alexandria, Virginia, address. Lisa had never lived in this house.

My mother died shortly after I graduated from high school, so although I would never stop missing her, I was used to her being gone. It was strange to be in the house without Daddy, though. As I put my clothes in my dresser, I kept expecting him to walk into the room and I had trouble accepting the fact that it was impossible. I missed our weekly phone calls and knowing he was only a few hours away. He'd been so easy to talk to and I'd always felt his unconditional love. It was a terrible feeling to know that there wasn't a soul in the world now who loved me that deeply.

He'd been a quiet man. Maybe one of the quietest people to ever walk the earth. He questioned rather than told. He'd ask me all about my own life, but rarely shared anything about his own. As a middle school counselor, I was the one always asking the questions and I'd enjoyed being asked for a change, knowing that the man doing the asking cared deeply about my answers. He was a loner, though. He'd died on the floor of the Food Lion after a massive heart attack. He'd been alone and that bothered me more than anything.

Bryan had suggested I have a memorial service for him, but I wouldn't have known who to invite. If he had any friends, I didn't know about them. Unlike most people in New Bern, my father hadn't belonged to a church or any community organization, and I was certain my brother wouldn't show up at a service for him. His relationship with our father had been very different from mine. I hadn't even been able to *find* Danny when I got to New Bern after Daddy's death. His cop friend Harry Washington told me he'd gone to Danny's trailer to give him the news, and I guess Danny just took off. He'd left his car parked next to the trailer, and Bryan and I hiked through the forest looking for him, but Danny knew those woods better than anyone. He had his hiding places. Now, though, he had no idea I was in town, so this time I'd surprise him. I'd plead with him to help me with the house. I knew better than to hope he'd say yes.

2.

Danny had no phone, so there was no way to reach him other than to drive out to his trailer. He lived deep in the woods on the outskirts of my father's RV park about ten miles from New Bern. As I turned onto the long narrow driveway leading into Mac's RV Park, the woods hugged my car so tightly I wondered how motor homes ever made it down the road. I reached the lane that ran parallel to the creek. The park was down the gravel lane to the right, but I turned left onto a rutted dirt road that would take me to Danny's trailer. I slowed way down, my teeth clacking against each other as my car bounced over the choppy peaks and valleys of the packed earth.

I came to the turnoff that led into the woods and made another left. The road here was barely more than a hiking trail. Someone would have to be looking for it to see it, and that was the way Danny liked it. Branches slapped against my windshield as I drove over rocks and tree roots. The few hundred feet to get to Danny's trailer always felt like an eternity on this road.

I finally spotted a glint of metal through the trees and I steeled myself for what lay ahead. Which Danny would I meet today? The affectionate big brother whose smile masked his sadness, or the angry, bitter man who could scare me with his fury? Either way, I hated that I was a counselor but I couldn't seem to help my own brother.

Driving forward again, I turned into the clearing. The trees formed an emerald-green cavern around the pine-needle-covered earth, and between Danny's small, ancient Airstream, his old Subaru, and the hammock strung beneath two of the towering longleaf pines, there was barely enough room for me to park. I'd brought him a couple of bags of groceries and I looped them over my wrist as I got out of the car and walked toward the trailer.

Danny opened the door as I got closer.

"Hey, Danny." I smiled brightly.

"Hey," he said. "I wondered when you'd show up." His expression was flat and hard to read, but there was a spark in his eyes that comforted me. He'd always been a good-looking guy and he still was, his messy collar-length hair a darker blond than it had been when we were kids and his pale blue eyes vivid against his tanned skin. He was too thin, his face all sharp angles and flat planes. I was glad, though, to see that his short beard was neatly trimmed. During the worst times, he let it grow long and scraggly. I'd come to see his beard as an indicator of how he was doing.

"I stopped by right after Daddy died," I said, "but I couldn't find you."

"And that surprised you?"

Okay, I thought. *The angry Danny today.*

I held up the bags. "I brought you some food and cigarettes." I'd bought some fruit for him—peaches and a melon and a pint of strawberries—but one whole bag was filled with the boxed macaroni and cheese he loved along with the Marlboros. I long ago gave up trying to make my brother into a healthy eater. Making him happy was more important to me. I'd stopped short at buying him booze. I was sure he had plenty of that already.

I reached up to hand him the bags and he took them from me, stepping back to let me in. As always, I yearned to reach out and hug him as I climbed into the trailer, but sometime over the years, our hugging had stopped. He was four years older than me, and until I was ten or eleven, I would have called him my best friend. That's when adolescence seemed to take hold of him and refused to let go.

"We need to talk," I said.

"Do we have to?" he asked in a way that told me he knew perfectly well we had plenty to talk about.

"Yes, we have to." It had been months since I'd been in his trailer and I'd forgotten how it listed to one side, giving me vertigo as I walked into the tiny space. His narrow bed was at one end, the built-in table and benches at the other, and they were no more than five steps apart. I knew he liked the confined space. He once told me he felt safe, contained that way. He was not a complete hermit, though. More than once, I'd come to the trailer to find signs that a woman had been there—lipstick on a coffee cup or a romance novel on the counter. You couldn't look like my brother without turning heads. My girlfriends used to drool over him when we were teenagers. I liked knowing he occasionally had company out here.

The window air conditioner cranked out a weak flow of cool air as I began putting away the groceries. I'd never really understood how he had power out here at all, but he'd somehow managed to rig up a generator that kept him cool enough in the summer and warm enough in the winter. The generator also kept his computer running. The laptop on the table was the one truly out-of-place item in the old trailer, which otherwise looked like it came straight out of the fifties. Danny had always been a technology geek. He was glued to that laptop by the fingertips, and I was glad, actually. He kept in touch with some of the guys he'd served with through e-mail, and I thought he needed that camaraderie. I only wished he'd keep in touch with *me* as well as he did with them. Sometimes I felt as though my e-mails to him went into a vacuum.

I put the milk in his refrigerator while he leaned against the counter, watching me.

"Bryan with you?" he asked.

"We broke up." I shut the refrigerator door. "It was my doing," I added.

"I thought you said he was 'the one.'"

I was surprised he remembered me saying that. "Well, I thought he was," I said. "But he's been separated from his wife for three years and he still wasn't doing anything about a divorce and I got tired of waiting." I was certain Bryan loved me, but as a couple, we were going nowhere. He had two great kids and I knew he still cared about his wife. I had the feeling I was in the way. "The writing was on the wall," I said. "It just took me a long time to see it."

"Good for you." Danny sounded sincere.

"I thought you liked him."

"I didn't like how he was stringing you along." Folding his arms, he leaned back and took a good look at my face. "And you know what?" he asked. "You look great. Like you got rid of a burden that's been weighing you down."

"Oh, right." I laughed. How could I look great when I felt so miserable? I was touched, though. Under his surly and sometimes caustic exterior, my brother was still a sweetheart.

He pulled a box of cigarettes from the carton I'd bought him, opened it, and lit one. He held the box out to offer me one, as though I might have started smoking since I last saw him. I shook my head as I slid onto one of the bench seats at the table.

His shotgun was directly in my line of view, propped against the wall next to the counter. He hunted small game in the woods and, as far as I knew, the shotgun was his only weapon. I hoped that was the case. Harry Washington told me that everyone in the police department saw Danny as a "loose cannon." Harry had served with Danny in Iraq and I knew he kept a protective eye on him. He'd e-mailed me a few weeks ago to tell me Danny'd been permanently banned from his favorite sports bar for getting in a fight with the bartender. He now hung out at Slick Alley, Harry said, a run-down-looking pool hall that gave me the creeps every time I drove past it.

My gaze lit on that shotgun again. I'd seen my brother's sudden bursts of anger firsthand, but I wasn't nearly as afraid of him using his gun against another person as I was of him using it against himself. Although the shattered leg he'd suffered in Iraq had taken a toll, his psychological injuries were far worse. To be fair, though, he hadn't been in the greatest shape before he went.

"How are you?" I looked up at him.

He took a drag of his cigarette, nodding. "Good," he said through a stream of smoke. Sitting down across from me at the table, he moved his laptop aside and tapped an ash into a jar lid.

"Are you taking your meds?" I asked.

"Get off my back, little sister," he said, and I knew

he wasn't. He hated the cocktail of medications the VA psychiatrist had put him on.

"Never mind." I folded my hands on the table as though I were about to start a meeting. "So," I said, "I'm Daddy's executrix, as you probably know, and I'm in New Bern for a couple of weeks to take care of his . . . estate." The word sounded silly attached to my father, and Danny made a derisive sound in the back of his throat. "You can have his car," I said. "It's only a few years old and—"

"I don't want his fucking car."

"All right." I backed off again. I'd deal with that later. "What about the house?" I asked. "I think we should sell it, but maybe you could live there if you—"

"No, thanks." He took a long slow drag on his cigarette, his eyes narrowed at me as though I'd insulted him by even suggesting he move into our childhood home. "You can decide whatever you want about the house and everything in it," he said. "All I care about is that this piece of land right here"—he pointed to the floor of the trailer—"right where we're sitting, is mine forever."

"We have to sell the park," I said, "but I don't think this area is technically part of it."

"It's not," he said. "It's totally separate."

"Okay. So I'll talk to the lawyer about making sure this land goes to you. Can you come with me to see her tomorrow?" I asked. "The lawyer? I'd like you to know what—"

"No," he said.

I nodded, unsurprised and knowing it was probably for the best. He would complicate things. Either he'd be so anxious he'd be unable to sit still, or he'd get angry and slam out of the room. Danny was anything but predictable.

"Okay." The smoke was really getting to me, but I planned to tough it out. "I have to clean out the house to be able to put it on the market. Can you help me with that? Not the physical-labor part, but we need to go through everything and—"

"Why don't you just hire someone to cart everything away?" He tapped the cigarette on the edge of the lid.

"Because . . . that's not the way it's done." I fanned away the smoke and leaned toward him. "Look, Danny, I need your help. Do it for me, okay? It wouldn't be for Daddy. It's for *me*. It'll be a massive job for me to handle on my own."

He stood up and squashed out the cigarette in the sink, running the water for a moment. I knew I'd gotten inside him by making the request more about me than about our father.

"This is so messed up," he said.

"What is?"

"Everything."

I tried to imagine what it was like inside my brother's head. In one of his more vulnerable moments, he'd told me that he always felt afraid. He reacted to every loud sound as though he was under attack. Nightmares put him back in Iraq, where he'd done things he refused to tell me about. *You'd never look at me the same way if I told you.* Daddy had tried to be there for him, but there was an animosity Danny felt toward my father that I'd never understood. Daddy finally gave up on him and I couldn't really blame him. But *I* wouldn't give up. It was that vulnerable Danny I tried to remember when he was being belligerent.

"Do you love me?" I asked now.

He raised his head sharply. "Of course," he said, and his shoulders suddenly slumped as though that admission had defeated him. He sighed as he turned to face me. "What would I need to do?" He suddenly sounded like a little boy, wanting to please me, yet afraid of my answer.

"Let me talk to the lawyer tomorrow and then figure out exactly what we need to do." *We.* I'd make this about both of us. "How about I get you a prepaid phone so we can communicate while I'm here?"

He shook his head. "Don't," he said, and I wasn't sure if he meant "don't get me a phone" or "don't make one more suggestion or I'll lose it." Either way, I thought we'd both had enough of a visit for one day and I stood up.

"You look good, Danny," I said, getting to my feet. "I love you so much." I did. He was all the family I had left.

I made up the double bed in my old bedroom that night. I could have slept in my parents' much larger room with its queen-sized bed, but I couldn't bring myself to do that. It still felt like their private space to me. I wasn't ready to invade it.

In the two weeks since I'd split from Bryan, bedtime had become the hardest part of the day for me. That was when we used to talk on the phone to say "good night" and "I love you." I missed those calls so much. For the first week after the split, I talked to Sherise every night instead of Bryan, and how she'd tolerated my whining and moaning, I didn't know. Now she was unreachable in Haiti, and I was an orphan.

I was still awake at midnight, staring at the ceiling. I would never sleep. I got up, walked downstairs, and made myself a cup of Sleepytime tea in the microwave. I was carrying it back to the stairs when I spotted my purse on my father's desk and remembered the purple envelope from the post office box. I took the envelope upstairs with me and climbed back into bed, sipping my tea as I examined the looping handwriting on the purple paper. *Fred Marcus.* No return address. I hesitated a moment before slitting the envelope open with my finger. The only thing inside was a postcard. On the front was a color photograph of a band. Bluegrass or country, maybe. Two women and two men, all of them carrying stringed instruments. At the bottom of the picture were the words *Jasha Trace.* The band's name, I supposed. On the back of the card was a tour schedule, and written where the recipient's address should go, in that same looping handwriting, *Can't wait to see you! Where should we meet up? xoxo*

Damn. Now I felt really terrible. Whoever Fred Marcus was, he wouldn't get this card because I'd taken it from his post office box. I should have left it there. Maybe even paid to keep his box open for a while.

With a sigh, I leaned over to toss the card and envelope into the trash can next to my night table. I had enough to deal with without taking on the problems of a stranger. Fred Marcus would have to figure this out on his own.

3.

_____

"So your father drew up this will three years ago." Suzanne Compton, my father's attorney, leaned across her desk to hand me a copy of the will. I paged through it on the edge of her desk. While I'd still been in Durham, Suzanne had helped me file information with the court and get into my father's bank accounts, but I'd put off dealing with his will until now when I could talk to her face-to-face.

"As I mentioned on the phone," Suzanne continued, "he split everything fifty-fifty between you and your brother's trust. The house. The RV park. His bank accounts. The only exception is that five-acre parcel that goes to Daniel alone. You'll take over as the trustee of his trust now, so we'll have to talk about your responsibilities in that regard."

I nodded. I knew about the trust, of course, but I hadn't realized I would now be in charge of Danny's money. He could only spend it on certain things to avoid losing his disability checks. I was relieved that my father had left the land to him.

"Your father had a small life insurance policy he apparently bought when he worked for the government," Suzanne said, "and it appears he kept up the premiums, so that's fifty thousand that also goes to the two of you."

"He never worked for the government," I said, wondering if she had her cases mixed up. "He's always just run Mac's RV Park."

"Well, it's an old policy." Suzanne rubbed the back of her neck beneath her blond chin-length hair. She looked a little sleepy as she flipped through some notes in what I assumed was my father's file. She couldn't be half as tired as I was after my mostly sleepless night. "He bought the policy in 1980 when he was with the U.S. Marshals Service," she said.

"U.S. Marshals Service? My father? I don't think . . ." My voice trailed off as a vague childhood memory came to me. Danny and I were working on a sand castle at the beach, watching a police officer arrest a couple of noisy drunks. *Daddy used to arrest people, too,* Danny had said. *He was a marshal.* I remembered the pride in his voice, but I couldn't have been more than five and had no idea what he was talking about.

Now I smiled. "When I was little, Danny told me our father used to be a marshal. That must be what he meant. In 1980—when you said he bought that policy—my family lived in northern Virginia outside Washington, D.C., so I guess it makes sense. But I had no idea he ever had a government job. He never talked about it."

"Well, it was a long time ago." Suzanne looked down at the will, clearly wanting to get on with business. "Now, your father was quite the collector, wasn't he? He told me the violins were the most valuable, but second to that was his pipe collection, and he wants that to go to Thomas Kyle."

"Seriously?" I sat back, surprised. Tom Kyle? He and

his wife, Verniece, were longtime residents at my father's RV park, but I barely knew them. Tom always struck me as a grouchy old man, though Verniece was sweet. When Daddy died, I'd asked Suzanne to work out an arrangement so that Tom could temporarily handle the reservations and payments for the park. As far as I knew, that had gone well.

"Is that something you want to contest?" Suzanne asked.

I shook my head slowly. "No," I said. "I'm just surprised. I guess Tom Kyle and my father were closer than I thought. It's nice my father left him something." I was glad to know Daddy'd had a friend he cared about that much. The pipes were probably worth a few thousand dollars. "Does Mr. Kyle know?" I asked.

"No. As executrix, you should notify him. You can have him call me with any questions and I'll draw up a document you and he will need to sign." She glanced down at the will again. "The only other thing he's spelled out here is that he's leaving his piano and ten thousand dollars to Jeannie Lyons."

The name didn't register right away. I hadn't heard it in years. "Really?" I asked.

"Do you know Jeannie? She's a real estate agent?"

"She was an old friend of my mother's from back when they were kids, but Mom passed away seven years ago." I remembered that Jeannie and my mother went away together every couple of years when I was growing up. A girls' getaway, my mother called it. They'd go to the beach or to Asheville, which was where Jeannie lived then, if I had my facts straight. "I didn't know my father stayed in touch with her."

"It's always possible your mother asked him to leave something to Jeannie," Suzanne said. "Do you—or your brother—have any problem with her getting the piano or the money?"

I shook my head. "Not if that's what my father wanted," I said. "Besides, Danny lives in a trailer and I have a tiny apartment." Then I added with a smile, "Plus, neither of us can play."

"Then you'll want to see Jeannie," Suzanne said. "She can help you with the house and RV park, too, if you plan to put them both on the market."

"I do," I said.

Suzanne turned to her notes. "I have here that your father had about two hundred thousand in savings at the time he drew up the will. So that, plus the insurance, plus the value of his house and the park, which Jeannie can help you determine, will be split between Daniel's trust and yourself."

The word *wow* crossed my mind, but it felt wrong to say it. I had six thousand dollars in my savings account at that very moment. I made next to nothing as a school counselor and I thought I was doing pretty well to have put away that much.

"A word of advice is not to go crazy spending," Suzanne said. "Sock it away. Find a good financial advisor. I can refer you to someone here, but you'd probably prefer someone in Durham. Just be careful with the money and let it grow. Maybe buy a house of your own. Get out of the tiny apartment. Hopefully this will help your brother out, too. How is he doing?"

"You know him?" I asked, not really surprised. Nearly everyone in New Bern knew Danny to one extent or another. He elicited a complicated set of emotions in people: gratitude for his military service, compassion for his injuries, and apprehension over his unpredictability.

"I've never met him personally," she said. "I set up his trust, though. It sounds like he's been through a lot." She gave me a kind smile as she closed the file on her desk, and I was grateful that she spoke about Danny with sympathy instead of disdain.

"He has," I said.

"Listen, one other thing," she said as we both got to our feet. "When someone dies unexpectedly the way your father did, they don't have the chance to clean everything up. You know, erase sites he's Googled or whatever. So don't dig too deeply into his personal things. Don't upset yourself."

I frowned at her. "Is there something you're not telling me?" I asked.

"No. I barely knew your father." She walked around the desk, heading with me toward the door. "When my own father passed away, though, I found some . . . pornography, that sort of thing, on his computer and wished I hadn't looked." She smiled sheepishly. "Just a little warning."

"I can't imagine my father being into porn," I said, my hand on the doorknob.

"You never know," she said. "Sounds like your father was full of surprises."

4.

I wanted an ordinary brother. One I could talk to reasonably about my appointment with Suzanne. A brother I could grieve with over our father. I was never going to have that brother, and even though I'd managed to guilt him into coming over to the house that evening, his anxiety was like a third person in my car as we drove away from the RV park. He said his Subaru was low on gas and he didn't have the money to fill it, so I'd picked him up, trying to hand him the hundred dollars I'd taken from his trust fund. He turned away from the money with an annoyed expression on his face. I couldn't blame him. It had to do something to his pride to be dependent on his younger sister for funds now.

I stopped at MJ's to pick up a pound of peel-and-eat shrimp and fries, my heart racing as I waited for the order to be filled, afraid I'd return to the car to find Danny gone. But he was still there, filling the air in my car with cigarette smoke. I said nothing. If he needed to smoke to get through this, fine. If he needed to drink, fine. I'd bought a six-pack of beer that afternoon. Whatever it took.

Before starting the car, I reached into my purse and

pulled out the phone I'd bought that afternoon. "Here's a prepaid phone for you so we can keep in touch," I said, holding it out to him.

"I really don't want a phone," he said.

"Just for while I'm here." I pressed the phone into his hand. "I put my number in the contacts, and your number is in mine." After a moment, he closed his fingers around the phone and slid it into his jeans pocket.

Satisfied, I started the car and we drove to the house, the scent of Old Bay Seasoning mixing with the cigarette smoke. I parked in the driveway, and we walked slowly across the lawn and up the steps to the front door. His limp was not as bad as it used to be, I thought, though I had the feeling his slow, stiff gait might be due to pain. Or maybe he simply wanted to put off going into the house as long as he could. It had been years since he'd been inside.

"Daddy has about two hundred thousand in savings," I said as we walked through the living room toward the kitchen, the sack of shrimp and fries in my arms. Danny turned his head left and right, taking in the room. I doubted anything had changed since the last time he'd been there. "Half of that money will go into your trust."

"What would I do with that much money?" he asked when we reached the kitchen. I knew it was a rhetorical question.

"Well"—I put the bag on the counter—"it'll be there if you ever need it." I'd already told him he could keep the land where he was living.

He immediately walked to the refrigerator and opened the door, pulling a beer from the carton. "How'd he end up with that much in the bank?" he asked, shutting the refrigerator door.

I reached into one of the cupboards for a couple of

plates. "He was a good saver, I guess," I said. "He didn't have many expenses. And he used to work for the U.S. Marshals Service, which I guess you knew?"

"Hm." He pulled open a couple of drawers before finding the one with the bottle opener. "He was crazy, wasn't he? Giving up a government job to come down here and run an RV park?"

I glanced at him as I took two of my mother's old Franciscan Ware plates from the cupboard. "Maybe he felt like you do," I said. "You know. Choosing a quieter lifestyle over the rat race of Washington, D.C."

He took a swallow of beer. "Not sure I could say mine is a choice," he said.

I nodded toward the back door, and Danny followed me onto the screened porch, where I set the plates on the oilcloth-covered table. The cicadas and crickets were singing their evening songs as I opened the bag from MJ's. I loved the porch. It reminded me of when I was a kid. All summer long, I'd read in one of the rockers. I could still remember a few of the books I devoured back then, when life seemed a whole lot simpler than it did right now.

"Do you remember hanging out on the porch when we were kids?" I asked as I opened the wrapper around the shrimp.

"Man, these plates!" Danny said as if he hadn't heard what I said. He looked down at the cream-colored plate with the hand-painted apples around the border. "Do we have to eat on these old plates?"

"What's wrong with them?"

"Just . . . it's like being fifteen again."

I wanted to prod. To ask him why being fifteen felt so terrible to him, but I'd prodded before and knew it would go nowhere.

"I actually love these plates," I said. "They remind me of Mom."

"Exactly," he said.

I wasn't about to get him a different plate. I took a handful of shrimp and pushed the cardboard container across the table to him. "Cover it with shrimp and you won't see the design," I said, and I was glad when he reached for the container.

"So." I peeled a shrimp, thinking I'd better get the subject off our family for a while. "I told you about my sorry love life. How about yours? Anyone special these days?"

His shrug was noncommittal. "They come and go," he said, "and that suits me fine." He ate a shrimp, then drained his beer and stood up. "I need another of these," he said. "Get you one?"

"No, thanks." I ate a few fries as I waited for him to come back. I hated how tense it felt between us. He seemed brittle to me tonight. Easy to break.

His bottle was already half empty by the time he sat down again, and his hands shook as he began peeling a shrimp. I wondered if he was on something. He'd smoked a lot of weed when he got back from Iraq, but as far as I knew, alcohol was his drug of choice these days.

"We have to talk about the house," I said, and I told him everything I'd learned from Suzanne. "The piano and ten thousand go to Jeannie Lyons, which I think is weird. She used to be a friend of Mom's, but I—"

"I know who she is," he said, taking another swallow of beer. "She tries to talk to me when she sees me around town, but I just put on my scary PTSD act and she leaves me alone."

I had to laugh. His delivery was deadpan and I had

no idea if he meant to be funny or not, but either way, I liked his honesty. "And you must know Tom Kyle," I said. "He lives at the end of the RV park?"

"Total asshole. He always wears camo pants, like he's trying to pass himself off as something he's not."

I nibbled a French fry. "Well," I said, "I don't know him very well, but he's been helping to keep the park going since Daddy died, so I appreciate that. And Daddy must have had some sort of relationship with him because he left him his pipe collection."

"What would anyone want with a bunch of old pipes?"

"Who knows?" I said. "But they're one less thing we need to deal with, so I'm happy about that. What I'll need the most help with is boxing stuff up to donate. You know, clearing everything out of the house so we can sell it." I fantasized about us working together for a couple of weeks, shoulder to shoulder. Maybe I could get him to really talk to me. To open up.

He stopped peeling the shrimp and looked out at the yard, nearly dark now. "Seriously," he said, "you better just hire somebody. I can't do it."

His voice was soft but sure, as though he'd been trying to reach a decision and had finally made it. "Why not, Danny?" I asked gently.

"Being here, I realize . . ." He looked at me, but only for a second before dropping his gaze to the remaining shrimp on his plate. "I just don't want to paw through all their old stuff. Things like these plates." He tapped his finger on the edge of the plate. "I don't want to see them."

"Okay . . ." I said, wishing I understood the enigma that was my brother.

"I have as many nightmares about our family as I do about Iraq," he added.

"I don't understand," I said. "I mean, it's not like you were abused or anything."

He lifted the bottle to his lips, tipping his head back to get the last drop. "There are all sorts of abuse," he said, setting the bottle down again.

"What are you talking about?"

"All I'm saying is, you need to hire somebody to help you with the house." There was an impatient edge to his voice now. "I'm washing my hands of it." He got up and walked into the kitchen. I heard the refrigerator door opening again as I stacked our dishes and began carrying them into the house.

The kitchen was empty by the time I got inside, but I could see him in the living room. I set everything on the counter by the sink and walked to the doorway between the rooms. Danny stood in front of the wall of vinyl albums, one hand in his jeans pocket, the other holding yet another fresh beer.

"What was the point of all this?" he said, lifting the bottle in the direction of the albums. The anger in his voice kept me from walking into the room. "You couldn't listen to this many records in a lifetime," he said. "Stupid waste. He was obsessed."

"It was his passion," I said carefully. I remembered our mother saying that Daddy needed his passions, and although she never said more than that, I knew she meant he needed something to keep him from thinking about the daughter he'd lost. "Do you remember how Mom and Daddy always talked about our family as though they'd only had two children?" I asked. "Like Lisa didn't exist?"

Danny didn't shift his gaze from the records, but I saw the quick flare of his nostrils. As kids, we'd both learned to respond the same way when people asked us how many kids were in our family. *Just two,* we'd reply.

"It was like we could never talk about Lisa," I said. "Even now, when I mentioned her, you shut down and—"

"This is so fucked!" he suddenly shouted. Turning, he raised his arm as though about to pitch a ball. He sent the beer bottle forward with enormous power, propelling it like a missile toward the wall with the pipe collection. I took a step backward as the sliding glass doors of the cabinet exploded into millions of pieces.

Danny spun around and stomped toward the front door.

"Danny!" I shouted, too stunned to move. He was gone, pounding down the porch steps before I could even absorb what had happened.

I stared at the cabinet, now unprotected by glass. Some of the pipes had fallen off their narrow wooden ledges. A few were on the floor. Jagged pieces of glass jutted from the edges of the cabinet like broken ice on a pond, and everywhere in the room—*everywhere*—glass glittered. Tiny crystal shards sparkled from nearly every surface.

I stood there numbly for a few seconds before remembering that Danny had no car. No way to travel the ten miles to his trailer other than by foot. I grabbed my purse and keys and headed out the front door after him.

New Bern was dark and quiet as I drove slowly in the direction I expected him to travel. I spotted him as he walked under a streetlight, limping badly, heading for the outskirts of town. Pulling over, I lowered the passenger side window.

"Get in," I commanded. He stopped walking, but

didn't look over at me. "Come on, Danny," I said. "Please."

I saw the moment he surrendered—that telltale slump of his shoulders that registered defeat. He walked to my car and opened the door. "Don't take me back to the house," he said as he got in the car. "Take me to my place, all right?"

"Absolutely," I said, giving up then and there on the idea of him helping me with the house.

We rode in silence for a couple of miles. I was unsure what to say that wouldn't send him bolting out of my car. After a while, he turned on the radio, pushing the scan button until he found something he liked. Hip-hop. The song playing was familiar and its pounding beat forced both of us to nod our heads in rhythm, whether we were in the mood for the music or not.

"The kids I work with love this song," I said, grateful for a neutral topic. Then I remembered the shotgun waiting for him in his trailer and it became all I could think about. I asked kids every day of the week if they had suicidal feelings, but now the words were caught in my throat.

"I'll go to the VA with you while I'm here," I said instead.

"What for?"

"Don't be dense, Danny," I said. "If you *are* taking your meds, they need an adjustment, don't you think?"

"No, I don't think."

"Let me go with you," I said. "You can't go on this way. When was the last time you saw a psychiatrist?"

"Fuck off," he said.

The dark road blurred in front of my eyes and I swallowed hard against the hurt, my fingers tight on the steering wheel.

After a moment, he reached over to touch my hand. "I'm sorry," he said. "I know you want to help, but you can't. Just accept it, okay? This is who I am."

I nodded, though I wasn't okay with it. Not at all. "Don't worry about the house," I said, turning onto the road that led to the RV park. "I'll take care of it." I made a left when we reached the rutted unpaved lane and we bounced slowly through the darkness.

"It's right here." He pointed to the nearly invisible break in the trees that led to the clearing and his trailer. I made a cautious left into the woods, then drove along the trail until my headlights picked up his car and the old Airstream. I stopped and turned off the ignition.

"I'm coming in with you," I said.

"No." He reached for the door handle.

The only thing in my mind was that shotgun. "Do you think about killing yourself?" I blurted out. When I turned to face him, I was surprised by the glint of tears in his eyes.

He didn't answer right away, and when he finally did, his voice was gentle. "I'm all right, Riles," he said. My heart felt a little pang of love at hearing the name he'd called me when we were kids. "Seriously," he said. "I am. I just couldn't be in that house any longer."

I reached into my purse and pulled out the folded twenties. I held them out to him. "This is yours," I said. "Take it."

He hesitated, then took the bills from my hand.

"I love you, Danny," I said.

He looked toward his trailer. "I'm just glad I can keep the land," he said as he opened the door and got out of the car. Those words heartened me. If he still cared about keeping the land, he was thinking of the future.

He wasn't about to blow his head off. Not tonight, at least.

I left my headlights on until he was inside his trailer, then I drove back and forth in tiny arcs until I was facing forward for the slow drive out of the forest, my mind consumed by the work that lay ahead of me. It wasn't only the house and my heart that needed to be repaired while I was here, I thought. Somehow, I had to also heal my brother.

5.

I couldn't remember the last time I'd been to Mac's RV Park. I tried to think back as I made a right turn onto the long narrow lane, driving in the opposite direction from the acres of woods that sheltered Danny's trailer. It must have been either last summer or the summer before that. I'd come to New Bern for a surprise visit and, not finding Daddy at home, I drove out here and found him working on the boat ramp. When he looked up and saw me, his smile lit up his face. It felt strange to pull into the park now, knowing he wouldn't be here.

My father kept his own small, aging RV in the first of the twelve sites, and I thought I'd check it out before driving to the Kyles' motor home. I parked next to the RV, then realized I had no key for it. I tried the doors, but they were locked, so I got back in my car and continued down the gravel road.

Mac's RV Park was not exactly a hot tourist destination. It was a funky little strip of land nestled between a wide, navigable creek and the Croatan Forest, and it offered no amenities other than electrical and water hookups and a boat slip. I wasn't sure how Mac's compared to other parks, but I'd always liked how each of the twelve sites was private at this time of year when the trees were full, cut off from the other sites by a patch of forest on either side. I could see a few other RVs through the trees and hear the distant laughter of kids playing in the creek.

The Kyles' RV sat on concrete blocks in the last site, close to the creek and shaded by the trees. A Ford sedan with fading green paint was parked behind it. Their RV was nearly as old as my father's, but much larger. A striped awning sagged above the door and the roof had caved in near the front of the vehicle where a tree must have fallen on it. It was a sad-looking thing, their motor home, and I guessed the Kyles were having trouble keeping it in decent shape. I hadn't seen Tom Kyle in years, but he had to be my father's age—pushing seventy. I wondered what he'd do with Daddy's pipe collection.

I parked behind the Ford and spotted Tom on the other side of the RV at a fish-cleaning table. He wore an undershirt and camouflage pants and appeared to be working on that morning's catch. He was a bigger man than I remembered. Tall and broad shouldered, he'd probably been muscular in his youth, but the years had taken a toll. He looked up when I closed my car door, squinting from behind silver-framed glasses as I walked toward him. I could tell he didn't recognize me.

"It's Riley MacPherson, Mr. Kyle," I said. "Frank MacPherson's daughter?"

He set down his knife and his expression changed. It was more of a frown than a smile. "Riley," he said. "Haven't seen you in a long time. How're you making out?"

"I'm all right," I said. "I'm down here to get the house and everything squared away. Thanks for taking care of things here at the park this past month."

He shook his head. "That was too bad about your father." He looked down at his hands, his fingers glittery with fish scales. "Things won't be the same without Frank around here."

"He left one of his collections to you, Mr. Kyle," I said. "His pipes."

"Verniece and me've been keeping up with the reservations and all," he said, as if I hadn't spoken. "Do you want to check over the books? Will you be handling that from here on?"

I could tell he didn't understand what I'd said. Whether it was his hearing or his cognitive skills, I didn't know.

I shook my head. "I came here to tell you that my father wanted you to have his collection of pipes," I said, raising my voice a bit. "I'm not sure exactly what they're worth, but he wanted you to have them. His lawyer will work out the details."

My words finally sank in. He nodded slowly, his eyes on the table and its three fish rather than on me. I couldn't read his face. "Well," he said after a moment, "that was nice of him." He looked out at the creek. "Anything else in his will we should know about?" he asked, surprising me. Had he expected more?

"No," I said. "The pipe collection is the only mention of you." All morning, I'd been picking up broken glass from around the pipes. I didn't think any of them had been damaged in Danny's sudden burst of anger.

I heard the creak of the door on the other side of the RV. "Who's here?" Verniece Kyle walked around the corner of the motor home.

"Verniece," Tom said, "do you remember Frank's girl? The little one?" he added quickly, as though he didn't want her to conjure up any thought of my sister.

Had they ever known Lisa? I didn't see how they could have.

"I surely do!" She smiled warmly at me and reached out to take my hand in both of hers. Her skin felt loose and satiny smooth. Her gray hair was neatly combed but it looked like she probably cut it herself, and she was overweight. Not obese, but her short-sleeved knit top stretched across her breasts and her stomach. "I'm so sorry about your daddy, Riley, dear," she said. "He was the salt of the earth now, wasn't he?"

I nodded. "Thank you." I was surprised she remembered my name. Maybe my father had talked about me to them.

"We never see your brother, do we, Tom?" she asked. "Even though he's no more than a mile down the lane." She let go of my hand. "I took some muffins over to him after we found out about your father, but he wasn't there, and I was afraid to leave them in case the squirrels or—"

"She has a little bit of news for us, Verniece," Tom interrupted. "You take her in the house and I'll clean up and come in and we can all talk about it."

"Come in, love." Verniece tugged gently on my forearm, and I followed her around the corner of the RV and up the steps into the dim interior of the trailer, where the air was only a few degrees cooler than outside. The window shades were lowered against the sunlight and it took a few seconds for my eyes to adjust. How did they tolerate this, living like moles in a hot airless tunnel?

"Some nice sweet tea?" Verniece asked as I sat down at the built-in table, larger than the one in Danny's tiny trailer. This RV was at least three times the length of his.

"Nothing, thank you," I said. "I'm fine."

She removed a photograph from the door of the narrow refrigerator and put it in front of me on the table, turning on the overhead light. "Do you remember our son, Luke?" she asked.

"I do," I said politely. I hadn't known Luke well. Living out here in the RV park, he'd gone to different schools from me. He'd been an outgoing, whip-smart kid, from the little I remembered. "Where is he now?" I asked.

"Colorado. He's studying to get his Ph.D. in something to do with computers."

"Did you have other children?" I asked, to make conversation. "I can't remember."

"No, he's our only one, and the reason I brought out his picture"—she gestured toward the photograph—"is because seeing you reminds me of him."

I tried to think of some connection between Luke and myself and finally gave up. "Why do I remind you of him?" I asked.

She sat down on the other side of the table, smiling at me with dazzling warmth. "We could have no children of our own," she said, "and one day, I confided in your mother about it and she told me about adopting you and put the idea in my head, and I said to Tom, why don't we adopt a baby, too? So that's how we ended up with Luke." She seemed so delighted by the connection between our families, that I hesitated to set her straight. But I had to.

"I wasn't adopted, Mrs. Kyle," I said gently. "I think maybe you have my family mixed up with some of your other friends."

Her eyes flew open and she sat back on the narrow bench. "Oh!" she said, color rushing to her cheeks. "I thought . . . You're right. I must have you mixed up with someone else." She suddenly stood up and opened the refrigerator door as if looking for something, but she made no move to reach inside. "Tom says I'm losing my marbles and sometimes I think he's right." She shut the door, picked up Luke's picture from the table, and put it back on the front of the refrigerator, her fingers trembling. I felt sorry that I'd upset her so much, but then she smiled at me again, collecting herself. "Well, whoever it was, they were about our age when they adopted," she said. "Fortyish. And we thought, if they can adopt a baby at their age, we can, too, and we got Luke when he was a year old. It was the best thing we ever did."

I smiled and said, "I'm so glad you got your son. You must be really proud of him."

"Oh, we are. And we miss him. We haven't seen him since Christmas."

"She telling you about Lucas?" Tom said as he stepped into the RV.

"Yes," I said.

"He's a perfect kid." He moved to the sink to wash his hands. He was too big for the space, and he filled the RV with the odor of fish and sweat . . . and a trace of alcohol, I thought. "The only imperfect thing about him is him living on the other side of the country. We wish we had an RV we could use to go see him sometime. A mobile home that's actually mobile." He put his hands on his hips and looked around him at his claustrophobic little home. "This one's been on blocks so long it's forgotten how to get up and go."

"That would be just wonderful." His wife sounded wistful.

"You tell her the news?" He nodded at me, and I told Verniece about the pipe collection.

"I'm sure it's worth a few thousand dollars, at least," I added.

Verniece glanced at her husband with a look I couldn't read, but then I thought I saw a spark of joy in her blue eyes.

"Well, God bless your daddy, that's all I can say," she said. "Would you feel bad if we sold them? I know how he loved all those things he collected, but we don't have much use for them."

"Not at all." I smiled. "The pipes will be yours to do what you want with them."

We chatted a little while longer and then I walked back to my car. I felt like Santa Claus. Not a bad feeling.

But as I drove away, it wasn't their smiling faces or their grief over my father I carried with me, but the certainty in Verniece Kyle's face when she told me it was my adoption that had inspired their son's.

Late that afternoon when the weather began to cool off, I put on my running shoes and headed downstairs. I'd taken a nap when I got home from the RV park. A sure sign of depression, I thought. But the truth was, Verniece Kyle's chatter about me being adopted had unsettled me in a way I couldn't quite explain. Of course she had no idea what she was talking about, but at a time when I already felt lost and lonely, her suggestion that my one and only beloved and mourned family wasn't my biological family was enough to leave me empty inside.

When I reached the living room, I noticed the mounting stack of bills on the table by the front door. I'd brought all the bills that had been forwarded to me in Durham, but I hadn't even looked at them. And now there was a handful more. I pictured the electricity suddenly being cut off to the house, the lights going out on me any minute.

Giving in to the worry, I picked up the envelopes and carried them to my father's desk. The rolltop was up and I could see Daddy's checkbook poking out from one of the many cubbyholes. I opened all the envelopes and laid the bills one on top of the other, then took a look at his check register, hoping he was better than I was at writing everything down so I could see how much money was in the account. The register was up to date as of a week or so before he died. If he had any automatic bill payments not reflected in the checkbook, though, I could be in trouble. I'd go to his bank tomorrow and look at his accounts with someone there before I started writing checks.

I was about to set down the register when I noticed the name Tom Kyle on one of the lines. My father had written him a check for five hundred dollars. What for? I wondered. I glanced through his register. The checks all appeared to have been written to utilities except for a monthly five-hundred-dollar check to Tom. Did my father owe him money? Was he paying him back for . . . what? I could think of no reason he'd be giving him money. There was only one way to find out, but I didn't see the rush. I'd ask Tom when I went back to the park to check out my father's RV.

I looked at the stack of bills again, this time with a sigh. One task of a thousand. I pulled the rolltop over the desk, covering the bills and the checkbook, making them disappear. They could wait one more day, I thought as I got to my feet. Then I left the house, walked down the porch steps, and started to run.

6.

_____

The real estate office where Jeannie Lyons worked was only a few blocks from the house, so I stopped in after my run the following morning. It was a hole-in-the-wall building, with pictures of homes for sale taped to the narrow front windows. Inside, a young woman with stick-straight blond hair sat at one of two desks and she gave me a broad, do-you-want-to-buy-something smile when I walked in.

"Good morning!" She got to her feet, holding her hand out to me.

"Hi," I said, shaking her hand. "I'm looking for Jeannie Lyons."

"Do you have an appointment?"

I shook my head. "I just need to talk to her for a minute," I said, although that was a stupid statement. Telling her my father was leaving her—someone I barely knew and hadn't heard him mention since my mother's death—the piano and ten thousand dollars would probably take more than a minute. "I'm the daughter of an old friend of hers," I said.

"Hold on a sec," the woman said, and she disappeared through a door in the rear of the office.

A moment later, Jeannie came through the same door. She was only slightly familiar to me. I'd been eighteen the last time I saw her, which was at my mother's memorial service. That day was such a haze to me that I couldn't really recall who was there. But I remembered Jeannie's eyes. They were enormous and an intense blue beneath deep brown bangs. Her bob was a bit edgy, one side tucked behind her ear, and although I knew she'd been the same age as my mother, she looked younger than my mother ever had. It was hard to believe she was sixty-four. I could tell right away that she knew who I was, but her smile looked uncertain. She held out her hand as she walked toward me. "Riley," she said.

"Mrs. Lyons." I nodded and shook her hand.

"Oh, call me Jeannie," she said, squeezing my hand with a warmth that didn't reach her face. "I'm very sorry about your father."

"Thank you." There was a moment of awkward silence and she looked at me expectantly. "I need to talk to you," I said. "Do you have some time now . . . or I could come back tomorrow?"

She glanced at the clock on the wall. It was eleven-fifteen. "I have some calls to make right now," she said. "How about we meet for lunch? I'll make reservations at Morgan's Tavern for noon. Would that work?"

"Yes, perfect." That would give me a chance to run home and change. "I'll see you then."

I was first to arrive in the restaurant and I gave the hostess Jeannie's name. She put me in a side room that was otherwise empty, and I couldn't help but wonder if Jeannie had told her we needed privacy.

I was looking over the menu when she arrived. She blew into the room with so much energy the air swirled around our table as she took her seat. "Sorry, sorry," she said, unwrapping her silverware from the napkin. "A million fires to put out this morning."

Sitting across the table from her, I could see that she looked closer to her age than I'd originally thought. Her jawline was blurry, her neck a little crepey, but she was still a youthful, vibrant-looking woman.

The waitress was at our table in an instant. "Your regular?" she asked Jeannie.

"Yes, but maybe we need a minute?" Jeannie raised her eyebrows in my direction.

"Fish tacos," I said to the waitress. "And my water's enough."

Jeannie smiled at me as we waited for the waitress to leave our table, and once we had the room to ourselves again, she leaned over to touch my hands.

"I'm so happy I finally have the chance to really get to know you!" she said. "You've grown into a lovely young woman, Riley. Your father told me as much."

"Thank you," I said, wondering if my father had actually used the word *lovely*. He told me often I was pretty. All through my growing-up years, he'd fed my self-esteem, even though I knew I'd disappointed him with my lack of musical talent. I didn't know what Danny's issues were with him, but to me, he'd been a good dad.

"You remind me of your mother," she said, tilting her head to study me.

"Do I?" So much for my adoption worries.

"Absolutely. I believe her memorial service was the last time I saw you? Seven long years ago. You were eighteen, right?"

"Right," I said. "You came all the way from Asheville. I'd actually forgotten that you moved here."

"Shortly after your mother's death," she said.

"And I guess you stayed in touch with my father after she died?"

"Oh, of course." She shook her head. "He was such a fine man, Riley. Your mother was lucky to have him." She took a sip from her water glass. Set it down. "And so was I," she added, her blue eyes watching for my reaction.

I didn't mask my surprise very well. "You . . . what do you mean?" She could mean only one thing, but I couldn't believe it.

She didn't answer. Just sat there staring at me, a small smile on her lips as she waited for me to state the obvious.

"So, were you . . . you were more than friends?" I squirmed. I was in utter disbelief over the idea of a romance between my father and *anyone*.

She gave a little nod. "I hope you don't find that upsetting," she said. "I like to think it would have pleased your mother. It was terrible for both your father and me when she passed away, and grief can really draw two people together. I miss both of them so much."

"Wow." I smoothed a wrinkle on the tablecloth, unable to look at her. "Why didn't he ever tell me?" I wanted to ask her how long it had been going on. How long after my mother's death had they started . . . seeing each other? "He never said a word about seeing someone," I said.

"Did you ever ask him?"

"No. I mean, I never thought to." I felt guilty, as though I should have known to ask him if he was dating. It never occurred to me.

"Well," she said, "your father knew how close you

were to your mother and was probably worried about upsetting you."

I hadn't been all that close to my mother, actually. I loved her and I knew she loved me, but she'd never been the type to share her deepest thoughts with her daughter.

"She's been gone *years,*" I said. "I'm sad he felt like he had to keep a . . . relationship from me."

The waitress arrived with our lunches. She set a bowl of lobster bisque and a glass of iced tea in front of Jeannie and the fish tacos in front of me. They looked delicious, but my appetite had taken a serious hit in the last few minutes.

"He had such a hard life," Jeannie said once the waitress walked away. "Losing your sister and then your brother's injuries, and then Deb—your mother—passing away on top of it all. So hard."

"I know."

"People your age . . . they don't think to ask their parents about themselves," she said, lifting a spoonful of soup toward her mouth. "It's all about 'me, me, me.' "

She must have seen my stunned look at her insult because she rushed on, her free hand on mine. "I don't mean that as nastily as it sounds," she said. "It's just your stage of life. It's normal. I was the same way in my twenties. My parents were nonpeople to me. I never realized they had full lives of their own. I didn't mean to lay a guilt trip on you."

"He was never a 'nonperson' to me," I said, withdrawing my hand from beneath hers. "I loved him."

"Of course. I'm sorry."

She was right in a way, though, I thought as I took a bite of a taco. I'd adored my father, but I'd relegated him to a little box in my mind labeled "reclusive, old, eccentric," hadn't I?

"And he loved you." Jeannie dabbed her lips with her napkin. "He was very proud of you."

"I wish he'd told me more about himself," I said.

"Well, he was a reticent man. He loved to gather information from other people, but he never was very good at sharing his own thoughts and feelings, was he? Still, he adored his family. He loved to show me those pictures . . . you know, that big box of family photos he has? He liked to reminisce. I think that's one thing that drew us together, since I knew your family so—"

"What big box?" I interrupted her, setting down my taco.

"The one in his bedroom closet. Don't you know it? There's pictures of you when you were little. Pictures of your brother and sister and mother."

"Oh, yes." I remembered no such box, but didn't want to tell her there was yet one more thing I didn't know about my father.

"And I'd show him pictures of your mother from when she and I were kids, back in our teen years. I met Deb when we were in the eighth grade in Arlington, Virginia, and we became inseparable."

"What was she like?" I asked. Suddenly, I felt terribly sad that I'd never asked my mother about her childhood. I'd never thought to ask either of my parents. Jeannie was right about the "me, me, me" part. And now I'd lost the chance.

"She was always the life of the party." Jeannie smiled broadly.

"*My* mother?"

"Absolutely! She was always getting us into trouble.

We'd hide other kids in our trunk to sneak them into the drive-in movie. We weren't allowed to be there with our boyfriends in the first place, because you know what went on in those cars." She laughed. "No one watched the movie, that's for sure. And she was always talking me into cutting school with her."

My mouth hung open. "This doesn't sound like my mother at all," I said.

"No? How do you remember her?"

"Super-Catholic and really . . . I don't know. Law-abiding. And depressed." And distant, I thought. You could be in the same room with my mother and barely feel her presence. "Antidepressants barely seemed to touch her sadness," I added.

Jeannie nodded. "She changed after Lisa passed away," she admitted. "That's very true." She looked at her watch. "So, Riley," she said abruptly, "why did you want to see me today?"

I would have liked to hear more about my mother but guessed Jeannie was pressed for time. "I saw Daddy's lawyer a couple of days ago," I said. "My father left you ten thousand dollars and his piano."

She sat back a bit from the table. "Oh," she said, and I couldn't read the emotion behind the word. "Well, that's very sweet." Her voice was strangely flat. "And I do love that piano. I have an upright, but I guess I can sell that and squeeze the baby grand into my living room."

"You don't have to take it," I said, trying to interpret her reaction. She was clearly not thrilled and that bothered me. He didn't *have* to leave her anything. "I'll be selling his things and I could sell the piano, too, and give you the money."

"No, no," she said quickly. "I'd love the piano. I don't mean to sound ungrateful." Then she smiled a sad, sad smile. "It's just hard to say good-bye, you know? The piano will be a good way for me to remember him. I know some piano movers, and I'll arrange to have them pick it up whenever's convenient for you."

"Perfect." I pulled one of my business cards from my purse, crossed out the number for the school where I worked, and wrote my cell number in its place. I handed it to her across the table.

"So, I assume you'll be selling the house and RV park and all his collections?" she asked, glancing down at the card.

I nodded. "Well, I'll sell the house and park, at least, but he did leave one of his collections to someone. The pipes will go to Tom Kyle. Do you know him?"

"Really?" She wrinkled her nose. "How odd."

"I thought so, too, at first," I said. "But I think the Kyles were closer to him than I realized. They've lived at the park for as long as I can remember and I guess my father probably thought he should leave them something. I think they can use a little extra cash."

She looked at my business card like it was the most interesting thing in the restaurant. "That was very generous of him," she said.

Everything out of her mouth sounded as though it had a double meaning. I set down my taco, feeling impatient. "Is something wrong?" I asked.

"No, no." She smiled. "Not at all. When did your father write that will?"

"Three years ago."

She nodded absently. Sipped her soup. "Don't you wish you could talk to him?" she asked. "I mean, we have to guess why he did what he did. Why the pipes to the Kyles? That collection has to be worth at least ten thousand."

"Seriously?"

"Seriously. Your father knew what he was doing as a collector. I'm not sure he knew what he was doing when he wrote that will, though." She pursed her lips. "He was not all that friendly with the Kyles. I always had the sense he disliked Tom Kyle, actually."

And I'd gotten the sense from Tom Kyle that the feeling may have been mutual. I looked down at my barely touched tacos. "Yes, to answer your question. I'd love to be able to talk to my father. I suddenly feel like I didn't know him as well as I thought."

"Have you been going through his things?" Her head was lowered toward her bowl, but her eyes were raised, watching me from beneath thickly mascaraed lashes. I wasn't sure what was behind her question, but it made me feel guilty. Again.

"Not really," I said. "I haven't known where to begin."

"Would you like help?" She looked excited all of a sudden, as though she'd been waiting for the opportunity to ask. "I'd be happy to do that." She set down her spoon and used her hands to help her talk. "I can track down resources for you," she said. "Appraisers for the collections. Then perhaps buyers. You really need to hold an estate sale and it so happens that my daughter, Christine, recently started an estate sale business, so she can help you set that up. She's very good."

"That would be awesome," I said sincerely, although I found myself leaning away from the table as though blown back by her sudden burst of energy. "I forgot you had a daughter." I wasn't sure I'd ever known.

"She's considerably older than you, so you never

really knew her. She's forty-two now, a couple of years older than Lisa would have been. They played together sometimes when they were little, before Christine and I moved to Asheville." She rolled her eyes. "When Lisa wasn't practicing the violin, that is. Your sister was a driven—and very talented—little girl."

"I know."

"Let me come over and go through the house to see what's there," Jeannie said. "When would be a good time? How long do you plan to be here?"

"I was hoping to be done in a couple of weeks, but I can see that's not going to happen. I have the summer off so—"

"Can your brother help?"

I shook my head, and it was clear I didn't need to explain.

"It's always a bigger job than you imagine," she said. "And with that particular house . . . I can certainly help you get it ready to go on the market, if you like, but I don't want you to feel pressured to use me just because—"

"Please. I'm sure my father would have wanted you to be the one to sell it, and I don't know the first thing about how to do it."

"You can let me take care of everything!" Her cheeks were flushed. "Christine and I will make it easy for you." She pushed her bowl to the side of the table, clearly more interested in talking now than eating. "Now, because of how your father has everything set up in that house—all the built-in cabinets and the way he transformed the living room into an office and everything—I think we'll have to do some renovations to make it look like a comfortable family home," she said. "Nothing huge. No tearing down walls or anything like that, but the cabinets need to go and his furniture is quite old and the kitchen and bathrooms are beyond dated. We should have the estate sale first to get everything we can out of there and then evaluate the need to do the kitchen and baths, because that would be an expense, though perhaps worth it in the long run." She was off and running and I sank lower in my chair, drowning under the deluge of her ideas. "The house has great bones," she continued, "but he let the outside get a bit rundown and with old houses like that, they can look haunted, don't you think?"

"Well, he spent so much time working on the RV park." I felt defensive, although seriously, the RV park looked like it took care of itself. Trees. Creek. Concrete pads. What was there to do?

"How about I get someone over to the house to do the lawn and trim the shrubbery?" Jeannie asked. "Maybe plant something colorful in the front for a little curb appeal?"

"That would be awesome," I said again. I didn't like her—she was pushy and hard to read and I felt resentful of all she knew about me and my family. But I was relieved to have someone to help me.

We settled up with the waitress—Jeannie paid for my barely touched tacos—and we walked out to the sidewalk. Standing in front of the entrance, I turned to face her.

"I'll call you in a day or two and figure out a time for you to come over," I said.

"Don't wait too long," she warned.

"No, I won't," I said.

She lifted my hand and held it tightly as she stared hard into my eyes. I felt gooseflesh rise on the back of my neck.

"I'm so glad to see you again, Riley," she said, finally freeing my hand.

I gave her a weak smile. "I'll call you," I said, and turned to head home, thinking all the way, *What the hell is wrong with that woman?*

7.

There *was* a big box of photographs on the top shelf of my father's bedroom closet. I carried it to his bed, which I'd stripped when I was in town the last time, washing the sheets and pulling the quilt up. I'd noticed then that the quilt had initials in the corner: "JL to FM." At the time, I hadn't thought much about it, too caught up in the sorrow over losing my father. Now I realized Jeannie had most likely made the blue and yellow patchwork quilt for him. A personal thing. Something for his bed.

I wasn't sure why that woman made me so uncomfortable. The fact that she seemed to have been closer to my father than I'd been, I guessed. The suspicion that she'd been happy to get my mother out of the way so she could take her place? That was unfair. My mother'd been her oldest friend—I knew that for a fact—and surely Jeannie was telling the truth when she said that her grief and my father's grief had drawn them together. It was the way she spoke to me. The way she stared at me, especially there on the street after lunch. I was trained, though, to look beyond behavior to motivation. Maybe she was simply uncomfortable with me. She didn't know how to behave with the daughter of her lover.

Whatever.

I sat cross-legged on the bed in front of the box and pulled out photographs by the fistful. For a man who fastidiously displayed his collections, my father was sloppy about the family photos. I spread them around me on the bed. Many of them were from the years before I was born. Baby pictures of Lisa, but not too many of Danny as an infant and even fewer of me. I knew that younger children were neglected when it came to photographs and the recording of every developmental milestone. My parents were probably tired by the time Danny and I came along. Lisa had been eleven years old when Danny was born, and I was sure he and I were surprises. Mom had been a devout Catholic and I doubted she'd used birth control.

As babies, Lisa and Danny looked very much alike. Fair-haired, blue-eyed, long faces. I was the odd one with a little mop of dark hair and dark eyes, a round face and a button nose I was glad I'd outgrown.

There were pictures of Lisa as a child of about five or six. She wore a ruffled pink dress and held a diminutive violin. Her smile was wide, and she still had every one of her small, perfect baby teeth. What had happened? I wondered. How did that happy-looking little girl turn into a teenager sad enough to kill herself?

In the middle of the box were two old VHS tapes. One was labeled "Lisa, April 1980" and the other "Rome Music Festival, June 1987." My heart sped up. I could see and hear my sister! The only problem was, I hadn't seen a VHS player anywhere in the house. I hadn't seen one *anywhere* in years.

I set the tapes on my father's night table and continued digging through the box. There was a picture of Lisa as a very young teen standing with a boy about her own age, both of them holding violins to their chins but smiling for the camera. On the back of the picture, someone had written "Lisa and Matty, '85." She would have been around thirteen. I had no idea who Matty was, other than a cute kid with a mass of dark curls and chocolate-brown eyes. I found another picture of the two of them at sixteen, standing back-to-back, a strand of Lisa's pale hair tangled in one of Matty's dark curls. Lisa wore a white oval-shaped pendant around her neck. Matty's smile looked genuine, but I thought Lisa'd had to work at hers. Or maybe I was reading too much into a photograph, one tiny fraction of a second, frozen in time.

I recognized Jeannie in one of the pictures. Her dark hair was long and she had her arm around my mother. Lisa, about eight years old in the picture, leaned against my mother's side and a black-haired girl a couple of years older and several inches taller leaned against Jeannie's. That had to be her daughter, Christine, the one who could help me with an estate sale. Everyone looked happy in this picture, my mother included. Her smile was wide, the tilt of her head playful. It was a jolt, seeing that relaxed and lighthearted side of her. But in this happy photograph, she hadn't yet lost her daughter.

As I looked at the picture of my mother, I remembered the weeks before her death from cancer. She'd wanted to be at home, and the hospice nurses taught Daddy and me how to care for her here in this bedroom. I'd nearly lived at her bedside night and day during those last weeks. I felt like I grew up that summer. I bathed my mother, managed her medications, held her hand. I told her every day that I loved her, and sometimes when Daddy wanted to take over from me, I resisted. I wanted every extra minute with her that I could have. My usually reserved mother was softer, more open, in those last weeks, and although our conversations were never deep or profound, we probably talked more than we did during my whole life. Her focus was on our future—mine and Daddy's and Danny's. Danny was still in the hospital in Maryland then and unable to travel. "You all need to stay in touch with each other," my mother had said. "You need to take care of each other." I hadn't done such a great job of that with Danny. He made it hard. I thought I'd stayed in good touch with my father, but now, knowing he'd been unable to be open with me about his life, I worried that I'd failed not just Danny, but everybody.

I set the picture aside, wondering if I should give it to Jeannie, but then I thought about the hundreds of photographs Jeannie most likely had of herself and her daughter over the years, and the few I had of my mother and sister, and I set the picture with the others that I would keep. I wanted to remember my mother this way, happy and content with her life.

The next picture I pulled from the box was of Danny in his uniform. The expression in his eyes was empty, as though he was surrendering to his fate. Or maybe I was once again reading too much into a picture with the benefit of hindsight.

There was another picture of Matty, the boy with the curly dark hair. He sat on a bench at a baby grand piano—ours?—between Danny and myself. I couldn't have been more than two and Matty had his hand on mine above the piano keys, as if he was trying to teach me to play. *Good luck with that,* I thought. Funny to see myself in that picture when I didn't remember Matty at all.

Beneath those pictures was a large framed photograph that made me gasp with recognition. I knew this picture. It was a professional shot of Lisa, Danny, and myself. Lisa and Danny sat side by side on a white up-holstered love seat and I sat on Lisa's lap. I couldn't have been more than a year and a half. That would have made Danny about five and Lisa sixteen. All three of us were dressed in white. My hair was the only dark thing in the whole photograph and I wondered if it had irritated the photographer. Had I messed up an otherwise ethereal composition? Danny grinned at the camera, a gap where one of his front teeth should have been. My head was turned to the side and I was reaching up, toward his chin. I felt a twist in my chest, looking at the picture. I'd loved him so much, my big brother. He'd looked out for me. I was always mystified when other kids said they hated their siblings or tried to get them in trouble. There was never any of that between Danny and me. I treasured this picture. I was glad my parents selected this one over their other choices—surely there had been one where I was looking directly at the camera? But this photograph, with my hand reaching out for my brother, said so much more. Was there any way, I wondered, to get that connection back?

And what did the photograph say about Lisa? She was only months from her death, and I swore I could see the pain in her face. She smiled for the camera, of course, like a dutiful daughter, but when people say "her smile didn't reach her eyes" . . . well, looking at this picture, I understood that phrase. Had she been thinking about her application to Juilliard when this picture was taken? Had the fact that she was talented enough to apply not been enough to validate her? What pressure she must have been under during her whole young life. *Child prodigy.* It couldn't have been easy for her.

I must have stared at the picture for half an hour, wishing I could change things for her, the sister I never got to know. "I'm changing things for other kids," I whispered out loud to the room. I hoped that, somehow, she could hear me.

I suddenly remembered the first time I'd seen this photograph. I'd found it tucked away, facedown, in the dresser drawer where my mother kept her scarves. I was seven. I'd recognized Danny and myself, of course, but I didn't know who the older girl was, though she was a little bit familiar. I carried the photograph into the living room, where my father was playing the piano and my mother sat on the couch, helping Danny with his homework.

"Who's this girl?" I asked, holding up the picture in its carved wooden frame.

All three of them looked at me, and then my parents looked at each other.

"It's Lisa," Danny said. "Don't you remember her?" I'd heard her name before, scattered here and there in conversations that went over my head.

"Come here, Riley," my mother said, patting the couch next to her. My father turned on the piano bench to face us as I took a seat next to my mother. I held the framed photograph on my lap.

"Lisa was your sister," my mother said. "She passed away when she was seventeen. You were not quite two."

I looked at the picture again. The girl suddenly seemed more familiar to me, yet I couldn't remember her. Not really. I couldn't remember ever talking to her or touching her. I didn't know much about death at that age. All four of my grandparents were dead, and the only one I'd ever gotten to know had died of a heart attack the year before.

I looked up at my mother. "Was it a heart attack?" I asked.

"No," Danny said. "She did it to herself."

"Danny!" my father snapped at him, and my mother gave him a little smack on his knee, but that cat was out of the bag.

I looked across my mother's lap at my brother. "What's that mean?" I asked.

"She drowned," my father said. "That's all you need to know."

"Why did Danny say she did it to herself?"

"She drowned on purpose," Danny said.

How could you drown on purpose? I could hold my breath for forty seconds and after that I needed air. I couldn't imagine how someone could drown herself.

"Why did she do it?" I asked.

My mother glanced at the picture in my lap, but only for a second. "Sometimes when a person is very, very unhappy," she said, "they forget that they'll someday feel better and they just want to end the unhappiness. That's what happened to Lisa. She felt so unhappy that she thought she'd never be happy again, and she ended her life. It was a terrible and very wrong thing to do. Don't *ever* think about doing anything like that, Riley," she added.

"If you ever feel that sad, you come tell us," my father said.

"I could never be that sad," I said, looking at the girl in the picture, still trying to wrap my head around the fact that she'd ever existed at all.

I never forgot my mother's words about Lisa feeling unhappy and thinking she'd never feel happy again. I thought about that every time I counseled a depressed kid. I thought about it every time *I* felt unhappy, reminding myself I would one day be happy again. I could use that reminder right now.

I carried the photograph into my bedroom and set it on the nightstand. I'd sort through all those other pictures soon and decide which ones to keep and which to toss. But this one picture, I would keep always. I smiled at it where it rested upright on the nightstand. The three of us, together. My family.

8.

It was searingly hot the next morning as I drove down the rutted road toward Danny's clearing, and even with my air conditioner blasting cool air in my face, I was perspiring. On the seat next to me was a key ring I'd discovered in my father's desk drawer. Most of the keys belonged to the various curio cabinets, but there was one that appeared to fit nothing in the house and I hoped it would get me into Daddy's RV. I'd also brought a few of the old photographs with me, hoping Danny might like to see them. Doubtful, but worth a shot. I actually wanted an excuse to check on him. I hadn't spoken to him since dropping him off at his trailer the other night and I knew he hadn't been in the best shape. He wasn't answering the phone I'd given him, either. I had a feeling he hadn't bothered to turn it on.

I turned onto the trail through the woods and nearly drove head-on into a police car coming from the direction of the clearing. *Oh, God.* Why was a cop coming from Danny's place? I was in a panic as I got out of my car, but then I got a look at the officer in the cruiser. Dark skin. Hair beginning to gray at the temples. Harry?

He grinned at me as he stepped out of the car, and my body nearly sagged with relief. "Hey, Riley," he said. "One of us is going to have to back up."

"Is everything okay?" I asked. He was in uniform, his navy blue shirt crisp-looking in spite of the heat. "How come you're here?"

"Just dropping some books off for your brother." That grin again. "Him and me got a little book club going."

"He's okay?"

"Why wouldn't he be?"

"Oh, I just freaked out when I saw your car. He was pretty down when I saw him the other night."

"He's fine." A shaft of sunlight pierced the trees and he shaded his dark brown eyes. "You don't see him all that often, so you're not used to his ups and downs," he said. "He's a survivor. It's the other guy that has to watch out for him."

"I know you keep an eye on him, Harry," I said. "Thank you."

Harry shrugged like it was nothing. "He's my brother," he said. "We all keep an eye on each other."

I knew what he meant by *brother*—they'd served in the army together and that bond would always be there—and yet I felt envious that Harry seemed more sure of his relationship with Danny than I did.

"I wish I could get him to move closer to me," I said.

He smiled. "How many times have we had this conversation, Riley?" he asked.

I laughed. "I know," I said. "I just wish I could."

"I've got to get rolling." He pointed to my car. "You okay with backing up? We're a lot closer to the road here than the clearing."

"Sure," I said, not looking forward to driving in reverse through the woods. I waved at him as I got behind the wheel again. I put the car in reverse and slowly backed out through the tunnel of trees. Once on the road, he drove past me with a wave, and I headed down the trail toward the clearing again.

When I pulled into the clearing, I spotted Danny lounging in his hammock, one hand holding a book open on his stomach and, in the other hand, a bottle of beer, and I wondered if he might have the right idea about how to live after all. I was the one scrambling around in a panic as I tried to sort out all the things I needed to do, while—at least from a distance—he looked like a man without a worry in the world.

I got out of my car, a tote bag containing the old photographs and the key ring hanging from my shoulder. When he saw me, Danny swung his legs over the edge of the hammock until he was sitting up, his sandaled feet barely touching the ground.

"You're not answering your phone!" I called, walking toward him across the pine-needle-covered floor of the clearing.

"Forgot to turn it on," he said.

"Why don't I believe you?" I aimed for a teasing tone in my voice, but wasn't sure I succeeded. "What are you reading?" I stopped walking a couple of yards from the hammock.

He glanced at the cover of the tattered-looking paperback and shrugged. "World War II fiction," he said. "I take whatever Harry brings me."

"I just saw him. We almost had a head-on collision on the trail." I dug my hand into the tote bag and pulled out the key ring. "I think one of these is for Daddy's RV," I said. "Do you want to check it out with me? Maybe you'd even like to have it?" I asked, hopeful. "It's not much bigger than yours, so you could move it here to your clearing and have two trailers. More space."

"I'm fine with what I've got." He pushed his feet into the ground so that the hammock swung a little.

"Should I sell it, then? His RV? Or I could see if the Kyles would like it."

"Whatever you want to do with it is cool with me." He held up his beer bottle. "Want one?" he asked.

"No, thanks." My phone rang and I pulled it from my pocket and checked the caller ID, though I was already sure who was calling. Jeannie Lyons had been badgering me since our lunch the day before, anxious to get moving on the house. She was way too pushy for my comfort level. I hit ignore and slipped the phone into my pocket again.

"Jeannie Lyons," I said to Danny. "She's going to help with the house. Did you know that she and Daddy were lovers?"

He stopped swaying the hammock, and the stunned look on his face told me he'd had no idea.

"Well, I wish you hadn't told me that," he said. "Revolting images playing in my head right now." He waved his hand in front of his eyes as if he could make the images go away.

I laughed. "It's just . . . weird, isn't it?" I asked. "*She's* weird. It's been going on for years."

"*Damn*," he said. "I didn't know the old man had it in him."

I reached into the tote and pulled out the framed photograph of Danny with Lisa and myself. "I found a whole bunch of pictures." I stepped in front of him and held out the frame. "I love this one," I said. "I love how I'm reaching toward you. Remember how close we were when we were kids?"

He barely glanced at the picture before lifting his eyes to mine again. "We were babies back then," he said. "Fucking innocents."

I lowered the frame to my side, disappointed. I could hardly bear how lonely his response made me feel. I had a box of treasures but no one to share them with. I wouldn't show him the others I'd brought with me.

"I found some VHS tapes of Lisa that I want to watch," I said, "only I had to order a VHS player, so I can't see them until it arrives. I'm guessing you don't have any interest in watching them with—"

"You couldn't pay me enough," he said. "I had to watch her perform thousands of times when I was a kid. That was enough."

I felt defeated. "Why are you so . . . *disdainful* about her?" I asked.

"You were too little to remember what it was like," he said. "Lisa was their princess. Their little violin goddess. Their *everything*. You and I could never measure up."

"I never felt that way," I said, defensive of our parents.

"Well, you were not even two when she died, so you lucked out." He sounded bitter. "The world revolved around her. When she killed herself, she took our parents with her. She turned them into zombies and you and I were left to fend for ourselves." He shook his head, looking down at the book where it rested next to him on the hammock. "This is pointless," he said. "Talking about the past. Totally pointless." He motioned toward the photograph, still clutched in my hand. "Why do you want to live in the past?" he asked.

"I don't."

"You're looking through old pictures. What's the use?"

I looked away from him and into the forest. I could feel the carved wood of the frame beneath my fingers. "It's because I feel alone, Danny," I said finally, turning toward him again. "I miss having a family, and I really wish you and I could be closer, but you won't even answer the phone when I call. I promise I won't call about helping with the house, okay? I get that you don't want to do that. But can we at least hang out a little while I'm here?"

"What would we do?"

"Anything," I said, exasperated. "We could go to the movies or out to dinner or . . . you could take me to your favorite bar." I remembered he'd been banned from his favorite bar and wished I hadn't added that. "Maybe we could go out with Harry and his wife some night. You could introduce me to your friends."

"Most of my friends are online."

"Well, then, you can tell me about them."

He smiled at me, the sort of indulgent smile an older brother might give his little sister. "You want me to be someone I'm not, Riles," he said.

"Maybe I do," I admitted. "I'll work on that, but could we at least see each other? We can hang out on your terms. Whatever you want to do. Just include me while I'm here, okay? Not every minute. Just sometimes. What do you like to do?"

"Read. Walk in the forest. Fish. And I like to get shit-faced drunk."

"I can do that." I smiled, game for anything. "Or I could be your designated driver."

"Maybe," he said. "But we stick to the here and now, all right? No old photographs"—he motioned toward the frame in my hand—"or old tapes or stories about Dad's sex life. Deal?"

"Deal," I said. And we shook on it.

9.

I drove away from Danny's trailer and turned right on the gravel road toward the RV park. *Okay,* I thought, *the way to deal with Danny is to focus on the here and now.* I felt some joy, as though I'd found a path into his troubled mind. I wouldn't bring up our family with him again. Though I bet he talked about the past with his online ex-military buddies. Wasn't that what those guys did? Relive everything that happened to them over there? Whatever. I'd leave the past in the past. I'd try to find a movie playing nearby that he might be interested in. I'd take him to dinner. We could talk about books. Some nice, safe topic. Maybe I *could* get him to move up to Durham, closer to me. There were more services for veterans up there.

But I was getting ahead of myself.

My father's small RV stood where it always had, in the first of the park's twelve sites. The old trailer had once been white with a green stripe down the side, but although the green was still in pretty good shape, the white had aged to a dingy yellow. I pulled up next to it on the concrete pad and was about to get out of my car when my phone rang again. Pulling the phone from my tote bag, I saw *Jean Lyons* on the caller ID. With a sigh, I lifted the phone to my ear. Might as well get it over with.

"Hi, Jeannie," I said, opening my car door wide to let the air in.

"Listen, honey, I'm swamped the rest of today and tomorrow morning," she said, "but I could come over tomorrow afternoon. Christine's dying to meet you, but she's tied up till next week, so I can get started on making an inventory of everything in the house. Then we can get cooking on—"

"Oh, I'm sorry," I interrupted. "I have plans for tomorrow." I was lying, but I needed one more day to myself without Jeannie in it. "The next day, maybe?"

"I have two showings that day." She sounded frustrated. "And you need to get going on this or we'll be putting the house on the market too close to the schools opening. We're way too late as it is."

"Tuesday?" I suggested.

"You know," she said, "you don't really need to be there tomorrow. You can go on about your business and I'll come over in the afternoon and get to work. I have a key so I can let myself in."

She had a key to the house? Well, of course she did, but for some reason, that creeped me out.

"I'd rather be there, Jeannie," I said. "I want to go through everything, too. We'll just have to wait a few days."

I heard her sigh. "All right," she said. "If you change your mind, let me know."

I hung up the phone and shoved it in the pocket of my shorts. Could she be any pushier? Picking up the ring of keys from the passenger seat, I got out of my car.

It took a few tries to get the key to turn in the rusty RV lock and the door creaked open on its hinges. I was nearly blown back by the heat and the scent of mold and mildew. I turned on the air-conditioning, relieved to find it still worked. In spite of the mustiness, the small space looked fairly neat. A threadbare navy blue spread was pulled over the narrow bed and the only thing on the built-in table was a small CD player, tucked close to the wall.

I went through the dresser and kitchen drawers and the one closet, but found little besides a few towels and some well-used rags. A couple of fishing poles stood upright against the wall next to the lavatory. The mini-refrigerator was empty except for three of cans of Pepsi and a nearly empty bottle of Chardonnay, and there was no food in any of the kitchen cabinets, although I did find evidence that mice had made the space their home sometime in the not-too-distant past.

A small TV sat at the far end of the kitchen counter, and a row of CDs, bookended by fist-sized rocks on the left and right, was lined up next to the small sink. No vinyl here, I thought. Taped to the wall above the CDs was a newspaper ad for a concert, and I recognized the picture of the four musicians from that postcard in the purple envelope, the one from the post office box in Pollocksville. *What a weird coincidence,* I thought. A child's stick-figure drawing of two smiling adults and two smiling children was taped next to the ad. Then there was a photograph of a couple of kids on a merry-go-round. I pulled it from the wall for a closer look. The girl was two at the most, the boy a few years older. Both redheads. They had to be brother and sister, but who were they? If Daddy had truly been close to Jeannie, maybe these were her grandkids?

As I retaped the picture to the wall, I saw the cover of the first CD in the row. Alison Krauss. My father listening to bluegrass? I pulled out a couple of the other CDs. Ricky Skaggs? Béla Fleck?

I was starting to feel like a trespasser. This couldn't be my father's trailer. I kept glancing out the dirty windows, expecting the real owner—or renter—of the RV to show up any minute, angry over my intrusion into his space. I replaced the CDs and had turned off the air-conditioning when I noticed the VHS player beneath the television. I stared at it for a moment in disbelief, then detached it from the TV, tucked it under my arm, and left the RV, locking the door behind me.

I put the VHS player in my car, then decided to walk rather than drive down to the Kyles' RV at the other end of the park. My feet crunched on the gravel as I headed east, and it was a pretty walk along the winding lane through the trees. Though the park was short on amenities, it had a natural beauty that I guessed had drawn my father to it to begin with. Through the trees, I could see more RVs than the last time I'd stopped by. The park was filling up for the weekend. I heard voices as I passed a couple of the RV sites, and at one point I smelled bacon frying, the scent heady and delicious.

As near as I could figure, my father had been in his midforties when we moved to New Bern, too early for him to have retired from the U.S. Marshals Service. Maybe he'd burned out or just needed to get away from the pressure and rat race of Washington. Both he and my mother had inherited some family money. Not a lot, but it had probably been enough to allow him to get out early if he wanted to after Lisa died. They could get a fresh start somewhere else. I would never know. It was too late to ask him all the questions I had now.

I reached the Kyles' dented old motor home. Their car was gone and I was afraid they weren't home, but as I neared the RV, the door opened and Verniece Kyle stood beneath the striped awning.

"Hello, Riley!" she called. "How are you, love?"

"I'm good." I smiled. I loved her sweetness. "Do you have a minute?"

"Of course. Tom's fishing and I'd enjoy the company. Don't you have the prettiest hair, the way the sun's shining on it."

"Thanks," I said, climbing into the RV.

"How about some coffee and we'll sit out on the patio?"

I'd already had two cups that morning, but I liked the idea of sitting with her, sipping coffee and chatting. Verniece wasn't much older than Jeannie, but I had a completely different response to her. Frankly, I liked having someone call me *love*, even if she probably used that endearment for everyone from her husband to the checkout clerks at the grocery store.

We carried our mugs out to the patio and sat down on a couple of blue-webbed lawn chairs.

"Do you get lonely out here?" I asked, nestling the mug in my lap.

"Oh, no," she said. "No more than any other housewife gets lonely. I like meeting all the newcomers to the park and of course there are those folks who come back year after year. It's a lot of fun. Plus, I'm really involved with the church. That's not Tom's thing. I need to be around people more than he does."

We sipped our weak coffee and talked about a few

of the people who had checked in the night before. Then I put my cup on the plastic table next to me and reached into my purse for my key ring.

"I stopped by my father's RV on my way here, and I wondered if you and Tom would like to have it," I said. I worked the RV's key free of the ring and set it on the table. "I know it's not in the best shape, but I figured you could sell it or rent or . . ." I shrugged.

"You don't want it?" she asked. "What about your brother?"

"He doesn't want it," I said. "I looked through it to be sure there wasn't anything I should keep, and it seemed like my father hadn't been inside it much in a while. Has someone else been using it, do you know?"

She shook her head. "Not that I know of. Your father was there a couple of times a month, I'd say. He liked to be close to the water, like Tom."

"Speaking of Mr. Kyle," I said, glad for the opening, "when I was going through my father's checkbook, I realized he's been paying Tom five hundred dollars a month and I don't know what that's for. I don't know if my father owed him money or what."

She stared at me blankly. I'd flummoxed her. "I have no idea," she said. "Are you sure about that? Maybe it was for . . ." Her voice faded away as she shook her head. "Well, I have no earthly idea what it was for, actually. Every single month?"

I nodded, but wished I'd kept my mouth shut and waited to talk to her husband about it. I had a terrible feeling I'd told her something no one had wanted her to know.

"Maybe Tom would want my father's fishing gear that's in the RV," I said, to change the subject.

"Sure." She let me change it, but her eyes were still

cloudy with confusion. "I'll tell him to look it over and see what he wants," she said.

We had a few more quiet sips of coffee.

"Did you remember who you had me mixed up with?" I asked after a while. "When you thought I was adopted?

"Oh, you're not still thinking about that, are you?" she said. "I should have kept my fool mouth shut. And it doesn't matter, does it, Riley?" she asked. "Adopted or not, you had wonderful parents and you turned out fine."

"You sound like you still think I was?"

She looked toward the creek, breathing loudly enough for me to hear. "I'm going to tell you something, Riley," she said, very slowly, as though her head and her mouth were not in agreement about what she had to say. "I don't know what your parents would think of me telling you this, but I'm a firm believer in knowing the truth about where you come from. I like to think your father would have done it at some point, but then he waited too long."

"What are you talking about?" I asked.

"We told Luke right from the start that he was adopted," she said. "He looked for his birth parents when he was nineteen, with our blessing. We felt we should be totally open with him about it. No secrets. I know your parents felt differently, but—"

"Verniece!" I said, exasperated. I was beginning to think Tom Kyle was right about her lost marbles.

She looked up at the sky through the canopy of trees and let out a long sigh. "Do you want to know the truth?" she asked.

I felt a chill run up my back. "Yes," I said, "though I think I *do* know the truth. I mean, I still think you have my family mixed up with someone else."

She scratched her cheek, slowly. Thoughtfully. She

looked out toward the creek again. "I met Tom in 1980 when I was thirty-two years old," she said. "I was a police dispatcher in Maryland back then. Now that was a job!" She gave me a rueful smile. "We were married a year later and immediately started trying to have a baby. It took a while for us to get pregnant and we were thrilled, but I miscarried right at twelve weeks."

"I'm sorry." I had no idea where she was going with this.

"I got pregnant again and miscarried again. Five times, Riley." She looked at me, the pain of those miscarriages still in her eyes. "It was a nightmare. I finally carried a baby to term, only to have her be stillborn."

"Oh, no," I said, trying to imagine it. "What a terrible blow for you."

"Terrible doesn't begin to describe it," she said. "I met your mother right after it happened. There was some function . . . your father and Tom worked together, did you know that?"

"*No,*" I said. "Tom worked for the U.S. Marshals Service?"

"Uh-huh."

"I didn't even know my father did until I met with his lawyer."

"Really?" she said. "Your family . . ." She shook her head. "Not very open with one another, were they?"

I started to speak, but didn't know what to say. It seemed she was right.

"Well, anyhow," she continued, "Tom and your father worked together, and there was . . . I don't remember exactly what it was—a big picnic or some outdoor get-together that was important for us to attend. Tom had trouble dragging me out of the house. I was extremely depressed after the stillbirth and could barely function.

But for some reason, I went with him. Your father was his supervisor and I think there was some expectation everybody turn out for this"—she waved her hand through the air—"this picnic or whatever it was. Oh! It was a retirement party for one of the marshals. This would have been '88. Or I guess '89. Anyway, there were lawn chairs and I ended up sitting next to your mother, who I didn't know very well at all, and all I could do was cry. She was a very kind woman, and when she saw how upset I was, she took my hand and walked me away from the crowd and we sat under a tree and I told her everything and sobbed and sobbed. And sobbed some more. She had a lot of sympathy. *Empathy*'s a better word for it. A lot of empathy. She held my hand while we talked. I was a stranger to her, but you know how women can sometimes get close very quickly."

I nodded, suddenly choked up. I missed my mother.

"After I'd told her everything, she asked me if we'd consider adoption and I said we were too old, but she shook her head. And that's when she told me."

"Told you what?"

"That she and your father had wanted more children because there was such a gap between your older brother and sister. They wanted Danny to have a sibling. But they weren't getting pregnant. Then they looked into private adoption and found a baby girl being put up for adoption here in North Carolina and they were able to get her. Get you."

Was she crazy? Or could she possibly be right? "This doesn't make any sense." I tried to keep my voice calm, but I felt it rising.

"She gave me hope. She said they planned to tell you when you were old enough to understand, but it sounds like they never got around to it. It never occurred to me that you still didn't know."

"This is *insane,*" I said, but I was more aware than ever before of my dark hair and dark eyes.

"I'm so sorry if I've upset you, Riley. The last thing I'd want to do is turn your world upside down. But like I said, it doesn't really matter if—"

"Are you absolutely sure it wasn't someone else you talked to that day? That it was my mother?"

"Honey, I'll never forget your mother. Not even a year after that day, she lost your sister and they moved down here. They were running away, coming down here, but you can't run away from some things." She shook her head. "You don't forget a woman who went through something like that."

"I'm still having trouble believing this," I said. I *didn't* believe it. My parents had not been the most open people in the world, but I couldn't imagine them keeping this from me.

"Do you wish I hadn't told you?" Verniece looked worried. "Tom said I should butt out."

"No, I'm glad you told me. I just . . ." I gave my head a shake, trying to clear away the crazy doubts that were filling it. "I'm still not sure it was my mother you were talking to."

She smiled. "I understand," she said. "I'm sure I'd feel the same way if I were you. But it was, Riley. I can promise you that."

I felt nauseous as I walked back to my car. The scent of bacon still clung to that one spot along the gravel lane and this time I rushed to get past it. I was nearly to my father's trailer when I spotted Tom walking toward me, carrying his fishing rod and basket.

"Hi, Mr. Kyle," I said when he was close enough to hear. "I have a question for you."

"What's that?" he asked. He had a stubble of gray beard I hadn't noticed the other day and he looked no happier to see me now than he had then.

"My father was paying you five hundred dollars a month," I said. "What was that for?"

"Doesn't matter now," he said. He started to walk past me and I could smell beer on him, as I had the other day. I wondered how much of a problem he had with alcohol.

"Tom?" I said, and he turned around, looking at me without a word.

"Do you think I was adopted?"

He scowled. "You need to stay away from here," he said. "Stay away from Verniece. She's not in her right mind and it upsets her, seeing you."

"What are you talking about?" I almost shouted. "If anyone should be upset, it should be *me*."

"Just stay away, all right? For your own good."

I opened my mouth to speak again, but he'd already turned away, leaving me with many more questions than answers.

10.

As I got back into my car next to Daddy's RV, I wished I could talk to my brother again. He'd been four when I was born. If I'd been adopted, was there a chance he would know? But I'd just promised him I'd stick to the present and put the past behind us—or at least, behind *him*—so I forced myself to turn left out of the park, away from Danny and his trailer.

My whole body felt different all of a sudden, as though my genes were reorganizing themselves inside me as I drove back to the house. Verniece Kyle seemed so sure of what she'd told me! Not the least bit crazy. She struck me as a woman who saw kindness in honesty. As a counselor, I agreed with her: truth was always better than a lie. As Riley MacPherson, whose grasp on sanity wasn't all that strong these days, I wasn't so sure.

When I reached the house, I struggled to figure out how to set up the dusty old VHS player so it would work with Daddy's relatively new flat-screen TV in the living room. I had to go online to figure it out, setting my laptop on the rolltop desk, and while I was on the Internet, almost without thinking, I Googled "how to learn if you're adopted." *Talk to older relatives,* one site suggested. Well, I would if I had any. Danny was my only hope there. *Search birth records.* Not as easy as it sounded, I quickly discovered. Birth records were not simply sitting on the Internet waiting to be found. *Check your birth certificate for place of birth.* My birth certificate was somewhere in my Durham apartment. I had no idea where. I'd probably been a teenager the last time I looked at that thing. I couldn't remember anything unusual about it.

When I finished searching the Internet, I sat in front of my laptop, my hands folded in my lap. I was nervous about watching the tapes. I had no memory of my sister from when she was alive. In all my memories of her, she was frozen in time in a photograph. I didn't know how I'd feel, seeing her in action. I was afraid of the grief. The loss. Danny complained about having to listen to her play far too often. I would have traded a year of my life to hear her just once.

According to the instructions I'd found on the Internet, I needed a particular cable to hook up the VHS player to the TV. I knew there was a drawer in the kitchen filled with all sorts of cables. I sat cross-legged on the floor in front of the drawer, pulling apart the tangle of cords and cables until I found the one I needed. Back in the living room, I had no problem connecting the tape player to the TV. I slipped the older of the two tapes—1980—into the player, sat on the sofa, and hit play.

The tape began, and I sat forward on the edge of the sofa, clutching the remote in my hand. The image was grainy, but clear enough that I could see a little girl dwarfed by a cavernous stage as she lifted a violin to her chin. I wasn't even sure it was Lisa, but as she began to play the camera zoomed close enough that I could see the fair hair. She would have been seven in 1980, I thought. A tiny, skinny, fragile-looking seven, and although her features were indistinct, I imagined the concentration in her face as she played. I didn't know the piece, but it was clearly complex and tears filled my eyes.

I moved to the floor in front of the TV, trying to get even closer to my sister, my throat so tight it ached. What incredible courage she had had to be able to stand on that huge stage in front of . . . I couldn't see the audience, but I imagined there were hundreds of people seated in the auditorium. Danny would not have been born yet, and I wondered if it would temper his envy of her to see her at such a tender age and realize the pressure she must have been under during her entire short life.

The tape was a little more than an hour long, and I watched every second of it, mesmerized. It contained bits and pieces of different recitals and concerts. In a couple of segments, Lisa performed with other children, although it was obvious she was the youngest, the tiniest of them all. In one piece, she was the only child in a sea of adult violinists. That segment hurt me the most to watch. Although she played with confidence and skill, I thought I could see the vulnerability in her. The tender innocence that any child of seven would have. How hard had she been pushed? I wondered if she was truly doing what she'd wanted to be doing. She'd never been allowed to have a real childhood.

"I'm so sorry," I whispered, reaching forward to touch the screen with my fingertips.

When the tape ended, I sat still for a moment before ejecting it and inserting the second. "Rome Music Festival, June 1987" the label read. Lisa would have been fourteen in 1987. This tape was much clearer, with a professional quality to it. It opened in what looked like the gate of an airport. A group of energetic teens appeared to have taken over the seating area, some of them standing, others sitting, all of them laughing and talking. I searched the faces for my sister. A few frowning adults sat in nearby seats, clearly not amused at finding themselves surrounded by a bunch of rowdy teenagers, probably Lisa's fellow music students. They were all about the age of the kids I counseled, thirty or forty of them, loud and goofing around while crammed into the waiting area. The scene, full of adolescent hormones and blossoming egos, would have been comical if I hadn't been so intent on finding Lisa in the crowd.

A brown-haired man appeared on the screen. He held his right arm in the air, and as if he'd cast a spell over them, the kids stopped what they were doing and looked in his direction. He was tall and slender, with a thin angular face that was just shy of handsome. He gave a slight nod, and the kids pulled their instruments from cases I'd barely noticed till that moment. They began to play. Violins. Violas. Cellos. As usual, I had no idea what music they were playing but it was a happy, bouncy melody that quickly had the sour-faced spectators not only smiling, but clapping.

I finally spotted Lisa. She stood to the side, nearly out of the camera's view. I recognized the boy next to her from the photographs in my father's box. Matty, with the curly dark hair. When that piece was over, the conductor or teacher, or whatever he was, motioned to Lisa and she moved forward. He lifted his baton, and she began to play a solo. She looked very much like a feminine version of Danny. She was so pretty. There was a fragility to her features, but it was clear that when it came to her violin, there was nothing fragile about her. She was in complete command. I knew she'd been good—I knew she'd been a prodigy—but I found her incredible talent heartbreaking. Somehow it had cost her. It had cost her everything.

I fast-forwarded through the tape and saw the same group of kids behaving like idiots at the Trevi Fountain and the Spanish Steps and in front of the Colosseum. My sister and Matty were always a little off to the side, talking together. Sometimes laughing. Not quite part of the crowd. Then the group performed with hundreds of other young musicians in front of an audience in an enormous, ancient-looking building with ceilings so high they weren't on the TV screen, and pillars as big around as the living room I was sitting in. At one point, Lisa stepped forward from the rest of the group as she had in the airport. Dressed in white, she looked like an ethereal angel as she raised her violin and began to play. To the far right of the screen, I saw the tall conductor again, and even though there was quite a distance between him and Lisa, it was as though a fine thread ran from his white baton to her violin, coaxing every note from the instrument. This music I knew: Mendelssohn's Violin Concerto in E Minor. My father listened to it all the time. The familiar piece used to drift through the rooms of our house until I was numbed by it, but I was anything but numb now, hearing Lisa play it. I swallowed hard, wanting both to turn off the tape and to play it over and over again.

When the camera closed in tight on Lisa's face, I leaned forward and saw the long fair lashes above her closed eyes, the delicate crease between her eyebrows, as if the music pained her. I wished so much that Danny was watching the tape with me. That I had someone to share the emotions with.

I made it through the first movement of the concerto before I needed to turn off the tape. I sat in front of the TV, crying until I could cry no more, overwhelmed with grief for the sister I'd never gotten to know. It had only been a couple of hours since I'd started watching the tapes, but it may as well have been a month for how changed I felt. Even though I'd never had the chance to know her, she'd been such an influence on my life and I was full of love for her. Yet I realized now that I'd made her up. I'd had to imagine what she'd been like because I had no way of knowing. Now suddenly, I'd seen her face. I saw how hard she worked. She'd been just a kid. Practically a baby in that first tape and a young and hopeful teenager in the second. All anyone would be able to see as they watched her perform was the skill and perfection; no one could see the toll her career was taking on her heart and soul.

What was it that caused her to break apart? That conductor—had he demanded perfection of her? Had my parents? Had the fame been too much for her? I ran my fingers through my hair, my tears falling all over again. I wished I could hug her! Hold her tight. I wished I could tell her she didn't need to be perfect; she only needed to be Lisa. I wanted to reach inside those tapes and tell that delicate young angel to hold on. *Someday,* I would promise her, *it will be all right.*

11.

"You'll be shocked what people will buy at an estate sale," Jeannie said as we poked through the items in my mother's china cabinet in the dining room. In my hand, I held an old green bowl that had clearly been broken in two and glued back together "Christine will want you to leave everything just as it is."

"Even broken dishes?" I asked, holding the bowl so she could see the crack.

"Absolutely," she said. "Artists use them to make jewelry and all sorts of things you can't imagine. So we want to leave everything in place. You don't need those boxes." She pointed to the three empty boxes I'd found in the basement. My plan had been to fill them with things to donate, but Jeannie had a different idea. "I do want to get a closer look at the collections and figure out what sort of appraisers we need to call," she said. "If there are any things you want to keep—items with sentimental value, for example—just set them aside. We can make a place for them in your father's upstairs office. For now, you can clean out those cabinets in the living room where he kept all his paperwork." She took the green bowl from my hand and put it back in the china cabinet. "Let's go take a look in there," she said, and I followed her into the living room. She stood in the middle of the room, hands on her hips, and both of us faced the ten built-in cabinets that ran the entire length of the living room beneath the windows. "I know he would just stuff insurance forms and all sort of things in there that can probably just be shredded. That can be your job."

"All right." I dreaded even opening those cabinets. I'd seen how Daddy crammed papers into them with as little care as if he was tossing them in the trash.

"Look at those hydrangeas!" Jeannie took a step toward the windows that overlooked the side yard. "How your father loved them," she said. "I wish he could have had one more summer. He was looking forward to it. His favorite season."

I hadn't known that about my father and it irked me that she did. But I was determined to be nice to her today. I really needed her help.

"What the hell . . . ?" She suddenly noticed that the sliding glass doors were missing from the pipe collection. "Where's the glass?"

I thought of making something up, but decided to tell her the truth. "Danny was over the other night and he got upset about something and threw a beer bottle at them," I said.

"That's terrible!" she said. "Your father always insisted Danny wasn't violent."

"He's not." I remembered Danny saying he'd put on his PTSD act for Jeannie, whatever that meant. "He was just angry. He'd never hurt a person."

"Are you very close to him?"

"I was when we were young. He was more withdrawn as he got older and we didn't talk as much. He became more like my father, I guess. Very introverted." I missed the Danny I'd grown up with.

"I don't think of your father as all that introverted," Jeannie said.

I worked hard to produce a smile. I was sick of her thinking she knew Daddy so much better than I did. "I guess we experienced him differently," I said.

"Oh, well." She smiled. "We both know he was a good man, and that's what counts."

I nodded. I would let it go at that.

Jeannie walked over to the pipes and lifted one of them from its ledge in the display case. "I've always been drawn to this one," she said. The barrel of the pipe was carved in the shape of a bird's head, complete with ruffled feathers and green beads for eyes. I noticed a serious tremor in her hands as she held the pipe. Was she nervous or ill? Whatever the cause, seeing that small weakness in her made me feel slightly sympathetic toward her. You never knew what demons people were dealing with.

"Would you like to have it?" I asked.

She looked surprised. "Oh, no," she said. "I wouldn't know what to do with it. I have to say, though, that I still can't get over Frank leaving this collection to the Kyles."

"Well, I guess they've helped him a lot with the park, and they—"

She made a sound of disgust. "I'll tell you something," she said. "I don't like to gossip, but you should know why this makes no sense to me. Tom Kyle was beholden to your father, not the other way around."

"What do you mean?"

Jeannie carefully replaced the pipe in the cabinet. "Your father was his supervisor back when they worked for the Marshals Service," she said. "Tom had an affair with a client he was supposed to be protecting and Frank found out about it. He should have canned Tom, but he didn't. He even helped him cover it up. Tom owed him his job and probably his marriage. So why would your father—"

"He's been giving Tom checks for five hundred dollars every month, too," I said.

Jeannie stared at me, and I saw a blaze starting in her eyes. "You're joking."

I shook my head.

"He could have given that money to me, if he was so hot to part with it," she said bitterly. "I'm underwater on my mortgage, and I thought that after a six-year relationship, he—" She shook her head. "Sorry," she said. "It is what it is."

Now I understood her lukewarm reaction to my father leaving her only the piano and ten thousand dollars. And I thought of the hundred thousand that would soon be in my own bank account.

"I'm sorry, Jeannie," I said. "How can I help? He left me more than I need right now, and—"

She bent over and put her hand on mine. "Don't even think about it, honey," she said, her features softening. "I'm sorry to lose my composure like that, and I'm fine. Truly. I just wish I understood why Tom and Verniece rated so high in his opinion."

"Do you know Verniece well?" I asked.

"Not all that well. They pretty much keep to themselves out there."

"She told me I was adopted."

Jeannie's blue eyes flew open even wider than usual. *"What?"* she said. "That's crazy."

Had the color left her face or was I imagining it? "She says my mother told her I was."

"She didn't even know your mother," Jeannie scoffed as she set the pipe back on its ledge again, fingers shivering. "Not really."

I hesitated before I spoke again. "Well, she admitted that," I said, "but according to Verniece, she was upset over losing a baby and my mother suggested that she wasn't too old to adopt. She said she and Daddy adopted me, and that's what encouraged Verniece and Tom to adopt a little boy."

"Ludicrous," Jeannie said. "Just utterly ludicrous. Think about it," she said. "Even if it were true, your mother wouldn't tell a near stranger, for heaven's sake. You know what a private person she was."

"Actually, I don't know that," I said. "I only know what she was like with me, not what she was—"

"Listen to me, Riley. I was her dearest, oldest friend and she still wouldn't tell me half the things that were going on with her. So the idea of her telling a woman she barely knew something that intimate is just plain silly."

"I guess." I felt only slightly relieved, especially with Jeannie admitting that my mother didn't tell her everything. Maybe my mother'd had a weak moment, touched by Verniece's pain, knowing she could say something to relieve it. Verniece was so sweet. I could understand how she might have inspired my mother to confide in her.

"Enough of that nonsense," Jeannie said. She picked up a notepad from the piano bench where she'd set it when she first arrived at the house. "I'm going to walk through the house and make a list of what needs to be done, starting with the collections upstairs. I can't wait for you to meet Christine," she added. "You're going to love her and vice versa. She really knows the value of things and ways to publicize a successful estate sale."

"I found Daddy's keys for the upstairs cabinets, if you need them." I thought of the key to his RV that I'd left with Verniece. "Do you happen to know if he let someone else use his RV?" I asked.

"Heavens, no! He loved that old thing. He called it his man cave. Even I wasn't allowed inside."

"It's strange," I said. "He has a bunch of CDs in there, but they're all bluegrass and country. When have you ever known my father to listen to bluegrass?"

"I haven't," she admitted, "but he knew that wasn't my thing, so he probably just didn't play it around me. He had very varied tastes." She looked at me. "And we've already established that you didn't know much about him, haven't we?" It wasn't a question; it was a dig, and the sympathy I'd felt for her moments earlier melted away. I did not like this woman! I didn't trust her. I just didn't. "So," she said, taking me by the arm and leading me over to the wall of cabinets. "You get started here going through your father's papers, and I'll work upstairs."

I felt steamrollered, but I also didn't care where I started working in the house. Suzanne had warned me to keep the last three years of my father's receipts for her to go through, but other than that, everything could be tossed. As Jeannie climbed the stairs, I sat down in front of one of the cabinets and opened the door, groaning when papers slipped from the shelves to my lap. I knew Daddy had a shredder in the upstairs office and I hoped it was heavy-duty. Taking a deep breath, I started piling the papers into a stack. I wondered if, buried somewhere in one of the ten cabinets, I might find documents related to my adoption. I hoped not.

About an hour later, I was getting bleary-eyed when I heard a sound from upstairs that made me stop my work to listen. Drawers opening and closing? Was she in his bedroom? I got up quietly and moved to the foot of the stairs. I would have thought little of the sound if she'd been slamming around up there, but there was something so sneaky in the slow, quiet sliding of the drawers . . . or whatever it was. Curious, I started up the stairs.

She was coming out of my father's bedroom when I reached the top of the stairs, and she jumped when she saw me. "Oh," she said, her hand to her throat. "You startled me!"

"I wanted to see how you were making out." I really wanted to ask her what she'd been doing snooping through his dresser drawers, but I kept my mouth shut.

"Oh, fine," she said, then she nodded toward the bedroom, as if she knew an explanation was needed. "I was looking for a few things I'd left here," she said.

She'd gone upstairs with a notepad, but now a white box rested on top of it. It was the size of a small shirt box or maybe the sort a manuscript would fit in. She clutched it and the notepad to her chest.

"Did you find them?" I motioned toward the box, and she looked down at it as though she was surprised to find it in her arms.

"Yes," she said. "Just some things of mine I'd forgotten about. Old . . . things I'd wanted to show him." She laughed nervously, and I almost felt sorry for her. From the color in her cheeks, I imagined the box contained a sexy negligee or worse. I remembered Suzanne telling me about her father's pornography and wished I could erase that thought.

"How'd you make out up here with the collections?" I asked.

"I think I know the appraisers we need to call," she said, heading for the stairs. She didn't let go of the box even to hold on to the handrail.

"It's going to take me a week to clean out those cabinets," I said from behind her on the stairs.

"I can imagine." She'd reached the last step. "We should get those pipes appraised before turning them over to the Kyles, too. And, oh, my God"—she chuckled—"we need to get a sense of how many vinyl albums he has so I can tell Christine. Do you know if he has more squirreled away anywhere? The attic, maybe?"

"I don't think so," I said, though I didn't know what, if anything, was in the attic.

We worked quietly for a short time, me sitting on the floor, Jeannie looking over the albums, but my mind was numb from hunting for the dates on medical bills and bank statements.

"I think I've had it for tonight," I said, getting to my feet. "Glass of wine?"

She let out a tired breath. "Just a half," she said. "More than that and I'll be asleep when I drive home."

I went into the kitchen and pulled two wine glasses from the cabinet above the dishwasher. Jeannie came into the kitchen, walking past me toward the powder room by the back door. She knew her way around this house as well as I did.

She was still in the bathroom when I carried the glasses into the living room, and I spotted her notepad and the box she'd been holding on the ledge by the pipe collection. I bit my lip, curiosity getting the better of me, though I wasn't sure I wanted to see what was inside that box. What if she'd stolen something? She was hurting for money and mad at my father for not leaving her more than he had, and she'd had access to his collections for a good hour upstairs.

I listened for any sounds from the powder room, but heard none. Then I moved her notepad aside and worked the cover of the box loose. The box was half filled with yellowed newspaper articles. The headline of the one on top read LISA MACPHERSON ASSUMED DROWNED IN APPARENT SUICIDE.

I let out my breath in a miserable "Oh." Why had he felt the need to save articles about Lisa's suicide? I ached for him and my mother. How must they have felt, knowing they'd been unable to prevent their daughter from taking her own life?

I heard the bathroom door open, but didn't make a move to cover the box.

"Oh, Riley, no!" Jeannie rushed toward me when she walked into the room.

I lifted the box in the air and turned my back to her, and she stopped, lowering her hands to her sides. "Honey, you don't want to do that," she said. "There's no good that can come from it."

"Why did he keep these?" I asked, tipping the box down again so I could look inside. I lifted the top article about her apparent suicide, and my hand froze when I saw the next headline. The font was huge, the letters thick and black, and I stared at them, confused and disbelieving as I tried to absorb what I was seeing: ACCUSED MURDERER LISA MACPHERSON ASSUMED DEAD.

12.

Slowly, I turned to look at Jeannie. She stood next to me, her hands now pressed to her face, her blue eyes brimming with tears.

I nodded toward the article, still in the box. ACCUSED MURDERER LISA MACPHERSON ASSUMED DEAD. "What is this?" My voice was a whisper.

She reached for the box and gently worked it free of my grip. "He never wanted you to know," she said, setting it back on the ledge. "I was hoping to get that box out of here before you stumbled across it. He would have wanted me to do that, but I wasn't sure where he hid it, and I've been so worried that you'd . . ." She shook her head. "Just close it up and throw it away, Riley. That's what he would have wanted."

She was talking quickly, trying to get my mind off what I'd seen. I reached into the box and pulled out the article that called my sister a murderer.

"I don't understand." I read the headline again. "I don't understand at all."

"I know," she said. "I know what you were told. That she killed herself because she was depressed and over-worked. Your parents never wanted you to know the truth."

"*What* truth?" I lifted the box again, carried it to the open rolltop desk, and sat down. I picked up article after article and that word kept jumping out at me from the headlines: *Murder, Murder, Murder.*

"That's why they moved here after Lisa's death." Jeannie walked to the piano bench and sat down heavily. "They wanted to get you and Danny away from all the accusations and everything. They wanted to get you away from a place where you'd always be known as a murderer's sister."

I looked over at her. "She did it? She actually killed someone? Who? Why?"

"It was an accident." Jeannie pressed her hand to the top of her head in aggravation. "Oh, your father would be so upset with me."

"Tell me!" I said.

"She was about to go on trial," Jeannie said, "and she believed she'd end up in prison for the rest of her life. The prosecution was going for first degree murder— 'planned and premeditated'—and that *would* have meant life in prison if they could prove it. But I think the real reason she killed herself was that she couldn't live with what she'd done. Accident or not, she'd killed someone. Lisa was only seventeen—a child!—and she couldn't get past the guilt."

"My God." I felt my whole body sag with the weight of the news. "Who was it?" I asked again. "Who did she kill?"

"His name was Steve Davis," she said. "He was her violin teacher."

I gasped, remembering the tall, slender conductor in the tapes. Was that who Jeannie was talking about?

"She *was* angry with him because he'd hurt her chance to get into Juilliard, but she never would have killed him over that," Jeannie said. "She was such a quiet, gentle girl. She never would have intentionally killed anyone over anything. It was all so unbelievable."

It *was* unbelievable, and I had so many questions. I paged through the articles until I found one of them with a picture of Steve Davis. He was definitely the man from the tapes. I pressed my hand to my mouth as I began to read the article to myself, while Jeannie sat quietly on the bench, waiting for me to learn the truth.

Lisa Beth MacPherson, the seventeen-year-old violinist awaiting trial in the murder of her former violin teacher Steven Davis, is missing and presumed dead. Ms. MacPherson's yellow kayak was found in the frozen waters of the Potomac River near Fort Hunt Park in Alexandria Monday morning, and her white Honda Civic was parked at the side of the road south of the Belle Haven Marina. Her book bag and a wallet containing her driver's license and more than thirty dollars in cash were in the vehicle. A blue jacket thought to be hers was found tangled in the icy reeds nearby.

Her father, Frank MacPherson, contacted police around eight o'clock Monday morning after finding an apparent suicide note in her bedroom. The contents of the note have not been made public, but a police spokesperson stated that the note indicated MacPherson's intention to kill herself, and her father identified the handwriting as hers. MacPherson's mother and younger siblings were out of town Monday morning.

Lisa MacPherson was out on bail in the October murder of Davis, who was forty-two at the time of his death. She was to be tried as an adult, and the trial was to begin this Wednesday. She was expected to testify that the shooting was accidental. MacPherson had planned to apply to the Juilliard School of Music for the fall 1990 semester, and Davis allegedly sent a derogatory letter about her to a colleague at the school, a fact prosecutors were expected to introduce as a possible motive. Davis had instructed MacPherson for most of her career, although at the time of the incident, she was studying with National Symphony violinist Caterina Thoreau.

Acquaintances stated that MacPherson had been extremely depressed in the months since her arrest. Upon hearing of her student's probable suicide this morning, Caterina Thoreau made this statement to the press: "This is tragic news. Lisa is the most gifted student I've ever had the pleasure to teach and her future was bright. I've always believed that the shooting was accidental, and given Lisa's sensitive nature, I can imagine how difficult it was for her to live with what happened. She held (Davis) in high esteem."

Davis, who lived in McLean with his wife, Sondra Lynn Davis, was teaching at George Mason University at the time of his death. The couple had no children.

The search for MacPherson's body continues.

I stared at the article, trying to comprehend it. "I always thought she killed herself because she was overwhelmed by how stressful her career had become and because she was worrying about getting into Juilliard, and . . ." My voice trailed off. I looked across the room at Jeannie, holding up the article I'd just read. "This is for real?"

Jeannie nodded. "I'm afraid so. I knew her quite well, Riley, and she was such a nice girl—studious and always with an eye toward her future. Your mother homeschooled her, as I'm sure you know, but she had friends even though she wasn't in a regular school. Other violin students, that sort of thing. She had a few rough patches . . ." She looked into the distance as if remembering some hardship of Lisa's. "But what kid doesn't?" she asked.

"Do you think she killed him because of the letter to Juilliard?" I asked.

"No, of course not! I believe that, for whatever reason, she got hold of your father's gun. Maybe to show him? I don't know. And she—"

"To show him? That doesn't make sense. Was it just lying around? It sounds like she was angry and intentionally shot him." My exalted image of my sister was rapidly deteriorating. I felt as if I was losing her all over again.

"Frank blamed himself," Jeannie said. "He always has. His service revolver was locked up in the den, but Lisa knew where it was. This was up in your Virginia house. Maybe Lisa just threatened Steve with the gun. Maybe she *had* lost her mind a little bit over that letter and she was asking him to make it right. That's what I've always pictured. She threatened him and maybe there was a scuffle and it went off. I don't know. No one will ever know. All I know was that it was heartbreaking.

Your mother never really recovered from all she went through."

"I'm in shock," I said honestly. "Is this why Daddy retired early from the Marshals Service?"

"Well, he was technically too young to retire, but it's why he left, yes. He and your mother wanted to move someplace where they could start over completely fresh for you and Danny."

"But Danny would have been six years old when Lisa died. He would have had some idea of what was going on, wouldn't he? He would have known why she really killed herself."

Jeannie looked old all of a sudden, her blue eyes tired. "You're right," she said slowly, "and I think they did your brother a huge disservice." She rubbed her temples. "I hate to criticize them, because I know they were surviving the best they could and they probably weren't thinking straight at the time. But they made up their minds that you and Danny should grow up not knowing about the murder, and so if Danny asked questions about things he'd heard, or things other kids said, your mother and father would tell him those kids didn't know what they were talking about. And like I said, they moved down here right away and did a pretty good job of starting fresh. The shooting and Lisa's suicide were national news, but somehow the kids down here didn't get the message, and to the best of my knowledge they left Danny alone about it. So he ultimately bought into the whole 'she killed herself because she was depressed' idea, same as you." She pressed her palms together in her lap. "And if he remembered things other children said, your parents would say he must be misremembering. I think that was a little cruel to him. It must have made him feel crazy sometimes. I think that's what led to him being so . . . disturbed. He had a lot of problems when they moved here."

"He was always getting into trouble at school," I said, remembering what my brother was like by the time he reached his teens. "He'd get into fights and wouldn't do his homework. And he argued with Mom and Daddy nearly every night." I remembered the fights. I'd cower in my room while my parents and Danny went at it, shouting and arguing about his grades and his foul language and the kids he hung out with. I'd been eleven years old, and I'd missed the big brother who'd doted on me and had always seemed like my protector. I'd put the pillow over my head to block out the noise.

"His school recommended that he see a counselor," Jeannie said, "but your parents wouldn't hear of it. They were afraid he'd say something about . . . the shooting and that Lisa killed herself, and then it would get out in New Bern and defeat the purpose of moving."

That really got to me. "How terrible for him," I said. "He needed help and they kept it from him." The thought of my brother's confusion tore me up. No wonder his feelings toward our parents were so bitter. I couldn't blame him. As far as I knew, they never did get him help. How could they trust him to hold tight to the family lies?

I wasn't sure who in my family I hurt worse for. The brother I'd adored, being told one thing while knowing another. My father, whose guilt over the gun must have haunted him his entire life. Or my mother, who lost her oldest child. And then there was my sister, the ethereal creature I'd seen on the tapes, struggling to live with the guilt of having taken a life. I dropped my head against the back of the chair and shut my eyes. "I wish I didn't know any of this," I said.

But now that I did know it, I had to know it all.

I sent Jeannie home, then sat up in bed reading every word of every article, including one that described the scene at our house when the police arrived: "Mr. Davis was found on the blood-soaked living room floor, MacPherson kneeling over him, a .357 Magnum in her hand. Davis had been shot in the temple and the eye and was pronounced dead at the scene."

That horrific description was going to give me nightmares.

Most of the other articles were repetitive, but I still read them all. It was nearly midnight when I reached the most personal, most painful-to-read item in the box. It was a handwritten note on a sheet of lined white paper, clearly a Xeroxed copy.

Dear Mom and Dad,

I'm so sorry for what I've put you through. I know what I'm about to do will make it even harder on you, at least for a while, but I'm sure a jury won't believe me about it being an accident and I can't go to prison. It terrifies me. I just can't do it. This is better for everyone in the long run. I love you and Riley and Danny so much and I'm sorry for any shame I've brought on our family.
Love, Lisa

13.

The forest was absolutely silent, the only sound the *hush-hush* of our footsteps as Danny and I walked over a carpet of long brown pine needles and tufts of neon-green weeds. I was in my brother's world, though not at his invitation. I'd shown up with the box of articles that morning, feeling anxious, wondering how much he remembered of the shooting and Lisa's suicide. How much he knew. But he didn't speak. He sat at the table in his trailer, his face growing nearly as red as his T-shirt as he scanned two of the articles, then shoved the box aside. Grabbing his shotgun, he pushed out of the trailer and into the woods. I quickly followed, terrified that I might have made the worst mistake of my life by bringing the box to him.

When I found him, though, he was walking slowly, as though he hoped I'd catch up to him. He didn't look at me, but kept his eyes forward, his gun propped against his shoulder, and I fell into step next to him. We walked that way in complete silence for ten minutes or more, and although I'd been nervous at first, I began to relax. There was something about the quiet out here. About the thick carpet of needles beneath our feet. All around us, for as far as I could see, the arrow-straight trunks of the pines shot into the sky, where they exploded into puff balls of long green needles. I glanced over my shoulders to see the same view in every direction. We were not on a trail, and I knew that without Danny at my side, I would be lost.

"How do you know where we are?" I whispered. It seemed wrong to break the spell of the woods with my voice.

"I just do." He pointed ahead of us. "That's where I like to go."

I looked ahead of us, but the landscape of tree trunks looked no different in that direction than in any other. Yet within a few steps, I understood. An oval of grass opened up in front of us, circled by pines so tall, they created a cathedral-like space below them. "Oh," I said. "I see why. It's beautiful."

He walked over to one of the trees and sat down on the cushion of pine needles near its base, resting the shotgun on the ground at his side. I sat next to him, and when I looked at him, he was slowly shaking his head, his eyes closed. I waited, and two or three minutes passed before he finally opened his eyes.

"You know how you think you remember things, but you're not sure if maybe you dreamt them?" he asked, looking out into the trees. "Or maybe even . . . made them up?"

"Yes," I said.

"Mom used to say I had a good imagination. I should be a writer, she said, because I made up such amazing stories." He sounded bitter. "She'd laugh them off, my stories. When I'd ask her if she remembered the day she and I came home from the grocery store and we heard two gunshots as we got out of the car, she'd say, 'Oh,

what a creative mind you have!' Or when I said something about remembering blood on the living room carpet, she'd say, 'If you have to make up stories, can't you
make up nicer ones?' "

"Oh, Danny." I touched his arm, relieved when he
didn't try to brush my hand away.

"I remember sirens," he said. "I thought they were
coming for you."

"For me?"

He nodded. "You were bleeding. You had a cut on
your head."

"I have a scar on my forehead," I said, lifting my
bangs to show him the small dent above my left eyebrow, but he didn't turn to look at me. He seemed lost
in his memory.

"You were screaming," he said.

I let my bangs fall over my forehead again. "Mom always told me I hit my head on a coffee table when I
was little, but I don't remember it."

"I thought that was why the ambulance was coming,
but that wasn't it, was it?" He shook his head as though
talking to himself. "It was for her teacher. That guy she
killed."

"Accidentally," I added. "You read the part about it
being an accident, right?"

" 'Shot through the eye,' " he said. "I *knew* that. I
knew . . ." He ran his fingers through his hair. "How did
I know that? Did I see it? Hear it?" He rubbed his temples hard in frustration, then looked at me. "I *knew* about
all this, Riles," he said. "I knew it, but I'd forgotten it."

"I think," I said carefully, not wanting him to go off
on his tirade about our parents again . . . and yet, maybe
they deserved it? "I think Mom and Daddy did their best
to make you forget it."

"I didn't have to go to school then," he said. "Mom homeschooled me for a while like she did with Lisa, though Lisa was gone." He frowned as if trying to remember. "She was always going away on trips and things, but . . . I guess she was in jail then? She must have been. I didn't connect the homeschooling with the sirens or anything. I thought I was being punished for something. They wouldn't let me go out and play." He was rambling, piecing things together in his mind. "I hardly knew her," he said. "Lisa. Eleven years older and always gone. Her schedule ruled our lives. The whole world revolved around her." He wrapped his hand around a fistful of pine needles. His face was still expressionless, but his voice was taut. Suddenly it softened. "I always liked you, though," he added, glancing at me. "You were a cool little kid."

I couldn't believe he was talking this way. Saying so much.

"You were my best friend," I said.

He dropped the needles. Rubbed his hands over his denim-covered knees. "I have this nightmare that comes and goes," he said. "It sucks. It's the worst one."

"Do you want to tell—"

"I thought it was about Iraq." He interrupted me, lost in his own thoughts. "But now I don't know, because Mom is in it. She's always in it. Always screaming."

I watched the muscles around his jaw tighten and release as I waited for him to say more, but he was done talking about his dream.

"Suicide is the coward's way out." He picked up a twig, playing with it between his fingers. "I mean, I feel for the vets who do it, and I get it. It becomes too much for them to carry around. Maybe they don't have a place like this to escape to."

I wasn't sure what he meant by "a place like this." Then I realized he was talking about this small patch of pine forest. His haven. I was touched that he'd allowed me to be there with him.

"So you don't have to worry about me and suicide, all right?" He glanced at me. "I know you do."

I was afraid of breaking the spell of warmth that had fallen over us, yet maybe I could take advantage of his mood to delve deeper.

"I *do* worry," I admitted. "I know you're depressed. If you'd stay on your medications, I think you'd be—"

"I'm not depressed."

Like hell, I thought. "How would you define your feelings, then? What do you—"

"I'm pissed off, is what I am!" He broke the twig in two between his fingers. The sound it made was barely audible, yet it made me jump.

"Who are you pissed off at?" I asked.

"Who am I *not* pissed off at would be a shorter answer," he said. "Our fucking government, for one. The shitty things they made me do over there. Made me . . ." He gave an angry shake of his head. "You don't even see people as human beings after a while when you're there, you know?" he said. "And I'm pissed at our parents. Our lying prick of a father and our ice queen of a mother. And our selfish bitch of a sister!" His face was red and damp with sweat, his breathing loud. "She took up all the air in our family. There was nothing left for anyone else."

"But," I said carefully, "did you ever stop to think of what it was like for her, growing up?" I asked. "The pressure on her?"

"Hell, no!" His anger shattered the sacred feel of the woods. "Nobody ever forced her to play the violin.

Nobody told her to kill her fucking teacher. Everything was handed to her on a silver platter and she took it all for herself!"

I ran my fingers through the pine needles. I could hear his hard, fast breathing and I made my voice as calm as I could to counter his rage. "I try to understand why people do what they—"

"Shut up with the counselor voice, okay?" he said. "I hate when you do that!"

I was stunned. "I'm only trying to—"

"You turn into some automaton, like you're programmed to say all this fake, warm, fuzzy shit that has nothing to do with reality." He looked at me, his face flushed. "You went to school for what? Five years? Six years? And then you think you're equipped to pick at people's heads when you haven't even lived in the real world yet? Maybe you can manage a thirteen-year-old. Fourteen-year-old. But you are *way* the hell out of your league when it comes to me, little sister."

I felt as though he'd picked up his shotgun and smashed the stock of it into my stomach. *"Danny."* I wasn't sure what else to say, the hurt I felt was so intense.

"You don't get me at all, okay?" He grabbed the shotgun as he jumped to his feet, sending my heartbeat into the stratosphere. He looked down at me, the pale blue of his eyes ice-cold. He leaned over so those angry eyes were no more than two feet away from me. "It's not my *mind* that's sick, Riley," he said. "It's my *soul*. And there aren't any drugs that are going to fix that."

He turned and walked back into the woods, his stride long and quick despite the limp, and I let out my breath in relief. I waited a moment, trembling, then got to my feet and followed him at a distance, my legs rubbery. I didn't want to catch up to him—I couldn't possibly talk with him right now after that outburst—but I needed to keep him in my line of sight. I would never be able to find my way out of the woods alone. Thank God for his red T-shirt! My eyes burned as I followed it from a distance, and I was crying before I realized it. I ached from the sting of his cutting words. Had he thought that little of me all along? Like I was nothing more than an undereducated charlatan with a "fake counselor voice"? Not only did I feel as though I'd just lost my brother, it seemed I'd never had him to begin with.

I thought about all he'd said as I followed him through the pines from a safe distance. I couldn't imagine what it was like to be Danny. To grow up with parents who told you your memories were crazy. Then to be commanded to do things—maybe torture people? Maybe kill them?—against your will. Against your values.

Maybe he was right. Maybe I *was* way out of my league. I'd been a terrific student—I hadn't wasted a moment of my time in school—and I knew plenty about healing the troubled mind.

But no one had taught me a thing about healing the soul.

14.

When I got home, hurt and shaken from the conversation with Danny, I took a yogurt from the refrigerator and sat on the porch, but I lost my appetite after the first bite. Danny had heard the gunshots. He'd seen blood on the floor. What else had he seen that my parents tried to erase from his memory? When I thought about that conductor from the Rome festival tape lying dead in the living room, shot through the eye, I felt sick to my stomach. I hadn't even seen the image that was troubling me, yet I couldn't get it out of my mind. What must life be like for my brother?

I put the yogurt back in the refrigerator, then returned to the porch with my laptop. Even with the overhead fan on full speed, I was hot, but I didn't care. I wanted to know something about the man who seemed destined to haunt me now. According to the newspaper articles, Steven Davis had had no children but he did have a wife. How had that woman fared without her husband?

I searched the archives of the *Washington Post* for his name, and quickly discovered how many different Steven Davises there were in the news. I added the word *killed* and that narrowed down my search significantly.

I found many of the same articles that my father—and mother?—had kept in the box, but there were more. His obituary, to begin with, which said that he started playing violin at age five, the same as my sister. He was a natural talent, the obituary read, and beloved by his students. He'd studied at Juilliard himself and played for five years with the National Symphony Orchestra.

Members of the symphony remembered him as "charming and a perfectionist, exacting and passionate about his performances." There was a picture of him with his violin, a black-and-white portrait in which he was unsmiling but not stern. Just flat-out handsome in this photograph, with a touch of gray in the dark hair at his temples and a perfectly symmetrical face that looked like it had been carved from stone.

I Googled his wife, Sondra Lynn Davis, and hit a page full of links to a blog: "Never Forgotten: A Meeting Place for Families of Murder Victims." I stared at the link for a full minute before finally clicking on it.

The image at the top of the blog was a heartbreaker. A couple stood with their backs to the camera as they watched the sun rise over a milky gray ocean. The man held the woman's hand to his lips, the gesture unmistakably tender and intimate. Even though the figures were mostly in silhouette, I knew who they were. I knew the man thought he was far too young to worry about dying.

Before I could get any more lost in the picture, I lowered my eyes to the introductory blog post.

NEVER FORGOTTEN:
A Meeting Place for Families of Murder Victims

On October 27, 1989, I lost my husband and best friend, Steve Davis. Steve was a brilliant musician. He performed for years with the National Symphony and later opted to teach at a university in northern Virginia so he didn't have to travel as much and could be close to home. He was a loving and devoted husband. He taught violin students privately, and that is where the end began. It wasn't the desire to make extra money that drove him to take private students, but a desire to help as many people learn as possible. This is how he ended up with Lisa MacPherson as a student.

Lisa started with him when she was just five years old. He taught her on a one-eighth-sized violin and she showed a great deal of promise, so he worked extremely hard with her. From the time she was small, she was as driven as he was. Of course, she was only one of his many students, but I think she reminded him of himself, since he started playing at the same age and with the same excitement. Every great teacher wants to inspire one of his or her students to reach amazing heights, and for Steve, Lisa was that student. She was clearly on her way to the top, thanks to his commitment to her. He lined up concert engagements for her, spoke to music schools on her behalf, and took her and his other most gifted students to Montreal and Rome to participate in music festivals. He put his heart and soul into his students.

I'd met all of Steve's students over the years. They were all talented and unique and intriguing. I believe every passionate musician is a little quirky, Steve included. But Lisa always struck me as more than a little quirky. I felt there was an instability there that had gone unrecognized and therefore untreated. Steve brushed off my concerns. As long as she played beautifully, he wasn't worried about her mental health. He should have been.

Lisa's commitment to her music began to deteriorate during her teen years, and her playing suffered as she explored working with other teachers. In his distress over how Lisa seemed to be derailing her own career, Steve wrote to an old friend at Juilliard, which was one of the schools where she was applying. He told this friend that Lisa had lost her edge and somehow word of his letter got back to her.

Steve felt so guilty over writing that letter. For a full week, he couldn't sleep and he grew quiet and hard to reach. Finally, he decided to go to her house to apologize. That's when she essentially ambushed him, shooting him in the head with her father's gun. He died instantly.

Lisa MacPherson was about to stand trial for his murder when she "drowned herself" in the Potomac River. However, her body was never recovered and I believe she faked her suicide. The police stopped looking for her, but I'll never stop searching. I hired a private investigator who found some leads, though he couldn't get the authorities to follow up on them. A $25,000 reward for information leading to her whereabouts remains in place, but in a way it doesn't matter. Nothing will bring my beautiful husband back.

Time doesn't heal. Maybe you no longer cry every single day but the pain is still there. Steve and I were working on having a family when he died. We'd waited a long time—maybe too long—both of us wanting to have established careers before we added children to the mix. I was undergoing fertility treatments at the time of Steve's death and we'd been optimistic about our chances. Our children would be in their late teens and early twenties by now if we'd succeeded, and I mourn the lost chance we had to create our family.

Ten years ago, I realized I am not alone in my sorrow. Thousands and thousands of other people have lost their loved ones to murder. That's when I started this blog. It's a place for you to share your own journey and where we can support one another. If you've lost someone you love to murder, you are welcome to share your story here.

I didn't know how many times I read that blog post, sitting on the porch in the breathless heat. I was looking between the lines for . . . something, I wasn't sure what. My emotions were in turmoil and I felt the confusion physically: a pain across my chest, a knot in my stomach. My sister's body had never been found, and the thought of her bones lying undiscovered somewhere in the river was unbearably upsetting. I thought of all the times my parents must have pictured Lisa taking her last breath, maybe panicking in that dark, ice-cold water before finally losing consciousness. No wonder they'd tried to protect Danny from the truth. And no wonder that, even when my mother had been in the same room with me, she often seemed so far away.

I was stuck on the phrase "I felt there was an instability there." I thought of the girl in the tapes again, always standing a little off to the side with Matty . . . unless she was called forward to perform. She hadn't fit in well with all those other teens, had she? Had there been mental illness that had gone unrecognized and untreated, as Sondra Davis suggested? I felt sorry for Sondra, still grieving for the children she might have had, and hiring investigators to find my dead sister. More than twenty years had passed, though, I thought. Sondra needed to let it go. I wanted to write to her, although I knew I never would. I wanted to give her my condolences and tell her I was certain, absolutely certain, that Lisa never meant to kill her husband. But then, it was easy for me to say she must have killed him by accident, because that would be the only reason *I* could imagine killing someone.

But she wasn't me, was she?

15.

_____

When I opened the front door the following morning, Jeannie and her daughter burst into the living room like they'd been shot from a cannon, and I stepped back to make room for all that energy.

"Riley, this is Christine," Jeannie said, setting her purse down on the table by the door.

"Riley!" Christine's grin split her face in two. Her dark hair was up in a ponytail, and her big eyes were brown instead of blue, but it was clear she and Jeannie were mother and daughter. "I'm so glad to see you!" She grabbed my hands in hers and the tote bag she was carrying slid from her wrist to mine. She pumped my hands up and down. "You were just a baby the last time I saw you, can you imagine? Just an itty-bitty thing!"

The same overwhelmed feeling I'd had at that lunch with Jeannie wrapped around me like a straitjacket. The nut had not fallen far from the tree.

"It's good to meet you, too, Christine," I said. "I'm glad you can help me out."

"Absolutely!" She lifted her tote bag from where it had landed on my wrist. "And this is a wonderful house.

I'm sure you have thousands of treasures in here. Mom told me all about your father's collections."

"Well, I have no idea if they're valuable or not." Nor did I really care. I just wanted someone to take over the daunting business of cleaning out the house while I focused on the emotional turmoil that my life had become.

"You're so pretty, isn't she, Mom?" Christine asked Jeannie. They scrutinized me from their stance inside the doorway.

"She's lovely," Jeannie agreed.

"You two!" I said, embarrassed. I walked away from them, heading for the kitchen, escaping their analysis. "Can I get you something?" I asked over my shoulder. "Bottle of water? Lemonade?"

"Nothing," Jeannie said.

"I'm good." Christine was following me into the kitchen, but she stopped at the cabinet containing the pipes and stood ogling it, hands on her hips. "Mom told me Danny broke the glass doors," she said. "He was really a sweet little boy back when I knew him. I guess that's changed, huh?"

I stared at her, wanting to defend Danny but too annoyed by her question to get the words out. I'd had no contact with my brother since we'd spoken in the woods the previous day, but that conversation was on my mind nearly every minute. I wondered if he thought about it, too, or if, once those harsh words were out of his mouth, he forgot about them. Maybe he drank them away along with the memories.

Christine picked up one of the pipes and examined it closely. "Oh, the appraisers are going to have a field day with these, aren't they, Mom?" she asked.

"I told you," Jeannie said, moving forward to put her

arm around her daughter's shoulders. Then to me, she said, "We have the appraisers set to come out this afternoon."

I felt the first teeny stab of worry. As much as I wanted the house cleaned out, I had the feeling I was going to lose control of everything in the process. Not that I felt very much in control to begin with.

"Please run everything by me before any major decisions are made," I said. "And remember that once the pipes are appraised, they go to Tom Kyle, not the estate sale."

"Oh, of course," Jeannie reassured me.

Christine picked up on my concern. "I'll just be making a general inventory today," she said. "I usually have a team working with me but one of them is pregnant on bed rest and the other's taking summer courses at the community college, so Mom will help me. We'll be sorting and pricing things once we get rolling toward the sale. As for this morning, I just want to get the lay of the land before the appraisers come." She smiled at me. "You don't remember me at all, do you?" She sounded sad.

I shook my head, doing my best to look apologetic.

"You were the cutest thing," she said. "I'd hang out with your sister." She laughed, a deep laugh, the sort that sounded like she smoked, although I couldn't smell tobacco on her. The last thing I wanted was somebody smoking in the house. "Not that your sister actually ever took the time to hang out," she added. "That girl had so much ambition." She shook her head sadly.

I wondered if she, too, knew my sister had killed someone? Did she know the real reason Lisa drowned herself?

"Well," I said, anxious to get the subject off my family. I spread my arms wide, taking in the whole house. "How do we begin?"

I started shredding the old paperwork in the first of my father's cabinets, while Jeannie and Christine made their way through the house. I could hear them chatting together from time to time, closet doors being opened and shut, the pull-down stairs to the attic being lowered. I was glad now that Jeannie had known my father so well. I told myself that he would have trusted her with this job. That eased my discomfort over having two people I barely knew pawing through his belongings.

Just breathe, I thought as I listened to them rattling through the house. *Everything's going to be fine.*

Around eleven, Suzanne e-mailed to tell me that Tom Kyle and I needed to sign a document, transferring the pipe collection to him. She'd reached him by phone, she said, and he was coming in the next morning. Could I come at the same time?

I had no desire to see Tom Kyle, although I wouldn't have minded talking to Verniece again. But I e-mailed Suzanne that I'd be there.

The appraisers, both men, arrived together as I was getting back to the shredder. Jeannie greeted them, introduced me, and then sent one of them upstairs to work with the lighters and compasses. The other man, a Santa Claus look-alike right down to the snowy white beard and round belly, pulled a chair in front of the pipe collection. "Nice stuff," he said to me as I refocused on the paperwork, but other than that he was a man of few words. I was glad he said nothing about the missing glass doors.

I was making egg salad in the kitchen a while later when Jeannie walked into the room.

She leaned against the counter. "Maybe you shouldn't sell Lisa's violin," she said.

I spooned mayonnaise into the bowl. "What would I do with it?"

"You never know." She shrugged. "You might have a talented child one day who wants to play the violin. Who knows? Maybe even Danny will have children one day. Even if the two of you aren't musical, you've got MacPherson blood in you. Maybe you'll pass that talent on to the next generation and it would be lovely for your son or daughter to have a MacPherson violin."

I thought she was trying to reassure me that I wasn't adopted and I appreciated the effort. "I guess I don't need to make a decision about the violin right now," I said.

"The appraiser upstairs says he's not an expert in stringed instruments, but he took a look at it and thinks it's quite valuable, so you might want to store it someplace safer than the house."

I nodded, stirring the egg salad in the bowl. One more thing to look into.

I felt her gaze on me. "Are you okay?" she asked.

I dropped my hands to my sides. "No, to be honest. How could I be okay?" I spoke quietly, aware of the appraiser in the living room. "My awesomely talented sister's a murderer. My family may not be my family. My brother's not doing great. And I miss my father." My voice broke, and Jeannie stepped next to me, her arm around my shoulders.

"I wish you'd never found that box of articles," she said. "It's my fault. I—"

"It's not your fault, Jeannie." I hunched my shoulders involuntarily, getting rid of her arm. "I had the right to know the truth and I'm glad I know it. It explains a lot."

"Your family was . . . *is* your family. Your blood family. That adoption nonsense is just that: nonsense. I am absolutely certain of that. I don't know who Verniece Kyle thinks she is, planting seeds of doubt in your mind. Can you put that worry to rest? Please."

The doorbell rang before I could respond. "Someone's here!" the pipe appraiser called from the living room.

"Oh! The piano movers!" Jeannie said.

"Today?" I didn't even know she'd contacted the movers, and I suddenly felt like running into the living room to block their path. I couldn't face more people in the house.

"Don't worry," she said, heading for the living room. "I'll take care of it. You don't have to do a thing!"

I stayed in the kitchen eating my egg salad sandwich while the movers hammered and grunted and yelled at one another in the living room. I didn't even peek into the room to see how they would take apart the baby grand. Instead, I sat at the small kitchen table, checking my friends' comments on Facebook. Bryan and I had unfriended each other, but I still went to his page to look at his profile picture every few days, staring at his smile and wondering if I'd made a mistake. He hadn't changed his picture in the two years that I'd known him. He stood against a pink sunset with his son and daughter, who had been three and four at the time the photograph had been taken and who were climbing up his body like little monkeys. The picture still made me laugh. I missed those kids almost as much as I missed him.

Looking at the picture, though, I felt glad of my decision. That was where he belonged. With his kids, and whether he knew it or not, with his wife.

The silence from the living room was sudden, and I could hear voices out on the front porch. I waited until they'd subsided, then walked into the living room, past the Santa Claus look-alike who was still working with the pipes. From the middle of the room, I stared at the enormous empty place where the piano had stood for as long as I could remember, and the breath went out of my body. I pressed my hand to my chest. I was only twenty-five, but I thought this month might kill me. If I was having this much trouble saying good-bye to a piano I couldn't even play, how would I ever say good-bye to the house I loved?

I dropped onto the couch as Christine trotted down the stairs carrying her iPad. "Whoa, look at that!" she said. "No piano! Mom went with the movers, I guess?"

I nodded. "I think so."

"The appraiser guy is almost done up there," she said. "He's loving those compasses!" She turned to the man at the pipes. "How's it going?"

He shut his computer. "Just about done," he said, running his hand over his beard. "I have a few things I need to check at the office, but ballpark figure is seventeen thousand."

"Wow!" I said, sitting up straighter on the couch. I'd had no idea the pipes were that valuable. Maybe that would take some of the grouch out of Tom Kyle.

The appraiser slipped his computer into a briefcase and headed for the door. "I'll get back to you with the exact figures and a certificate in a few days." He spoke to Christine rather than me and I didn't bother getting up as she ushered him out of the house. Once back in the living room, she sat down at my father's rolltop desk, sideways on the chair so she was facing me, her iPad resting on her thighs. "How's the shredding going?" she asked.

"Slowly," I said. "I'm afraid of tossing something that turns out to be important."

"Oh, you don't have to be supercareful," she said. "I'm sure most of it is tossable." She smoothed her bangs across her temple and I saw the damp skin of her forehead. The attic had to be unbearably hot to work in and I suddenly felt sympathy toward her.

"Must be challenging, going through someone else's stuff," I said. "I feel like I've left you a mess, but Jeannie said not to throw anything away except the old paperwork."

"She was absolutely right," Christine said, "and I love going through someone else's stuff, so don't worry about the mess." She touched the screen of the iPad. "Mom and I will be in again tomorrow, if that's okay with you. I know you want to get this thing rolling."

"The sooner the better," I said.

"A few items I need to go over with you." She tapped the screen again. "The computer on the desk in the office upstairs. Docs that go?"

I nodded. "It was my father's. I guess I should clean the hard drive first."

"Exactly. We can do that for you, but you might want to be sure there's nothing you need on there before you let us have it."

"All right."

"I found keys lying here and there around the house and I put them in a plastic bag and left them on the shelf in that office," she said. "You should go through them to see if you need to keep any of them. And you should be putting things you want to hold on to in that office, too. Mom knows that room is off-limits, except for the lighters and compasses and instruments, of course."

"And my bedroom," I said. "Make that off-limits, too."

"Of course," she said. "What about your brother's old room? There's nothing in there, really, but would he want to—"

"He won't care," I said.

"If we find anything that looks like a personal item or a family heirloom, we'll put it in the office, too," Christine said. "How's that?"

"All right," I agreed. "I want to keep that one violin, at least for the moment."

"Lisa's," she said. "The one with the violet on the tag?"

"Yes." I looked up at her. Tipped my head. "Did you know about . . . what she did?" I asked.

For the first time, I saw a shadow pass over her features. "I was living abroad when it happened and not in much contact with Mom at the time, so I only heard about it later when I got home," she said. "That was after your family moved down here. I was shocked. I knew Mom felt terrible. She really liked Lisa and wished she could have talked to her. Helped her somehow."

"It sounds like Lisa was beyond help," I said.

"Yeah. That happens." Her bangs had flopped over her forehead again, and she looked at me from beneath them. "Mom told me you didn't know and you found some articles about it. That must have been a shock."

"It was," I said. "It still is."

"Well," she said, getting to her feet again. "Hopefully that'll be the last shock you have as we clean out the house."

16.

"You look like shit," Tom Kyle said as he sat down across from me in the waiting room at Suzanne Compton's office the following morning. I'd run to the attorney's office from home and knew my face glistened with perspiration under my visor. It was the first time I'd seen Tom out of his T-shirt and camo pants. He'd shaved, combed his sparse gray hair, put on khakis and a blue short-sleeved dress shirt. But the clothes hadn't seemed to change his ornery disposition, and I wished my father had left him absolutely nothing. I thought of him cheating on Verniece, maybe even putting some high-level government work at risk when he did so. What my father had liked enough about this man to help him cover up his affair was beyond me.

I wanted to say something snotty to him in response to his crack about the way I looked, but I needed more information from him and didn't think that was the way to go about getting it. If he knew why Verniece was stuck on me being adopted, I wanted to know, and if he knew why my father gave him those checks every month—and left him the pipe collection—I wanted to know that, too. I decided to play on his sympathy, hoping that beneath that rough exterior, he actually had some.

"I know," I said, aiming for a self-deprecating smile. "My life is kind of a mess right now."

He studied me from beneath his bushy gray eyebrows. "Your father left you a lot to deal with," he said.

I nodded. "And I just feel really alone." I rubbed my palms on my damp thighs. "It's overwhelming."

I thought I saw sympathy in his face, but it was quickly replaced by his usual scowl.

"That brother of yours is more a hindrance than a help, I take it," he said.

"Well, he has his own problems to deal with."

Tom glanced at the reception desk. Suzanne's secretary wasn't at her desk, and although we were alone in the waiting room, he still lowered his voice. "You ever think he's a suicide risk, like your sister?" he asked. "We hear gunshots coming from down there sometimes and Verniece gets worried. She wants to go check on him, but I say it's best we leave him alone."

That sounded like Verniece, worrying about other people. "My sister's situation was totally different," I said. "Danny won't hurt himself . . . or anyone else, either, so Verniece doesn't need to be concerned. He's just hunting out there." I wondered if Tom knew the real reason Lisa had killed herself. Probably. Steven Davis's murder had been such a big deal in the news back then. I thought Danny and I had been the only people kept in the dark about what really happened.

"Well," Tom said, "let me know if we can do anything else to help with the RV park." He leaned forward, elbows on his knees. "It's our home, you know," he said. "We've lived there more than twenty years and I'm not sure where we'll go once you sell it."

He stared at me so intently that I had to turn away. There was something other than kindness in his offer of help, but I wasn't sure what it was.

"Hello, Riley." Suzanne walked into the waiting room, hand outstretched toward me. "And you must be Mr. Kyle."

We both shook her hand, then followed her into her office where we sat nearly side by side across the desk from her.

"Riley," she said, scrutinizing me from her side of the desk, "are you all right?"

"I'm fine." I must have looked even worse than I'd imagined. I wanted to get back to the house. Christine and Jeannie were again culling through my family's possessions, and it felt strange to leave them there alone. Christine's rough edges were beginning to chafe me. She was impatient and not exactly a diplomat when assessing my family's old possessions.

"Okay," Suzanne said, getting down to business. "I've drawn up this document transferring ownership of the pipe collection to you, Mr. Kyle. Have you had it appraised yet, Riley?"

I nodded. "The appraiser thinks it's worth about seventeen thousand." I watched Tom's face, but it was impossible to read. I'd just told him he was seventeen thousand dollars richer and he seemed unmoved. "How do we do it?" I asked. "I mean, do I deliver the pipes to him, or—"

"I think it's best if Mr. Kyle comes over and packs them up and takes them away. They're his now."

We talked with Suzanne awhile longer, signed a couple of documents, and then walked quietly out of her office together. Once outside, I saw his old Ford in the driveway.

"Don't take everything so hard, Riley," he said as he walked away from me toward his car.

I didn't know what to say to that, so I kept my mouth shut and kept walking. He was backing out of the driveway by the time I reached the sidewalk, and he suddenly called to me through his open car window.

"Riley?"

I looked over at him. "Yes?"

"That sister of yours who killed herself?"

I waited for him to say more, but it appeared he was waiting for me to respond. "Yes?" I said again.

"She didn't," he said, and he gave his car gas, swinging the tail into the street, then taking off before I even had a chance to register those two words.

PART TWO

17.

___

Alexandria, Virginia

Lisa

The glow of the streetlight spilled into her bedroom, and from her seat on the edge of her bed, she saw the outline of Violet's case, the sweet worn black leather shoulder. She looked away. Her father had said Violet couldn't go with her. She'd argued with him. If she killed herself, it made sense that she'd take the violin. She'd never leave it behind. But he gave her a look that told her Violet was the least of their problems and she'd said no more about it.

Powdery snow fell like dust beneath the streetlight and she shivered. She couldn't get warm these days, no matter how many layers she wore. Tonight, her teeth chattered and she felt sick. She hadn't been able to eat in days. Her mother thought it was because of the trial and worried that the jury would take one look at her pale sunken face and bony shoulders and think she was a junkie. "You have to eat, Lisa," she'd pleaded. "The jurors will think you're on drugs."

She didn't want to think about her mother tonight.

Her father came to her bedroom door. She couldn't see his face in the darkness. He'd said to leave the lights off in case a neighbor was awake and curious.

"Are you ready?" he asked.

She stood up from her bed. "No," she said, but she picked up her backpack and the bag with the towel and empty hair dye box and every strand of her hacked-off long blond hair and walked past him into the hall. This was the sort of thing you could never be ready for.

He caught her arm and turned her toward him. "You need to leave this here." He touched the pendant at her throat.

"But I'd be *wearing* it, Daddy!" she said, touching the oval of white jade. Beneath her fingertips, she felt the design carved into the stone. "I never take it off."

"You have to," he said. "It's too identifiable."

Giving in, she returned to her room and unfastened the necklace, but rather than leaving it in her jewelry box, she slipped it into the pocket of her jeans. There was no way she could leave it behind.

Back in the hallway, she followed her father out the front door, pulling her hat low on her head because it was so cold and her hair was still damp.

"Sh!" Her father said, although she hadn't made a sound. He walked ahead of her to the driveway and pulled open the driver's side door of her car. "No lights till we get to the parkway," he whispered.

She nodded, and he closed the door more quietly than she'd thought a car door could be closed.

His car was behind hers and they both backed out of the driveway slowly, with only the streetlight to guide them. She followed him down the road, the chattering of her teeth echoing inside her head. "Good-bye, Ansel Road," she whispered. The car filled with the scent of the hair dye she'd used, and she wondered if the same scent was in her bedroom. How long would it stay there?

Would her mother notice it when she came home from Pennsylvania? Worse, would the police?

Then she pictured Violet abandoned in her room. She imagined her mother reading the note she'd left. And then she thought about her mother and Riley and Danny up at Granddad's house in Pennsylvania, not knowing anything was going on. "The kids shouldn't be here right now," her father'd said to her mother when he insisted she get Riley and Danny out of town. "Not with the press hounding us like this." Her mother had agreed without really knowing what she was agreeing to.

Riley. Danny. Mom. She would never see any of them again. Her heart seized in a way that sent a prickly pain down her arms.

"Don't think!" she told herself. Her voice sounded weird inside the dark car. She couldn't let thoughts of her family derail the plan. She couldn't think of anything except what she needed to do now. Tonight.

Her father had told her his idea only a few days earlier. He'd come into her room in the middle of the night. Sat on the edge of her bed. Presented it to her in great detail and she knew he'd been thinking about it a long time. She listened, first in complete disbelief, then in gratitude that he would do this for her. He would save her. She had a choice, he said: spend the rest of her days in prison or live out her life as someone else. Some other girl who was free as a bird. She didn't see that she had much of a choice at all.

They didn't pass another car as they headed for the George Washington Parkway that ran along the river. That was good, since they were driving blind. The darkness on the road made this eerie night even eerier, and she put on her wipers to brush the dusting of snow from her windshield. Every time they passed beneath a street-light, she saw the shadow of her kayak fall across the hood of her car and hoped she'd tied it tightly enough to her roof. She'd asked her father to tie it for her because she was too shaky, but he said she had to do everything herself in case the police had a way of figuring out she hadn't acted alone.

When her father turned onto the parkway, he put on his headlights and she did the same. The snow was coming down harder and she kicked up the speed of her wipers. They passed only a few other cars. The fewer the better.

They drove for a while. She knew they were headed for the Belle Haven Marina and then some little road she'd never been on. Her father had it all figured out and she had to trust that he knew what he was doing. They reached the turn for the marina, and she followed him into the driveway that led to the parking lot, but instead of continuing to the lot, he turned onto a narrow road that cut through the woods. His car lights blinked off, and she turned hers off as well, and then it was almost impossible to see. The bushes scraped the sides of her car. After a while, her father pulled his car into the woods, nestling it in a narrow space between the trees. She knew she was supposed to stop driving then. He'd explained all of this to her. So she stopped and waited and he got out of his car and into her passenger seat, kicking the snow off his shoes before letting his feet rest on the floor.

"You're doing great," he said, patting her shoulder with his gloved hand. "Just great. Keep going now, nice and slow."

She gave the car a little gas.

"That's it," he said. "Perfect. We're so lucky with this

snow. It's supposed to get a lot heavier before morning and it'll cover our tracks when we walk back to the car. I wasn't sure how we were going to handle that."

She didn't want to hear that he'd been unsure about anything.

After a while, he told her to turn on her headlights to see where they were. She flipped her lights on and saw the snow falling ahead of her, and beyond that, too close for comfort, the river.

"Perfect," her father said again. "Stop right here. Turn off your lights."

Once the lights were off, she couldn't even see her gloved hand when she held it in front of her face. How was she going to do this without being able to see?

He handed her a flashlight. "Keep it pointed to the ground," he said. "The woods are thick right here, but we can't risk too much light. Can you get your kayak down on your own in the dark?"

"Yes," she said. She got out of the car, closing the door as quietly as he had back in their driveway, and reached up blindly for one of the straps. She'd taken her kayak off her roof herself a hundred times, but never in the dark and never in the cold and certainly never wearing gloves. It took less than a minute for her fingertips to go numb, and she couldn't get the strap undone. She thought of last summer, before everything happened, when they rented the place in Rehoboth and her mother let her take Riley out in the kayak on the calm water of the Intracoastal Waterway. She remembered Riley's sense of wonder as she waved to the birds. She remembered bending over to kiss the top of the little girl's head, how she let her lips linger against the silky dark curls as she breathed in Riley's scent, still more baby than little girl back then.

Her eyes stung, and her fingers lost their grip on the strap. She pounded her fist against the window. She kicked the door.

"Hey, hey," her father said, getting out of his side of the car and coming around to hers. He put his arm around her and she leaned against him.

"I can't do this, Daddy," she said.

For a long moment, he said nothing, just held her and rubbed her back. "You don't have to, sweetheart," he said. "It's an option, that's all. It's your choice."

She pressed her forehead into his chest, thinking. Her nose ran and she wiped it with the back of her glove. *My choice.* Her own attorney had told her that her case was unwinnable. She was afraid of prison. She was afraid of those hard women. Those real criminals. She was terrified of being locked up, unable to escape. Unable to breathe. Even when they put the handcuffs on her in her living room that day, she started to scream. How did people stand being locked up with no way, absolutely no way, out? She imagined her mother telling people, "I have three children, but one's in prison." The humiliation Riley and Danny would face. It was already bad enough for Danny. He didn't understand exactly what was going on, but he knew kids were talking about him. He'd always been a happy, bubbly kid, and suddenly no one wanted to be his friend.

"I'm just scared," she said.

"I know. Me, too."

"I want to do it," she said.

"There's no going back."

"I know." She turned away from him and reached up again for the kayak. "I can do it myself."

"You sure?"

"Yes." The front strap came free and she started to work on the rear strap, ignoring the numbness of her fingers and thinking of nothing other than getting her kayak in the water.

Her father waited in the car while she carried the kayak over her head to the river. He'd picked a good spot for her to put in. The bank eased down to the water. No nasty rocky drop-off. She risked shining the flashlight into the river and saw that it was already starting to freeze along the bank and was choppy and frothy and wind-whipped farther out. She was afraid she wouldn't be able to shove the boat far enough into the water for the current to grab it, but she gave it a great push and the river ripped it from the bank, just like her father had predicted. With the last of her strength, she tossed the paddle as far out in the water as she could. Then she remembered she was supposed to put her jacket in the kayak. Too late now. She took it off and tossed it hard across the water, but the wind blew it against the shrubs along the bank and out of her reach. She stared after it for a moment, shining the beam of her flashlight on it. Nothing she could do about it now. The snow landed on her throat and she pulled up the collar of her sweater, her fingers barely able to grip the fabric.

Her father checked her car with his flashlight to make sure she hadn't left anything incriminating inside. She took the bag with the towel and empty box of hair dye, but left her backpack in the car, as they'd planned. Her driver's license, her wallet with the pictures of Riley and Danny and Matty—everything was left behind in the backpack. Then her father took off his jacket and put it around her shoulders and they trudged through the thick woods to get back to his car. They could have walked along the road, but he said he was worried about tracks, even though the way the snow was coming down now she thought they'd be okay.

By the time they got back to his car, they were both freezing. He turned on the heat and she took off her wet gloves and held her hands in front of the vent.

"Has to be the coldest night of the year," her father said.

"You have a jacket for me, right?" she asked.

"It's in the backseat."

She turned to look in the backseat, but it was too dark. "And a new backpack?" She worried he might have forgotten something. There was so much to remember.

"No backpack. You have a new purse. It's with the jacket."

"A purse? Daddy, you know I never carry a purse."

"*Lisa* never carried a purse," he said. "Ann Johnson does." She was Ann Johnson in all her new documents.

She started to unfasten her seat belt to reach behind her for the purse and jacket, but he put a hand out to stop her. "Wait till we have some light," he said. "I want to get away from here." He began carefully backing the car out of the narrow lane. It took forever, and by the time they were again on the parkway and he put his lights on, she was horrified to see that the dashboard clock read two-thirty.

"You're not going to have time to drive me to Philly and be back home by morning!" she said. That had been the plan, and it was already falling apart. He needed to "discover" she was missing in the morning. He was supposed to go to her room to make sure she was up and ready for her nine o'clock appointment with the attorney, and he'd find her gone and the note in her place.

"We're okay," he said calmly. "I'm not taking you all the way to Philadelphia." He glanced at her, but it was too dark to read his face. "Don't panic," he said.

"What do you mean, you're not taking me to Philly? I'm supposed to be on that eight o'clock train!"

"You will be. Don't worry."

"How?" He was really scaring her.

"Now listen. You remember a man I work with? Tom Kyle?"

"I have no idea who that is!" She knew she'd met a man with that name somewhere, but she was too upset to admit it to her father.

"Well, you'll probably recognize him. We're meeting him at the rest stop on 95 and he'll drive you to Philly."

She felt ice run through her body. "He knows?" she asked. "You told him? You said absolutely no one! Tell absolutely no one. That's what you said. You—"

"Stop it." He stared straight ahead at the road. "Don't worry. I know what I'm doing. Tom will keep his mouth shut."

"How can you be so sure? I can't believe you didn't tell me. I wouldn't have—"

"Lisa!" he shouted, shutting her up. "It's set, all right? I promise you. I absolutely guarantee you. You'll be safe."

She went quiet. She'd never liked it when he yelled at her. He was a soft-spoken, calm person, and those rare times he yelled shook her up.

He turned onto the Beltway and they didn't speak for half an hour, not until he'd exited onto 95. Then he suddenly broke the silence.

"I'll always love you, no matter what you've done," he said.

He would always believe she was a murderer. Tears

clogged her throat. The truth or a lie, she knew it didn't matter to him. Her parents would love her regardless of anything she'd done. She'd tested their love to the limit during her lifetime.

They came to the first rest stop and he pulled off 95 and into the empty parking lot.

"He's not here." She stated the obvious.

"He will be." He left the car running so they'd have heat and could use the wipers to keep the windshield clear. "Let me see your hair," he said.

He turned on the overhead light to look at her as she pulled off her hat. He rubbed his hand over his chin. "Maybe we should have gone with the wig." He sounded nervous. "Wear your hat as much as you can and stick to yourself on the train. Your picture's been all over the news for months." He pointed to the bag on the floor by her feet. "Give me the bag," he said, and she handed it to him.

She watched as he got out of the car, walked through the few inches of snow, and tossed the bag in the trash can by the brick building that housed the restrooms. She was tempted to lower the visor mirror to look at her hair again, but decided not to depress herself any more than she already was. She'd had long pale blond hair all her life. She wasn't going to like the girl she was becoming.

Daddy shook off the snow and got back in the car, looking at his watch. Then he reached into the seat behind him and grabbed the jacket and purse, handing them to her. In the overhead light, she saw that the purse wasn't new at all. It was some thrift shop thing and nothing she'd ever buy for herself, but she wrapped her hand around the straps, trying to get used to the feel of them. She'd never owned a purse and her shoulder already missed the thick strap of her backpack.

"Did you remember the suitcase?" she asked, worried. She'd totally forgotten about it herself.

"In the trunk." He turned to look back at the entrance to the rest stop, then checked his watch again.

The suitcase held only the new documents she'd need and some clothes her father had bought for her. She couldn't risk taking any of her own. Her mother would know they were missing. She had no idea if the police would believe the suicide story or not. They might think she ran. They'd look at airports and train stations. That's why she was taking off from Philly instead of D.C. Even so, it was a huge risk. When the police came to the house in the morning, Daddy would point out that Violet was still in her room. "She'd never leave without her violin," he'd say. He'd pretend to notice that the kayak was missing. He'd have to be careful not to point out too much, though. He'd raise suspicion. They'd ask if she'd been depressed lately, and he would be able to honestly answer yes. She was certifiably depressed. They'd made her see a shrink, who'd said she should be watched carefully. She felt terrible that her mother would think she hadn't watched her closely enough and that she should never have gone to Granddad's this close to the trial. She didn't want her mother to blame herself.

"Now, listen to me, Lisa," her father said. "I want you to memorize something. Do not *ever,* under any circumstances, write this down, okay? Just keep it in your head."

"What are you talking about?"

"I've opened a post office box," he said. "It's only to be used in a dire emergency. I won't be able to check it often, at least not for a while, but you'll have it if you need it."

She suddenly felt as though she could breathe. She had a way to reach him!

"What's the address?" she asked.

"Dire emergency," he warned. "Understand?"

She nodded.

He rattled off the address: PO box 5782, Pollocksville, North Carolina, and she frowned.

"North Carolina? Why would you have a post office box in—"

"It doesn't matter. And the name it's under is Fred Marcus. Don't ever address anything there to my real name."

"Okay."

"Say it back to me."

"Post office box 5782, Pollocksville, North Carolina. What's the zip code?"

"That's too much to remember. And what's my name?"

"Fred Marcus."

"Good," he said. The snow had stopped and he turned off the wipers. "Now, when you get to San Diego, I suggest you head to Ocean Beach. I was there once a long time ago, and I think you'll blend in. Find a cheap motel room." He glanced at her and she felt his worry. "Not so cheap that you don't feel safe," he added. "Get a job and look for something better as soon as you can."

She was barely listening. "I wish you hadn't told Mr. Kyle," she said.

She thought he wasn't going to answer her, but after a minute he spoke. "We needed him to get your documents," he said. "He does them for the Witness Protection Program. I don't handle them anymore. I'd set off alarm bells if I tried."

"But . . . now he knows."

Daddy looked at her. "Trust me, Lisa, he's not going to breathe a word."

Headlights suddenly swept through the inside of the car, and she turned to see a pickup pull into the parking lot.

"Here he is," Daddy said, then added, urgency in his voice, "What's the name and address of the PO box?"

She repeated them one more time.

"Good girl."

The truck pulled up next to their car. She didn't budge, suddenly paralyzed with fear, as the man opened the door of the truck and stood up, tugging a knit cap low on his forehead. He was tall. Broad shouldered. Her father got out of the car, reaching out to shake Tom Kyle's hand, but the bigger man kept his own hands in his pockets. Daddy knocked on the window to hurry her up. She fumbled with the door handle, nerves and her still-damp gloves making her clumsy. Finally out of the car, she couldn't look Tom Kyle in the eye. Her father opened the trunk and handed her the suitcase, which was so light she knew she'd have to be careful not to let anyone else lift it or risk raising suspicion.

None of them spoke. Mr. Kyle put the suitcase behind his seat in the pickup, and for just a moment, she wondered if her father had a different plan for her than the elaborate one they'd concocted. Could Tom Kyle be taking her someplace other than the train station in Philadelphia?

He glanced from her to her father. "I'll wait in the truck," he said.

When Mr. Kyle was in the truck, her father pulled her wordlessly into his arms. "Stay in the ladies' room at the train station till there are more people around," he said into her ear. "Mix in with crowds. Guard your purse—there's money in it—and guard the documents in your suitcase. Keep your wits about you." He hugged her hard. "And most important of all, never pick up a violin again, Lisa, understand? *Never.* You have to hide your light under a bushel from now on. Promise me." It wasn't the first time he'd told her she could never play again. She would attract too much attention, he'd said. People who knew music would figure out who she was.

"I promise," she said.

"I love you, Lisa," he said, pulling away. She couldn't see his eyes, but she heard the tears in his voice. She'd never seen her father cry.

"I love you, too," she said.

She climbed into the cab of Tom Kyle's truck. He didn't say a word, and she cried silently as he drove out of the parking lot, full of doubt over what she was doing.

The snow started again and Mr. Kyle took it slow, even though they saw a couple of plows and the road was in decent shape. Not a word passed between them for nearly an hour and it was either that he knew she needed to cry in peace or he didn't know what to say. Or, possibly, he simply didn't care. By the flat, sort of angry look on his face, she thought that might be it.

After a long time, she turned to him. The snow had let up and he was driving faster. "Why are you doing this?" she asked, her voice loud in the truck after so much silence.

He was quiet as though he hadn't heard her. Then he finally spoke. "I don't have anything to say to you," he said gruffly. "I don't want to hear your excuses for why you killed an innocent man over a fucking college application. I don't want anything to do with you."

She turned back to the window, her eyes burning. He scared her. Why her father trusted him to keep this quiet when he was obviously disgusted by her, she had no idea. She wished she could tell her father she thought Tom Kyle could be a danger to them, but as she clutched her purse close to her body, reality hit her hard: she might never be able to tell her father anything, ever again.

18.

Riley

I was sure I broke my own record for speed as I ran home after the meeting with Tom and Suzanne. *She didn't,* he'd said. Didn't what? Kill herself? Was there any other possible way to interpret what he said? How could he know something like that? I wondered if he'd read Sondra Lynn Davis's blog. Sondra didn't believe Lisa had killed herself, either. Maybe Tom had read her blog and bought into the theory.

Or maybe he knew something no one else knew. Either way, I felt sullied just by having him talk to me about my family.

I didn't bother changing out of my running clothes when I got home. I spotted Christine and Jeannie working in the dining room, the curio cabinet doors open as they culled through my mother's beloved china and old vases.

"Do you have a minute to—" Christine started to get to her feet, but I cut her off.

"Sorry!" I said. "I'm in a rush."

I grabbed my purse and keys from the table by the front door, got in my car, and headed for the RV park.

* * *

I sprayed gravel behind me as I drove through the park and I didn't slow down until I reached the end of the lane and saw that Tom's car wasn't behind the Kyles' RV. *Damn it!* Still, I parked in the shade by the trees, got out of my car, climbed the steps to the motor home, and pounded on the door.

"Hold your horses!" Verniece called from inside, and I heard her heavy footsteps as she came to the door. I pounded again, unable to stop myself. She pulled the door open, a look of annoyance on her face that softened the instant she saw me.

"Riley! What's all the knocking about? My goodness!"

"Where's Tom?" I asked.

"Oh, please don't tell me he didn't show up for the meeting with the lawyer." She looked pained. "Every once in a blue moon he stops off for a drink in the daytime, even though he knows better, and then he forgets—"

"He was there. The meeting went fine. But when he left he said something that—" I stopped speaking, winded as if I was still running. "Can I come in?" I asked.

She looked at me with real concern, reaching out to touch my arm as though she thought I might need steadying. "Let me come out there," she said. "More comfy than in here. We'll sit in the shade. Would you like something to—"

"No." I backed down the steps to the concrete pad. "No, I don't want anything. I just need to talk to Tom!"

"All right, all right," she said, descending the steps. "You're worrying me. You seem like such a calm person most of the time, and to see you like this is . . . well, what's the problem? You said the meeting went fine, so—"

"He said my sister didn't kill herself."

She stared at me a moment, her face a puzzled mask. "Sit down, dear," she said after a moment, lowering herself into one of the old webbed chairs.

"I don't want to sit." I stood in front of her. "I just want to know why he said that."

"Sit," she said again, motioning to the other chair, and I reluctantly dropped into it. My right knee jumped up and down as though an electric current ran through it.

"Why would he say that?" I asked.

"I honestly don't know," she said. "I'm a tad stunned that he would. He has a bit of a mean streak that comes out every once in a while, but I can't imagine, even in his foulest moods, that he'd tease you that cruelly."

"So, you don't think it's true? That she didn't kill herself? You think she did?"

"Oh, honey." She reached out to rest her hand on my arm. "You know why she took her life, right?"

"Guilt and fear," I said. "She was afraid she'd end up in prison."

Verniece nodded. "She killed someone and she was going to have to pay," she said. "I know they didn't find her body, and some people believed she'd faked her death to avoid going to prison, but the Potomac is a big river, and they couldn't search everywhere." She spoke kindly, the way she had spoken to me about my supposed adoption, and there was something about Verniece's voice—her whole demeanor—that had a way of calming me.

I felt tears collect in the back of my throat. "I want it to be true." I twisted my hands together, rubbing them back and forth. "I want her to be alive. I need my *family,* Verniece. I'm managing everything to do with the house and Daddy's estate and I'm worried about Danny and . . . I feel like I'm a little kid with too much on her plate."

"You poor dear! I never should have told you about your adoption, at least not now, when you're dealing with so many other things."

"My mother's best friend knows nothing about that," I said firmly. "I really think you have my mother mixed up with someone else."

She looked at me a moment before nodding. "Maybe," she said, and I knew she was saying it only to placate me. "Maybe I'm remembering wrong."

"Where can I find Tom right now?" I asked.

"He's probably stopped off for a nip someplace where you wouldn't want to go." She looked toward the road as though expecting to see his car any moment. "Tom's a good man and he's been a good husband for all these forty years," she said, "but the bottle has a bit of a hold on him, I'm afraid."

I thought about the affair my father had kept hidden for Tom. I felt sad for Verniece, being stuck with a man like that. Feeling like she needed to defend him.

"Do you know when he'll be back?"

"Oh, you never know with Tom." Verniece smacked a mosquito on her bare knee. "And depending on how much he's had to drink, you might not get any clear information out of him," she added. "Better to try to see him in the morning. You can bet that when I see him, I'll ask him what he meant about your sister. All I can think is that you must have misunderstood him."

"I don't know what else he could have meant."

"I'll talk to him. But"—she let out a sigh—"I should tell you something, Riley. It might explain why Tom would say something so hurtful to you."

"What?" I braced myself, not sure I wanted to hear.

"See," she said, "your daddy was planning to give us the RV park." She tightened her lips together as though afraid she'd said too much.

"He *was*?" I remembered the look Tom had given me in Suzanne's office when he mentioned the park.

Verniece nodded. "He and Tom had been talking about it for a while, and now with your father gone . . . if we seemed ungrateful about getting that pipe collection, that's why. Tom expected so much more. He thought we'd be able to sell the park and have a little easier time of it in our later years."

I was shocked. Why on earth had my father been so generous with Tom Kyle? "Oh," I said, "I had no idea. I'm sorry."

She shrugged. "That's life, I guess. But my husband is bitter about it. I'm afraid he was just taking it out on you with what he said about your sister."

I looked down the gravel lane, wishing I would see his car coming around the bend. "I wanted it to be real," I said quietly.

"I know, dear, but sometimes we have to face the truth." She shifted in her chair. "I was actually there at the river that day," she said.

"What day?" I asked, confused.

"The day after it happened. You remember we lived up there, since Tom worked for the Marshals Service?" She looked into the distance as though she could visualize the scene. "I saw the yellow kayak caught in the ice out in the middle of the river. The police and firefighters and everyone were there, and they looked overwhelmed by how they'd get to the kayak, much less how they'd find a . . . someone under the ice. Your sister could have been out in the Chesapeake Bay by then, honey."

I shivered, although the temperature was well into the eighties. "I just wish it could be true," I said. "I don't remember her. I never got to know her. But I need her right now."

She looked at me kindly. "You can lean on me, Riley," she said. "I know I'm not your mama or your sister or even an aunt, but you can talk to me anytime. All right?"

I made myself smile at her. "All right," I said. "Thank you."

19.

San Diego

Lisa

Her legs were like rubber when she got off the train in San Diego after three days and nights of a miserable, anxiety-ridden journey. She'd felt paranoid during her waking hours on the train, afraid she would be found out and led away at any moment, and her sleep had been full of the nightmares that had haunted her ever since that horrible day in October. They were bloody dreams. She didn't know the people in them, only that they bled. And bled. And bled.

Waking up that final morning in the tiny cubicle her father had reserved for her—so tiny she had to lift the bed to use the toilet—she'd noticed her hip bones poked up beneath the thin blanket. All she'd been able to eat on the train were saltines, and she'd had to force them down. She'd gotten her period the second day of the trip and had to make do with paper towels and toilet paper until the train reached Chicago and she could buy what she needed as she waited for a different train to L.A. For most of the trip, though, she slept, trying to block out thoughts of what her mother was going through, thinking her daughter had killed herself. Matty would be hurting, too, wondering if there was something he could have said or done to stop her from taking her life.

Clutching her suitcase and purse, she followed the other passengers out of the San Diego train station, wincing at the blinding late afternoon sunlight, the sky a more vivid blue than she'd ever seen. A line of cabs was parked beneath a row of palm trees, and she climbed into the backseat of one of them and asked the driver to take her to Ocean Beach.

"Where in Ocean Beach?" he asked as he pulled away from the curb.

"Um, a motel?"

He chuckled, glancing at her in the rearview mirror. "You want a nice motel or a cheap motel?" he asked.

She thought of the three thousand dollars her father had left in her purse. A lot of money, but how long would it last? *Find a job,* her father had said, but all she could think of doing at that moment was crawling into a bed where she could sleep away the rest of her life.

"Cheap," she said.

Thirty minutes later, the cabdriver pulled up in front of an old motel only a block from the ocean. It looked rundown and dingy, but that close to the beach, how bad could it be? She lugged her suitcase out of the back of the taxi—she couldn't believe it had felt so lightweight to her only a few days earlier. Now she could barely lift it to the sidewalk. Her hands shook as she peeled bills from the wad of cash in her purse, and when she reached through the window to pay the driver, the money fell from her fingers onto the floor of the cab.

"Oh!" she said, trying to open the door, but the driver waved her away.

"No problem!" he said, and she watched him drive off, leaving her alone, and only then did she realize that the blue sky had clouded over and dusk was closing in. She needed a room.

She carried her suitcase into the bare-bones lobby of the motel, where a man, as big and broad as Tom Kyle, stood behind the counter, brazenly smoking a joint. She froze just inside the doorway.

"Ain't got no rooms," he said. "Come back tomorrow."

She couldn't move. Couldn't speak. Her brain was too tired to comprehend what he'd said, and the scent of the marijuana alone made her dizzy.

"You okay?" he asked.

"I need a room," she managed to say. "Where can I get one?"

"Saturday night in Ocean Beach?" he asked. "Nowhere. Stay on the beach, like everyone else. Then you come back tomorrow. Maybe a room for you then." He sucked on the joint, filling his lungs, holding it in. "You okay?" he asked again in a stream of smoke.

She had no voice to answer. She turned and walked outside.

The sky had turned an inky blue in the few minutes she'd been inside the motel. The air grew chillier by the second as she walked the half block to the beach and she was glad she had her jacket. The man was right. There were people on the beach, a mixture of vibrant, healthy-looking people her age, some of them winding up a volleyball game, all of them packing up to leave, and the bedraggled men and women who, she was certain, had no home to go to. They huddled alone or together against the seawall, and she guessed they were settling in for the night. She stood at the entrance to the beach, paralyzed, unsure what to do as darkness fell around her.

She clutched her purse in one hand, her suitcase in the other. People stared at her. She stood out, and that was the one thing she couldn't afford to do. Walking onto the sand, she took a few steps to a vacant area by the seawall. She set her suitcase flat on the sand, sat down on it, and hugged her arms across her body, pressing her purse and the money inside it to her chest. Everyone's eyes were on her. The homeless people. Staring. Wondering who this strange new girl was. What if someone called protective services? She was only seventeen. They could take her in, couldn't they? And then the questions would start. Questions she could never answer. Daddy would be furious at her for botching this. But then she remembered she was eighteen in all the documents she carried. Birth certificate. Social Security card. Driver's license. Protective services wouldn't be able to touch her.

She couldn't let herself sleep. As soon as it was dark enough, she took the money from her purse and crammed the bills into her underwear, flattening them against her breasts and her hips. She heard some of the people talking. Heard laughter. The clink of bottles. *"Fred Marcus,"* she whispered to herself. *"PO box 5782. Pollocksville, North Carolina."* And she repeated it over and over again, like a prayer.

Her muscles grew stiff as she sat like a statue, trying not to draw any attention to herself. The darkness terrified her. She felt like a target for anyone who wanted to hurt her. Rob her. But no one bothered her and she had nearly begun to relax when she saw a light bobbing along on the beach near the seawall. People began calling out, "Hey, Ingrid, over here!" and "Ingrid! Ingrid!" They came to life as the beam of light found them, and she caught a glimpse of the woman who seemed to know them all and who stopped and chatted with each of them.

She hugged herself harder as the woman and her light drew closer, and her fingers toyed nervously with her pendant where it rested snugly in the pocket of her jeans. There was nowhere to go and her mouth was dry as dust as she waited for the light to find her. When it finally did, she blinked and turned her head away.

"Hey." The woman carrying the light dropped to the sand in front of her. "You're new," she said. She rested the lantern on the sand so that it reflected off the wall, and her face, while shadowy, was suddenly visible. Blue eyes. Straight nose. Wide smile. "I'm Ingrid," she said. "What's your name?"

She was afraid to say the words *Ann Johnson*. Afraid the name would somehow give her away. She felt the jade pendant beneath her fingertips. "Jade," she whispered, then tried to wet her lips with her dry tongue. "Jade," she said again.

"Beautiful name." Ingrid reached into a bag she carried and pulled out a bottle of water. "Here, baby," she said, handing her the bottle. "And do you like chocolate chip or oatmeal?"

She didn't know how to answer. She didn't even understand the question.

"Cookies, sweetheart," Ingrid said. "I try to bring them out here a few nights each week."

She doubted she could eat a cookie, but knew she needed to try. "Oatmeal," she said, and took the plastic-wrapped cookie Ingrid offered her.

"Is this your first night in O.B.?" Ingrid asked.
She nodded.
"And how old are you, honey?"
"Eighteen."

Ingrid hesitated, then picked up her lantern again and got to her feet and Lisa—*Jade*—had to stop herself from grabbing the woman's leg and begging, *Please help me!*, but the last thing she needed was a stranger in her life. A stranger who, in better light, might recognize her face. Steven's murder had made national news. It had even been written up in *People* magazine. Her father had been foolish to think that changing her hair color would be enough to protect her.

"Stay safe, honey," Ingrid said as she moved away from her, and Jade fought back a sob as she watched the light move on down the beach.

In the morning, she hobbled stiffly to a small coffee shop, where she used the bathroom. Her reflection in the mirror was a shock, not only because of the brown, unwashed hair but also the dark circles below her eyes and the tight, sickly white skin stretched across her cheekbones.

In the café, she drank a carton of juice and ate half a bite of Ingrid's oatmeal cookie before her stomach let her know it was a mistake. She was so exhausted after a sleepless night that the people milling around her in the café seemed like figures in a dream. At a table by the window, she spotted a man reading *The New York Times,* and wondered if there was a story about her in the paper. The *Times* had covered the murder, of course. Would it also cover her suicide? The man glanced in her direction, and she let a few strands of her hair fall over her cheek like a veil.

Back in the motel, the same man as the night before sat on the stool behind the counter and he said he'd have a room ready for her by noon. She cried, she was so relieved. One-twenty a week, he told her. She had no idea if that was a good price for this dumpy old place or not. She'd never been on her own before. She'd traveled more than most kids her age. All the concerts. All the festivals. But some adult—her parents or Steven or Caterina—had always taken care of everything and all she'd needed to do was show up and play her twenty-thousand-dollar violin. She knew now, as she waited for her room on a hard plastic chair in the lobby, with its grimy floor and stained walls, that she'd been spoiled.

Sitting there, she clamped her suitcase between her knees, knowing she was perilously close to drifting off to sleep. At noon, the man gave her a key and she walked outside, up the stairs and down a long exterior walkway to a room that was no bigger than the prison cell she belonged in. Although it was daylight and the sun shone through the filmy glass of the window, two roaches marched across the floor in full view. Jade barely took note of them. All she saw was a bed that looked like it had clean sheets beneath a thin green blanket. She locked the door, pulled the curtains closed, and fell onto the bed to sleep away this horrible new reality that had become her life.

She didn't fully wake up until noon the following day. She'd gotten up a few times, awakened by laughter or shouting or, on one frightening occasion, pounding on her door, but other than that and a couple of breaks to use the filthy toilet in the bathroom, she slept. When she opened her drapes that second day, a man was peering straight into her room, his craggy face pressed against her grimy window. She screamed and whipped the drapes closed again. She didn't dare go out there. The night she spent on the beach seemed like ages ago.

Like someone else's life. She'd been very lucky she'd made it through that night safely and had lost none of her precious cash.

Sitting on the bed in the dim light, she nibbled the remaining third of that woman Ingrid's cookie, wondering how she would get more food, even though she still had no appetite. But she needed to eat to survive. She felt so weak and trembly, she wasn't sure she could make it down the motel steps to the street. *I could die in this room,* she thought. But she couldn't go outside with that creepy man out there. She crawled under the covers again. When she closed her eyes, all she could see was the image of her mother rocking Riley to sleep in her arms. Riley had on her pink-footed pajamas and Jade imagined the scent of baby shampoo and her mother's hand lotion. If only she could erase the past few months and be back with her family! She fell asleep, longing to touch them.

The next morning, she awakened to a knock on the door. She stared at the door from the bed. The sun peeked into the room through the gap between the door and the door frame. It was the only way to know day from night in the room. The knocking came again.

"Jade?" a woman's voice asked. "It's Ingrid, honey. Please open the door."

Jade hesitated a moment, sitting up in the bed, thinking, *It's a trap. Don't open it. Don't open it.* But her need for kindness, for a grown-up to take over her life and put it in some kind of order, was too strong and she slowly moved the covers aside.

"I'm coming," she said, her voice a croak as she got out of the bed. She could smell her filthy hair as she moved across the room, and she was still in the clothes she'd been wearing since getting off the train. Lisa would never have let herself fall apart like this. But Lisa was dead and gone.

She cracked open the door, blinking against the sunlight, and got her first real look at Ingrid. She wore loose white pants, a loose white flowy top, and green flip-flops. A very, very long braid hung over her left shoulder, and the color of her hair was a dull mixture of beige and brown and gray. Her eyes were as blue as Jade's, but Ingrid's stood out because of her tan. Crinkly lines fanned out from her eyes, and her neck had a leathery look, but she wasn't very old. Maybe in her early forties. Jade's mother's age.

Ingrid smiled. "Do you remember me from the other night on the beach?" she asked.

Jade nodded.

"I asked around and someone told me they thought you got a room here. But I don't think you really belong here, do you?"

Jade wasn't sure what she was asking, but no. She didn't belong here. She shook her head.

"I don't live too far from here," Ingrid said, "and I have a little cottage I rent out. My tenant moved out last week and I can let you have it for a little more than what you're probably paying here. Would you like that?"

Could she trust her? Had Ingrid called the police about her? Jade's brain was too foggy to think it through. She remembered the screaming and shouting outside her room during the night hours. The old man's craggy face pressed against her window. She nodded. "Yes," she said.

"Then pack up your things and let's go."

They had to walk. Ingrid explained that she had no car and didn't need one in Ocean Beach, where everything was at her fingertips. She rolled Jade's small suitcase for her, saying nothing about how light it was when she took it from her hands. Jade wanted to ask how far it was to her house—she wasn't sure she could walk more than a block, she felt so weak and sick. Her stomach was concave and her muscles so slack that it was difficult to hold herself upright as they walked. But it was wrong to ask. Wrong to complain about anything at all when this woman was being so nice to her.

"Look at you, in that heavy jacket and hat," Ingrid said as they walked. "You must have come from someplace cold?"

"Maryland," Jade said, trying out the lie. Ann Johnson was from Bethesda, Maryland. At first she'd thought it was stupid that her documents made it look like she was from Maryland when that was only one state over from Virginia, but her father said it would be easiest for her. Growing up in Virginia, she knew a lot about Maryland. If anyone asked her about it, she could sound like she'd actually grown up there.

"Well, you can burn those winter clothes," Ingrid said cheerfully. "You're a California girl now."

They walked a few blocks in silence, the shops and palm trees and people a blur, and Jade was breathing hard through her mouth by the time Ingrid pointed to a low wooden bungalow. It was tiny and looked old, like all the other houses on the street, but it was painted a deep turquoise, and purple flowers grew on vines all over the front yard. It looked like a real home. It looked like more than Jade felt she deserved.

She followed Ingrid up the cracked sidewalk to the front door of the bungalow. Ingrid opened the unlocked door and ushered her inside. They were in a small living room dominated by a green tiled fireplace and a huge, fat-cushioned brown couch. Jade could see three doorways from where she stood, all of them arched. "This is my house," Ingrid said. "Your little cottage is out back." Jade felt Ingrid scrutinizing her face and wished she could hide behind more than her filthy hair. Was Ingrid comparing her face to one she'd seen on TV that morning? She thought of the photographs of her that had made the news since Steven's death. In nearly every one, she was holding Violet. Her father had been right not to let her bring the violin with her.

"I've never been farther east than Iowa, where I'm from," Ingrid said. She stood in the arched doorway between the living room and a yellow kitchen. "But I've been out here since I was eighteen. Your age," she continued. "As soon as I graduated, I hightailed it out of town." She laughed and Jade tried to smile. "I didn't regret it for an instant," Ingrid said. "I had some friends in San Diego, though. How about you? Do you know someone here?"

She shook her head. "I wanted a fresh start," she managed to say. "Just . . . really fresh."

"And you look like you could use one," Ingrid said. "Utterly exhausted, aren't you. Come on. Let me show you your new home." She reached for the suitcase, but this time Jade grabbed the handle herself.

"I've got it," she said.

She followed Ingrid through a tiny yellow kitchen and out the arched back door. They were in a small yard, where a minuscule turquoise cottage sat in a tangle of vines and pink flowers, looking like something out of a fairy tale.

"So this is your little abode." Ingrid motioned to the cottage. "You can pick your own oranges for your morning juice." She pointed to a couple of trees in the middle of the yard. "The man at the motel said you were paying one-twenty a week, so this will be one-thirty. Will you be able to manage that?"

Jade nodded. This time, she knew she was getting a bargain.

"Don't carry a lot of cash with you," Ingrid said, pointing to her purse. "It's pretty safe around here, but there are drugs and users, just like everywhere. I'm sure you met some of them on the beach." She smiled. "You need to open a bank account, even if you only have a little money. Don't risk losing it. You've got to be smart."

They'd reached the little front patio—just big enough for two small white metal chairs and an identical pair of large potted plants. Jade touched the leaves. They were thick, rubbery and shiny, and they felt like velvet between her fingers.

"When I decided to ask you if you wanted to stay here," Ingrid said, pointing to one of the plants, "I bought these for you to have on the patio. Do you know what they're called?"

She shook her head.

"They're jade plants," Ingrid said. "Like your name."

Before she knew what was happening, Jade started to cry. It was an out-of-control sort of crying that took over her whole body and spirit, and she wasn't even sure what started it. That Ingrid was so nice, she guessed. So nice to a girl who was lying to her face. She sobbed into her hands, unable to hold herself together one more second.

"Oh, you're so worn down." Ingrid put an arm around her shoulders. "Come inside and get unpacked and you can take a nice bath. There's no shower, but you can wash your hair in the tub or the sink. Then after you've had a rest, we're only two blocks from a market where you can stock your fridge and pantry." Ingrid lowered her arm to her side as Jade wiped her wet face with her fingers. "You're all skin and bones," Ingrid said, and Jade wondered if she thought she was one of the drug users she'd been talking about.

She let Ingrid guide her inside the cottage to a tiny living room. Ingrid pulled open the blinds of the only window in the room, while Jade looked around her. A giant brown couch, identical to the one in Ingrid's house, took up most of the room, along with two chairs that looked like they came from someone's old dining room set. There was a TV in the corner. She wanted to turn it on. She needed to see if Lisa MacPherson's suicide was on the news. Instead she followed Ingrid into the bedroom, which was only a little bigger than the double bed, the same size bed she'd had at home. A dresser was wedged between the bed and the window that looked out on the orange trees. "And here's your bathroom," Ingrid said. The bathroom, too, was tiny—just a toilet and sink and one of those old claw-foot tubs. Ingrid was right. She needed a long soak in that thing.

"Linens come with the cottage." Ingrid pulled open a little cupboard that held faded pink towels and pink floral sheets. "There's a Laundromat on Newport Avenue," she said. "Not far. And if you need to make local calls, there's a pay phone right in front of it. You can use my phone in an emergency."

"Thank you so much," Jade said, and for the first time since leaving home, her voice sounded a little more like her own, though quiet and weary. "This is amazing. And I'm going to do what you said. Take a bath. And then a nap."

Ingrid pressed a key into her hand and looked her in

the eye. "You'll be safe here," she said, and Jade could only hope she was right.

For the next two days, Jade stayed in the cottage. She drank water from the tap but ate nothing, afraid to go out. Afraid to be seen. She trusted Ingrid, but not one hundred percent, and she waited for the knock on the cottage door that would spell the end for her. She cowered in the corner of the couch evening and morning, watching the news. There was absolutely nothing about her on it, although she knew she was probably the only story the newscasters back home were talking about. Here, it was all about a serial killer who was stabbing women to death in their homes and the Leaning Tower of Pisa being closed to the public because it was leaning too far. If the San Diego news had ever mentioned Lisa MacPherson's suicide, they were done with it now.

In bed at night, she longed for her mother. A word she hadn't uttered in years—*Mommy*—was nearly always on her lips. She wanted to be a small child again, like Riley, being tucked into bed by her mom. She remembered her mother leaning over to kiss the tip of her nose before saying her prayers with her, God-blessing everyone they knew, including Steven. Now, though, the bedtime prayer she repeated each night had nothing to do with God and everything to do with a post office box in North Carolina. She needed to keep that address front and center in her mind, although she felt certain her father hoped she'd never try to use it.

Was he relieved these days? He'd spared the family from the spectacle of her trial, which would have been in its third day by now. The media circus was over for them. Had he done this for her, she wondered, or for her family?

On the third morning, there was a knock on her door. Through the window, she saw Ingrid standing between the jade plants, something in her hand. Ingrid gave her a wave and Jade knew she had no choice but to open the door. She hadn't spoken to her landlady since the first day.

"I brought you some banana bread," Ingrid said, when Jade pulled the door open. "Come sit out here in the sunshine with me. You've got this place all closed up and you're missing some beautiful weather." She tilted her head, peering closely at her. "Are you all right?"

"I'm fine," Jade said. "Just still worn out after . . . not sleeping well on the train. And the beach and the motel."

Ingrid looked like she didn't believe her. "Come on," she insisted. "Sit with me out here. Let's have a chat."

Jade followed her onto the patio, terrified of what Ingrid had to say and blinking against the bright sunlight.

"I don't mean to pry," Ingrid said, as they sat down on the white metal chairs, "but I'd like to help you, and to do that I need to know what's going on with you. You're ill, right? You can tell me. Is it AIDS?"

"AIDS?" She was shocked. "No!"

"Well, I'm relieved to hear that," Ingrid said, although she didn't look completely convinced. "You remind me of a friend I lost to that damn disease, so I was worried. It's that . . . you're so thin. You look like you haven't eaten in months. You're so pale and just . . . you have those dark circles around your eyes."

She knew she looked sick. The shirts her father had picked up for her at Goodwill hung from her shoulders and she would soon need to get a belt to keep her jeans up. Her breasts had always been small, but now her bra puckered over them.

"I'm not sick," she said. "I've just been . . . I guess I'm nervous, moving here, starting a new life on my own. I have no appetite."

"Honey." Ingrid leaned toward her. "Are you on the run from someone who hurt you?"

She tried to laugh as if the question was absurd. "Not at all," she said.

"Pregnant? I'm sorry to be so personal," Ingrid added quickly. "I only want to help."

She wanted to tell Ingrid everything. She was so nice. But of course she couldn't. She'd never be able to tell a soul.

"Not pregnant. Not sick." She made herself smile. "I'm okay. Really."

"You need to have some food in the house." Ingrid handed her the loaf of banana bread and she held it on her lap. "Have you been out at all?" she asked. "Have you been to the market?" She pointed north of where they sat. Or maybe it was south. Having the ocean on the west coast was confusing her after living her whole life with it on the east. "I have a cart I use if I need to buy more than I can carry a block," Ingrid said. "You're welcome to use it. I keep it in the shed." She motioned to a tiny building at the back of the little yard. It was overgrown with a white flowering vine.

"Thank you."

"Are you up to walking over there?" she said. "If not, I can pick up some things for you later."

Jade had the feeling Ingrid still thought she had AIDS.

"I'll go this afternoon," she said. She would, too. Ingrid was right. She had to get out. She had to see how people reacted to her. She had to know she was safe here.

* * *

Inside the cottage, Jade looked at herself in the bathroom mirror. She was a disaster. Her hair was clean now, but it hung limply around her pale face, and her eyes were red-rimmed. Although she'd dyed her eyebrows, her eyelashes were their usual white and if that wasn't a giveaway, she didn't know what was. She had to get mascara. And more of that dye for when her roots started coming in.

She put on her sandals and grabbed her purse. Once on the street, she walked in the direction Ingrid had pointed. North. She was winded by the time the market came into view. There were loads of people on the street and most of them seemed to be close to her age. Blond boys on skateboards. Long-haired girls with holey jeans and cutoff T-shirts. They glanced at her. Some even smiled and said hi. She was not in northern Virginia any longer. People were happy and friendly and unrushed here. The sun shone brighter and crisper. Nobody was thinking about the murderous girl from Alexandria.

Once in the market, she realized she should have brought Ingrid's cart with her. She limited what she bought so it would fit in two paper sacks, picking out some fruit and chicken breasts and a paperback cookbook called *Healthy Cooking on the Cheap*. She paged through it for a chicken recipe and bought the rest of the ingredients she'd need to make it. She'd never learned to cook. Her mother always said she'd rather have her practice the violin than do housework. She bit back tears at the memory of her mother, and that's when she saw the little girl. She was tiny, no more than two, crouching down in the pasta and rice aisle with her back to Jade as she poked at a plastic bag of noodles. A woman—most likely the child's mother—stood nearby, reading the labels on jars of pasta sauce. The girl's black hair shimmered in two high pigtails. Jade stopped in the middle of the aisle, staring, willing the girl to turn around and be Riley. *If only!* The little girl chattered to herself as she poked the bag, and Jade fought the urge to pick her up, swing her around, and bury her face in that chubby little neck that she was certain would smell exactly like Riley's. But when the girl looked up at her with the face of an adorable stranger, the magic spell was broken, and Jade quickly walked past her toward the checkout counter before the child's mother could catch her staring.

She walked back to Ingrid's as fast as she could with the bags in her arms. They weighed a ton and she had so little strength. She was out of breath after the first block, and she couldn't get her heart to slow down. It was even skipping beats, the way it had the day she was arrested and the police dragged her down to the station. She'd been nearly comatose in the back of that police car and her chest had felt like it had a pinball banging around inside it. Her jeans had been stiff with blood; her hands sticky and red. She didn't care then if she died. A heart attack would have been just fine with her. She'd wanted it to be over, because she knew that whatever was ahead of her was going to ruin her life. She felt a little the same way now. Her life no longer seemed to matter. If she dropped dead on the street, they'd find this girl, Jade, this girl who didn't exist, and they'd try to contact her family, only to discover her family didn't exist, either.

By the time she got back to the cottage, she was sweating and crying. She dumped all the groceries in the kitchen, flopped onto her bed, and stared out the window at the orange trees. Did Jade have anyone who loved her? The family she ran away from—did they love her? What did it matter, she told herself. They were make-believe people. The people who loved Lisa—her parents and Riley and Danny and Matty—now only loved the ghost of Lisa. Except for Daddy. Nobody else knew she was still here. Nobody else knew the hollow girl she was turning into.

20.

Riley

In spite of Verniece's warning to wait a day to talk to Tom, I couldn't do it. I went back to the park after dinner and was relieved to see him and Verniece sitting in the webbed chairs on the patio, two beers on the small table between them.

I parked at the end of the gravel lane and they watched me as I walked toward them.

"Would you like a beer, Riley dear?" Verniece asked when I reached the patio. I thought she looked nervous, her smile shaky.

"No, thanks." I lowered myself into the third chair without waiting for an invitation. A mosquito promptly landed on my thigh, another on my wrist. I swatted one and missed the other, but I didn't care.

"Look." Tom sat forward, not waiting for my questions. He still wore the shirt and pants he'd had on at Suzanne's office. "I was only saying what the police said. They never found her body. It was suspicious, that's all."

"So you don't know anything?" I heard the plea in my voice. *Please tell me you know something!* "You were just guessing?"

"Exactly," Verniece said. "He was just guessing."

Tom lifted his beer and took a long pull on it. He glanced at his wife. "They found more than one set of footprints in the area where her car was parked, like she had help," he said.

"Tom," Verniece protested.

"Like someone helped her fake her suicide," he added, in case I wasn't following him. I was. Very well.

"How do you know about the footprints?" I asked.

He shrugged. "I read it in the paper somewhere. Your sister's so-called suicide was written up all over the damn place."

"My father cut out a ton of articles about what happened," I said. "I read them all. There was nothing about two sets of footprints."

"Well, he must have missed one," he said. "I didn't pull it out of thin air. What's it matter, anyway?" He narrowed his eyes at me. "You want a murderer in your life? You want to have to split your inheritance with someone like that?"

"Tom . . ." Verniece had red splotches on her throat.

"If my sister *is* alive, I want the chance to know her." I felt the threat of tears behind my eyes.

"Oh, see now what you've done?" Verniece snapped at her husband. "Stop teasing her. What's wrong with you, old man?"

Tom leaned back in the chair with a sigh. "I didn't mean to get you all worked up."

"He didn't mean it, Riley, truly," Verniece said.

"But . . . you honestly don't believe she killed herself?" I couldn't let it go. I would keep the possibility alive as long as I could.

"No, I don't," he said. "I think she's probably still alive and free as a bird somewhere."

"Stop it!" Verniece leaned over to smack him on the arm. "She's vulnerable. Can't you see that? I told her about her adoption and upset her to bits and now you're filling her head with all sorts of crap!"

"I'm not adopted," I said tiredly, then looked at Tom again. "It's just the way you said it. You know, when you were in your car before you drove off? Like you knew for sure."

"I was pissed off," he said. "But that doesn't change what I believe. About her being alive."

We were both ignoring Verniece, who was making tsking sounds of distress.

"Verniece told me my father said he was going to give you the park," I said, "but there's nothing about that in his will. There's nothing to indicate that at all, and I'm sorry if you had your hopes up. I honestly think the pipe collection was pretty generous."

The look he gave me was evil. "You have no fucking idea." He got to his feet so quickly I drew back in my chair, afraid. Picking up his half-empty beer bottle by the neck, he walked away from us toward the creek. I watched him go, wishing I hadn't mentioned the park. Wishing I hadn't come at all.

I looked at Verniece. "I'm sorry," I said. "I didn't realize it was such a sore subject."

She let out a long sigh and brushed a fly away from her damp face. "We're hurting for money a little right now," she said. "That's all. You know how it is . . . well, you don't know, actually." She smiled. "But you reach a certain age. You're on a fixed income, yet expenses keep going up. Your house is falling apart." She laughed mirthlessly, pointing to the dented RV behind her. "It gets a little frightening."

"I'm sorry," I said again. I felt wealthy, my share of

Daddy's money on its way to my own bank and more to come when I sold the house and the park. I'd done absolutely nothing to earn that wealth. "You know you can stay here without paying any rent until I sell the park." *Oh, God.* Where would they go then? "I hope the pipe collection will give you a little bit of a cushion."

She wore a sad smile, reaching over to touch my hand. "I'm sure it will," she said. "And don't you worry, now. We'll be fine."

I felt far worse as I drove away from the Kyles' motor home than when I'd driven toward it half an hour earlier. I wanted to believe my sister was alive, and yet I knew there was a good chance Tom was toying with me.

Two sets of footprints, he'd said. Was he making it up? Even if he wasn't, what did it mean?

All I knew was that I didn't want to be alone with this possibility another minute. I drove past the exit of the RV park and onto the rutted lane that would take me to my brother's trailer.

21.

San Diego

Jade

She played the violin in bed at night.

She had no instrument, of course. She would honor the bargain she'd made with her father, no matter how difficult. She would never play again. But just like a boy without a guitar could play an air guitar, she played the air violin. She'd lie on her back and hold Violet beneath her chin as she stroked the bow across the strings, playing Bach or Mendelssohn, until the instrument grew too heavy for her arms to hold. And then, every single night, she'd cry until her head was stuffy and she'd struggle to fall asleep.

She missed her violin so much. She'd never been one of those children whose parents had to force them to practice. Instead, they'd had to force her to go outside and play. To Jade—to Lisa—the violin had been a reward. Even when she was eight or nine and the neighborhood kids were out riding their bikes on a Saturday morning, she'd wake up with her fingers twitching, ready to pick up the bow. Her violin had gotten her through some terrible times and now, during the loneliest, scariest time of her life, she didn't have the one thing that could calm her.

Sometimes she couldn't believe what had happened to her life, as though it was a nightmare and she would wake up, excitedly working on her applications to Juilliard and the other schools she'd been applying to. Maybe Juilliard wouldn't take her, thanks to Steven, but some school would want her. "Oh, Lisa has such a bright future!" everyone said. Now, Lisa had no future at all, and Jade's looked empty as well. She wondered if there was a way out of her dilemma. Maybe her lawyer hadn't thought of everything. Now, though, even if there were a way out, her father would end up in prison, too. She couldn't let that happen.

In the mornings, she'd eat a piece of toast she wasn't hungry for and watch the news. Even though a month and a half had passed since she'd left home, she still worried that her face would pop up on the television, but it never did. Each day without any mention of Lisa MacPherson, she grew a bit braver. She walked a little farther through the neighborhoods with their bungalows and wild gardens. When people smiled at her, she made herself smile back, and she doubted anyone knew that it was only her facial muscles making the expression and not her heart. At the beach, she'd watch the surfers ride the waves in their wet suits. She looked with new sympathy at the homeless people who had let her share their beach for a night without harm. A few times, she accompanied Ingrid as she carried her baked goods out to the hungry in the dark. It seemed the least she could do.

Newport Avenue, the main street in Ocean Beach, ran between Ingrid's neighborhood and the beach, and both sides of the street were lined with antiques shops and consignment shops and yoga studios and little eateries, but there was one store that drew her in nearly every time she passed it: Grady's Records. The first time she set foot inside the shop, she spent an hour going through old vinyl and cassettes and new CDs, and for a while, she forgot the ache in her chest. She went through everything—the classical, the rock, the folk, the country, the gospel. Everything. She needed music! How had she survived all these weeks without it? If only she could buy some of the CDs, but she had no way to play them and she was afraid to touch her shrinking bank account. She needed a job, but although she could get onstage in front of thousands of people and perform for hours, the thought of walking into one of the shops along Newport Avenue and asking for work scared her. But Grady, the blond, long-haired owner of the shop, gave her a warm smile every time she came in, and she was slowly working up the courage to ask him if he needed help. If it annoyed him that she spent so much time looking through his albums without making a single purchase, he never said a word.

Grady's felt like home to her for another reason that had nothing to do with music. The first time she walked into the shop, her eyes had been drawn to a poster on the wall. Grady had tons of posters, all of rock groups except for this one. It was a photograph of a model, Nastassja Kinski, lying naked on the floor with a python wrapped around her body. It was not the first time Jade had seen that picture. If the police went through her room at home after her "death," they would find the same photograph tucked deep in her T-shirt drawer. She'd first seen it when she was eleven years old, lying on her stomach on the living room floor, looking through a magazine with Matty. He'd turned the page and there was Nastassja and the snake. "Gross!" Matty had said, contorting his face into the expression of disgust that always made her laugh.

"Gross," she'd agreed, but later, when she was alone, she cut out the picture and stared at it for hours before slipping it into her drawer, fascinated by the way the snake coiled around the woman's body, hiding and exposing, hiding and exposing.

To see the same poster on Grady's wall when it had nothing whatsoever to do with music felt like a sign to her. This was where she wanted to work.

Surrounding herself with music in the record store wasn't enough to kill her homesickness, though. Her longing for home, for her family, for Matty, for Violet, seemed to grow bigger and more heartbreaking with each passing day. Back when she thought she'd end up in prison, she'd asked Matty to watch over Riley and Danny for her, and she comforted herself with the thought that he was staying in close touch with them even though he now thought she was dead. She pictured him coming over to the house, acting like a big brother to Riley and Danny. Reading to them. Maybe taking them to the zoo or a movie. If only she could be with them.

One day, when she couldn't shake the sense of having lost everything, she went to the bank and changed a twenty-dollar bill for quarters, telling herself she needed the change for the Laundromat, even though she knew that twenty dollars' worth of quarters was overkill. Then, while her clothes were swooshing around in the washing machine, she walked to the nearby pay phone. She left the door open a crack to cut the urine-and-alcohol scent of the booth, then piled her change on the small metal shelf beneath the phone.

She stared at the dial. It was five o'clock on the East Coast. Her mother was likely at home, making dinner. Jade only wanted to hear her voice. That was all. Maybe she'd be able to hear Riley chattering in the background.

She wouldn't speak, though. Wouldn't dare to. But she needed that connection to her family. She needed it desperately.

She dialed her old home number, adding quarters as the mechanical voice commanded. Holding her breath, she waited through three odd, tinny-sounding rings before someone answered.

"The number you have reached has been disconnected." The voice was mechanical and disinterested, and Jade stared wide-eyed at the dial.

Oh, no. They'd had to change their number twice after her arrest, so she supposed her suicide had caused a new rash of unwanted calls, but her heart sped up at having no way to reach her family. Their new number would be unlisted, for sure. Nevertheless, she had to try. She called information and asked for a Frank MacPherson in Alexandria.

"There is no number for a Frank MacPherson in Alexandria," the operator said.

"You mean, you can't give it out, right? It's unlisted?"

"No, there is no number. There's a Peter and a J.T."

Had they moved? That seemed unthinkable. "What about . . . Arlington?" she asked. "Anywhere around Washington?"

The operator had a Fiona, but no Frank, listed or unlisted, and Jade finally hung up in defeat. Where were they? Where was her family? Were they running away from the reporters? Or were they running away from *her*?

Did Matty know where they were? Her comforting image of him remaining a part of her family's life disintegrated. If they'd moved away, how could he stay involved?

Then, although she hadn't intended to, she dialed

Matty's number. He had his own phone number, separate from his family's, and it only rang in his bedroom. She would settle for his answering machine. Anything! She just needed to hear the voice of someone from her old life. Someone she knew cared about her.

He picked up. "Hello?" he said.

Oh, my God. She touched the phone as if she was touching him. He sounded so familiar, so close by, and it was all she could do to stop herself from speaking.

"Hello?" he asked again. "Who's this?"

Might he guess? There was no one in the world she was closer to than Matty. Didn't he know she would never kill herself? She waited, wanting him to say, "Is this Lisa?" Instead, though, he hung up.

Walking back to the Laundromat, she was in a fog. She tried to picture her house in Alexandria with new people living in it, hurt that her family had moved on without her. Even though she knew it could never happen, she'd fantasized about finding some way to go home. Now "home" didn't exist anymore. She felt dizzy thinking about it, like she was floating out in space forever.

In the Laundromat, she opened the washing machine, reaching in for her wet, twisted clothes.

What had she expected? She had to stop thinking about herself and start thinking about what was best for Riley and Danny and her parents. She'd turned their lives inside out. A move would definitely be the right thing for Danny. He could start fresh at a new school where no one knew about her. And Riley, barely two years old now, would never have to know about her murderous, suicidal sister at all.

She blotted her eyes with the damp towel in her hands.

She knew that would be for the best.

22.

Riley

I couldn't find my brother. When I drove into his clearing after seeing the Kyles, his car was parked next to his trailer but there was no answer when I knocked on the door. He wasn't suicidal, he'd said, but I couldn't stop myself from dragging a concrete block over to the trailer so I could stand on it to peer into a window. There was no sign of him inside. Of course, there was no sign of his shotgun, either, which did nothing to ease my mind. He was probably in his favorite place in the woods, but I would never be able to find that oval of grass on my own. I sat on the Airstream's step, pulled my phone from my pocket, and tried calling him, unsurprised when he didn't pick up.

I found a scrap of paper in my car and tucked a note between his door and the jamb. *I need to talk to you. Please call. Please let me know you're okay.* I drove away without much hope of getting a response.

That night, I tossed and turned until two A.M., more awake than I'd been when I went to bed. I finally decided to get up and tackle my father's computer. I had to see what needed saving from the hard drive before I turned it over to Christine. Maybe concentrating on that task would clear Tom and Verniece—and my worry about my brother—from my mind.

I walked barefoot down the hall to Daddy's office and switched on his small desk lamp. The house was deathly quiet as I sat down at the computer. When I pressed the power button, the old machine let out a human-sounding gasp that broke the silence and sent a chill up my spine. The clunky monitor was slow to come to life, and once it did, I groaned. It wanted a password. Great.

In movies, people always managed to come up with the appropriate password to hack into a computer. A child's name. An anniversary date. Something obvious. I tried every possible combination of letters and numbers I could think of without luck before heading back to bed. Maybe Jeannie would have some idea of a password he'd use, I thought as I lay awake staring at the dark ceiling. She seemed to know everything else about him. If she didn't know what it was, I'd have to ask Danny for help. He knew everything there was to know about computers, and if anyone knew a way to get into my father's files without a password, it would be him. How I'd get him to come back to the house, though, was another question entirely.

And of course, I'd have to find him first.

I was just waking up the following morning when Jeannie and Christine arrived. I heard their car doors slam outside, their muted voices on the front porch as they let themselves in with Jeannie's key. In a moment, one of them would knock on my bedroom door, badgering me about my father's cabinets or the computer or whatever. My house was not my own.

I got out of bed, brushed my teeth, then threw on my running clothes. I managed to escape down the stairs and out the front door without them seeing me, and I headed for the river at an easy jog, still yawning from my mostly sleepless night. When I reached the path along the river, I spotted five kayakers paddling south. I slowed down, then stopped altogether, standing at the railing near the river's edge as I watched the kayaks cut through the water in a chevron shape. The lead kayak was yellow, like my sister's had been. *Weird timing,* I thought, as my mind drifted back to the conversation with the Kyles.

Two sets of footprints.

I pulled my phone from my shorts pocket and dialed Danny's number. No answer. Turning around, I started for home, running now. I went in the back door to find Jeannie rooting around in one of the kitchen cabinets. She looked up in surprise and opened her mouth to speak, but I grabbed my keys from the key rack, gave her a quick wave, and left before she could ask me anything.

Danny was still not in his trailer, but this time his car was gone as well and I guessed he was either at the store or in a bar. I sat in the sweltering heat of my car, remembering the e-mail Harry had sent me about Danny hanging out at Slick Alley these days.

I turned the key in the ignition, hoping I'd see his Subaru in the Food Lion parking lot rather than at the pool hall, for both our sakes. I jostled my car back and forth in the tight clearing, then headed back to New Bern. Fifteen minutes later, I spotted Danny's black Subaru in the Slick Alley parking lot. The building itself was a one-story, flat-roofed rectangle of concrete that had once been painted white but now blended into the gray sky behind it. SLICK ALLEY BILLIARDS was hand painted in green letters above the door, and on the side of the building, someone had painted a picture of a busty blond woman as she bent over a pool table to take a shot. Lovely.

It was not yet eleven in the morning, but there were already ten cars in the lot. I parked between the Subaru and a green truck and got out of my car before I could change my mind. When I pushed open the front door of the building, a dozen male heads turned in my direction and I wished I was wearing something other than my running shorts and tank top. The place was like every stereotype I'd ever seen of a pool hall—murky light, smoky air, faint background music interrupted by the muffled *thwak* of pool balls hitting one another at the tables. A row of booths lined the left wall of the room, and as my eyes adjusted to the dim light, I saw my brother in the last booth, a book in his hands and his eyes on me. He didn't wave. Didn't rise. I walked toward him, ignoring the looks and comments and lip smacking of the pool players as I passed them.

Danny was alone in the booth, except for a full bottle of beer and one empty, and I slid onto the bench across from him. The fake leather seat felt sticky beneath my bare thighs.

"What the hell do you think you're doing?" he asked.

I'd expected to tell him about my conversation with the Kyles, but knew I couldn't do it here. I had no idea how he'd react to anything I said about Lisa. "I need your help getting into Daddy's computer," I said instead. "It's password protected."

"You shouldn't be here."

"Well, I don't know how else to get to talk to you, Danny," I said. "You won't use the phone I got you."

"Why do you need to get into his computer? You should just wipe the drive clean and chuck it."

"I have to see if there's anything important on it before I get rid of it. I need your help. Please."

He shook his head. "I told you. I'm not going in that house again."

I sighed. "I'll bring it to you, then," I said, not looking forward to lugging the computer around with me. "It's a big clunky old PC. You don't need the monitor, right? Just the computer?"

He didn't answer. Instead, he gave me a flat look I couldn't read, his blue eyes catching the faint light from the front windows. I wanted to ask him if this was how he spent his days—sitting alone in this sticky booth in this disgusting building. Did he even know these guys at the pool tables? Was there anyone here he could call a friend? Yet, that's not what came out of my mouth at all.

"The other day, when you said those things to me about not being a good counselor, I was hurt," I said, the words spilling out in an unexpected rush. "I worked hard for my degree, Danny, and I'm good with the kids I counsel. I know I am. Maybe you're right that I'm out of my league when it comes to someone like . . . someone who's been through what you have. But you don't have to belittle me or cut me down the way you did." I leaned forward to make my point. "It really upset me," I said.

He tightened his hand around his beer and my whole body went stiff, afraid of what he was doing to do, but he only lifted the bottle to his lips and took a long swallow. When he set the bottle on the table again, he looked at me. "I'll come to the house to help with the computer," he said, sliding out of the booth. "You don't need to bring it over."

It took a moment for his words to register, and I knew this was his way of apologizing. I felt strangely euphoric as I slid out of the booth, and he waited for me before heading toward the door. He walked next to me, a shield between me and the cretins at the pool tables, and for the first time since we were kids, I felt the protective arm of my brother slip around my shoulders.

Outside, I started to ask him if he was okay to drive, but thought better of it. He seemed perfectly sober. I had the feeling his tolerance for alcohol was pretty high, and anyway, the last thirty seconds had left me with a sense of joy that I didn't want to damage.

"Follow me?" I asked, opening my car door. I was suddenly afraid this was a ploy to get me off his back. Maybe he'd drive away from me once we got on the road and I'd be stuck trying to track him down again. But I didn't think so. The way his arm had felt around my shoulders seemed to change everything. At least, for me it did.

Driving home, I remembered Jeannie and Christine were at the house. *Oh, great.* It was one thing for Danny to be there with me alone. Another for him to have to deal with those two.

I was relieved to see that Jeannie's car was gone when we arrived and I figured they were on a lunch break. I pulled into the driveway and Danny parked on the street. We met on the lawn and walked together up the front steps, and as soon as I opened the door, I could see Christine in the dining room.

"Where have you been?" she called to me as we walked into the living room. "A collector was here and bought the lighters and compasses. Isn't that great? But we have thousands of questions for you." She appeared in the doorway between the dining room and living room, and when she spotted Danny, she let out a squeal. "Danny MacPherson!" she said. "Oh, my God! I haven't seen you since you were a little boy!" She started toward him, arms outstretched, but I stepped between them before she was anywhere within touching range and she wisely stopped walking. "You are *gorgeous,*" she said. "Seriously. Wow."

"I can't do this." Danny headed for the door, but I grabbed his hand and nearly dragged him toward the stairs.

"Later," I snapped at Christine, shooting her a look that could melt steel.

Danny offered absolutely no resistance as I led him up the stairs, holding his hand as if he were a small child. I walked him past his old room without a word and into our father's office, where I let go of him to shut the door and turn the lock.

"Who the hell . . . ?"

"Jeannie Lyons's daughter," I said. "Christine. Do you remember her?"

He shook his head and walked straight to our father's desk. "What's she doing here?" he asked as he sat down at the computer.

"Remember I told you she and Jeannie are setting up an estate sale? And then Jeannie'll list the house and the RV park for me. For us. I'm sorry she ambushed you. It's like having two pit bulls in the house. They're in every room every time I turn around, and they treat the house more like it's theirs than mine."

Danny stared at the computer screen. "You have no idea what his password might be?"

"No."

He looked up. "Do you know where his boot disk is?" Our voices seemed to echo in the room.

I shrugged. "I don't know if he even has one. This computer's so old."

"Let's start looking." He got to his feet, and while he looked through Daddy's file cabinet, I checked the drawers of his desk.

"This is it," Danny said after a few minutes. He was crouched over the bottom drawer of the filing cabinet holding up a white-sleeved disk. He sat down at the desk again. "See if he has an external hard drive somewhere. You should copy everything to another drive before you wipe this one clean."

"I have one." I picked up the small, brand-new hard drive from the shelf by the door and handed it to him. Christine had given it to me days earlier, hoping it would encourage me to attack the computer. I sat down on the only other chair in the office—an upholstered antique in the corner—as Danny got to work. Only then did I realize that the glass-fronted cabinetry on the east and west walls of the room now stood empty. The lighters and compasses had been sold, Christine had said. No wonder our voices seemed to echo. Although I'd had no attachment to those collections, the emptiness in the room suddenly struck me hard. It was as though Daddy was disappearing from the house bit by bit.

Lifting my bare feet to the chair, I wrapped my arms around my shins and turned away from the empty cabinets. Danny inserted the boot disk into the computer and I watched the reflection of the screen light up his pale eyes, mesmerized. Christine was right; he *was* gorgeous. I remembered what Jeannie had said about keeping Lisa's violin for one of our children. Could Danny ever have a child? A healthy family life? I wanted that for him so much. As much as I wanted it for myself.

"I'm in," he said, after another few minutes had passed.

"Hooray!" I clapped my hands together. "Oh, Danny, thank you."

"What do you want the new password to be?" he asked, his fingers still on the keyboard.

The first word I thought of was *Lisa,* and I quickly moved it as far to the back of my mind as it would go. "Just . . . anything," I said. "It's only for a couple of days. How about New Bern?"

"Weak as hell," he said, but he typed it in. "You've got *newbern.* No caps, no spaces. You need to see anything on here right now?"

I shook my head. "I'll do it tomorrow." I smiled. "That's my new slogan. Why do something today if I can put it off till tomorrow? I'm driving Christine and Jeannie crazy."

He didn't respond as he hooked the computer up to the external hard drive. "Just let this stuff copy over," he said, hitting a couple of keys. "It'll take a few hours. Then you should check the drive to make sure everything came over smoothly before you wipe this sucker clean."

"Great," I said.

"I'm out of here," he said, standing up. "You want to distract the pit bull downstairs so I can leave?"

"I need to talk to you about something else first." I stayed in my seat, trying to get my courage up. "A few things related to the Kyles."

"What about them?"

"Sit down again, okay?"

He resisted a moment, his eyes burning into mine, and I was relieved when he gave in and sat down.

"Well, first of all," I said, lowering my feet to the floor, "they told me that Daddy promised the RV park to them. That he was planning to give it to them."

"So give it to them." He shrugged. "What are we going to do with it?"

"It's valuable land, Danny," I said. "You may not care about the money, but frankly, I do. It's for our futures. And there's more," I added quickly before he could get his temper up. "I know Lisa's not your favorite subject, but we need to talk about this."

"I don't care what you do with her violin," he said, his gaze darting in the direction of the five violins still propped against the wall.

"That's not what I was going to talk about," I said. "Tom Kyle thinks she didn't kill herself."

Danny scoffed. "How would he know?"

"He read somewhere that there were two sets of footprints by Lisa's car. You know, where she put the kayak into the river?" Danny frowned and I wasn't sure if he was following me. "Do you remember her friend Matty?" I asked. "A boy?"

"Vaguely." He stretched his neck to the left and right, as if I might be boring him.

"Well, I keep wondering . . . Maybe she *didn't* kill herself," I said. "Maybe Matty helped her get away."

He laughed, but there was no humor in the sound. "Wouldn't that just fit?" he asked. "Everything always went her way. She could kill that guy and stroll away, free as a bird. She's probably sitting in Tahiti sipping a martini right now. I honestly wouldn't be surprised."

"I don't know what to think," I said. "I read every one of those newspaper articles Daddy had in that box and there was no mention of two sets of footprints, so—"

"So, Kyle is yanking your chain." He leaned across the corner of the desk to get closer to me. "He's a son of a bitch, Riles. I'm serious. You shouldn't give him the time of day."

"But why?" I asked. "Why would he say that?" I wanted it to be true. I wanted Lisa to have escaped. To be alive.

"Because he's an asshole. Don't let him under your skin."

"The thing is," I said, "if there's any chance she *didn't* kill herself, no matter how small, I think we should pursue it." I ran my fingertips over the frayed fabric on the arm of the chair. "I mean, I know she probably did it, but what if she didn't?" I looked at him. "What if we have a sister out there?"

"Listen," he said. "If she's alive, all that means is that we have a sister who intentionally left her family behind," he said. "And that includes us."

I nodded to let him know I heard him. My voice was caught in my throat.

"It wouldn't be like she's lost and wants to be found," he said. "Even if she missed us, her whole reason for faking suicide would be to avoid prison. And if we found her, that's where she'd end up."

I honestly hadn't thought of that. Stupid of me. All I'd thought about was the slim chance of having a sister again. "That's not what I want," I said.

I was sure he didn't hear me. He looked thoughtful, staring at the dark screen on the monitor. "And that's where she belongs," he said finally. He lifted his gaze to me. "Damn," he said. "It'd be nice to see her finally pay for what she did."

23.

Jade

She spent most of the morning realphabetizing the rock albums. In the five months since she started working at Grady's, she must have done that a hundred times. The kids who came into the shop mixed them up so badly she thought it must be on purpose. That never happened with the classical albums, which stayed in perfect alphabetical order. Classical fans, who tended to be older and less wasted, kept things orderly.

She'd built up a small, carefully selected collection of her own CDs now. Grady gave her a discount, saying she was his best customer. He thought she was amazing, the way she knew so much about music and musicians, but the truth was, she was dumbing down everything she knew.

Grady was working behind the cash register that morning while she organized the albums. His curly blond hair fell over his shoulders and Jade knew that many of the teenaged girls who came into the shop were only there to get a look at his amazing green eyes. He also had a pierced eyebrow, adorned with a small gold hoop. It had looked bizarre to her at first, but now that she was used to it, she liked it and wondered if she should get her own eyebrow pierced. It would make her look even less like Lisa MacPherson.

She worked slowly that morning, her mind only half on the records. Today was Danny's birthday. Wherever her family was living now, they would be going out to dinner tonight. That was their tradition—celebrating birthdays in a restaurant. She could picture it. Even though they'd moved someplace else, she still imagined them in the Chinese restaurant on Route 1 in Alexandria, which was where they usually went for a celebration. They'd sit at the table by the aquarium so Riley and Danny could watch the fish. Riley would be in one of those restaurant high chairs . . . or, now that she was two, would she be big enough for a booster seat? And Danny was seven! Unbelievable. She supposed she'd think that to herself every year: *I can't believe Danny's nine or ten or fifteen or twenty.* God, that was so depressing.

It was September. She would have been settling in at Juilliard right now, if things had gone according to plan. She didn't want to think about that or it would make her crazy. Instead of studying where she'd dreamed of studying her whole life, she was hiding out like a fugitive. Not *like* a fugitive; she *was* a fugitive. She was thinking about that impossible fact when an old man walked into the shop. He headed straight for the classical section, so it was clear that he'd been there before, although Jade didn't remember seeing him. He was short and mostly bald, with wire-rimmed glasses and a mustache, and he wore an ancient sweater very much like the ancient sweater her father always wore in the winter months. It was beige with patches on the elbows, and even though he was much older than her father and looked nothing like him, she felt like walking up to him and asking for a hug.

Instead she walked up to him and asked if she could help him find something.

He smiled at her. "I doubt it," he said. "I've been looking for a certain record for years. It was my late wife's favorite, but it's obscure." He rested his hand on top of the Bach albums. "We owned it when we lived in England long ago and we left all our records behind. I checked here about a year ago and, of course, no luck. I've tried the big record stores and no luck there, either. So I was passing by and thought I'd check again. And anyway, I wanted to pick up a few other albums if you have them. I love looking through the old records you have here."

"What was it?" she asked. "Your wife's favorite."

"Well, that's part of the problem. I can't remember the artist. The record had both a Bach and Mozart concerto and the cover had two little statues on it and the violinist was Italian." He chuckled. "Not much to go on, I'm afraid."

Her heartbeat quickened. It was plenty to go on, actually. She knew the record he was talking about. He was right—it was obscure, and she hoped she wasn't about to give herself away, but she couldn't play dumb with this. She began humming the melody of the Mozart and the old man's eyes widened as he grabbed her arm. "That's the concerto! That's it!"

"And you're looking for Gioconda de Vito," she said.

"Oh, good Lord. That's right! That's the violinist! How did you know?"

She felt Grady's eyes on her. She was sure he wondered the same thing.

"Oh." She shrugged. "My family was always into classical music and I remember that one."

"Amazing! Do you have any idea where I could find it?"

She was definitely going to make his day. She couldn't stop smiling. "I do," she said. "We got a bunch of records from an estate sale the other day and I went through them. They're still in the back room, but the one you want is in one of the boxes. It's mono, though."

"Mono's fine! That's what we had in England."

"We have it?" Grady asked from behind the counter. He looked as surprised as the old man.

"Uh-huh. It'll take me a few minutes to dig it out." She looked at the man. "Can you wait?"

"Yes, yes, of course!"

"Give me a minute." She started toward the back room. As she neared the door, she heard the man say to Grady, "She's a wonder," and Grady said, "She knows more than I do."

The boxes from the estate sale were stacked in one corner of the back room, and she was happy to see the one she wanted was on top. She opened it and pulled out album after album, finally finding the prize. The black cover with its two porcelain statues was a little faded from being tucked between other albums for a few decades, but she pulled the record from the sleeve and held it up for a better look. Pristine. Probably worth a hundred bucks. She carried the album back to the man, who'd found three others that he wanted. He took it from her with tears in his eyes and tried to press a twenty-dollar bill into her hand, but she shook her head.

"I'm just excited we had it for you," she said. She really was. She couldn't remember the last time she'd felt so happy.

"What's your name?" he asked her.

She almost slipped. In the eight and a half months she'd lived in Ocean Beach, she hadn't slipped once, but he'd touched that part of her that was still so connected to Lisa. "Jade," she said.

"Oh, what a beautiful name. Beautiful name for a beautiful girl. I can't thank you enough. I'm Charlie, by the way."

"Glad to meet you, Charlie."

She stepped behind the counter to slip a note to Grady. *Worth $100,* it read, though she hoped he wouldn't charge that much. Grady looked at her note, then at Charlie's glistening eyes. "Ten for this one," he said, touching the album. "Five for each of the others."

Charlie paid, thanked her again, and left. When she returned to the rock albums, still smiling to herself, she felt Grady's gaze on her.

"You're spooky," he said after a minute.

"Spooky?"

"Just . . . that was amazing."

She shrugged like it had been nothing, and moved Neil Young out of the Bs and into the Ys.

"How come you're not in school?" Grady asked.

"What?" She looked up quickly, panicked by his question. What was he asking? "I graduated in '89," she said. Another one of her many lies. She'd barely started her senior year when everything fell apart.

"I mean college," he said. "You're smart. You're not a stoner. You don't seem broke. Why aren't you in school?"

"Oh," she said. "I wanted some time off after high school."

"You planning to go?"

"Eventually."

"Do you know you can have in-state tuition at San Diego State after you've lived here a year? It's super-affordable."

"I didn't know that," she said, running her fingers thoughtfully over the tops of the albums. She hadn't thought about being able to go to college since her escape. Her life had been all about surviving. Pretending. Lying. She hadn't thought about actually living the rest of it. But a state school? After coming a hairsbreadth away from Juilliard? She felt like a snob for thinking that way. She'd been cut down to size pretty quickly.

She knew Grady'd graduated from San Diego State University with a degree in business and then opened the record store. "Are you glad you went?" she asked. "I mean, you're not exactly using your degree here."

He laughed. "Oh, I use it and it's good to have. And college was a blast. You need to have some fun, Jade. You're very serious, you know?"

She could hardly disagree. "I know," she said.

"I don't know what you went through with your family and everything that you needed to get away from, but I can tell it took a toll," he said. It was the first time he'd talked to her about anything personal and he must have seen her discomfort. "Sorry to get in your business," he said, "but I like you. I don't want to lose you as an employee, but I think you need to go to school and cut loose. You could still work here part-time."

"I've only lived in California eight months," she said. "But I'll think about it."

"What would you major in?" He was looking down at the CDs on the counter, marking them with pricing stickers and acting like her answer didn't matter, which made her wonder if it was a trick question. If she said *music,* would he somehow guess who she was? And of course, she couldn't major in music, but she'd never considered anything else. "I have no idea," she said.

"You'd make a great teacher, I think."

"I'll think about it," she said again, wondering how you went about taking the GED test, since she had no high school diploma. She'd need to retake her SATs, a thought which made her groan to herself. But then she pictured herself in the front of a classroom of little kids. Kids like Danny and Riley. She might like that, she thought, and for the first time since leaving home, she thought that maybe, just maybe, she could have a future.

24.

Riley

"Good morning!" Jeannie said as she and Christine walked into the kitchen, accompanied by their usual explosion of energy. I'd hoped to be out of the house by the time they arrived, but no such luck. Instead, I was standing next to the counter eating a bowl of granola, and I nodded to them, my mouth full.

"I finally have some comps for the RV park to show you." Jeannie held her laptop in the air, then seemed to notice I was eating. "Come in the living room when you finish and we'll go over them," she said.

"All right." I turned around and I rinsed my bowl in the sink, letting half the cereal slide down the garbage disposal. My appetite was shot these days.

"You know, Riley," Christine said as she opened the dishwasher for me, taking the bowl from my hand and putting it inside as though I wasn't doing it quickly enough to suit her. "You haven't put anything in your father's office yet. There must be *something* that you want to keep."

I was sure there *were* things I wanted to keep, but the truth was, all I seemed able to do for the past two days was sleep in the daytime and lie awake all night, thinking about Lisa. Torturing myself with the thought that she might still be alive. The last thing I felt like doing was going through my family's belongings. I didn't want to look at a vase or a shirt or a pen or a lamp and be flooded with memories. I'd rather have Christine take everything away than face more of my sad and confused feelings.

"I'll try to get to it today or tomorrow," I promised.

"Well, it would be good if you could," she said, shutting the dishwasher, "because we're going to start slapping prices on everything soon. And it'd be a drag to do all the work of figuring out the value of things and *then* have you decide you don't want us to include them in the sale."

"I know," I said. "I'll do it."

"And what's happening with your father's computer?" Christine nudged.

"I'm getting ready to clean the drive," I lied. I hadn't even thought about the computer since copying everything to the hard drive.

"And . . ." Jeannie reappeared in the doorway between the kitchen and living room. She motioned to the long row of built-in cabinets beneath the living room windows. "You were really cooking with your father's paperwork for a while," she said. "How's that going?"

It wasn't. "I have a lot more to do, but there's no rush for that, is there? I mean it's not like his paperwork will be included in the estate sale."

They both looked at me with the exact same expression: concern tempered by impatience.

"Well, it has to be done," Christine said, walking past her mother into the living room. "I'll be in Danny's room if you need me."

"Fine," I said, with a bit too much annoyance in my

204 | Diane Chamberlain

voice, and Jeannie didn't miss it. She put a motherly arm around me and walked me into the living room in the direction of the couch. I let her lead me, too tired to resist.

"I know this is hard, Riley," she said. "I know you're feeling overwhelmed. You just need to rely on Christine and me a little bit more and not worry about anything. All you need to do—your *only* task—is to get through your dad's paperwork by July twentieth when we have the estate sale. And—"

"July twentieth?" I asked. "That's only a couple of weeks away! You were supposed to check with me before setting a date."

She looked surprised. "I thought Christine talked to you about it," she said.

I folded my arms across my chest. "No, she didn't," I said, "and you have to change it."

"We can't change it, honey. The advertising is already in place, but don't worry. We'll have everything ready by then. I promise. Please stop stressing about this, okay?"

I gave in, dropping my arms to my sides. Somehow, I would have to make this work. "Fine," I said, though I knew my voice made it clear it was not fine at all. I wished they'd picked a date a month away. Or even *two* months.

"Good." Jeannie put her arm around me again. "Now, sit down and let me grab my laptop and I'll show you the comps."

She didn't let go of my shoulder completely until I was sitting on the couch. She got her laptop from the table by the door and sat next to me, opening the lid. Hitting a few buttons on the keyboard, she pointed to some listings for land as they popped up on the screen.

"I won't bore you with all of this because I can tell you're not in the mood, but by looking at the comps for undeveloped land along the creeks and backing up to the forest, as well as looking at other RV parks and campgrounds, I think we can safely say the land your dad's park is on, with the improvements, is worth about ten thousand dollars an acre."

I hadn't expected it to be that high. "How many acres is it?" I asked.

"Just under twenty. Twenty-five if you include the land Danny's trailer is on, but I know we can't touch that."

"That many?" I pictured the park and its small RV sites. Each one of those sites stretched down to the creek and back to the woods, though, so I guessed twenty acres made sense. "I didn't realize it was that valuable."

"Yes, it is. Isn't that lovely? So I propose we—"

"Jeannie," I interrupted her. "Do you know anything about my father promising the park to the Kyles?" I was quite sure she didn't, given her reaction to Tom Kyle being left the pipe collection.

She stared at me. "Where on earth did you hear that?" she asked.

"They told me. The Kyles. They're upset because he said he would give them the park in a couple of years and they've been counting on it. I guess they don't have much money."

Jeannie's blue eyes were even bigger and rounder than usual. "Oh, my God, Riley," she said. "They're trying to pull a fast one on you."

I remembered Danny saying that Tom Kyle was yanking my chain.

"Well, even Verniece said it, and she's—"

"She's a sweet old bat, I know," Jeannie said. "But

she's the one feeding you the load of crap about you being adopted, too, right? Stay away from them, Riley. They don't care about you, and you really need people around you who'll support you, not mess with your head." She tapped her fingertip on my temple.

"But could Daddy have said it?" I asked. "Promised the park to them?"

"*No!*" She frowned at me. "He didn't like the Kyles. I admit I'm lost about the checks he was giving Tom Kyle and why he'd leave him the pipes when he knew I could use a bit of that cash." She let out an aggravated breath. "Although three years ago, which is when he wrote that will, I was in better shape, so it probably never occurred to him I'd be in need. But the idea of him leaving them a valuable piece of property is preposterous."

My phone rang before she finished her last sentence and I pulled it from my shorts pocket. The number was unfamiliar and it took me a moment to realize it was Danny's cell phone. I jumped to my feet, amazed he would call. "I have to take this," I said to Jeannie as I headed for the front door and privacy. Once on the porch, I lifted the phone to my ear.

"Danny?"

"Come over," he said. "I have something to tell you."

25.

―――――――――――

Jade

She needed a car.

After sailing through the GED, she'd been admitted to San Diego State for the fall semester on the strength of new SAT scores—not nearly as good as Lisa MacPherson's scores had been—and an essay about growing up in Maryland with her fictional family. She planned to study hard and keep her head down, and she guessed that in a few years, she'd be a teacher. Not a career she'd ever imagined for herself, but she had to do something worthwhile with her life, and if she couldn't play music, working with children was the best thing she could think of.

San Diego State, though, was fifteen miles from Ocean Beach. She planned to continue living at Ingrid's and working at Grady's, the two places she felt safe, so a car was an absolute must. And that, she decided, constituted a dire emergency.

She'd been so good about not getting in touch with her family! Yet she longed for them, and sometimes she felt so forgotten. She knew her father had created the ruse to save her from a far worse fate, but did he miss her? Did he even think about her anymore?

She opened her own post office box under her new name, Ann Johnson. Then, sitting at the kitchen table in her little cottage, she wrote a long, heartfelt letter to her father, weeping through every sentence. She couldn't send it. She didn't dare. She dried her tears and started over.

> *Dear Fred,*
> *I plan to attend school, majoring in education. The only problem is transportation. Although I'm working and will continue to do so, I don't have enough money to buy a used car. I hope you can help.*
> *Sincerely,*
> *Ann*

She sat back from the table and read the note aloud, stumbling over the cold sound of the words. The formality, when what she really wanted to write was, *I miss you so much! How is everyone? Tell me about Riley. Please tell me she's still the happy little girl at four that she was at two. Is Danny all right? Has he forgotten that terrible day? Is there any way—ANY WAY—I can see all of you? Please!*

She folded the letter in thirds and put it in an envelope. There was a good chance he would be angry, but so was she.

She began checking her post office box three days after mailing the letter and of course it was empty. Her spirits sank each time she saw the hollow space behind the glass window in the small metal door. But on the nineteenth day, a shadow blocked the glass. She opened the door and pulled out a long fat envelope. There was no return address, but the postmark was from Pollocksville, North Carolina, and she let out a joyous yelp before she caught herself. Her address was written in block print she would never recognize as her father's, but it could be from no one else. She trembled as she put the envelope in her purse, and she nearly ran all the way home.

Sitting on the big couch in her living room, she carefully slit open the envelope. There were bills inside— twenty one-hundred-dollar bills—and tucked in the middle of the stack, this note: *You are loved and missed.* She held the note close to her heart. Of the twenty-one items in the envelope, this was the most precious.

She bought a rickety old white VW bug for four hundred dollars from an aging hippie in Ocean Beach and put the rest of the money in her bank account. She also got a California driver's license. Even after living in San Diego for a couple of years, she'd felt nervous walking into the DMV, turning in the fake Maryland license, having her new picture taken. The process was easy, though. Facing her fear turned out to be the only hard part.

Late in July, she made her first drive to the university to take a special placement test. The test took two hours to complete and struck her as easy. When she'd finished, she wandered around the campus. She would have denied even to herself that she was looking for the music building, but there it was—standing between the building where the test had been held and the parking lot—and because it was so hot out, she told herself it made sense to cut through the building to cool off.

The sound of an oboe greeted her in the hallway. It was only playing scales, briskly, then slowly, then briskly again. She was due to work at Grady's in an hour, but she slowed way down as the oboe began to play an étude, the haunting sound echoing through the deserted hallway.

The air in the building began to smell like Violet. She walked even more slowly, filling her lungs with the woody, dusky scent, knowing it was only in her imagination but not caring. The oboe accompanied her down the hall until she went through the first set of double doors that led outside. In that small vestibule were two bulletin boards, both covered with posters. She stopped. Would it hurt to go to a concert? Nonmusicians went to concerts all the time. She moved from poster to poster to see who'd be in San Diego over the summer. There were so many performances she would love to see! Then one small poster made her stop and stare. THE STUDENT STRING ORCHESTRA OF THE PEABODY CONSERVATORY. Her heart pounded. Matty'd had early acceptance into the Peabody Conservatory at Johns Hopkins. Surely he went; it had been his first choice. He would have finished his sophomore year by now, and the chance that he might be touring with the string orchestra for the summer made amazing, wonderful, extraordinary sense.

She studied the poster for the longest time, squinting at the dark photograph of the orchestra, but it was impossible to make out faces. She committed the date and time to memory, fantasizing about seeing Matty, and maybe if she was very brave—or very stupid—talking to him. She was going to that concert. There was no way she would miss it.

She left the music building, her heart skittering in her chest. She nearly ran the rest of the way to her car, feeling so alive and excited that she couldn't walk slowly. She doubted the concert would be a sellout, but she would get her ticket right away. She needed a good seat. She needed to sit close enough to be able to scrutinize every musician. She would die if Matty wasn't one of them.

But she would also die if he was.

The concert was poorly attended, so much so that she felt embarrassed for both the string orchestra and for San Diego State that it couldn't turn out a better crowd for a classical concert. The poor attendance, though, had enabled her to get an excellent seat in the middle of the second row and she got there early, sitting alone in the row, staring at the stage and barely breathing as she waited for the musicians to take their seats. *Please be here,* she pleaded to Matty in her head. *Please, please.*

Ever so slowly, the seats around her filled. The audience was made up mostly of music students and they talked and laughed like they were in a classroom rather than the small auditorium. She envied them, not for their camaraderie, although that was certainly part of it. She envied them for being able to study music. They could go home tonight and pick up their instruments, while all she could touch was air.

When the lights dimmed, a hush fell over the students and polite applause echoed in the building as the musicians took the stage. She recognized Matty right away. He went directly to the first chair of the second violins, and she caught her breath, pride welling up inside her. He was only heading into his third year at Peabody, and already in a leadership role. He'd always been a strong and passionate musician, though he'd never been at her level. But he was doing well. He was being appreciated.

His dark hair was still a wild mass of curls, but although she wasn't quite close enough to make out his features, she could tell from the shape of his face alone that they had changed. What if he'd changed along with them? she thought. What if he'd come to hate her?

The orchestra opened with Barber's Adagio for Strings and no one in the audience seemed to breathe as the wistful music filled the space. She hadn't anticipated the pain, although perhaps she should have. Why had she thought seeing him, hearing him, was a good idea? It hurt so much. She couldn't possibly talk to him. It wouldn't be fair to ask him to keep a secret so enormous. She loved him too much to put him in that position. It hurt, too, to see him doing the thing she longed to do: play the violin. Watching him was agony in too many ways to count.

Still, as she sat there choking back tears, she imagined going backstage after the performance. Finding him. Pulling him aside. Pressing a finger to his lips to keep him from saying her name. She would wrap her arms around him and settle into the safety of his embrace. But the fantasy was only a fantasy, and when intermission came and she stood up, she knew she wasn't going backstage. She was leaving the theater, moving away from temptation. Away from the danger.

26.

Riley

"There were definitely two sets of footprints in the area the night Lisa supposedly killed herself," Danny said the moment I walked into his trailer. He sat barefoot on his bed, his back against the wall and his computer on his lap.

"How do you know?" I sat down on the bench seat by the table.

He lit a cigarette and inhaled, his gaze never leaving my face. "I hacked into their data system."

"*Whose* data system?" I asked, perplexed. "The Kyles'?"

"The state police of ol' Virginny." He smiled. "They need much better security."

"Danny! Tell me you're kidding. How did you do that?"

"Do you literally want me to tell you how or would you rather just know what I found out?"

"Can they catch you?" That thought wiped all others from my mind. The last thing Danny needed was time in prison.

He shook his head. "Very doubtful. I'm sure no one up there is looking at records from 1990."

"They were using computers back then?"

He nodded. "At least partly. I got the feeling they were just starting to digitize. I'm sure they had more on the case than I could get my hands on."

"You're amazing." I laughed. I couldn't help it; I felt proud of his skill, even if he'd used it for something illegal. "What did you find out?"

He took a pull on his cigarette. "It snowed pretty heavily that night," he said through a stream of smoke, "and that apparently screwed up the investigation. But there were definitely signs of two people being there. Here's the weird thing, though." He moved his computer from his lap to the bed and leaned forward, his elbows resting on his knees. "That second set of footprints? They withheld that tidbit from the media. There's no way Tom Kyle could have read about them anywhere."

"How could he know, then?"

"That's a really good question, isn't it?" He blew a smoke ring toward the ceiling. "They're sure the second set of prints was from a man's boots, but—"

"Matty," I wondered out loud. "Remember I told you about him? They were really close friends, and we have pictures of—"

"Matthew Harrison," Danny said. "Assuming it's the same guy as the one mentioned in the police report, that's his full name. They questioned him because he was there the night she killed her teacher, so—"

"He was?"

"Yes, but they don't think he had anything to do with it. He didn't get there till after the guy was shot. But since he was already on their radar, they questioned him about the suicide. Turned out he was out of town the night she supposedly killed herself."

"Oh, my God!" I said, excited now. "Supposedly? Did the police think she—"

"Don't get your hopes up," he said. "Most likely, she did it, but—and don't freak out about this—one of the theories they were looking at was that the second set of prints might have belonged to someone who killed her and made it *look* like suicide."

"But she left a note, remember?"

"Could have been faked. And the other set of tracks could have been from before she was in the area, or it could have been someone who saw her abandoned car and was checking it out." He stubbed out his cigarette in the glass ashtray on his bed. "Like I said, the snow made checking out the scene a challenge. Anyhow, it seems they stopped looking into it, so it's a cold case at this point."

"If she's alive, I want to find her," I said.

"Well, good luck with that wild-goose chase," he said, "but if you *do* happen to track her down, let me know, so I can give Harry a call. He loves a cold case."

"Danny." I stared at him and he stared right back. "You're teasing me, right?"

"When have you ever known me to tease?"

As a boy, he'd teased me relentlessly and good-naturedly, but the grown-up Danny had lost that playful side. "I know you didn't like her," I said. "I know you blame her for everything that's ever gone wrong with our family. But you were only six when she died . . . or disappeared. You never really knew her."

"You need to accept the fact that she's a murderer, Riley." He shook another cigarette from the pack on his bed.

"She never got to have a trial," I said.

"And whose fault was that?" he asked as he lit the cigarette.

I stood up. "If I find her," I said, "I just won't tell you."

He leaned back against the wall again, his face momentarily clouded by a puff of smoke. "That's probably a good idea," he said.

27.

Jade

She sat on the cool floor in the hallway of the music building, leaning against the wall outside a classroom. Inside the room, an ensemble rehearsed a Bruch concerto. They were good. A dull ache traveled down her arms as she listened to them, and her throat was tight from the effort of holding back tears. She'd skipped her child development class to sit here and listen, like an addict who couldn't stay away from her next fix, and she knew she was in trouble.

Her first few weeks of college had been an out-of-body experience for her. The campus swarmed with students and she didn't remember ever feeling a part of something so enormous. Having been homeschooled all her life, she found it hard to adjust to moving from one classroom to another. The structure was so impersonal; the crush of students daunting.

She was quiet in her classes, afraid to draw attention to herself, and she didn't interact with her fellow students. The only people she could sincerely call her friends were Grady and Ingrid and some of the regular customers, like Charlie, who came in every week to talk music.

The ensemble reached her favorite part of the concerto and she rested her head against the wall, shutting her eyes to listen. She didn't know why she tortured herself this way, hanging out in the music building, but she couldn't stay away.

When the ensemble had finished rehearsing, she opened her eyes and noticed a bulletin board on the wall across from her. Unlike the boards where she'd found the poster about Matty's concert, this one had small typed or handwritten notices: students advertising instruments they wanted to sell. She caught her breath. Standing up, she crossed the hall to scan the notices. There were three violins, none anywhere near the quality of Violet, but there was a Jay Haide for five hundred dollars. More than her car had cost her, but probably in better shape.

She'd gotten in the habit of using Ingrid's phone on those rare occasions she needed to make a call. It was cheaper, easier, and less disgusting than using a pay phone, but it came with the possibility of Ingrid overhearing the conversation. She could usually wait until Ingrid was working in the garden or taking cookies to the homeless on the beach. This afternoon, though, she was too impatient. She needed to call about that Jay Haide violin before it was snapped up by someone else, and it didn't matter if Ingrid was in the kitchen or not.

So Ingrid chopped vegetables to toss in a stockpot while Jade placed the call. The girl—her name was Cara—was a senior, and she told Jade that she was moving up to a nineteenth-century Amati. They made plans to meet in one of the practice rooms at San Diego State the following day. Jade had hoped Cara could meet that evening. She would have turned around and driven all the way back to school if Cara had been free, but she said she had classes and then a date with her boyfriend.

When Jade hung up the phone, Ingrid handed her a chunk of the celery she was chopping.

"A violin?" She looked amused, as though she thought Jade had lost her mind.

"I used to play when I was a kid," Jade said, "and I kind of miss it."

"Cool." Ingrid scooped the celery pieces into the pot on the stove. "I can't wait to hear you play."

Jade shrugged, as though buying the violin was no big deal. "Oh, well, it's been years," she said. *Two years, nine months, and about fourteen days, to be exact.*

"Well, good for you for pursuing a passion," Ingrid said. "Stay for dinner? Turkey soup?"

Jade shook her head. "Thanks, no. I have homework." Ingrid was really nice but Jade tried not to spend too much time with her. She no longer worried about being recognized, but she did worry about the police showing up at Ingrid's door one day, asking questions about her strange tenant.

She barely slept that night, she was so excited about the violin. The excitement, though, was tempered by thoughts of her father. *Never pick up a violin again, Lisa,* he'd warned her. He'd be furious if he knew, but she would be very careful. She'd play only in her cottage. She had no reason at all to play anywhere else.

Cara was twenty-one and extraordinarily beautiful. Total California girl, Jade thought. The kind she could picture surfing rather than cooped up in the music building at San Diego State. But Cara was a good violinist, and Jade sat mesmerized as she played the opening section of "Czardas" by Monti. She watched Cara's tanned and toned bare arms work the bow and her long fingers sail over the strings, and she was unsure whether she was more taken with the violin or the violinist.

Cara finished playing, then handed the instrument to Jade. Holding a violin beneath her chin for the first time in so long felt like holding a friend she'd thought she'd lost forever. She played some scales and arpeggios to hear the sound and warm up her tense, tight fingers. Then she played a bit of Vivaldi's Concerto in A Minor, and she didn't have to work hard at sounding like a novice. It had been so terribly, painfully long.

She gave Cara five one-hundred-dollar bills, then carried the violin across campus to her car, hugging the case tightly in her arms as if it were a baby.

San Diego was in the midst of the hot, dry Santa Ana winds of autumn, and even though her cottage felt like a sauna, Jade closed all the windows, stood in her living room, and played. Although her left hand and bow hand worked seamlessly together, her fingers felt weak from too much time away, and they moved sluggishly at first. Her control of the bow was imprecise, but none of that mattered. She cried with happiness and sorrow as she played. She'd lost so much. Her home. Her family. Her future. But in her hands she held the one thing with the power to bring her joy, and she played her new best friend until the early hours of the morning.

28.

Riley

I pulled into the circular drive of the oceanfront house in Myrtle Beach and sat there a moment, thinking through what I planned to say to Caterina Thoreau. Caterina—not Steven Davis—had been Lisa's violin teacher at the time she supposedly killed herself. I'd found her name in several of the newspaper articles my father had saved. She was the only person still alive who'd truly known my sister around the time of her death—if indeed she was dead. I felt a desperate need to talk to someone who had known her well and, I hoped, cared about her.

Caterina had been remarkably easy to find. Now seventy-six, she'd retired from the National Symphony ten years earlier and moved to South Carolina to be near her daughter. I found her phone number online and told her who I was and that I wanted to talk to her. After expressing her shock at hearing from me, she invited me to her home. I didn't let the fact that her home was nearly four hours from New Bern stop me. I would do whatever I needed to do to get answers about Lisa.

The bonus of driving to Myrtle Beach was getting away from the insanity in my house. When I'd first arrived in New Bern, I'd wanted to get the house cleaned out and on the market as soon as possible. Now I wanted to slow everything down, but with Christine and Jeannie on a rampage as they tore through the rooms, I wasn't sure I could make that happen. I'd told them I was visiting a friend in Virginia and would be home some time this evening. Christine opened her mouth and I was sure she was going to get on my case about my father's paperwork, but I left the house, shutting the door behind me, before she had a chance to say a word.

Caterina Thoreau had the front door open by the time I got out of my car. She was dressed in white capris and a frothy blue tunic that matched both the sky and the ocean I could see through the glass wall behind her. She reached her hand toward me with a smile.

"Lisa's sister!" she said, physically drawing me into her house with her hand in mine. "I'm so happy to meet you!"

"You, too," I said.

She led me into a high-ceilinged living room and settled me on one of two white sofas while she poured us each a mimosa. Through the glass wall, the ocean seemed close enough to touch.

"What an awesome view," I said.

She nodded, handing me my glass. "I'm very fortunate." She sat down on the other couch, curling her bare feet beneath her. She was a beautiful woman. Her hair was as white as the sofa, and her blue eyes sparkled in a face that time had treated kindly.

She took a sip of her mimosa. "I've been thinking so much about Lisa and your family ever since your call." She shook her head sadly. "What a terrible time that was," she said. "I remember your parents so well. They tried to do everything right with your sister and look what happened. It was all very sad. How old were you when she passed?"

"Not quite two, so I don't remember her at all, really," I said. "I guess I'm talking to people who knew her to try to understand her better." What I was really doing, I thought, was trying to find out if Lisa was dead or alive.

"Oh, we all wanted to understand her better," she said. "To this day, when I think about her, I shake my head. It's hard to believe what she did and . . . how it all turned out." She smiled sadly at me, holding her glass on her thigh. "How can I help?" she asked. "What would you like to know?"

"Just anything you can tell me," I said, hoping she was one of those people who liked to talk. "You probably know my family moved from northern Virginia right after Lisa took her life," I said, and she nodded.

"They disappeared," Caterina said. "No one seemed to know where they went."

"They moved to North Carolina," I said, "and they hid the fact that she'd killed her teacher—Mr. Davis— from my brother and me. We only found out recently when I came across some old newspaper articles."

Caterina's mimosa froze in the air halfway to her lips. "Oh, my," she said after a moment. "No wonder you're curious. You need to fill in a lifetime of blanks, don't you?"

I nodded. "Exactly."

"Well." She leaned forward to set her drink on her glass-topped coffee table. "I only started working with Lisa when she returned from studying with that 'mystery teacher,' and—"

"Mystery teacher?"

She hesitated. "You wouldn't know, I guess. Were

you even born then? That's what started everything spinning in the wrong direction, in my opinion." She put her feet flat on the floor so that she could lean toward me. "First of all," she said, "I want you to understand that I adored your parents. You had lovely parents. Your mother in particular was a very sweet woman, and I don't blame either of them for anything that happened. But Lisa did very well with Steve. For heaven's sake, look at the level he took her to!" She raised her hands in the air. "I first heard about her when she was only eight years old. 'You *must* hear this girl!' people would say. The young stars in the violin world were Asian at that time, so Lisa stood out, especially with that white hair of hers." She reached for her glass and took a sip of the mimosa. "Steve was extremely proud of her, as well he should have been." She sat up straight and looked out toward the sea, then gave a little shake of her head as if clearing away a sad memory. "He did have a possessive streak, I guess you could call it. In Lisa's case, I didn't blame him. To put years into a student and then to have that student go to some unknown teacher?" She shook her head with a look of disdain. "We all thought your parents had lost their minds."

"Why did they switch?" I asked.

"Who knows!" She set down her drink. "Your parents kept it very quiet because they knew they were going to get a lot of criticism. I think they worried Steve would interfere, and he probably would have. I'm sure he did all he could to find out who it was, but I don't know that he ever did."

"Wouldn't he—and you—have known all the violin teachers in the area?"

"Oh, see, that's the thing." She'd been about to pick up her glass again, but stopped. "It wasn't someone in the area," she said. "She went *away* to study for the entire school year with this person—or perhaps it was a conservatory—who knows? We never found out. At any rate, whoever it was utterly ruined her."

My brain felt like a pinball, spinning in one direction then another. I remembered Sondra Davis mentioning some other teachers in her blog. "What do you mean, 'ruined her'?" I asked.

"Her playing deteriorated terribly that year," Caterina said. "It was quite tragic, really. That's when your parents asked if I'd take her on. I was so shocked. I said I'd assumed she'd go back to Steve, and your mother said Lisa felt she'd outgrown him, but I think she was embarrassed to go back to him when she was playing so poorly." She lifted her glass from the coffee table and took a long swallow. "I knew Steve would be furious with me if I took her on—he could be so petulant!—but I was drawn to the opportunity to work with a talent like your sister. How could I refuse? So I didn't." She smiled. "But then she came to my home and I heard her play. I nearly wept. It was hideous! Plus she'd lost her confidence." Caterina set down her glass again. "I asked her to explain the other teacher's approach, but she couldn't. I'm sure that . . . *charlatan* . . . came to your parents and said, 'Here's what Steve is doing wrong and here's how I can help,' and they thought, 'Oh, Steven Davis, he teaches five-year-olds! It's time to move Lisa to someone better.'" She rubbed her arms through the gauzy fabric of her sleeves. "Steve wouldn't talk to me after I agreed to teach Lisa," she said. "He never spoke to me again. Neither would Sondra, his wife, and we'd been friends for many years."

"Wow," I said. "He really was . . . petulant." I repeated her word. It seemed to fit.

"Indeed," she said. "Sondra was not a very happy woman, even before Steve's death. They struggled to have children. Very frustrating for her, I know. I don't think she's ever moved on. It's sad, after so many years, to still be living in the past that way."

"That *is* sad," I said.

"Well, anyway, to Lisa's credit, she knew she had lost ground and she worked hard. We slowly turned around the mess the other teacher had made of her playing, and her joy started coming back." She lifted her glass and drained it. My own drink was nearly untouched. "By the time she was ready to apply to schools, she had an excellent chance at Juilliard," Caterina said. "I was certain she'd get in because she'd gotten her confidence back." She turned away, eyes suddenly glistening. "I'll never understand it, what happened. Why Steve was so cruel. There's no other word for it. You know he interfered with her application to Juilliard?"

I nodded.

"He was an idiot. And I made the mistake of telling her, so I've always blamed myself."

So that's how Lisa found out about the letter Steven sent to Juilliard. "What happened wasn't your fault," I said.

"Well, I still wish I could undo it. She was more fragile than I ever guessed, and your father was foolish enough to keep a gun where she could get it." She teared up again. "Just . . . terrible." She stared out the window at the sea, and for a while, neither of us spoke. She suddenly stood up. "When I knew you were coming, I asked my assistant to find a video I have of her practicing for an audition. I had all the old tapes transferred to DVDs. What a task! Would you like to see it?"

"Yes," I said, although I remembered how hard it had

been to watch the tapes I'd found, and that had been in the privacy of my own living room.

Caterina walked over to the television, picked up a remote, and then sat down next to me so we were both facing the TV. She turned it on and my sister appeared on the screen playing a vibrant violin solo that sent her fingers and the bow flying over the strings. This video was crisper than either of the ones I had and Lisa's face was full of emotion as she played.

"There's that pendant," Caterina said.

"Pendant?"

Lisa finished her piece, lowering the violin from beneath her chin, and I saw what Caterina was talking about. Lisa wore a white disc on a chain around her throat. I remembered seeing it in the photograph of her standing back-to-back with Matty. The pendant appeared to have a design engraved on it, but I couldn't make it out.

"She always wore it," Caterina said. "She said the teacher she'd stayed with that year had given it to her." She looked at me. "Now tell me that isn't strange," she said. "The teacher who ruined her playing—and Lisa freely admitted that was the case—gave her this pendant and she never took it off, at least not when I saw her."

On the TV screen, Lisa lifted the violin to her chin again and played something slow and bittersweet this time, and we watched for a while in silence. Except for the opportunity to see my sister play one more time, I felt disappointed in this visit. What had I expected? That Caterina might have secret knowledge about Lisa's whereabouts? That she might have hidden her in her basement after her faked suicide? But now, I was out of questions and Caterina was out of answers, so we sat and listened to the music of the girl she thought was dead and I wanted to be alive—and I wondered about that mystery teacher who'd given her the pendant she'd cherished. Could he or she have the answers I needed? Or was I looking for answers that didn't exist?

29.

Jade

"Are you Jade?" the woman asked.

Jade sat on a chair in the hallway of the music building, her violin in its case. She'd gotten there early, excited and nervous for the audition that would let her change her major from education to music education. She'd become a realist about how far she could take her playing this last year. She knew she couldn't be a soloist again, and she had to let go of the Carnegie Hall fantasy she'd had all her life. She wouldn't even dare to play in a symphony orchestra. But she could teach music. She'd thought about it a lot. She could help kids live the dream she'd lost.

She'd watched the other students waiting for their auditions as they sat in the hallway. Most of them looked like high school seniors and they appeared so nervous she felt sorry for them. She was every bit as jittery, but for a different reason. They worried they wouldn't be good enough to get in. She worried about finding the balance between being good enough to get in, but not so good that she'd draw attention to herself. And she *was* good. In the year since she'd bought her violin, she'd played for hours every night. She missed Caterina

Thoreau's guidance more than she could say, but she taught herself—she drove herself—well. She bought reams of sheet music. She played all night long, sometimes, shutting her cottage windows no matter how hot it was outside, or she played in the practice rooms at school, even though she had to be sneaky about it, since she wasn't yet a student in the school of music. With any luck, soon she would be.

The violin had amazing sound for a relatively inexpensive instrument. It had opened up under Cara's playing, and it could be bright when the music demanded it as well as warm and mellow when that was what she wanted. It wasn't Violet—no violin could compare to Violet—but it was by far Jade's most treasured possession.

"Yes, I'm Jade," she said to the woman, getting to her feet. She followed her into the classroom where a panel of three men and two more women sat, ready to judge her. She thought of all the times she'd imagined her audition for Juilliard. The people in front of her were not Juilliard professors, but they still took themselves seriously. She could tell by the lack of smiles, and the way they stared at her made her uneasy. Could they see Lisa MacPherson in her face? Her father had warned her against doing this, and for a moment she was afraid he'd been right.

She played Kreisler's "Sicilienne" and the second movement of "Aus der Heimat," and she thought it went okay. She stayed emotionally detached from her playing, knowing from experience that was the ticket to mediocrity.

"Very nice," the woman who'd led her into the room said when she'd finished, and a few of the others nodded.

"With whom did you study?" one of the men asked.

"My father, actually." She'd practiced the lie and was pleased that it slipped out easily. "He never pursued the violin seriously, but he was well trained and he taught me."

"That's remarkable," the man said. "And you've had no other instructor? No concert experience?"

She shook her head. She knew she was drawing attention to herself by her very effort not to. It was unusual to play as well as she had with no formal training. They stared at her. *Oh, God,* she thought. Did they think they'd discovered a diamond in the rough? A musical freak of nature? She needed to offer more of an explanation. "I played as a hobby, really," she said. "My father and I played together around the house, just for fun. I never considered music as a career, though. I'd always wanted to be a teacher. But last year, while I was an education major, I really missed playing. And then I realized I could have both. Music and a teaching career." She smiled uncertainly.

They still stared. "All right," the woman said finally. "We'll contact you in two to four weeks."

She left the room. She knew they would talk about her once she was gone. She couldn't lift a violin without attracting attention. It had been that way her entire life. As long as no one looked into her story—called her mythical father in Maryland, for example—she'd be okay. She should have said he'd died.

But then they'd be talking about her even more.

30.

Riley

The morning after my trip to Myrtle Beach, I finally got around to checking the external hard drive in my father's office, reassuring myself that every speck of data from his computer had been saved. Then I began erasing the files on his computer, making good progress until I got to the e-mail. I was curious to see the last e-mail I'd sent him. I wanted to know that the last message he had from me had been loving and had left him with a good feeling the morning he went to the Food Lion.

He seemed to have no organization in place for his e-mails. The messages from collectors—and there were zillions of them—were mixed in with my e-mails and e-mail from Jeannie as well. I knew her e-mail name—Jlyons—and nearly every other message seemed to be from her. I found my last one, written the day before he died.

We can come down on the 24th and stay through the weekend, if that works for you.

It took me a minute to remember what I'd been referring to—Bryan and I had planned to visit my father for the Memorial Day weekend. That seemed so long ago now. I sighed at the impersonal message. I wished I'd signed every single e-mail "Love, Riley." Would that have been so hard to do?

The next message was from Jlyons and I couldn't help myself. I clicked on it.

> How about I make your favorite and I'll pick up a Redbox movie? Love, your Little Genie.

I cringed. Was that his pet name for her? I had no idea what it meant, nor did I ever want to find out.

I clicked on the next e-mail, feeling nosy now.

> Frank, I have the beautiful meerschaum pipe you're looking for. Excellent condition. The carving of the woman is a rich even-toned amber color. Let me know if you'd like a picture. I'd ask $150, as I have no real need to part with it.

That was the type of e-mail I expected to see in my father's in-box. I clicked on the next one.

> That is the best birthday card ever. You are amazing! Love you, Celia.

I stared at that one. Who the hell was Celia? And did Little Genie know another woman was sending "love you" notes to my father . . . who may have had a more interesting life than I'd ever given him credit for? This last year, he'd gotten into creating cards online for every occasion, but I couldn't remember any I'd received that I would have called "amazing."

"Hey, Riley." Christine appeared in the doorway.

"Can you come down to the kitchen for a minute? I'm pricing things and I need to talk to you about the stuff in the cupboards."

I glanced up at her, then back at the screen. "I'll be there in a minute," I said. "I just have to do a couple more things here."

"It would be great if you could come down now," she said. "I'm making good progress today and you don't want to stop me when I'm on a roll."

Go away, I thought to myself as I listened to her footsteps clicking down the hall.

I tried to return my attention to the e-mail, but I could hear Christine clattering around downstairs in the kitchen and decided to get whatever she wanted over with. With a sigh, I shut down the computer and went downstairs. I walked into the kitchen to see that she had nearly every plate and glass and pot and pan out of the cabinets and stacked on the countertops and the table.

"Wow." I stood in the doorway.

"Oh, great, you're here," Christine said. She waved her arm through the air to take in the mess she'd made. "So I'm in the middle of pricing everything in here," she said, "and once I have all the kitchen stuff organized, I don't want you moving things around. So you should probably get some paper plates and plastic silverware and, you know, plastic cups to use for the rest of the time you're here. Unless there's something you desperately need me to leave out for you."

I stared at her in disbelief. "Christine! I'm going to be here at least a few more weeks."

"Well, the sale's set for July twentieth, regardless," she said. "Are you really going to want to stay here when the house is emptied out?"

"*Yes,* I *am* going to want to stay here!" I spotted the

Franciscan Ware plates that reminded me so much of my mother. The plates I loved and Danny hated. "Look," I said to Christine. "I need you to leave out at least four of these plates and four glasses and four bowls and sets of silverware so I have things to use."

Christine let out her breath in frustration. "I've asked you and asked you to let me know what you want to keep," she said, "and you haven't told me *anything*."

I had to admit she was right. "I'm sorry about that," I said, "but I need to be able to live here for a while after the sale, all right?"

She was looking behind me, and I turned to see Danny in the living room. He stood awkwardly, hands in his pockets, motioning me into the room with a nod of his head.

"I've got to go," I said to Christine. "Leave me a medium-sized pot and a frying pan, too. Please." I turned away from whatever else she might say and followed Danny out the front door to the porch.

I shut the door behind us. "That woman is making me crazy," I said.

"I don't like the way she looks at me."

"She thinks you're hot."

He rolled his eyes as he sat down in one of the rockers.

"How come you're here?" I asked, sitting down myself.

"I want to talk to Tom Kyle about this whole 'two sets of footprints' thing," he said. "It's bugging me. Something's fishy and I want to find out how he knew. You should come with me."

I didn't answer right away. I wanted to talk to Tom again myself, but how would I explain knowing that the information about the footprints hadn't been released to the media? And if I did find a way to talk to him, I didn't want Danny there. I didn't trust my brother's motivation. I was afraid he'd run wild with anything he learned. "You haven't talked to Harry about this, have you?" I asked.

"There's nothing to talk to him about," he said. "Not yet, anyhow."

"How would you explain to Tom Kyle what you learned about the footprints?"

"I'll figure it out." The determination in his face was rare to see. Danny lived day to day. He hung out on his computer. He drank. He smoked. I remembered my father saying, *"I wish he'd find some sort of* project." It seemed he'd found one now.

"You really want to punish her, don't you," I said.

He scowled as he got to his feet. "Leave the psychoanalysis out of this, okay?" He looked down at me. Crammed his hands into his pockets. "I'm going to talk to him with you or without you," he said. "Do you want to go or not?"

31.

___

Jade

"Hey, Charlie," she said when the old man walked into Grady's. She always loved seeing him. She loved all the regulars, but she'd never forget the connection she and Charlie had made when she found him the album he'd wanted for so long.

"Afternoon, Jade," he said. "You must be gearing up for your senior year, aren't you?"

She nodded. She'd worked a lot of hours this summer, trying to bulk up her bank account, but she was looking forward to getting back to school. She'd long ago figured out how to handle being a student at San Diego State—by keeping to herself, for the most part. She didn't think her fellow students thought she was cold, exactly, but they saw her as a commuter with a busy life outside of school. At least she guessed that's what they thought. She didn't play her violin well enough to garner much attention or admiration, modeling herself after another student in her classes who was good but not great. She watched that student's progress and followed her path, settling for "just good enough." Yet, in her own cottage, she let Lisa MacPherson out for hours every night. She loved her old self. She needed her. She sometimes felt as though Jade and Lisa were two different people. In the daytime, though, she was often tired. It was exhausting, living two lives.

"So after this year, you'll be able to teach?" Charlie asked.

"No, I have another year to get my credential. Then I'll be able to teach." She was actually looking forward to teaching. After three years of college, she was beginning to think she'd be pretty good at it. "Are you looking for anything special today?" she asked him.

"No, but my granddaughter is." He looked over his shoulder toward the door. "She's visiting from Portland, Oregon. She stopped in the bakery next door, but she'll be here in a minute. I'll look at the jazz till she gets here."

"All right," she said. He'd mentioned a granddaughter from time to time and Jade was glad she was visiting him. Somehow, she felt responsible for Charlie. She worried about him living alone and she missed him those weeks he didn't stop in. She wasn't sure of his age and he didn't seem the least bit frail, but he was an old man and she knew he'd adored the wife he'd lost. She knew, too, that he loved coming into Grady's and feeling like family here. She was hypersensitive to loneliness.

She was busy adding new CDs to the classical section when Charlie tapped her elbow. She looked up. "Jade," he said, "I'd like you to meet my granddaughter, Celia."

Next to Charlie stood a young woman a little taller than him and a little older than Jade. Her dark brown hair was cropped very short on one side, a little longer on the other, and a lock of it fell across her temple. She wore black shorts and a gray Indigo Girls T-shirt with short capped sleeves. One of her slender arms was draped around her grandfather's shoulders, and she smiled at Jade, who felt hypnotized by the young woman's silver-gray eyes. It was impossible to look away from those eyes, and Jade didn't want to. She spoke as though everything was perfectly normal—*Hello, Celia. Nice to meet you. How long are you here for? Your grandfather said you're looking for something in particular*—but she couldn't pull her gaze away from Celia's, and Celia didn't seem to mind one bit. It was like a Vulcan mind meld. The strangest thing. Jade could see her future and Celia was part of it.

"Grandpop said you know every record that's ever been recorded," Celia said.

"Well . . ." She blushed, and she wasn't usually a blusher. "Now you've made me nervous," she said.

"I'm looking for an old album by Robin Flower. I can't find it anywhere."

"*1st Dibs*?" Jade asked, though it wasn't really a question. Somehow she knew which one Celia wanted. Celia didn't have to tell her.

"That's it," she said. They were still staring at one another.

"We have it on vinyl. No CD, though."

"Perfect," Celia said.

"I told you," Charlie said to her. "Told you she was good."

She managed to tear her gaze from Celia's to look at him and saw the mild amusement on his face, as though he'd known all along there'd be a quick and intense connection between Jade and his granddaughter.

Charlie stepped away from Celia's arm and gently

pushed her in Jade's direction. "You two find the Robin Flower record," he said. "I'll be in the jazz section."

"I love your grandfather," Jade said as she and Celia started riffling through the albums. She knew exactly where the Flower record was, but she didn't want to get to it too quickly. Celia's shoulder was pressed against hers, and Jade watched the muscles and tendons in Celia's forearm as she moved the albums. She felt heat rising up her chest and into her cheeks and her knees shivered. It was at once the most disorienting and delicious feeling she'd ever experienced, even though she was afraid she might need to sit down right there on the floor to keep from keeling over.

"He loves you back," Celia said. "He said he always comes in on the days you work." Her hands were beautiful. They were a warm honey color, like the rest of her, the fingers long and slender with short rounded nails. "He said you're a music major. Violin, right? No wonder you knew the Robin Flower record."

It took her a moment to find her voice. "Right," she said.

"And he said you want to teach. I teach, too."

"Really? What grade?"

"I teach math at a community college in Portland."

"Wow!" She suddenly felt very young. "Here it is." She pulled out the album and handed it to Celia.

"Cool!" Celia lifted the album into her honey-colored hands, then looked at her. "Grandpop said to ask you over to dinner tonight."

Jade had the feeling he'd said *If you like her, ask her over.* And Celia liked her.

"I'd love that," Jade said.

They stepped back from the records and Jade was almost afraid to look at her again and feel that other-worldly pull of her eyes. But she did it.

"How old are you?" Celia asked.

"Twenty-two. I sort of got a late start with college because I needed to work for a while first. So I'm only going into my senior year now." She blathered on when what she really wanted to say was, *You are so amazingly beautiful!* "How old are you?" she asked.

"Twenty-five. You'll come over tonight?"

"Yes."

"Sevenish? You know where he lives?"

She nodded. "I'll bring wine?"

"No, don't. We'll have everything. Just bring yourself." She rested her perfect hand on Jade's forearm, tightening her fingers ever so slightly, and for the rest of the day Jade kept touching her arm where Celia had touched, and each time, she felt the heat rise up her chest to her face as she ticked down the hours until seven.

Although she knew which bungalow was Charlie's, Jade had never been inside it before. His walls were covered with paintings, large and small. She didn't know much about art, but she had the feeling the work in his living room was original and possibly valuable. She'd known he wasn't a poverty-stricken old man, given the amount of money he spent in Grady's, but besides the art on the walls and the shelves filled with records—so much like her father's collection—there was nothing in his modest, cozy house to make her think he was wealthy.

There were, however, two guitars and a mandolin resting in cases against one of the living room walls.

"Who plays?" she asked, standing in the middle of the room.

"Both of us," Celia said. "The mandolin's mine. I brought it down with me from Portland. I'm not that great on the guitar, but Grandpop is. How about you?"

"I can play a little mandolin," she said. "Though it's been forever."

"We should have told you to bring your violin over," Charlie said.

It was just as well they hadn't. She wasn't sure she'd have been able to resist.

They ate pasta primavera on Franciscan Ware Apple–patterned plates that were exactly like the ones Jade had grown up with, but she said nothing about that because the girl who grew up using those plates had to be dead to her. Still it was eerie, eating off them.

They told her all about Celia's family while they ate. She'd grown up in San Diego until she was fourteen, when her father was transferred to Portland, and she finished high school there. She had a brother, Shane, who lived a few hours away in Seattle and they were a close-knit, music-loving family.

"They were kind of shocked when I came out," Celia said easily, as though she knew it would be no surprise to Jade, and it wasn't. The Indigo Girls T-shirt. The Robin Flower record. And yet, the way Jade had felt standing next to her in Grady's—*that* had been a surprise, and she wasn't sure what to make of her feelings. She found it hard to look at Celia across the table without feeling that telltale heat rising up her throat to her cheeks again.

"Were they okay with it?" Jade asked. "With you . . . coming out?"

"Not right away. They thought it was a phase." She laughed.

"I knew it wasn't a phase," Charlie said to her. "I told them they'd better just accept it or lose you."

"Grandpop likes to think he saved the day, but they would have come around."

"I saved the day," Charlie said with certainty, as though he had some insider knowledge about what had gone on.

"They came around pretty quickly, whether it was anything Grandpop said or not," Celia said. "I think they were just worried they'd never get any grandkids from me."

They asked Jade about her family, and she ached as she lied. She ached because she loved Charlie and she had the feeling she could easily love Celia and every member of her family just from hearing about them, and everything she was telling them was total fiction. She told them how she'd needed to escape from her terrible parents, and the lie felt simply awful. She wished she could tell them about Riley. About Danny. But the truth was, she no longer knew much about her family. She didn't even know where they lived. Charlie and Celia looked at her with so much sympathy. How could they even relate to the lack of support she'd described? Did they think it was her fault for not working it out? She didn't like her false self any better than she did her real self, and that made her very sad. She wanted to tell them how her parents had loved her in spite of her mistakes. How good they were. Instead she turned them into an evil couple bent on ruining her life.

"I'd love to hear you two play," she said, nodding toward the living room and the instruments as she tried to get the focus off herself.

"Good idea," Celia said, pushing back from the table. "Let's clean up and make some music."

Jade helped Celia in the tiny kitchen while Charlie put the Robin Flower record on his stereo. He had top-of-the-line equipment, which didn't surprise her, given his love of music. Working in the kitchen, she felt Celia's arm brush against hers more than was absolutely necessary. Yes, it was a tiny space, but they still seemed to find themselves next to each other more than was needed to wash and dry. And Jade loved it, the touching. She loved it so much that she was disappointed when the dishes were done and the counter clean.

When they joined Charlie in the living room, he was sitting on his futon, taking one of the guitars out of its case. Celia turned off the stereo and looked at Jade. "Why don't you play my mandolin," she said, "and I'll just mess around on the other guitar?"

Jade shook her head. "No, that's okay," she said. "I'd love to hear you two play together."

Celia sat on the other end of the futon from her grandfather as they lit into "Roll in My Sweet Baby's Arms" on the guitar and mandolin. Jade sat on a nearby chair, grinning. They were brilliant together! They played a bunch of traditional tunes Jade didn't know, and then a few familiar old Beatles songs.

She listened to them play awhile longer and she clapped and even sang along for a bit . . . and then she reached the point where she couldn't take it anymore. She suddenly got to her feet and they looked up in surprise.

"I have to get my violin," she announced.

"All right!" Celia said.

"Go with her," Charlie said to Celia. "Too dark to be out there alone."

It wasn't really too dark to be alone. Oh, there were parts of Ocean Beach Jade wouldn't want to be in alone

at night, but the three blocks between Charlie's bungalow and her cottage were perfectly safe. Still, she
wouldn't turn down more time with Celia.

They walked quietly for a while before Celia spoke.
"It took real courage to leave your family like that when
you were only eighteen," she said after they'd walked a
block. "Do you ever hear from them?"

Jade shook her head. "No," she said. "They don't even
know where I am and I want to keep it that way."

Celia was quiet a moment. "Was it because you're
gay?" she asked without looking at her, and Jade was
stunned by the question. Did she look gay? Her hair was
still down to her shoulders and she thought she looked
pretty feminine. Maybe, though, looks had nothing to
do with it.

She hesitated. "I don't think I am," she said, then
added, "Although right now, I'm a little confused."

They were passing beneath a streetlight, and she
could see the slight smile on Celia's lips. Jade had the
feeling Celia knew more about her than she knew about
herself.

Celia touched her arm. "It's okay," she said.

She thought about the way she felt every time she
looked at the Nastassja Kinski poster in Grady's, and she
remembered the day she'd bought her violin from Cara
and the electric jolt she'd felt watching Cara play.
Matty'd told her once that he wondered if she was gay
and just didn't know it yet. She'd thought he was joking, his feelings hurt because she said she didn't care if
they ever kissed or not. She looked at Celia's profile.
That was not the way she felt right now. She wished
Celia would try to kiss her. She wouldn't resist.

Neither of them spoke for half a block.

"That's my place." She pointed toward Ingrid's

bungalow. "I live in a little cottage behind the house." She pushed open the gate to the walkway. "Down here," she said, and Celia followed her down the narrow path.

"This is really cute," Celia said when Jade flicked on the living room light. She was embarrassed by all the papers and music scattered all over the place. She'd never had anyone other than Ingrid inside the cottage. "How do you afford it, working at Grady's?" Celia asked, then she blushed. "Sorry," she said. "That's so personal."

"Ingrid takes pity on me," Jade said. Ingrid had never once raised her rent. "Plus the in-state tuition is great. I'll need to find a teaching job as soon as I'm out, though." She was worried about that. How many schools were hiring music teachers these days?

She picked up her violin case. "I bought this from a student who was trading up," she said. "I had a better one before I left home, but had to leave it behind."

"I'm sorry." Celia touched her shoulder, a look of sympathy on her face. "Whatever it was you went through with your family," she said, "you didn't deserve it."

Jade couldn't look at her, she felt so choked up. She was glad when she turned out the light and they walked outside into the darkness again.

Sitting once more in Charlie's living room, Jade felt her hands shake as she tuned the violin. She knew what she was going to do, and she knew there was danger in it. "Want us to start and you join in?" Charlie said kindly. He and Celia sat on the futon, waiting for her to finish her painstaking tuning. "What's your favorite song?" he asked.

"I'll play it for you," she said, and she lifted the violin to her chin and began to play Bazzini's "Dance of the Goblins," her eyes shut so she could lose herself in the music. Forget where she was. Forget she was taking a risk, playing one of the most technically challenging pieces of music she knew. Forget she was pushing the bushel aside and letting her light explode from beneath it like fireworks.

When she'd finished, she opened her eyes to the silence in the room. Celia's hands were prayerlike, pressed to her mouth, and above them her gray eyes were wide.

"Holy shit," Charlie said into the still air of the cottage.

Jade's arms trembled as she lowered the violin to her lap. "That's it," she said. "That's my favorite song." *Please don't tell,* she thought.

"Where did you learn to play like that?" Charlie asked.

"I studied a lot as a kid." She shrugged her shoulders. She hadn't played well out of a need to show off. Not at all. It had been a need to let out a little of who she really was to people she cared about. People who cared about her.

"Why aren't you making this your life's work?" Celia finally found her voice. "Why San Diego State? Why not a conservatory?"

"Juilliard," Charlie said, making Jade jump. It was as though he knew.

"Because I had to leave home," she said. "I had to give it up."

"No!" Celia said. "You can't. You have to get back to it."

"It's a gift," Charlie said. "You have a responsibility to use it."

"I want to teach," she said. "That's all I want right now." She nodded toward his guitar. "Let's play together."

It took them another minute to recover from what she'd done. They could tell she was hurting, she thought. That she needed the relief they could offer. So, in their kindness, they began playing. The three of them played until two in the morning, and this time when Celia walked Jade home to her cottage, it surprised neither of them when she took the violin case from Jade's hands and set it next to the couch, then drew Jade toward her, her hands warm against her rib cage, her lips pressing gently against hers.

"Stay," Jade said when they'd pulled apart, and Celia nodded.

"I don't have a phone for you to let Charlie know you won't be coming home, though, and you—"

Celia pressed her fingertip to Jade's lips. "I told him not to worry if I didn't come home tonight."

"Oh." In spite of how open the three of them had been with each other all evening, Jade felt a little shock. "What did he say?"

"He said to be good to you. He said you're very, very precious." Celia smiled. "But I'd already figured that out."

32.

Riley

"What are you two doing here?" Tom Kyle said when Verniece let us into the stifling hot RV. Verniece had that jittery look that I'd seen in her a couple of times. I imagined life wasn't pleasant for her when her husband was upset and I hated being part of the cause. They didn't ask us to sit down, and the four of us stood awkwardly in the small kitchen. I was next to the door, one hand on the doorknob, nervous about my brother and his unpredictable anger. Already, I couldn't wait for this to be over.

"We have a few questions," Danny said. "You laid some news on my sister and you owe us an explanation."

"About what?" Tom nodded in my direction. "What's she been telling you?"

Verniece reached toward the refrigerator. "Would you like—" she began, but Tom put his arm out to stop her from opening the door. I was disappointed. I would have loved some of that cool refrigerator air to seep into the RV.

"We don't need to entertain them," he said to Verniece. He looked at Danny. "Get to the point, all right?

It's going to rain this afternoon and I want to get some fishing in before the downpour."

"We're supposed to get an inch or more," I said, like this was a pleasant visit between neighbors.

"How did you know there was a second set of footprints at that marina where our sister's car was found?" Danny asked.

Tom couldn't seem to look my brother in the eye. He fiddled with a pill bottle that sat on the counter. "Why are you dredging up that old nonsense?" he asked. "It's like I told her." He nodded toward me as if he'd forgotten my name. "I read it somewhere."

"But that information was withheld from the media, Tom," I said. "You couldn't have read it."

"Really?" Verniece looked puzzled. "I remember reading about it, too. At least I think I did. It was so long ago."

I wondered if Danny could be wrong. Maybe the information had made it to one of the papers after all.

"You couldn't have," Danny said to Verniece. "So, come on. Out with it. How did you know?"

"Please think back, both of you," I said, almost gently, trying to counter my brother's harsh tone. "Try to remember how you heard about it."

They fell silent. Tom folded his beefy arms across his chest and looked into space, like he was considering the question. Verniece gave him a stubborn glance as she reached for the refrigerator door again. She opened it and took two bottles of orange soda from inside the door, then handed them to Danny and me.

"Here, Riley," she said. "You look like you need to cool off."

My phone rang as I took the bottle from her, and I

pulled it from my pocket to check the caller ID. Christine. No surprise there. She'd be annoyed when I didn't pick up. I set the phone on the counter and twisted the cap off the bottle. I took a long swallow, then pressed the cool bottle against my neck. Did they have any air-conditioning blowing in this trailer at all? How did they stand it?

"You know what I bet it was?" Tom said finally, as though he'd thought the question through and come to a conclusion. "I was with the U.S. Marshals Service back then. I knew people. The state police got involved with that case. FBI, too. I had a few buddies in both places, so maybe I didn't read it. Maybe I heard it from one of them."

"And then you probably told me sometime over the years," Verniece added. She looked relieved to have an answer.

"And what did your buddies make of those two sets of footprints?" Danny asked.

Tom shrugged. "That maybe it was some kind of setup. You know. Like the second person got her out of there somehow."

"Why would they . . . your *buddies* . . . jump to that conclusion?" Danny asked.

"How the hell would I know?" Tom snapped. He leaned forward to look out the window above the sink. "Clouds coming in," he said impatiently. He pushed between us to open the door, clearly showing us the way out. "We're done here," he added.

Danny hesitated, and I tensed, unsure what he was going to do or say. Finally, he turned toward the door. "For the moment," he said, and I was relieved he was letting this go, at least for now.

I held my soda bottle in the air as I followed him out of the RV. "Thanks, Verniece," I said. I hoped my smile conveyed an apology.

"He knows more than he's saying," Danny said once we were in his car. He had a faraway look in his eyes, as if he was trying to solve a puzzle.

"Well, he didn't want to talk to us, that's for sure." I adjusted the air-conditioning vent so the cool air blew on my face. "But what could he possibly know? Don't you think the police would have gone over any evidence with a fine-tooth comb twenty-three years ago?"

"Who knows?" Danny asked as he started driving down the gravel road. "Could've been a bunch of incompetents working on it. All I know is, something doesn't add up, and I—"

"My phone!" I interrupted him, patting my shorts pocket. "I left it on the counter."

He pressed the brake and I reached for the door handle. "Don't back up," I said. We'd only driven thirty yards or so from the Kyles' RV. "I'll just get out here." I opened the door and got out. "Be right back," I said.

I started toward the RV at a jog, annoyed with myself. The last thing I felt like doing was seeing Tom and Verniece again right now. I slowed to a walk as I neared the motor home and was circling the rear of it when I heard shouting. I stopped walking. The voice I heard wasn't Tom's or Verniece's and I was suddenly afraid to move. Had someone else been hiding in the trailer? But then I realized it *was* Verniece's voice I was hearing, although she sounded nothing like the Verniece I'd come to know and like.

". . . might as well have gone straight to the police,

you jerk!" she yelled. "He's friends with Harry Washington! How are we supposed to—"

Tom shouted something unintelligible, and whatever Verniece said after that was muffled and lost . . . except for the word *Riley*. I rested my hand against the rear of the RV. Verniece was always so soft-spoken. So sweet and gentle. This was a side to her I hadn't imagined existed. Beneath my palm, I felt the metal siding vibrate with their voices, but they spoke more quietly now, too softly for me to understand them.

I coughed loudly to give them a moment's warning, then walked around the side of the RV and called out, "Verniece!" Their voices fell completely silent as I neared the steps to the door. "Verniece? I forgot my phone."

I heard a scrabbling movement from inside, and in a moment Verniece opened the door, my phone in her hand. "Here you are, love." She smiled and reached out to hand it to me. Her face was bright red and shiny with perspiration. "Wouldn't want to forget that, now, would you?"

"No," I said, unable to return her smile. "Thanks."

I turned and walked back to Danny's car, wanting to look over my shoulder to see if they were watching me. *Might as well have gone straight to the police, you jerk!* I didn't know what she was talking about. All I knew was that, for now at least, I'd keep what I'd overheard to myself.

33.

Portland, Oregon
Jade

"A special toast!" Celia's father, Paul, raised his wine glass high in the air above the broad dining room table, which nearly sagged under the weight of an enormous roast turkey and huge bowls of potatoes and vegetables and stuffing. "To Celia's friend Jade," he said. "We're happy she could share Christmas dinner with us for the first time and we hope it won't be the last."

"Thank you," Jade said from her seat next to Celia. She smiled across the table at Celia's brother, Shane, and his wife, Ellen, a petite, very cute strawberry blonde, as they raised their glasses in the air.

She was in love. Deeply, wildly, passionately in love. She and Celia had spent that one week together in Ocean Beach before Celia had to go back to Portland to teach. Then Celia returned to San Diego for a few days after Thanksgiving, staying with Jade instead of Charlie that time, although they were careful to include Charlie in everything they did. Well, *almost* everything. He loved that Jade and Celia were together. He told them so a million times.

After that visit, Jade knew she wanted to tell her father about Celia. She needed to share the joy she felt

with someone who'd care. Was it a "dire emergency"?
Yes, she told herself. From an emotional perspective, it
was. Maybe her father didn't bother checking his post
office box any longer, although she checked hers every
month, hoping for a peek into the world of her family.
But since the day three years ago when she'd received
the money for her car along with his one-line note—*you
are loved and missed*—there'd been no communication
at all between them.

She wrote a carefully worded message:

Dear Fred,
    *Just to let you know, I've met someone I care
deeply about. Be happy for me. I'd love to know
how everyone is doing.*
Ann

She mailed it, imagining the note languishing in her
father's dusty old post office box, never to be read.
Maybe she should have risked adding her return address
in case his box had been closed, but it was too late.

Only a week later, though, she had a reply.

Ann,
    Be cautious. A friend can easily become a foe.
Yours,
Fred

P.S. We are fine.

It wasn't the response she'd been hoping for—far
from it—and the cool tone of the note hurt so much that
she broke down in tears in one of her classes and had to
leave. What did "we are fine" mean? She wanted details!

Riley was seven and Danny twelve, and she longed to know them. How did Riley like school? Did she love music, the way Lisa had? Did she play an instrument? Did her hair smell the way it used to, like sunshine and baby powder? How was Danny doing? Did he miss his big sister? And had her mother recovered from Lisa's "suicide"? She wanted to know, but it was clear her father would not be the one to give her the answers.

Now she found herself surrounded by someone else's family. She'd met Celia's parents, Paul and Ginger Lind, for the first time the night before on Christmas Eve, when everyone gathered to open presents. She'd been nervous, meeting them, but they acted as though they'd known her—and loved her—all her life.

There was another nonfamily member at the Lind Christmas dinner. Travis was a longtime friend of Celia's. His long curly blond hair reminded Jade of Grady, though Travis wore his in a ponytail. She thought he was a cousin at first, he fit so easily into the family, and she could tell he'd shared many holidays with them. Like everyone else at the table except Charlie, who had flown to Portland with Jade, Travis was a teacher. He taught at the community college with Celia. Paul and Ginger taught high school, Shane and Ellen taught elementary school in Seattle. They all asked Jade about her own plans to teach, and she felt their approval when she told them she wanted to teach music on the middle or high school level. They asked her nothing about her past, and for the first time, she felt as though her past was unimportant. It had nothing to do with who she was now.

"What's the story of your necklace, Jade?" Ginger asked halfway through the meal. "It's so intriguing."

Jade touched the pendant at her throat. This was the

first time she'd worn it since leaving home. A sign of how safe she felt with Celia's family. "It was a gift from a friend," she said. "I like it because it's jade, like my name."

"White jade?" Ellen asked. "I've never heard of it."

Jade nodded. "The Chinese call it mutton fat jade," she said.

"Mutton fat!" Ginger laughed. She had a girlish laugh that Jade was quickly coming to love.

"What does the Chinese symbol mean?" Shane asked.

"This side means 'hope,' " she said, touching the pendant, "and this side"—she flipped it over to expose the second symbol—"means happiness."

That launched a discussion of heirloom jewelry, with Ellen describing her great-grandmother's cameos and Ginger, her grandmother's emerald earrings. Jade listened, touching her pendant over and over again during the rest of the meal, thinking about how easily she'd lied about the meaning of the symbols and wishing she could tell someone the truth.

Everyone helped clean up after the meal, even the men. Jade's father had never been one for cooking or cleaning, so it surprised her when Paul put an apron over his sweater and jeans. "The sooner we get cleaned up, the sooner we can jam," he explained.

Celia had told her that her family was known for its jam sessions, but until they'd finished the dishes and moved to the living room, Jade hadn't really understood. Suddenly, all the instruments came out. Charlie and Shane played guitars. Paul and Travis played banjos and Celia the mandolin. Although Ellen and Ginger didn't play instruments, Ginger sang along and Ellen banged a tambourine. Jade had brought her violin at Celia's insistence—Celia didn't have to twist her arm too hard. She wanted Jade to play the "Dance of the Goblins" she'd wowed her and Charlie with the night they first met, but Jade knew she would never again play for anyone the way she had that night. That had been too great a risk. And anyway, playing with Celia and her family, her violin turned into a fiddle. They played mostly bluegrass with some country and old rock thrown in, and the evening passed at lightning speed.

After a couple of hours, the older generation and Ellen went to bed, and that was when the music changed to something more serious and intense. The four of them—Celia, Shane, Travis, and Jade—sounded incredible together. They all knew it, too. Jade had chills as they played, the chemistry between them magical. Ironically, she was the weakest musician of the four of them. Classical violin and fiddling were different animals. Travis also knew how to play the fiddle, though, and he gave her tips, and she started to fall in love all over again with the instrument in her hands.

She thought about her father while they played, wondering what he'd make of her playing bluegrass . . . and how he'd feel about her bonding so closely to another family. She remembered his note—*a friend can easily become a foe*—and it angered her.

She watched Celia as they sang and played. She wasn't worried about Celia ever becoming a foe, but she knew she could never tell her who she really was. Celia was a happy person in a happy family. Telling her would be like throwing a handful of dirt into a glass of clean water. She couldn't do it.

* * *

On Sunday, she went to Celia's church with her. Jade had given up on church long ago, but she knew it meant a lot to Celia, who said her church was an "open and affirming" congregation. That meant gays and lesbians were welcome, Celia explained, but Jade was still stunned when Celia held her hand during the service.

"So," Celia said as they drove away from the church, "what did you think?"

"Totally different from the Catholic church I grew up in, that's for sure," Jade said.

Celia glanced at her. "Do you believe in God, Jade?"

It wasn't something Jade thought about often. "I'm not sure," she admitted, liking that with Celia, she didn't have to lie about her opinions. "I believe something set everything in motion. That's as close as I come to God, I think. I don't like religion, to be honest. Religion seems to have twisted the idea of God into a way to control people."

Celia smiled at the road in front of them. "Yeah, I know," she said. "For me, it's all about the people in the church. Taking care of each other, you know what I mean?" She glanced at Jade again. "I love my church. If any single one of those people you saw there today had a problem or a crisis, everyone else would reach out to help."

That wasn't the church Jade remembered from her childhood. When her family had a crisis—the crisis she'd brought on them—no one reached out to lend a hand. Instead, they pushed them away.

That night, after Celia fell asleep, Jade went out on the balcony bundled up in a quilt and looked out over the city. The air was cool and misty and she could see the lights of Portland below. Everything looked so beautiful. She felt choked up. Celia was the best person she'd ever known. The kindest, warmest, smartest—and sexiest—person ever. And she was in love with Jade.

But Celia didn't know her. She didn't know Jade was a liar and a fake. Would she still love her if she knew? Jade would never be able to put that question to the test.

34.

Riley

As soon as Christine arrived the following morning, I left the house for a run. I'd timed it that way. Every minute away from Christine was a good minute. But as soon as I descended the porch steps, the Kyles' old Ford pulled up to the curb in front of my house.

Oh, no, I thought. I'd wanted an hour's peace. Was that too much to ask?

The passenger side window of the car rolled down and I could see it was Verniece rather than Tom in the driver's seat.

"Riley, dear!" Verniece called, all sweetness and light. "Can we talk for a minute?"

I stood with my hands on my hips. I looked behind me at the house, knowing Jeannie would show up any minute and wouldn't be happy to find Verniece there. Crossing the lawn, I pulled the car door open and got in. After hearing bits and pieces of Verniece's argument with Tom the previous day, the older woman no longer gave me that warm cuddly feeling.

"We can't talk here," I said. "There's too much going on."

"Oh, that's fine." Her voice shook the way it had that

first morning, when she told me how my so-called adoption had inspired them to adopt their son. She put the car in gear and gave it a little gas. "How about we find a shady spot to sit by the water? It's too hot to stay in the car."

"Fine," I said. "What's going on?"

She ignored my question, seemingly focused on her driving, and I didn't press. I would find out soon enough.

She parked in the lot near Union Point Park and we sat on a bench in the shade of a couple of trees. I looked toward the river. In the distance a couple of kayakers paddled slowly away from shore.

"This is really hard for me," Verniece said. "Extremely hard. I feel like I'm under Tom's control, sometimes." She shrugged. "Embarrassing to admit that, but that's the way it is."

Spit it out, I thought. The fact that I could no longer trust her made me angry. Since my arrival in New Bern, Verniece had been the one person I thought I could count on to have my best interests at heart. I'd been wrong. *No one* in this town had my best interests at heart.

She waited for me to respond to what she'd said, and when I didn't, she nervously plowed ahead.

"First, I have to get your promise that you won't tell your brother what I'm going to tell you," she said.

"I can't promise that," I said.

"Please, Riley. There's information you should know, but if you tell Danny and he tells . . . anyone, well, frankly, it will ruin my life. Mine and Tom's. And I didn't tell you this before, but I'm very ill." She looked at me. "Heart disease." She laid her palm flat against her chest. "I'm looking at open heart surgery soon, and all this is taking a toll on my health." When I didn't respond, she continued. "You probably wonder why I stay with a difficult old coot like Tom," she said. "I'm sure it's hard for someone like you to understand. You're young and healthy with marketable skills, but I have none of those qualities. So I put up with what I have to to survive."

I nodded in spite of my desire to remain cool and detached from her this morning. I understood what she was saying. Probably a lot of women her age were in the same boat.

"All right," I said. "Just tell me what you want."

"Okay." She took in a deep wheezy breath and I thought she might be telling me the truth about her heart. "I know this will sound terrible . . . it *is* terrible," she began, "but Tom is desperate. Well, we both are, I guess." She laughed nervously. "The thing is, Tom knows more about your sister's . . . disappearance than he was letting on yesterday. I don't know all what he knows," she added quickly, "just that he wasn't telling you and your brother the truth."

"Her disappearance?" I said. "You mean, he knows for certain she didn't kill herself?"

Verniece nodded, and my own heart skipped a beat. "That's what he says," she said. "And he told me to let you know"—the corner of her mouth twitched—"that he'll tell you where she is in exchange for the deed to the RV park." She looked toward the river instead of at me so she didn't see the shock in my face.

"I can't possibly do that!" I said. "You're talking about extortion!"

"Oh, no, it's nothing like that!" she said. "And I do know it's a terrible thing to ask and I'm so embarrassed, but remember, it *is* what your father wanted, and . . ." Her voice faded away. She wrung her hands in her lap.

"It's all Tom's idea," she said. "This is a part of him I never knew existed." She grabbed my hand. "Please don't say anything to Danny!" she pleaded. "Tom wants you alone to have the information. You deserve to know what happened to your sister, but surely you don't want the police involved, and your brother . . . we just don't know what he'd do if he—"

"Is she still alive?" I drew my hand away from hers.

"She was alive the last time he saw her."

"*Saw* her?" I pressed my hand to my own chest and felt my heart thudding beneath my palm. "He actually saw her?"

"He says he was involved, but I don't know how exactly. It sounds crazy to me. But he knows a lot, Riley. He has a good idea where she is."

I did the math in my head. Twenty acres at ten thousand dollars an acre. Was finding my sister worth two hundred thousand dollars? Danny couldn't care less about his half and we already had my father's money plus whatever we got for the house. I knew Verniece was playing good cop/bad cop with me, pretending she was an innocent victim of her husband in this scheme. I knew that in my head, but my heart didn't give a damn.

"I'll do it," I said.

"Oh, my good Lord!" Verniece slapped her hands on her thighs. "You will? Oh, thank you, thank you, Riley! You've just given me a future!"

"I'll come over this afternoon and Tom can tell me how to find her and then I'll have my father's lawyer draw up whatever papers we need to turn the park over to you."

She lost her smile. "Tom said we need you to do that first. Get the documents taken care of first."

Whatever, I thought. "All right."

"And you won't tell Danny any of this?"

I shook my head. "No," I said. At least I wouldn't tell him right away, although I hoped I could someday. "I don't know how quickly Suzanne—my father's lawyer—can get this done, though."

"Well, Tom said it has to be soon. Before he loses his nerve."

What absolute gall, I thought. I pulled my phone from my pocket, and she panicked.

"What are you doing? You didn't record this, did you?"

"Relax," I said. I wished I *had* thought to record her. "I just want to put your number in my phone. I'll call you when I have the papers drawn up."

"Oh." She gave me her number and I added it to my contacts.

"You won't regret this, Riley," she said. "I think Tom knows a lot and can really help you." She stood up. "Come on and I'll drive you home."

I shook my head, not budging from the bench. "I'll run," I said.

She looked worried as she reached down to touch my shoulder, tentatively, like she wasn't sure her touch would now be welcome. She drew her hand away quickly, and I thought she must have felt the cold stone my shoulder had become. "We'll wait to hear from you," she said.

I watched her walk away, then stood up and started running toward the waterfront. Was I really going to go through with this? It was insane. And risky. I'd have to track Lisa down with care, keeping Danny out of it. Keeping the authorities out of it. I needed to protect her. If I hurt her by finding her, I'd never forgive myself. And if she'd ever cared about me, if she'd ever loved her little sister, that love would vanish like vapor. I would ruin her life. I'd ruin *her*.

Two weeks ago, I was the proud owner of six thousand dollars. If it took every new cent I was due from my father's estate, I would spend it to find Lisa. I was certain Daddy would have wanted that. My eyes filled with tears as I ran, and I brushed them away with the back of my hand, but they were instantly replaced by more. How my parents must have tortured themselves over Lisa's suicide! I was sure Daddy would have given up everything he owned to learn the truth. I'd do this for him as much as for myself.

FEBRUARY 1996

35.

San Diego
Jade

Dear Fred,
My life is good and full and I'm loved and pro-
ductive, but there is a gaping hole in my heart that
I can't heal without your help. I need to know DE-
TAILS about everyone. It keeps me awake at
night, wondering and worrying how you all are.
Please. If you still love me at all, please do this
for me.
Love, Ann

MARCH 1996

Dear Ann,
I'm happy to hear you're doing well. You
haven't been forgotten, nor will you ever be. I hope
you know that.
You ask for details, so I will do my best, but
only this once and you must destroy this letter the
second after you read it. Knowing you, you'd want
me to be honest about the state of affairs here at

home, so that is what I'll be. I'm sorry if this worries you.

We are a family falling apart at the seams.

Your mother has never recovered from losing you. She's very withdrawn and is on antidepressants. They help somewhat, but I miss the joyful woman she used to be. We are living in a nice part of North Carolina and she found a church she likes, but she's made few connections. I believe she's afraid to leave D and R unsupervised for a minute. She carries some blame for everything that happened and nothing I say can change that.

D has grown quite challenging to manage. He'll be thirteen in September and, to be honest, we dread his teen years. He's always angry, at what I don't know. He's a troubled boy who gets in fights at school and is sullen and hard to communicate with. I suppose this is simply a matter of the hormones getting a head start. We're considering homeschooling him again, or rather your mother considers it, but I don't think she has the energy to homeschool anymore. I don't know if that's the answer, anyway. He looks more like you every day.

R is growing into a beautiful girl. She is sweet, polite, and does well in school but she can be clingy with your mother and is overly sensitive, in my opinion, and I've tried to toughen her up with little success. She cries at the drop of a hat and is the type of child who finds stray puppies and kittens wherever she goes. D adores her and he's a different boy around her. They are very close and you'd be pleased. She is not musically talented AT

ALL. We have not pushed either her or D. They both hated piano lessons, and there is no point.

If the weather is good on R's birthday, I plan to take her and D to the beach for the day to fly our homemade kites. (Do you remember the kite you and I made?) I don't know if I'll be able to persuade your mother to join us. Either way, we'll have dinner at a restaurant on the way home. Yes, I still try to hold on to some of our traditions. R loves this place called the Sanitary Fish Market (what a name for a restaurant!) because all the diners eat together at long tables and she thinks that's bliss. I expect one of these times she'll break out singing "Kumbaya." It's a blessing that R doesn't remember our family as it used to be. This is the norm for her—a perpetually sad mother, a preoccupied and worried father, and a confused and angry brother.

As for me, I'm sure you've gathered I'm no longer in my old line of work. I'm focusing on my collections now and have a small side business where I can work outdoors.

So there you have it, Ann, the wrap-up of the M family's lives. Trust me when I say I want to know all about yours, but I'll have to do without. We can't continue this back-and-forth. There are people who remain suspicious.

Again, destroy this letter. I cannot say that forcefully enough.

With love,

Fred

36.

Riley

"So, what's up, Riley?" Suzanne asked from her side of the desk. "You sounded upset on the phone."

I was relieved that Suzanne had a cancellation for that afternoon and was able to see me. I told myself it was a sign that I was doing the right thing, and I needed to do it before I lost my nerve.

"I did?" I asked innocently. "I'd just gotten back from a run so I was probably out of breath. Everything's fine, but I do need your help." I folded my hands tightly in my lap. "I discovered that my father had wanted to update his will to have the RV park go to the Kyles, so I wanted to talk to you about how to make that happen."

She tilted her head as though she might have misunderstood me. "Well," she said slowly, "there's no way to change the will now."

"Oh, I know that," I said. "But I . . . Danny and I . . . want to carry out our father's wishes and somehow transfer the park to them. I just need you to tell me how to do that."

She frowned as I spoke. She must have thought I was the most generous person in the world. "Well," she said, "the first thing I'd advise is that you give this a whole lot of thought, Riley. You're talking about valuable property. Jeannie can give you an idea of its worth, and—"

"She already has. She thinks we could get about two hundred thousand for it. But we can't take it, knowing Daddy wanted someone else to have it."

She leaned back in her chair, slipping on her reading glasses although there was no paperwork that I could see in front of her. "How did you find this out?" she asked.

I was glad she couldn't see my hands from where she sat, since I was now wringing them in my lap. "Jeannie mentioned something about it," I lied. "So did Verniece Kyle. And then as I was cleaning out my father's desk, I found a 'to do' list where he said he needed to talk to you about rewriting his will, and in parentheses it said 'Park to the Kyles,' so I knew then that it was true. What Jeannie and Verniece said."

I was a terrible liar. I always had been. Suzanne shifted in her seat, squinting at me. "Are you making this decision under duress?" she asked.

"Not at all," I said. "It's our decision. We just wouldn't feel good about keeping it."

"It's very generous of you and your brother, Riley, but I wish you'd talk to a financial advisor before you make a huge decision like this. Are you aware of the tax implications?"

Tax implications? That gave me pause, but I didn't want to sound like I hadn't thought this through.

"Yes." I nodded.

"That you'll have to file a gift tax form with the IRS?" she asked, as if she didn't believe me. "You don't have to actually pay taxes on the gift until you reach the lifetime limit, but you're only twenty-five and you never know how much—"

"I've thought about it a lot, Suzanne," I interrupted.

"We want to do it, and the sooner the better. I really want to get the estate taken care of so I can go back to Durham and my life."

"Well, that's what worries me," she said. "That in your rush to get back to your life, you're not making the wisest decisions."

I leaned forward. I needed to get this over with. "How do we do it?" I asked. "Do you need to draw up a contract or what?"

She sensed my impatience and gave in to me with a small nod of her head. "It's called a gift deed," she said. "It's really quite simple. As grantor, you sign the deed over to the Kyles. As grantee, they sign it as well, accepting it without special warranty. They can have a title search performed, which I'd recommend, but they can waive that if they so choose. Then I, or rather my secretary, will deliver the deed to the courthouse to be recorded and we're done. It's that simple."

"Perfect," I said. "When can we do this?"

"I can draw up the form this afternoon and you can all come in tomorrow afternoon to sign it."

You all. "Does Danny need to come, too?" I asked. I was his trustee. I was counting on him not needing to sign.

"No," she said. "The only problem with us doing it tomorrow is that I won't be able to get the deed to the courthouse until Monday, so it won't be recorded until then."

"That's fine."

"Usually"—she peered at me above her reading glasses—"the language in a gift deed states that the transfer is being made in consideration of love and affection between the grantor and grantee."

My stomach knotted at the words. "Just leave that out," I said.

She gave me a worried smile. "Will do," she said, and I had the feeling she didn't believe for a moment that I wasn't making this decision under duress.

37.

Morehead City, North Carolina
Jade

Sitting in a rental car in front of the Sanitary Fish Market Restaurant, she took off the giant sunglasses she'd bought for this trip. She was afraid she was on a very big, very expensive, wild-goose chase. She'd sat there for nearly three hours and now daylight was fading and it would be even harder to see people going into the building.

Putting the car in drive, she moved it a bit closer to the entrance so she could see more clearly in the dimming light. It had been a beautiful day, and with so many families on spring break, the restaurant appeared to be filling up. She'd counted on that. She'd counted on being able to blend into the crowd, but it was beginning to seem as though it didn't matter.

Grady had wanted her to work this week, but she told him she was going up to Portland to see Celia. The truth was, Celia's break fell at a different time from hers. Even Celia didn't know where she was right now. No one did, and that thought put a lump in her throat. *No matter how many people care about you,* she thought, *if you can't be open with them about who you truly are, you are still alone.*

She'd tried to sleep in the car the night before after flying into Raleigh, but it had been too cold and she couldn't quiet her brain. She kept thinking about the drive here to Morehead City, the small North Carolina town that was home to the Sanitary Fish Market her father had made the mistake of mentioning in his letter. She'd worried about getting lost and all the other things that could go wrong. Riley could wake up with the sniffles. The weather could keep them home. By the time morning came and she actually started the drive, she was wiped out.

She'd waited until she was nearly to Morehead City before putting on the oversized sunglasses and Halloweenish black wig she'd bought, worried that her dyed hair wouldn't be nearly enough of a disguise. Then she found the restaurant, parked the car, and waited. Now it seemed the whole trip had been for nothing.

Then, in the spotlights from the restaurant, she saw a man and woman and fair-haired boy walking up the sidewalk toward the entrance. A girl ran ahead of them and Jade leaned forward, holding her breath. Despite knowing full well that Riley was now eight, she'd been looking for a small child.

"Oh, my God," she whispered. Her breath left a smudge of fog against the car window, and she quickly erased it with her fingers so nothing was in the way of her view.

Her mother's dark hair was short now, tucked behind her ears. She walked next to Jade's father, but they weren't holding hands as they used to and there was a good six inches of air between them. *My fault,* Jade thought. Her father hadn't said as much in his letter, but between every line about her family falling apart, she'd felt the blame.

In the light from the restaurant, her father looked completely gray. That was a shock. But he smiled as he called out something that made Riley turn around and wave to him.

Danny and Riley . . . she wouldn't have recognized them. Danny was tall and gangly, his hair absolutely white, the same color hers would be if she didn't dye it. He walked a little hunched over, like he'd grown tall too quickly and was uncomfortable with his height.

Then there was Riley. Oh, my God, Riley! Jade wished for more daylight so she could see her clearly, but she could tell that the little two-year-old was gone and in her place was a slender, pretty child with dark wavy hair. Riley ran back to her parents and took her father's hand, swinging it, giving a playful hop every few steps. Jade swallowed hard. She'd done the right thing, all those years ago. The right thing.

She waited for them to walk into the restaurant and then gave them a few extra minutes to be seated. Putting on her dark glasses and adjusting her wig, she took a deep breath and got out of the car.

The restaurant was set up with rows of long picnic-type tables and it was crowded, for which she was relieved. She was seated about four tables from her family, where she had a perfect view of Riley and her father, but her mother and Danny had their backs to her. She sat across from an elderly couple and was glad they seemed to have no interest in talking to her. Her glasses were so dark she could barely see the menu and she worried she stood out. She was probably the only person in the restaurant who was eating alone, and she was certainly the only person wearing a cheap wig and sunglasses, yet no one seemed to notice her.

She ordered stuffed flounder, but she couldn't eat. All

she could do was stare. Riley had changed so much. She grinned up at the waitress and seemed to be ordering from her own menu like a grown-up. She'd forgotten everything about that blood-soaked day six and a half years ago, Jade was certain of it. That was just what she'd hoped for—Riley's memory wiped clean. What she saw four tables away from her was a family that had moved on without her. She was still there somewhere—in her father's careful hiding of the truth. In the pain in her mother's heart. In Danny's acting out, and maybe in old family pictures Riley might stumble across one day. But she'd been moved aside to make way for their future. It was what she'd wanted, yet the pain of witnessing it was nearly too much.

When the tears started behind her glasses, she laid a twenty-dollar bill next to her plate and stood up, ignoring the surprised look of the elderly couple across from her. She walked quickly out of the restaurant and back to the rental car. Sitting there, she let herself sob as the evening turned to night. It felt good in a way, letting out the tears she'd held in for so long. When she finally stopped crying, she dried her damp face with a tissue and started the car. Then she drove away from Morehead City, leaving the past behind for good.

38.

Riley

As soon as I'd signed the gift deed in Suzanne's office late Friday afternoon, I headed for the RV park. Tom and Verniece had already signed the simple form—I'd intentionally waited until they'd left Suzanne's office before going in, not wanting to see them any more than was absolutely necessary. I asked Suzanne for a copy of the form bearing both our signatures so I could show it to Tom and Verniece in case they doubted my word.

They were waiting for me inside the trailer. We sat down at the built-in table, the two of them on one side, me on the other. "Here's a copy of the signed form." I placed it between us on the table. "Everything's set and Suzanne will record the deed on Monday. Now you tell me where my sister is," I said to Tom, acting as if I were the one with the power in this small, hot space when I knew that was not the case. My body seemed to know it as well, because I heard the tremor in my voice.

Tom and Verniece looked greedily at the form, but Verniece suddenly shook her head. "We should wait till the deed's recorded," she said, her voice sharp. It was the same voice I'd overheard the day I'd left the phone in their RV. She seemed to catch herself, as if remembering she was supposed to have a sweet and loving persona with me. "I mean," she said, "wouldn't that make the most sense?"

"She's right," Tom said to me. "That's how we do it. After that lawyer lets us know it's been recorded, you come back here and I'll tell you everything."

"No." I folded my hands on the table. "You tell me *now*. I'm not waiting all weekend to find out what you know. I'm giving you a huge chunk of my net worth." The words slipped out of my mouth. I wasn't even sure what *net worth* meant, but I hoped I sounded like I'd thought everything over very carefully and knew what I was doing.

"You don't understand what *I'll* be giving up," Tom said. "I'm putting myself at risk by telling you anything. And one thing you better know is that I'll deny it all if you so much as whisper a lick of it to anyone in authority. Or to your brother."

"Hush now, Tom." Verniece put her hand on his arm. "Let's keep this civil. I think you should go ahead and tell her what she needs to know. She's trustworthy." She reached across the table to squeeze my hands where they were folded together. "Aren't you, love?"

I didn't answer. I let my eyes burn into Tom's, and I could see the moment he decided to back down.

He got to his feet. Walked over to the refrigerator and pulled out a beer. "I owed your father," he said, popping the top on the beer with a church key. He turned to face us, leaning back against the counter as he raised the bottle to his lips. "Verniece knows all this, so don't worry about that," he said. "I got involved with a female prisoner I was transporting when I was with the Marshals Service. Stupid move. Frank was my boss and he found out. He should have canned me, but instead he covered for me. Gave me a second chance." He looked down at his beer. "But," he said, "I ended up paying for that second chance about ten times over."

"What do you mean?" I asked.

"Your sister didn't kill herself, but she wasn't the mastermind behind the scheme."

I felt a chill in spite of the heat in the RV. "Do you mean . . . you?"

"No, honey," Verniece said. "Your daddy."

I suddenly felt nauseated and sat back from the table, dropping my hands into my lap. What the hell kind of game were they playing with me? Were they going to feed me lies in exchange for the park? "I don't believe you," I said.

"Look," Tom said. "I promised to tell you what I know. I didn't promise to pretty it up for you."

I tried not to let the shock show on my face. Daddy? It was impossible. He was the most honest person I knew, and he'd grieved for Lisa. My whole life, I'd felt his grief.

But I thought of those two sets of footprints in the snow where Lisa had left her car. "What are you saying?" I asked. "That my father helped her . . . do what? Make it look like she killed herself?"

"Exactly," Tom said. "They put the kayak in the water and she got in his car and then he drove her halfway to Philadelphia. That's where I came in." He set the bottle down on the counter. Folded his arms across his chest. "I picked her up in a rest area and took her the rest of the way to Philly."

I felt the blood drain from my face. I couldn't breathe. There seemed to be no air at all in the trailer and Tom and Verniece grew wavy in my vision. Beneath the table, I pressed my hands together hard.

"Are you all right, Riley?" Verniece asked, and I ignored her, my eyes on Tom.

"Did my mother know anything about this?" My throat was so tight that the words barely made a sound. "Did she know Lisa didn't kill herself?"

Tom shook his head. "Nobody knew," he said.

"How do I know you're telling the truth?" I asked. "My father would never—"

"Your father would never what?" He laughed, but the sound was mocking. "Save his firstborn from a lifetime in prison? I personally don't think she was worth saving, but apparently, he did."

I felt tears fill my eyes. I didn't want to cry in front of them. I had to be strong in here, but the thought of Daddy doing all he could—breaking the *law*—to save my sister, tore me up inside.

"I didn't want any part of it." Tom lifted the bottle to his lips. "Your sister had to be a sociopath, with all that crap she handed the police about it being an accident and everything. I didn't care a bit about her. I did it because I owed your father and needed to keep on his good side."

I wiped a tear from my cheek. "Why Philadelphia?" I asked. "Why did you take her there?"

"He took her to the train station," Verniece said.

"To go where?"

"How would I know that?" he said. "I didn't want to know."

"Do you mean you don't know where she is?" I asked, my voice rising.

"Tell her about the new name," Verniece said quickly. I knew she wanted to keep me calm, but if he didn't actually know where I could find her, I was going to lose it completely. That had been the deal: he'd tell me where she was in exchange for the park.

"I made her a set of documents," Tom said, "same as I'd do for someone in the Witness Protection Program."

"So he gave her a new name and everything," Verniece said.

"What name did you give her?" I asked.

"Ann Johnson. Usually we tried to give someone in witness protection a name with the same initials. Easier that way. But your father wanted something completely forgettable, so that's what I gave her."

My sister has a name. Words I could say out loud. Words I could Google. But Ann Johnson? "There have to be thousands of Ann Johnsons," I said.

"That was the point."

"You said documents. Plural," I said. "What else did you give her?"

"She had a driver's license with that name and a Maryland address. She had a Social Security number."

"Do you know what it is?" I asked.

"Hell, I can hardly remember my own Social Security number," he said with a bitter laugh. "I have no idea." He took another swallow of beer. "So," he said, setting the bottle on the counter again. "I've told you all I know. Now you have a name and you know she got on a train in—"

"You said you could tell me where I could find her!" I felt panicky. That was what Verniece had promised, wasn't it?

"I never said that," he said.

I looked at Verniece and she recoiled a bit from whatever she saw in my eyes. "I didn't say he knew exactly where she is, Riley," she said. "But you have a whole lot more information than you had just a few minutes—"

"I can tell you she was alive and healthy twenty-three years ago," Tom interrupted her, "and I can tell you how she disappeared. That's all I promised. And I paid for it. I failed a lie detector test in '93 because I protected your father and sister when I said I never used my official role for anything outside official business. I should have just let them hang."

"Oh," Verniece said, "you would have failed it anyway because you were lying about that tramp you had a—"

"Shut up, woman!" Tom shouted. "You don't know what you're talking about."

Verniece clamped her mouth shut, though I had the feeling if I hadn't been there, she would have let him have it the way she had when I'd overheard her a few days before. She had to keep up her sweet-and-innocent act for my sake.

"This is why my father's been paying you five hundred dollars a month all these years," I said. Suddenly the pieces of the puzzle were falling into place.

"A small price to pay to keep his daughter out of prison, don't you think?"

"What I think is that you haven't told me much of anything," I said bitterly. "So Lisa was alive twenty-three years ago, with a name that's impossible to track down, and she got on a train to who-knows-where."

"You know what, Riley?" he said. "Did you ever stop to think that if Lisa wanted to see you, she would have found *you*?"

He'd hit a nerve I hadn't even realized was raw and tender, and the pain was too much for me. I stood up, and grabbing the copy of the signed form from the table, I tore it in two.

"That's only a copy!" Verniece said.

"This is what I'm going to do to our deal," I said, tearing the paper into quarters, then eighths. "I'm calling

Suzanne to tell her I've changed my mind and not to record the deed."

"You can't do that!" Verniece looked up at me, a shocked expression on her face. "We signed the paper! The real form!"

"I can do it and I will," I said, hoping I was right. "This is over."

"You little bitch." Tom growled. He took a step toward me and I tried unsuccessfully not to flinch.

"Riley." Verniece groaned. "That's not playing fair! He's telling you everything he knows. You don't want him to make things up just to satisfy you, do you?"

"No, but I *do* want him to tell me something that's worth two hundred thousand dollars," I said. "We're done."

I pulled the door open, then leaped down the steps. Once I hit the ground, I ran all the way to my car, terrified Tom might come after me with a shotgun. When I got into my car and hit the locks, though, I looked back at the trailer and saw there was no one in sight. My hands shook as I started the car. I turned it around at the end of the lane and headed out of the park, and only when I reached the main road did I pull over to the shoulder and start to cry. What had I expected? That he would know right where I could find her?

Sitting there, I called Suzanne's number and was relieved to get her voice mail. I was too embarrassed to talk to her at that moment. I cleared my throat, hoping she couldn't tell that I'd been crying.

"Suzanne," I said, "this is Riley MacPherson. I thought about some of the things you said and I've decided not to gift the park to the Kyles after all. I'm sorry for the hassle. Please don't record the deed. Thanks for helping me think it through."

I hung up the phone and sat there staring blindly at the trees by the side of the road. *Daddy knew.* All these years, he'd known the truth. Could he have told my mother? I didn't think so. Not the way she grieved. You couldn't fake that kind of grief. I thought only my father knew, and I wondered if somewhere, buried deep in the sea of paperwork in those living room cabinets, there might be a clue to Lisa's whereabouts.

And if there was a clue, I was going to find it. I would attack the paperwork with a new vengeance. No more stopping to shred every unwanted sheet of paper. I had no time for that. I would search through it all for something, anything, that would tell me where I could find my sister.

39.

Jade

"Hi, Charlie," she said as the old man walked into Grady's carrying an armload of LPs. She gave him a kiss on the cheek and took the records from him. "Ready to turn these in?" Every time he came into the store lately, he brought more records to sell to Grady. He'd reached the age where it was time to pare down, he'd told her, but even though he was turning in ten or twenty a week, he was buying at least five to replace them, so it was going to be slow going.

She set the pile of records on the counter in front of Grady, who would tally them up while Charlie wandered through the aisles, looking for something new.

"I'm going through some boxes in the back," she said to them. They were the only people in the store, and she usually looked forward to catching up with Charlie, but today she needed to be alone.

"Let me know if you come across anything back there that I can't live without," Charlie said.

"I will."

Sitting on a stool in the back room, she pulled old vinyl albums from one of the estate sale boxes. She barely noticed the records, though. She was thinking about what she'd discovered at school that morning: before she started her fifth year at San Diego State, the year in which she'd get her credential that would allow her to teach, she needed to be fingerprinted. It was the law for anyone who taught, anyone who worked with kids. How stupid she'd been not to realize that she'd have to be fingerprinted to work in a school! Blindly sifting through the records in front of her, she realized that the last four years of her life, at least from an educational perspective, had been wasted. She could never teach. Not music. Not anything. And she had no idea now what she was going to do.

It was momentarily quiet in the store. Grady always had music going, but Enya's *Watermark* had just ended and Jade knew he was figuring out what to play next when she heard the jingle of the bell on the front door.

"Can I help you?" she heard Grady ask.

"Maybe," a deep male voice answered. Something about the voice made her still her hands on the records to listen. "I'm a private investigator," he said. "My name's Arthur Jones and I'm trying to find this girl."

She lowered her hands from the box to her lap. *Be calm*, she told herself. Ocean Beach was full of runaways. People were always searching for their missing kids in this town.

"This is an old picture," the man said. "She'd be twenty-three now. She's probably changed her looks. Maybe wears a wig or dyed her hair."

She pressed her fist to her mouth, waiting. For a really long moment, no one said a word. "Looks like some kind of promotional shot," Grady said finally.

"Right. She's a violinist, as you can see. She was one of those prodigies."

She shut her eyes. She could guess which photo he was showing Grady—the one they'd splashed all over the news after Steven's death.

Six years, she thought. For six years, she'd been safe. She'd believed it could last forever.

"She doesn't look familiar," Grady said, and she let out her breath.

"No?" Arthur Jones said. "I showed this to someone on the street out there and he thought he saw a girl who looked like her working in here."

"Bunch of space cadets out on the street." Grady sounded annoyed.

"Let me see it," Charlie said.

"Well, she'll look different now," Arthur Jones said. "Older, like I said, and try to picture her with a different hair color or maybe cut short."

"Pretty girl," Charlie said. "Why're you looking for her?"

"She's wanted for murder," the man said, just like that. She heard Grady laugh.

"That's funny?" the man asked.

"Just, she doesn't look like much of a murderer," Grady said. "What did she do? Hit someone over the head with her violin?"

"No, she shot a guy in the head with a .357 Magnum." Silence.

"Damn," Charlie said after a moment. "You've got to be kidding."

"So, you're just going around to all the stores, showing that picture?" Grady asked.

"We know she's a musician and we're pretty sure she's in San Diego," Arthur Jones said, "so checking music stores makes sense, don't you think?"

How did they know she was in San Diego? How did

they know she hadn't killed herself in 1990, for that matter? She thought of those letters she'd exchanged with her father the month before. Had they been a terrible mistake?

"Well, I don't think she's been in here," Grady said.

"I know everyone in Ocean Beach and I've never seen anyone who looks like her," Charlie added. "I think you're barking up the wrong tree."

"Anyone else here I can show her picture to?" the man asked.

"No," Grady said quickly. "Slow day."

"All right, then. Thanks for your time."

She heard the jingle of the door, but didn't move. Should she go out the back door to the alley? And then what would she do?

Slowly, she slid off the stool on legs that threatened to give out on her and walked into the shop. The two of them stood there like statues, staring at her, Charlie with an LP in his hands, Grady behind the counter.

"You're white as a ghost," Grady said, and Charlie held up his free hand.

"Just tell me you didn't do it," he said.

She swallowed, her throat dry as a piece of toast. "I didn't do it." What else could she say?

"That's good enough for me," Charlie said.

"How long till it occurs to him to check the music department at State?" Grady asked, and her heart nearly stopped beating.

"I have to leave," she said. "I have to leave Ocean Beach."

"Go to Celia," Charlie said. "But tell Ingrid you're going someplace else."

She nodded.

Grady opened the cash drawer, counted out five

twenties and handed them to her. "We'll miss you," he said, then added, "We love you, Jade. Take care."

She cleaned out her cottage quickly. She had little to pack and less that she cared about, but she thought she'd better take everything. Her fingerprints were all over the place! She hoped that private investigator never spoke to anyone who would lead him to Ingrid and this cottage. If he was only looking at music shops she'd be safe, but if he took that photograph to the market, someone there was sure to recognize her. And as Grady said, the music department at State . . . oh, God. How could this be happening?

It took her four trips to carry everything she owned out to her car. She had the one suitcase she'd arrived with. Her textbooks, which she imagined she'd never need again but didn't want to leave behind in her room. Her laptop computer. The violin and music and music stand. That was it. With every trip to her car, she scoured the neighborhood for Arthur Jones, wishing she'd gotten a look at him. She didn't know who to fear.

Once the car was full, she found Ingrid hoeing in her small garden behind the shed.

"Ingrid," she said. "I'm sorry to do this so quickly, but I have to go home."

"Home?" Ingrid stopped her work and looked at her in absolute shock. "You mean, to your family in Maryland?" Jade hadn't so much as mentioned that nonexistent family in years.

Jade nodded. "My father somehow found out I'm going to State and he got a message to me that my mother's really sick."

Ingrid didn't say a word. She stared at her, and Jade had to fill the silence.

"And honestly," she said, "I've been missing them. I just have to go. So my rent's paid up till the end of the month . . . is that okay? Do I need to give you more? I could—"

"No, Jade." Ingrid held the hoe upright at her side. "That's fine. I'm sorry about your mother." She laid down the hoe and walked over to her, putting her hands on Jade's shoulders. "You've been the best tenant I could ask for, but I've always felt you should go home," she said. "Be with your family. What about school, though?"

"I'll have to transfer. It's okay. Family's more important." She choked up a little at that. She wished she *could* go home.

"Are you driving all the way to Maryland?" Ingrid lowered her arms, a worried look on her face. "That will take you days."

"I know. That's why I'm going right away. I don't want to leave my car here." Was she making any sense or digging herself in deeper? "Thanks so much for everything," she said.

"Let me get you some food to take with you." Ingrid took a step toward the house, but Jade grabbed her arm.

"That's all right, thanks," she said, afraid that with every second that passed, Arthur Jones was getting closer to her. "I'll be fine."

She had one more stop to make before leaving Ocean Beach: the bank. She still had nearly two thousand dollars in her account. She took the money in cash, stuffing it into her purse, and hoped that she hadn't set off some kind of alarm in the teller's head. She was sure she looked like the frightened, guilty woman she was.

* * *

She made it all the way to a rest stop near a town called Redding in northern California before she absolutely had to sleep. Even so, she only managed to doze for about an hour, cramped in the backseat of her car, before fear woke her up. Maybe she should have called Celia before heading to Portland, but she was afraid of what Celia might say. What if she told her not to come? Everything was going wrong for her all of a sudden, and if things went wrong with Celia, too, she couldn't take it. She didn't know how she'd explain showing up at her apartment out of the blue, though. Suddenly she felt like she didn't know Celia well at all. Charlie'd said to go to her, though, and he knew her best.

She was numb from worry and the road by the time she reached Celia's apartment the next afternoon. Celia wasn't there, and Jade sat on the landing outside her door. She had to pee and she was starving as she went over and over in her mind what she planned to say to her. She had it worked out, a long and elaborate string of lies. But when Celia walked up the steps, her face registering surprise at seeing her there, Jade burst into tears.

And then she told Celia everything. *Everything.* Even the things Daddy had no idea about.

Even the things he couldn't possibly guess.

PART THREE

40.

Riley

Once I pulled myself together after leaving the message for Suzanne, I drove the rest of the way home with a thrill of excitement running through my body. Lisa was alive! Unless she'd met with some terrible illness or accident—but how likely was that? She was only forty years old. I would find her, and nothing would stop me. I knew, though, that I'd have to be cautious. That meant not telling Danny what I knew, for starters. I'd look for Lisa in a way that put her in no danger, remembering what Tom had said: *If Lisa wanted to see you, she could have found you.* She had to be afraid of being found. Did she know Daddy was dead? Did she know about our mother, for that matter? Would she care if she did?

When I walked in the house, Christine grabbed my hand. "Where've you been?" she asked. "We hit the mother lode in the attic!" She dragged me into the dining room where she had completely covered the table with knickknacks and stacks of old books and other odds and ends I'd never seen before. I yanked my hand away from her, not at all in the mood to deal with details of the estate sale.

Jeannie walked into the room, her arms overflowing with old sewing patterns.

"Look at these!" she said. "Deb must have saved these from when we were teens just learning to sew. Check out the styles on the packages!"

I looked around my mother's warm, cozy dining room, now turned into a junk store. I saw the gleam in Christine's eyes and the dress patterns spilling out of Jeannie's arms onto the floor. The two of them were now more familiar with the house of my childhood than I was, treating it like their own. I wanted them gone.

"I can't take this anymore!" I shouted, my voice so loud even I was surprised.

Jeannie stopped walking toward the table, a few more of the patterns falling from her arms. Christine held a small ceramic horse frozen in midair.

"What are you talking about?" she asked. "What can't you take?"

"This!" I waved my arm through the air above the table and the hundreds of items from the attic. "The mess in my house! People in my house! I really—"

"Honey"—Jeannie dropped the patterns onto one of the dining room chairs, where they spilled like a fountain onto the rug—"you just need to let Christine and me handle everything. I've told you. There's absolutely nothing you have to do."

"I need some peace and quiet," I said, trying to lower my voice. Trying to keep myself calm. "I know you two are doing a ton of work and I appreciate it, but I need some time to myself."

They looked at one another. "We could go get a cup of coffee and come back in an hour," Jeannie suggested to her daughter.

"*No.*" I looked from one of them to the other. They

wore puzzled expressions as if I were speaking a foreign language. "You don't understand," I said. "I need *days* to myself. Maybe *weeks*."

"But the sale is in eight days, Riley," Christine said, "and we're making fabulous progress, but we have a lot more to—"

"You'll need to move the sale," I said.

"What do you mean, 'move it'?" Christine said. "We can't cart all this stuff someplace—"

"I mean, postpone it," I said.

"Oh, no." Christine finally caught on. "The date is already set and we're—"

"I don't care!" I gripped the back of one of the dining room chairs. "I hate this! I hate people in my house, taking it apart bit by bit until I don't recognize it anymore!" My voice rose to a hysterical pitch and it felt good. "I just lost my father, and now I'm losing the house I grew up in!"

"You should have thought of that before you hired me." Christine put her hands on her hips. "Everything was 'rush rush rush' and now suddenly the brakes are on?"

"Christine." Jeannie moved to her daughter's side, a hand on her arm as she tried to calm her down, but that did nothing to temper the anger in Christine's eyes.

"Yes," I said, more quietly now. "The brakes are on. I'm not ready to let go of everything. You need to wait until I am."

Complete silence fell over the dining room. Finally, Jeannie spoke. "All right," she said, "I'm sorry if we've been in your way, Riley. I wanted to make things easier for you, not harder. Let Christine and me organize this mess we made today, and then we'll postpone the sale and we won't come back until you're ready. How's that?"

"That would be excellent," I said. "Thank you."

"Mother!" Christine shot a look of daggers at Jeannie.

"Of course that means the house won't go on the market until late in the season," Jeannie said. "We can't get the repairs and painting and everything done until after the estate sale, but maybe we can—"

"It'll be fine," I said calmly, heading for the living room. Suddenly, though, I turned back to face them. "Oh, but the RV park?" I said to Jeannie.

"What about it?" she asked.

"You can put that on the market right away."

41.

In my bedroom, I closed and locked my door, then sat in the armchair by the front window waiting for them to leave. I could hear them downstairs; the dining room was right below my room. Their voices were muffled, but I imagined they wondered what had gotten into me. I didn't give a damn. It had been such a relief to tell them to go. I'd still be uncomfortable, living in a house that had been turned upside down, little price tags on every lamp and chair and dish, but I could deal with that, and my own bedroom was an untouched haven.

A half hour passed before I heard the front door close. From the window, I watched Jeannie and Christine walk down the porch steps and across the lawn to their cars in the driveway. I smiled, watching them go. Once they'd driven away, I sat down at my desk and turned on my laptop.

How to begin?

I Googled "Ann Johnson" and immediately knew the name was going to be of absolutely no help. I tried searching for images of women with that name. Pages upon pages of Ann Johnsons showed up on my computer, all looking at me with such haunting expressions that I couldn't stand it and I closed down Google altogether.

I sat with my hands in my lap, staring at the screen. With his tech skills, would Danny know of some way of finding her I'd never think of? I shook my head to rid it of the idea. It didn't matter. Even if he did, I couldn't involve him. Maybe I could hire a private investigator, but would a PI have a legal obligation to tell the police if he or she managed to track Lisa down?

And then I remembered that someone *had* hired a PI: Steven Davis's wife, Sondra. And she, I knew, would be easy to find.

It took me only a few seconds to locate her blog again. "Never Forgotten: A Meeting Place for Families of Murder Victims." My gaze fell to the bottom of the page, where I clicked on the word *contact,* and a form appeared below Sondra Lynn Davis's e-mail address. I chewed my lip for a couple of minutes, thinking through what I was about to do. Then I began typing.

Sondra, my name is Riley MacPherson. I am Lisa MacPherson's younger sister. I was only two at the time of your husband's death, and I'd never been told the truth about my sister's role in it. I stumbled across your blog. I wonder if you could tell me if the private investigator made any progress in finding my sister or if he came to the conclusion that Lisa did actually kill herself, which is what my family has always believed.

I'm sorry for your terrible loss, and I'm sure you're helping a lot of people through your blog.

I read it over several times, adding the sentence about believing that Lisa had killed herself only on the third reading, so that I gave nothing away. I added my phone number and signature, and then hit send.

I went for a run with my phone in my hand in case Sondra saw my message right away and called me back, but it wasn't until I'd gotten home, taken a shower, and settled down on the floor in front of the living room cabinets that the phone finally rang. The number on the caller ID was unfamiliar and I held my breath after I said hello.

"Is this Riley MacPherson?"

I knew who it was without her telling me. "Sondra?" I asked.

"Yes." Her voice was youthful, although I figured she was at least sixty. "I was so shocked to get your message," she said.

"I'm sure it seemed strange, out of the blue." I turned to lean my back against the cabinets. "My father died recently and I found articles about . . . everything that happened. And then I found your blog and realized that you thought Lisa might still be alive, and I just wanted to see if you ever learned anything from your private investigator."

She was quiet a moment. "You didn't know she killed Steven?" she asked finally.

"No," I said. "I wasn't even two at the time, and all my parents told me was that she was depressed."

Sondra didn't speak and for a moment I thought we'd been cut off.

"Sondra?"

"Your sister's out there somewhere, you know," she said. "She was never punished for what she did. It's disgusting. My husband was so gifted, and he would have done anything for her and his other students. I think

Lisa's rise in the music world was too fast for her own good. She was spoiled and selfish, and—"

"Why do you think she's . . . out there?"

"The PI we hired found evidence."

"What kind of evidence?"

"A couple of people recognized her from a photograph. This was in San Diego."

"San Diego! Why was he looking there?"

"I got a tip that she was in California. Someone— anonymously—sent me a note saying she traveled to San Diego by train."

I could guess who that someone was. I was so glad I'd called Suzanne to stop the gift deed.

"Of course I received loads of other tips, sending the investigator on a hundred wild-goose chases," Sondra said. "But this was the only one that got a nibble."

"Did you tell the police?" I asked.

"Of course. They did nothing," she said. "They believed she was dead and that I was obsessed. Which I *was,* but with good reason. If the PI had found nothing, I would have let it go. Eventually."

"So . . . you said some people recognized her picture?" I prompted.

"Yes. She'd changed her hair, of course, but they were certain it was the same girl. They said she worked in a shop in Ocean Beach, which I guess is part of San Diego. The PI talked to the shop owner. He denied knowing her, but the PI thought he was lying. I don't think the police even followed up on it." Sondra sounded bitter. I supposed I would feel the same way. "I'm absolutely certain Lisa was living there back then," Sondra said. "The PI was sure of it, but he just couldn't find her."

"So, did he keep looking?"

"Of course, but without any luck," Sondra said. "And my money was drying up, and without being able to get the authorities interested . . . it was immensely frustrating."

"I can imagine," I said, trying to sound empathetic. "Can you tell me the PI's name?"

"Well, I could, but he died about ten years ago so there's not much point." She hesitated. "Are you going to look for her?"

"Oh . . . well, honestly, I tend to think the police were probably right about her killing herself."

I heard her sigh. "You know what my most fervent wish is?" she asked.

"What?"

"I'm sixty-three years old," she said. "I only pray that I live long enough to see your sister found and brought to justice. That's my hope and I won't ever give up on it."

When I got off the phone, I sat in a rocker on the back porch, opened my laptop, and looked for any Ann Johnsons who lived in San Diego. I searched for my sister's features in each photograph that popped up, but I was beginning to think Lisa was wisely living a reclusive life. She probably turned away every time someone pulled out a camera.

It was growing dark, the crickets singing in the yard. I closed my computer and went into the kitchen to scavenge for something to eat. My mother's Franciscan Ware was piled on the counter, a small price sticker attached to the bottom of each plate and bowl and cup and saucer, and I stood there removing those stickers with a sense of relief. Those dishes belonged to my childhood. I planned to keep every one of them forever.

* * *

I didn't wake up until nine the next morning, and I lay in bed, stretching for a while, glad to have the house to myself. It was so quiet with nobody rummaging through the rooms. I planned to go through more of my father's papers that morning, searching for something—*anything*—that might lead me to Lisa. But I suddenly had a different idea.

I got up and carried my laptop back to the bed with me. Surfing to one of the travel sites, I plugged in "New Bern to San Diego," and a few minutes and seven hundred dollars later, I was booked on a flight for that evening.

42.

It was tourist season and all the hotels near the San Diego beaches were packed. So, after I arrived, I picked up my rental car and drove east through the darkness to reach a hotel in Mission Valley, where I'd been able to make a reservation. It was ten at night by the time I got there—one A.M. New Bern time—but I was wide awake. I sat in my room, staring at my phone, realizing I had no one to text that I had arrived safely. I'd left a phone message for Danny, telling him I was going out of town for a few days to see a friend, and now I felt sad and lonely. I missed Bryan. I missed Sherisc. No one knew where I was and the one person I'd told I was going away, I'd lied to.

As usual, I couldn't sleep. Why should a change of coasts make any difference in my insomnia? I was anxious to do what I'd come here to do. I surfed the Internet on my laptop in bed, trying to make myself tired. At two in the morning California time, I gave in, took a Benadryl, and finally drifted off to sleep.

Most of the shops in Ocean Beach seemed to be on the main road, Newport Avenue, and I managed to find a parking place a couple of blocks from the beach. I had a few pictures of Lisa with me in my tote bag and my plan was to go from shop to shop asking anyone over the age of thirty if my sister looked familiar to them. A long shot, but it seemed like the only shot I had.

I'd never been to California before and it felt like another world. The sun was unnaturally bright as I walked along the sidewalk, and the palm trees that lined the avenue looked like tall skinny pompoms. The sidewalk was packed with people of all ages. A lot of students, I thought. Young mothers with kids in tow. Aging hippies. There were all sorts of shops. Antiques. Surf shops. Jewelry. A Pilates studio. Had Lisa walked on this same street? I wanted that to be true. I knew decades had passed—and maybe Sondra was wrong and she'd never been in Ocean Beach at all—but I felt oddly close to her here.

After talking to people in fifteen stores, I took a break in a coffee shop, feeling discouraged. I'd quickly discovered this was a young town, full of people who were barely walking when Lisa would have lived there. In each store, I'd shown the framed picture of Lisa, Danny, and myself, telling whoever I spoke with that the girl in the photo was my sister who had run away when I was two. I'd selected that picture because she was close to the age she would have been when she'd worked in Ocean Beach . . . *if* she'd worked in Ocean Beach . . . and she wasn't holding a violin. I'd worried that the violin might give her away as the famous prodigy she'd been, but I quickly realized that was a pointless concern. Twenty years was a very long time. None of the shopkeepers recognized my sister, and I began to wonder if I should be speaking to the straggly old hippies instead.

After my break, I resumed my hunt. I was about to

skip the Pilates studio—had anyone even heard of Pilates twenty years ago?—but at that point I thought I had little to lose.

The ponytailed blond woman behind the counter in the dimly lit studio was no more than twenty-two, and she shook her head when I showed her the photograph. But an older woman, her gray hair in braids, stood next to me at the counter and she touched the edge of the carved frame with her fingertip.

"Oh, I remember her," she said. "Only her hair was darker."

I felt my heartbeat kick up, but I was afraid to get too excited. "That would fit," I said. "I'm sure she dyed it. Where do you remember seeing her?"

The woman leaned her elbows on the counter to study the photograph. "She worked at this music store that used to be across the street." She pointed through the window. "Grady's. I went in there a lot. I wish it was still there. I'd rather support an indie shop than buy all my music online, you know? She had a funny name, I can't remember what it was." She looked at the receptionist. "What was it?" she asked, as though the young woman could possibly know.

"Got me." The receptionist laughed.

My brain had perked up as soon as she said *music store*. That fit. It fit perfectly. The funny name did not.

"Her name was Ann Johnson," I said.

"Really?" The woman looked at the picture again. "Maybe I'm wrong, then. I don't remember her name, but I know it wasn't Ann."

"Well," I asked, my hope fading a bit, "do you have any idea where she is now?"

"Oh, God, no. I haven't seen that girl in"—she looked

toward the ceiling, thinking—"I don't know how long. You should try to find Grady," she said. "The owner of the store."

"Do you know where I can find him?" I asked.

"There's a jewelry store a block up." She pointed east. "On this side of the street. The jeweler Sal was good friends with him."

I'd already been in that jewelry store, but I hadn't met a Sal.

"Thank you so much," I said, and I slipped the photograph back into my tote and headed out the door.

A funny name, I thought as I walked the block toward the jewelry store. That worried me. But the music store fit so well, and that gave me hope. I wanted to hold on to that hope as long as I could.

The young guy in the jewelry store told me Sal would be working the next day, and I decided to wait till then to resume my search. Funny how I could run a half marathon without a twinge, but my feet ached from the stop-and-go walking through Ocean Beach.

I drove back to my Mission Valley hotel, took a long soak in the tub, and then spent the evening Googling "music store," "Grady," and "Ocean Beach." On various music Web sites and blogs, I found people reminiscing about Grady's Records from back in the day. The shop apparently closed down in the late nineties. I searched for any reference to a female employee, with a "funny name" or not, but no one mentioned anyone from the shop other than Grady himself, and I finally went to bed for another long and restless night.

Sal was not a very trusting guy.

When I arrived at the jewelry store the following

morning, the gray-haired, bearded jeweler sat at the worktable in the window, and he wore a blank expression as he looked at the picture of my sister through his safety glasses.

"Never seen her," he said, resting his soldering iron on the table.

"Someone told me she might have worked at Grady's Records years ago," I said. "And that you might know where I can find Grady."

"Rad shop," Sal said with a nod. "Grady closed it down around 2000 when vinyl officially tanked. He could open it up again now, though, and have customers lined up for blocks."

"Can you tell me where I can find him?"

He looked suspicious as he slipped his safety glasses to the top of his head. "You going to cause him any kind of grief?"

"No," I said. "Of course not. I just want to see if he remembers my sister."

He stroked his beard, considering the request. I thought I looked pretty straight and innocent in my blue capris and black T-shirt, my hair in a ponytail. Apparently, he thought so, too. "He's a sound engineer at the stadium," he said.

"Where's the stadium?"

He gave me directions back to Mission Valley, and I remembered passing a stadium not far from my hotel.

I thanked him for his help, then walked slowly to my car, reluctant to leave the beach. I was so sure I felt the vibrations of my sister in this town.

It took a lot of walking around the aging circular stadium and many questions of many custodians before I found the guy named Grady, but I did finally find him. He sat in a small room in the middle of a half circle of monitors of varying shapes and sizes. His back was to me, his hair in a curly gray ponytail.

"Excuse me?" I said.

He swiveled his stool around to face me and I was mesmerized by his see-through green eyes.

"You lost?" he asked.

"No," I said. "I'm looking for you if you're Grady. Do you have a few minutes to talk?"

"Depends on who's asking," he said, but he smiled warmly.

"My name is Riley MacPherson." I waited to see if my name meant anything to him, but he looked at me blankly. "I think . . . there's a very small chance you might have known my sister," I said. "Did you ever have a girl working for you by the name Ann Johnson?"

He lost his smile and stared at me. "No," he said, but the look in his eyes told me he knew that name, and I felt my own eyes fill with tears.

"Please talk to me," I pleaded. "I don't want to hurt her. I promise."

He was still looking hard at me, but I saw something inside him begin to bend. "You're too young to be her sister," he said.

Oh, my God, I thought. *He knew her.*

"My family was very spread out in age," I said. "But I promise you. I am." I wiped the corners of my eyes with my fingertips.

"Why would you think I know her?" he asked.

"I'm pretty sure that a private investigator talked to you about her long ago. Do you remember?"

He shrugged. "Some guy came in with a picture of a girl and I said I didn't know her," he said. "And that's what I'm saying to you, too." He swiveled his chair around so his back was to me again.

"I flew all the way from North Carolina to try to find someone who knew her," I said. "Please."

I saw his shoulders sag and heard him sigh. He turned back to me.

"Why do you want to find her?"

"I thought she killed herself when she was seventeen," I said, and his pale eyes widened, "but I recently found out that she faked her suicide. That she's probably still alive. I never got to know her. Our parents are both dead. She and my brother are my only family."

He was frowning at me now, gray eyebrows nearly knitted together. "When's the last time you saw her?" he asked.

"When I wasn't quite two."

"Shit." He ran a hand over the thinning hair at his temples. "Well, it seems to me if she wanted to see you, she would have found *you* instead of you having to look for her."

I winced. The same thing Tom Kyle had said to me, almost word for word.

"I think she was afraid of hurting me or our family by being in touch," I said. Or, more likely, I thought, she was afraid of *us* hurting *her*.

"Convince me you're her sister," he said. "You don't look like her."

I reached into the tote bag hanging over my shoulder and pulled out the framed picture of Lisa, Danny, and me, all of us dressed in white.

He held it on his knee and let out his breath. "Wow," he said. "This is your brother?"

"Yes. Danny. He doesn't know I'm here. He . . . he was in Iraq," I added. "His life's kind of a struggle."

A whole array of emotions passed over Grady's features, and he looked down at the picture awhile longer in silence.

"Please help me," I said.

After a moment, he stood up. "Not sure I can." He handed me the photograph. "But let's get out of this claustrophobic room and talk."

He led me out of the room and we walked down the wide corridor and then out into the bowl of the huge stadium itself. The brown plastic seats were completely empty, and we sat down high above a sunlit green field.

"What's your name again?" he asked.

"Riley," I said. "You knew her, right?"

"Did she really kill someone?" He looked at me. His green eyes were startling in the sunlight.

"Is that what the PI said?" I asked.

"Yes. Was that bullshit?"

I shook my head. "She shot a man, but it was an accident. I think she got scared then and faked her suicide." I'd leave my father out of the story. "I didn't know about the shooting. My whole life, I grew up thinking she'd killed herself because she was depressed." I told him about finding the box of newspaper articles and my conversation with Sondra Davis. "Which is how I found out that she'd worked in Ocean Beach. And then I met a woman who recognized her and she said she worked for you."

He didn't say anything.

"Did she? Work for you?"

He nodded.

"Oh, my God." A chill ran across my arms. "I can't believe it. A week ago I thought she was dead. Thank you! Can you tell me about her? What was she like?"

My words came out in a rush. "Do you have any idea where she is now?"

"I don't know where she is," he said. "I haven't seen her since she left, which was the same day that PI came into my shop. I knew she was running from something, though, and I have to tell you," he said, "I don't think she'll want to be found."

I turned my face away from him, afraid I was going to cry again. "I won't hurt her," I promised. "That's the last thing I want to do."

"She was an awesome girl," he said, as if trying to console me, and his words *did* give me some comfort. I needed to hear them. I didn't know my sister at all.

"Thanks for telling me that," I said.

"She knew everything there was to know about music, but I didn't realize till that private investigator showed me her picture that she was a serious violinist."

"A child prodigy," I said.

"How have you tried to find her so far?" he asked.

"All I know is that her name was Ann Johnson," I said, "which is not much to go on."

"She always went by Jade, though."

"Jade?"

"It was her nickname."

"So . . . maybe I should be searching for Jade Johnson instead of Ann?" I asked.

"I'd definitely try that." He looked far below us, where two men had appeared on the field, kicking a soccer ball back and forth between them. "Was Ann Johnson her real name?" he asked. "I always wondered."

I shook my head. "Please don't ask me to tell you her real name. I just can't." I stared down at the men, one of them heading the ball toward an invisible goal. "I'm so scared for her," I said.

"Why?" he asked. "Is something going on now that's making you afraid? I mean, I'm assuming if she's still on the run, she's been safe for a long time."

"What's going on now is that I'm trying to find her," I said, "and I don't want to screw up her life in the process."

"All right," he said. "I get it."

"Do you still have records on your employees from back then?" I asked. "Is there a way to get her Social Security number?" A Social Security number would be like gold, but he shook his head.

"Sorry. Those hit the dustbin a long time ago."

"Do you have any idea where I should look?" I asked, point-blank.

He hesitated, but not for long. "As far as I know, she went to Portland to stay with her girlfriend, Celia," he said. "Whether that lasted or not, I don't know." He looked at me. "You know she was gay, right?"

My look must have told him I'd had no idea. "I'd never heard a word about that," I said. "But then, there was a lot I never heard about in my family." It took me a moment to recover from the surprise, only then realizing that he'd given me two new pieces of information: "Portland" and "Celia."

"Do you know Celia's last name?"

He shook his head. "I knew her grandfather, Charlie, really well. His last name was Wesley, but he was on her mother's side."

"Can I talk to Charlie?"

He shook his head. "He passed away years ago," he said. "Good man. He left me all his vinyl, but I'd closed the store by then. He never talked about Jade after she left, and I never asked questions. I figured the less I knew, the better."

"I'm trusting you to keep this quiet." I pressed my finger to my lips.

"You can trust me," he said. We looked down at the bright green field for a long moment. "Here's what I think," he said finally. "I think if Jade's made a new life for herself, you should leave her alone."

My eyes stung. He was probably right, but I couldn't do that.

"I need my sister," I said, when I thought I could trust my voice. "I thought she was dead. I just want to . . ." What *did* I want? Was I going to hurt her by finding her? I felt my lips tremble. "I need my sister," I said again.

He rested a big hand on my shoulder then, nodding. "I think you'll do the right thing," he said. "And if—when—you find her, tell her Grady says hello."

43.

I was able to get a standby flight out of San Diego the following morning. I'd considered flying to Portland, but what would I do once I got there? Portland was a big city and I had so little to go on. I stayed up half the night searching the Internet for a Jade Johnson, thinking that would be much easier than finding Ann, but I was wrong. There were over eighty Jade Johnsons on Facebook alone. I studied their pages until my eyes ached and I finally fell asleep with my computer wide open.

I had to change planes in Charlotte, and as I waited for the puddle jumper to New Bern, I checked my phone for messages. Only one, and it was from Jeannie. "I'm concerned about you," she said. "I'm stopping over tonight to check on you. Don't worry. I won't be staying and I won't be doing any work there, but I don't feel good about the way we left it the other day—a lot of hard feelings on both sides, I think—and I just need to make sure you're okay."

I groaned. I should call her. Tell her I was fine and not to come over. We could talk next week. But I didn't even feel like speaking to her answering machine, much less to her. I'd deal with her later.

My flight was late and I tried to doze sitting up in the chair, but all I could think about was my conversation with Grady.

She was an awesome girl.

Every time I remembered him saying that about Lisa, I smiled. Suddenly, I felt as though I knew her. Hearing about her from my parents, or more recently from Jeannie and Caterina, had never had that impact on me. But now I knew she was *awesome*. Grady hadn't based that assessment on her musical ability. He hadn't even known about that. He'd based it on the person she was, separate from her violin. That was the person I wanted desperately to find.

44.

Jeannie didn't even knock before walking in the front door early that evening. After my blowup the other day, I would have thought she'd have the sense to at least knock before barging in, but no. I was sitting barefoot on the living room floor surrounded by piles of paid bills and statements and tax documents pulled from the cabinets. I'd already filled two big black trash bags with paper I'd have to shred later, but I didn't want to take the time to do it now. If there was something—anything—related to Lisa in those cabinets, I wanted to find it. So far, I wasn't having much luck. Most of the documents were ancient utility bills and medical records I saw no point in keeping.

"Well!" Jeannie stood in the middle of the room, smiling. "I see you're finally making some real progress."

I glanced up at her, but said nothing. She was dressed in white slacks and a navy blue blazer with a gold TOP REALTOR pin on the lapel.

"Maybe you just needed a little space from Christine and me," she added.

"You're right." I shoved another fistful of paper into

one of the trash bags. "I needed some time on my own, that's all."

"I understand. Oh! Look at this!" She'd spotted the photographs I'd taken with me to San Diego where they now lay on the coffee table. She picked up the picture of Lisa standing back-to-back with Matty, locks of their hair tangled together. "Is this the most darling photo or what?" she asked.

"It really is." I had to agree.

"I haven't seen this picture in a long time," she said. "They look like Siamese twins here, don't they? That's what they were like. You hardly ever saw one without the other." The pink of the setting sun poured through the window and across Jeannie's smile. "She's wearing the necklace I gave her," she said.

I'd been about to toss another stack of papers into the trash bag, but lowered my hand to the floor.

"What did you say?" I asked.

"This necklace." Jeannie tapped the picture with her fingertip. "I gave it to her. It's jade. Lisa always wore it, and that touched me so much. It had Chinese symbols carved on the front and back. They meant 'long life' and 'joy,' or something like that."

I set down the stack of papers and leaned back on my hands. "I was told that one of her violin teachers gave her that pendant," I said.

"Told by whom?" Jeannie frowned.

"I don't remember," I said. I was certain that's what Caterina had said—that the teacher who had "ruined" Lisa's playing had given the pendant to her. Of course, maybe Lisa had lied to Caterina. I knew for a fact that my sister was not the most honest person.

"What teacher?" Jeannie asked. "Steven Davis? Caterina Thoreau?"

"The one in between them," I said. "I heard—or maybe I read somewhere—that Lisa went away to study with another teacher and that's the one who gave her the necklace."

Jeannie stared at me and I couldn't read her expression. "Well." She looked flustered. "Maybe I have it mixed up with another necklace." She quickly set the photograph back on the coffee table.

"Do you know who it was?" I asked. "The teacher Lisa went away to study with?"

"I really don't recall very much about those days," she said. "It was so long ago. Christine had taken off with a bunch of her friends to live overseas, and I was beside myself worrying about her." She looked pointedly at her watch. "And now I've got to run. I just wanted to stop in to be sure you're doing okay. I'm thrilled to see you're making progress and I know Christine will be happy to hear it."

She left without saying good-bye. If it had been anyone else, I would have thought her behavior in the last few minutes was very strange, but given that it was Jeannie, it seemed in keeping with her character.

With a shrug, I went back to pulling paperwork from the cabinets, setting aside anything that looked important from the last three years, and tossing the rest. But as I worked, I wondered which story about the pendant was the truth. Did it really matter, though? I couldn't imagine why.

I'd nearly reached the last cabinet, the one closest to the wall of vinyl records, by eight o'clock. I had five garbage bags full to overflowing in the middle of the living room. I'd found absolutely nothing to give me a clue to my sister's whereabouts, but I had a sense of accomplishment at finally getting this task off my list of things to do.

I had to move the big upholstered armchair aside to get into that last cabinet, and as soon as I opened the door, I knew this one was different. There were actual file storage boxes inside, three of them, not a loose paper to be seen, and I was instantly filled with sadness. These must have been my mother's files. On the front of the first one, she'd written the word *Appliances* in her distinctive handwriting. On the second box, *Kids*. On the third, *Marriage License, Insurance, Misc*.

I pulled out the *Kids* box and set it on the floor. I felt the tiniest flash of fear at the possibility of finding adoption papers inside, but I no longer believed a word out of Verniece's mouth. I didn't know what her motivation had been to feed me tales. Maybe it had been part of her and Tom's diabolical plan to wear me down.

I lifted the lid and saw that the box was crammed full of file folders. Again, seeing my mother's neat writing on the tabs of each folder made my heart contract. I tugged out the file containing our old report cards. Danny's and mine were the usual computerized cards, but my sister's were handwritten forms that must have been used in homeschooling. I'd been a model student, according to my elementary school teachers' comments. Danny, not so much, and I felt terrible reading about his difficult childhood, especially from my perspective now as a school counselor and knowing how he'd been lied to—manipulated, really—by our parents. *There are all sorts of abuse,* he'd told me.

I read the comments from his teachers. "Danny wants to be good, but he lacks self-control, leading to fights with other students and misbehavior in class." I read only two years of his report cards before shoving them back into the box. It was too painful to think of how he must have felt, knowing deep in his heart that his sister had killed someone but being told he was "misremembering."

In the box was a thick white folder devoted to Lisa. Awards she'd won. Certificates of Achievement. I was reading through that file when I noticed the heading at the top of the next folder: *Birth Certificates.* I remembered reading that Internet article that suggested looking at your birth certificate to figure out if you were adopted. That felt like months ago now rather than a couple of weeks. *Check your place of birth,* the article had suggested. I reached into the folder and pulled out our three certificates. Lisa and Danny both had been born in Mount Vernon Hospital in Alexandria, Virginia, but my birth certificate told a different story. "Place of Birth: Mission Hospital, Asheville, North Carolina." I stared at it in confusion for a moment before remembering the first time I'd seen the certificate. I must have been about ten years old and I remembered asking my mother why I'd been born in Asheville. *Daddy and I were visiting Mrs. Lyons in Asheville when you were born,* she'd told me. That had made perfectly good sense to me at the time, but suddenly I thought it strange. I was eight and a half pounds when I was born. I couldn't have been very early. My parents had lived in northern Virginia then. Would they have traveled six or seven hours from home so close to my mother's due date?

They found a baby girl being put up for adoption here in North Carolina, Verniece had said.

A feeling of horror began to wash over me. I remembered meeting Christine for the first time. The way she'd gripped my hands. The way she'd proclaimed, *You're so pretty, isn't she, Mom?*

"Please, no," I said out loud. I thought of Christine's wavy dark hair, so much like my own.

I stared at my birth certificate awhile longer, looking at my parents' names. I desperately wanted them to be my biological parents! I had to know. I had to. I reached for my phone.

45.

Jeannie was in the middle of writing up an offer for a house buyer when I called her, but she must have caught the quaking of my voice because she said she'd be over the second she was finished. I spent the next hour shredding my father's dated utility bills and medical records. It was blessedly mindless work and slow going, and I'd only made it through one of the trash bags by the time Jeannie pulled into the driveway.

I opened the door and walked barefoot onto the porch, watching her as she got out of her car and hurried up the sidewalk, her white blouse neon bright in the darkness.

"What's going on?" she asked, shading her eyes against the porch light with her hand. "You sounded upset on the phone."

Wordlessly, I sat down on the top step and she climbed up to sit next to me. "What's the matter?" she asked.

"I found a copy of my birth certificate." I looked at her squarely. "Tell me the truth, Jeannie. Is Christine my mother? Are you my grandmother?"

Her eyes flew open. "No!" she said. "Of course not! Why on earth would you think that?"

"Don't lie to me!" I snapped. "I can't handle any more . . . lies and deception."

"What are you talking about?"

"I was born in *Asheville*," I said. "I'd forgotten that, but I just found a copy of my birth certificate. Verniece said my parents found a baby to adopt in North Carolina. How do you explain my being born in Asheville when my family lived in Virginia?"

Jeannie looked into my dark front yard, not speaking right away. "Christine left home when she was seventeen," she said finally. "She was living in Amsterdam when you were born, most likely so stoned she didn't know her own name. She's only been clean a few years, now. That's one reason why this estate sale work is so important to her. She wants to make a career out of it. She needs that."

"Oh," I said quietly, aware that Jeannie had revealed something painful to me. I was too wrapped up in my own thoughts, though, to pursue it. "Then why does it say Asheville on my birth certificate?" I asked. For a fleeting moment, I thought Jeannie herself might be my birth mother.

She looked toward the street again and let out a heavy, defeated sigh. "Lisa never went away to study the violin," she said. "She was living with me in Asheville, waiting to have her baby." She turned toward me, her face ghostly white in the porch light. "To have *you*."

It took a moment for her words to sink in. I felt queasy, the porch spinning around me, and I gripped the edge of the step to make the world hold still. "Oh, no," I whispered. I stood up, ignoring the dizziness as I walked blindly down the steps and onto the dark lawn. The grass felt strange and cool beneath my bare feet. I took a few steps toward the street, then turned to look at the house I'd grown up in. The living room windows glowed with a golden light, and the porch light illuminated the ornate trim and a patch of peeling yellow paint. All of it blurred in front of me. I'd led a counterfeit life inside those four walls.

Jeannie's gaze was on me and she perched half on, half off the top step as though she might need to run to my side any moment to hold me up. She was saying something, but she may as well have been in the next town. No words could make it through the buzzing in my head.

I sank onto the lawn, only vaguely aware of Jeannie rushing down the steps toward me. How could my parents have kept this from me my entire life? I'd been lied to. Whispered about. They were never going to tell me the truth.

But then I thought of Lisa, who had never had the chance to live in this house. What fear and pain she must have endured. What shame and embarrassment. And her *career* . . . No wonder her playing had suffered. There was no mystery teacher. Only a mystery child. Me.

Jeannie had reached my side. I heard her hard breathing as she sat down next to me in her crisp Realtor suit and rested a hand on my shoulder. "Are you all right?"

I looked wordlessly at the sky. The stars and moon were nothing more than a fog of light and dark.

"No one ever wanted you to know," she said softly.

I shut my eyes, holding still until I could find my voice. "What happened?" I asked finally, looking at her. "They sent her away when she was pregnant and told everyone she was studying with another teacher?"

"That's exactly it," she said. "Deb—your mother—called me in tears and asked if Lisa could live with me during her pregnancy. With her being so famous in music circles, Deb and Frank were worried about her getting a lot of negative attention and ruining her career. She was already four months along when she told your parents. At first she planned to put her baby up for adoption, but as she got closer to her due date, she realized she couldn't do it. So your parents decided to adopt the baby—adopt *you*—when you were born." She raised her hand to my cheek to brush away a strand of hair. Her touch felt tender. "Lisa stayed with me a couple of months after you were born so it wouldn't seem so obvious to the rest of the world that the baby was hers. And they told Steven and everyone that she'd decided to study with someone else for that period of time."

I was too stunned to say a word.

"You have to forgive your parents," Jeannie said. "They'd always planned to tell you the truth when you were old enough to understand, but with everything that happened with Lisa—the charges against her and her suicide—they felt it was best for you never to know any of it."

"So . . . you *were* the person who gave her the pendant."

She nodded.

I thought of the photograph on the coffee table inside the house. Lisa and Matty. *Like Siamese twins,* Jeannie had said. "Was Matty my father?"

The reflection of the porch light bounced in her eyes as she nodded. "We always thought so, though Lisa adamantly denied it, so your parents never talked to him or his parents about it. Lisa said it was a boy she met at one of the music festivals she went to. The one in Rome. I suppose that's possible, but Lisa and Matty were so inseparable, and when you were born with that full head of dark curly hair, we all just assumed. They were so young, her and Matty. They may have been . . . I don't know, experimenting or whatever. She never told him, as far as I know. She talked to him on the phone a lot when she was with me, but I'd overhear her telling him about violin techniques she was learning, when the truth was, she barely picked up the violin while she was in Asheville. She was quite depressed." Jeannie's voice cracked. "I always wished I could have helped her," she said. "Done more for her. She probably should have been on medication."

"I need to get that picture," I said, standing up. The muscles in my legs shivered as I walked toward the house. I climbed the porch steps and walked into the living room. It felt like days had passed since I'd been in that room, going through the cabinets. I picked up the photograph of Lisa and Matty from the coffee table. It suddenly seemed even more precious to me and I held it tenderly. When I brought it outside, Jeannie was sitting on the top porch step again, blotting her eyes with a tissue. I sat down next to her, holding the picture on my knees so that it caught the light. That curly mop of Matty's hair seemed like a dead giveaway. "Do you know where he is?" I asked.

"Matty? I have no idea. He was still studying with Steven Davis right up until Steven's death, as far as I know."

"His last name is Harrison, right?"

She nodded, then rested her hand on my knee. "Lisa was a good girl, Riley," she said. "She became very dear to me while we lived together. I felt like I'd failed with Christine and I really wanted to help Lisa, and she was so easy to be with after dealing with my own difficult daughter. She helped around the house while I worked. I was an accountant for a group of doctors' offices in Asheville. I had a dog and he got so attached to Lisa, he nearly ignored me, and he grieved for her when she left. So did I, actually." She smiled. "I got to know her very well. Probably even better than your parents did, because she felt like she could be more open with me than with them. You're a counselor. You know how that is sometimes."

"But she didn't tell you if it was Matty?"

"And I never pressed." She changed position on the hard step. "That's how I got her to talk to me," she said. "By not pushing her. I loved her." Her eyes clouded over again. "I was sad when she returned home. I missed her. She was such a dear soul."

How could she leave me? I thought, feeling more alone than ever. *She faked her suicide and left me and never looked back.* How could I ever move past that fact? But I couldn't say any of that to Jeannie. She still thought Lisa was dead.

"Were my parents angry with her?" I asked. "For getting pregnant, I mean?" With a jolt, I realized that my father had been my grandfather. My mother, my grandmother. Danny was actually my uncle. I hugged my arms across my chest, suddenly terribly sad. In the space of a few minutes, I'd lost the family I'd known. I'd lost my only brother.

"If they were angry, they didn't let me see it. Once they accepted what was happening and made the decision to adopt Lisa's baby, I think your mother was excited."

"Were you there when I was born?" I asked.

Jeannie hesitated, then sighed, as though she'd made

up her mind to answer any question I had. "Let's go inside," she said. "I can't sit on this hard step any longer."

I followed her into the house and we circled the hulking trash bags to reach the couch. She sat down heavily, taking the photograph of Lisa and Matty from me to look at while she talked.

"She called me at work one morning to say her water had broken and the contractions were starting," she said. "She knew what to expect, because we'd talked about it a lot. I called your parents right away so they could set out for Asheville. They left Danny with some friends. Your parents didn't make it in time. I was able to stay with Lisa in the delivery room. I can't lie and say it was a piece of cake. That she didn't suffer. She was afraid and so was I, but we muddled through together." She smiled into the distance and I knew Jeannie really had loved my sister. My *mother*.

"And then she cuddled you," Jeannie said. "Covered you with kisses. I don't think she would have been able to give you up for adoption to anyone other than her own family. She couldn't have parted with you. She loved you very much."

I blinked back tears at the thought of Lisa cuddling me.

"Her pendant." Jeannie pointed to the photograph. "I gave it to her right after you were born," she said. "I lied when I told you what the Chinese symbols meant. The symbol on the front actually meant 'mother' and the one on the back meant 'daughter.' She said she'd never take it off."

When Jeannie left, I sat on the couch in the dark living room, staring into space. I was more numb than anything else. I had a living, breathing mother somewhere.

Now I wanted to find her more than ever, but she didn't want to be found.

Then, as I sat there in the dark, I began to think about the living, breathing *man* who was, in all likelihood, my father.

46.

I found him.

Despite his relatively common name, Matthew Harrison was easy to track down. Still sitting on the couch at one in the morning, computer on my lap, I discovered his professional Web site and dozens of photographs of him. He wore his hair almost exactly as he had as a teenager—in a thick mop of dark curls—and he was a good-looking man with a killer smile. He was forty, the same age Lisa would be now.

He lived in Baltimore and taught at the Peabody Conservatory at Johns Hopkins University. I stared at his pictures for over an hour, searching for—and easily finding—myself in his features. He was married with twin daughters, his biography said. Were they my half sisters? Did I have family living in Baltimore? I searched for pictures of those twin daughters every way I could think of without success.

All that nearly sleepless night, I kept getting out of bed, turning on my computer, and staring at the man I thought was my father. I began to think of what I'd say to him when I spoke to him, because I planned to call him first thing in the morning. I absolutely had to. He'd been so close to Lisa. Did he know she was still alive? Could he know where she was?

At seven-thirty, I made coffee, my nerves jangling as I watched it brew. I carried a cup of it into the living room, sat down on the couch, and anxiously waited until nine before calling the conservatory.

"Oh, Mr. Harrison just left for Japan with a youth group," the woman who answered the phone told me. My heart plummeted, and I felt momentarily confused, still picturing him as the kid in the photograph—a teenager traveling with a youth group—when he was more likely their teacher. "You can leave a message on his voice mail, though I don't believe he'll be checking it until he gets back in two weeks," the woman said. "Would you like me to transfer you?"

"It's urgent," I said. After a night of planning this call, I didn't see how I could put it off another minute, much less two weeks. "Is there a way to reach him now?"

"I'm afraid not," she said. "I can give you his work e-mail address if you like."

"All right," I said. I jotted down the address she gave me, knowing I wouldn't use it. This was not a conversation for e-mail. I was afraid of hitting send and never hearing back. I'd have to wait for his return.

That night, I lay in bed, my eyes squeezed shut, thinking of how my world had changed in the last couple of days. I wanted my old life back, the one where I knew exactly who I was, but that life was gone.

I gave up on sleep and turned on my night table lamp. Next to the lamp was the novel I'd barely touched since leaving Durham and, next to that, a day-old copy of the

New Bern newspaper, the *Sun Journal*. Craving distraction, I picked up the paper and began leafing through it. At the bottom of one of the pages, I spotted an ad for an upcoming concert in Union Point Park—the same ad I'd found taped to the wall of my father's RV, with the same photograph from that postcard addressed to Fred Marcus. Jasha Trace. Two men and two women stood on a narrow path that stretched forever through a field. Each carried an instrument: a banjo, a guitar, a mandolin, a violin. And the violinist wore an oval-shaped white pendant.

I sat up quickly, sucking in my breath. Leaning my elbow on the night table, I held the grainy photo under the light. I should never have thrown that postcard away. What had been handwritten on it? Suddenly I remembered what Tom had said about the aliases used in the Witness Protection Program. *We try to give them a name with the same initials,* he'd said. Frank MacPherson. Fred Marcus. Owner of the PO box. Both of them, my father. *Oh, my God.* Daddy'd been in touch with Lisa! He knew this was her band.

I jumped out of bed and pulled on my shorts and T-shirt, cursing myself for giving the Kyles the key to my father's RV. I remembered the bag of keys Christine had left for me in my father's office. Racing into that room, I switched on the light and moved things around on the shelf until I found the small plastic bag. I shoved it in my pocket as I headed downstairs. In the kitchen pantry, I looked for the flashlights Daddy usually kept there. Christine must have moved them, no doubt sticking a price tag on them in the process. I would have to do without.

Outside, the air was still. Even the crickets and frogs were asleep. I got into my car and drove through the darkness to the RV park, pulling as quietly as I could onto the gravel lane, turning out my lights as I drove onto the cement pad next to my father's RV. The park was quiet and dark, the trees blocking the moonlight. Turning on the overhead light in my car, I searched through the keys, trying to remember what the key for the RV had looked like. I found a couple of possible candidates and clutched them in my hand as I got out of the car.

I used my cell phone to light the RV door as I tried the first key. It fit, though it took some jiggling before the door creaked open. Inside, I turned on the weak light that ran above the kitchen counter, relieved that the interior of the RV looked the same as it had the last time I'd been inside. Tom hadn't touched it yet. There was the row of CDs bookended by rocks, and the newspaper ad was still taped to the wall next to the picture of the little girl and boy. I pulled the photograph of the children from the wall. I had no idea who they were, but they'd meant something to my father. The picture was going with me.

I searched through the CDs. There were three by Jasha Trace. Each of the jewel case covers had a different photograph of the four musicians, and in every picture, the violinist wore the white oval-shaped pendant. The photographs were somewhat stylized, making it difficult to make out the musicians' features even when I held the CDs directly under the light. The violinist's hair was not Lisa's white-blond, nor was it dark, but somewhere in between. The other woman's dark hair was short on the sides, but it fell over her temple in the front. Both of the men—one dark-haired, the other blond and wearing glasses—looked a little shaggy, their hair dusting their collars.

I opened one of the jewel cases and pulled out the booklet inside. It contained page after page of lyrics, and the musicians' names were listed at the bottom of each song: *Jade Johnson*. Yes! *Celia Lind. Travis Sheehan. Shane Lind*. Celia's husband? Maybe Jade and Celia were not a couple after all?

I carefully pulled the ad from the wall and held it under the light. *Jasha Trace. Free Concert in Union Point Park. July 13 8 p.m.*

I touched Lisa's face, then the pendant with the Chinese symbols. *Mother* and *daughter.* I pressed the picture tightly to my heart and sat there for a moment, my eyes shut.

My mother was coming to New Bern.

47.

Back at the house, I listened to the CDs while I sat at my father's rolltop desk, searching the Internet for Jasha Trace. I tried to separate Lisa's voice from Celia's as I listened to the music, unsure which was which and wishing I knew. Some of the songs were rousing, while others were achingly pretty, a poignant sound track for the information I was discovering. Details were easy to find now that I knew which Jade Johnson I was looking for. They were less easy, though, for me to read.

Jasha Trace had a Web site with a biography of each member, and I read the fiction of Lisa's life. Jade Johnson had supposedly grown up in Los Angeles, the only child of a doctor and a nurse, both of whom were conveniently deceased so no one could possibly verify the story of her childhood. She learned to play the fiddle at the age of thirteen and taught herself several other instruments over the years. She'd lived in Portland for a few years before relocating to Seattle in 1999, where she'd been a fiddle-playing busker at Pike Place Market and the manager of a café. She lived with her wife and musical collaborator, Celia Lind, and their two children.

Her wife. Her two children. I stared at the photograph

of the little boy and girl I'd taken from the wall of my father's RV. Lisa's children? Was I related to these two red-haired little kids? How had my father gotten this picture? These CDs? Had he stayed in touch with Lisa all these years? Had they communicated through the post office box?

There was an excellent picture of the whole band on the Web site. Forty-year-old Jade Johnson looked so different from the old pictures I had of Lisa. I guessed she'd dyed her telltale white-blond hair brown all these years. She was somewhere between plain and pretty and she appeared to wear no makeup, although she must have dyed her pale eyebrows to match her hair and used mascara on her blond lashes. In the one close-up picture I found on her bio page, I saw that her eyes were a vivid blue, like Danny's. She wore a wide smile that gave her a carefree and confident look.

I continued searching through the Web site, and then landed at Wikipedia, where I was able to piece together a bit more of Lisa's life.

Jasha Trace

Jasha Trace is a Seattle-based American folk group made up of Jade Johnson, Travis Sheehan, and siblings Celia and Shane Lind. Although they played music together most of their adult lives, the foursome did not perform in public until 2006. Their first appearance was at Spoon and Stars, a café Johnson manages in Seattle. Their name, *Jasha Trace*, came from combining the first letters of each of their names. They describe their music as "Celtic Scottish Bluegrass." Celia Lind and Johnson collaborate on the songwriting and the foursome works out their arrangements together.

Jade Johnson and Celia Lind, who self-identify as lesbian, were married December 29, 2012, a few weeks after same-sex marriage was legalized in the state of Washington. They have two children, Alex born in 2001 and Zoe born in 2004. Lind is the biological mother of both their children, and Johnson legally adopted them shortly after their births.

I stood up from the rolltop desk and walked around the room, hugging myself, my fingernails digging into my arms. I felt hurt. Cast aside and forgotten. The sadness that had dogged me since Daddy's death and the breakup with Bryan washed over me with full force. I felt so alone. I'd been an unwanted complication in Lisa's life. She'd created a new future for herself. A new family. The last thing she'd want now would be for her past to crash into her present.

The pink light of dawn drifted through the living room windows and I was exhausted, physically and emotionally. I sat down at the desk again. Behind me, I heard the CD player click noisily from the second CD to the third, and another Jasha Trace song began, the sound of the band now familiar to me.

Love you, Celia.

The words suddenly popped into my head, and I sat up straight, remembering them from my father's e-mail. I'd thought he might be having an affair with a woman by that name. Maybe I'd been way off base.

Jumping to my feet, I raced up the stairs to his office, where the computer still sat on his desk—I'd never gotten around to cleaning the drive on that thing. I turned the computer on and typed *newbern* in the password field, nearly holding my breath as I waited for the old machine to chunk to life. It took me a few minutes to find Daddy's e-mail and a few more minutes to search for messages signed *Celia*. There weren't many e-mails from her, and I read them the way they came up in the search, in reverse chronological order, spread over many years.

May 18, 2012
That is the best birthday card ever. You are amazing!
Love you, Celia.

I looked in his sent file to see if he'd sent the birthday card via e-mail, but he didn't seem to keep much of the mail he'd sent. The next e-mail from Celia was from four years earlier.

February 7, 2008
F, it was so kind of you to send that note. I know you didn't know Charlie, but he meant so much to J and me—including the fact that he introduced us. It hurt J that she couldn't go to the service in San Diego, but it was way too risky. We are fine. Love you, Celia.

I remembered that name: Charlie. Grady had mentioned him. He was Celia's grandfather. Daddy must have been in very close contact with Lisa to know about him and to know that he had died. I searched, but I couldn't find a single e-mail that appeared to be from Lisa. I had the feeling he'd deleted hers but was less concerned about these few from Celia.

July 26, 2006
F,
J made her plane. She has to change in Charlotte. She's very upset. Take care of her, please.
Love you, Celia

I stared at that one for a long time. My mother died on July 28, 2006. Suddenly, an incident that had always mystified me made sense.

I'd stayed home with my mother every single day after my high school graduation, turning down a waitressing job because I didn't want to leave her side. Hospice was involved by then and I knew she didn't have long.

The day before my mother died—the twenty-seventh— my friend Grace asked me to go with her to the beach. I told her I couldn't; I needed to stay with Mom. Grace actually cried, nearly hysterical. She said she needed to get away for a few hours. She needed to talk about a problem she was having with her boyfriend. My father said it wasn't good for me to be cooped up at my mother's bedside every day and he insisted I go with Grace.

Grace and I lay on the beach for a couple of hours while she told me about a truly ridiculous fight she'd had with her boyfriend. She didn't sound all that upset about it and I was annoyed that she'd talked me into leaving my mother because she wanted someone to hang out with at the beach. I confronted her about it, angry. I called her selfish, and she finally said, "Don't blame me! Blame your father! He called me last night and told me you needed a break and I should make up some excuse to get you out of the house for the day."

I panicked. Was today the day my mother would die? Did he somehow know that and not want me there? I grabbed my towel from the sand. "We're going home!" I said to Grace, and started for my car at a run.

An hour later, we were back in New Bern. I dropped Grace off at her house, then drove to mine. There was a strange car in our driveway. I parked at the curb and was crossing the yard when Daddy came rushing down the porch steps toward me.

"What are you doing home?" he asked. He was pale, his face drawn as though he'd lost weight overnight.

"Grace told me the beach was your idea!" I said. "Why did you want me gone? What's going on?" I started to walk past him, but he stepped in front of me, grabbing my shoulders.

"You need a break, Riley," he said. "It's not good for you to be here, day in and day out."

"Who's here?" I asked, nodding to the car in the driveway. I looked up at my mother's window and saw a face that disappeared so quickly I might have imagined it. "Who's that?" I asked.

"Just one of the hospice nurses." His voice shook. That terrified me.

"Is Mom dying right now?" I asked. Then a fresh fear ran through me. "Is she *dead*?"

"No, no, honey." He pulled me close to him. He smelled of sweat. The scent made me think of exhaustion more than exertion.

"I don't care about taking a break, Daddy," I said. "I want to be with Mom."

He looked me straight in the eye. "Listen, sweetheart. You've been wonderful with her. You've been such a help and she knows how much you love her. But you've been here every minute since school ended, and the truth is, your mom and I need a day together. Just the two of us. Please don't be hurt by that. We just—"

"Oh." I felt embarrassed that I hadn't thought of that myself. "I wish you'd told me. I would have understood."

"I was afraid—"

"It's okay. I'll just . . ." I looked toward my car, pondering my next move. "I'll go over to Grace's. What time . . . when can I come home?"

He pulled his wallet from his pants pocket, took out a couple of twenties, and pressed them into my hand. "You and Grace go out on the town tonight." He nodded toward the house. "Give Mom and me till ten or eleven. Okay?" He smiled, and I was relieved to see his pallor disappear.

I hugged him. "Tell Mom I love her," I said.

I was sure now that he didn't tell her. I was sure he didn't mention my name at all when he returned to the room where my two mothers sat. I pictured them holding hands.

I remembered coming home that night. My mother seemed different to me. Lighter, somehow. She smiled when I came into her room to kiss her good night, and I thought, *Daddy was right. They needed a day together, just the two of them.* Now I knew it had been the visit with Lisa that had put the smile on her face. In spite of the fact that I felt hurt over being left out of that family reunion, I was grateful to Lisa for making it happen.

The very next morning, Mom was gone. Daddy and I ate a lonely, tasteless dinner that night. I told him how unfair I thought it was, that out of a family of five only three of us were left. "It's just you, me, and Danny now, Daddy," I'd said, and he'd turned his head away from me.

Back then, I thought he'd turned away because my words were too painful to hear, and I regretted them. Now I realized he'd turned away because he knew they were not the truth.

October 2, 2004

Mr. M (I'm not sure what to call you),

I wanted to let you know J's in the hospital. She lost the baby yesterday morning. It was another boy and we are both brokenhearted. The doctor has no idea why this happened, but I'm sure I know—she's so worried about Danny and it's taken a toll on her. She hasn't been the same since you let her know how badly he was hurt in the attack. She's so afraid he won't make it. The night after she got your note, she carried her fiddle out on our patio and played "Danny Boy." It was so beautiful. Some neighbors who heard her play it told me they cried. Of course they didn't know about Danny, but they knew something terrible must have happened for her to play so mournfully.

She thinks it's her fault. She knows that's irrational, but that doesn't make any difference. She's never been sure there's a God, but now she suddenly is and she thinks He's punishing her. First, her mother's cancer diagnosis. Now Danny's injuries. She's paranoid that something bad will happen to R next. I wish you could actually *talk* to her. She really worships you and is so grateful for how you helped her. My family loves her so much, but all our love can't make up for everything she's lost—and of course, my family doesn't actually *know* how much she's lost.

She talks about R a lot now. I know you don't want her to have a picture of her, but she could use it right now. She feels so lost. It doesn't matter how many children we have, there will always be a place in her heart reserved for R. The other night, she put on that pendant that reminds her of R and said she's never taking it off again.

If you think it would be safe, you could talk to her

on my cell phone instead of hers. Or maybe you have
another idea?
Love, Celia

That was the last e-mail from Celia. Or I guess it had
really been the first. I was sorry to hear that Lisa had
lost a baby, but I knew that one line from the e-mail
would be swirling around in my head for days: "It
doesn't matter how many children we have, there will
always be a place in her heart reserved for R." Was there
still a place for me in Lisa's heart? Was there room? I
needed to find out.

48.

Between searching the Internet for Lisa and reading Celia's e-mails, I'd been up the entire night. I went to bed at seven in the morning, exhausted and excited. I lay there unable to sleep, knowing that I could no longer keep what I'd learned to myself. I had to share it with the one other person who'd understand how I felt. The one other person who had loved Lisa . . . and who—unlike my brother—I was certain would never cause her harm.

I waited until eight o'clock before dialing Jeannie's number. I paced the living room floor, cell phone to my ear. "Please tell me I didn't wake you," I said when she answered.

"I'm up." She sounded worried. "What's wrong?"

"Are you home? Can I come over? I need to talk to you." I hadn't been to Jeannie's house, but I knew exactly where it was.

"I'll come there," she said. "I'm dressed."

"Could you?" I was glad for the offer. I didn't trust myself to drive.

"I'll be there in a few," she said.

I brewed a pot of coffee and sat on the couch, so tired

I felt as though I might be dreaming. I must have drifted off, because I didn't hear Jeannie's car pull into the driveway and I jumped at the sound of the doorbell. Morning light poured into the living room when I opened the front door.

"My God, honey, you look like hell." Jeannie ran her hand down my arm as she came inside. Her touch was warm and concerned, and it made me want to trust her.

I shut the door, then stood with my back to it. "Lisa's alive," I said, nearly whispering as though I was afraid someone might be able to hear me.

She opened her mouth to speak, but couldn't seem to find the words. I could tell she'd had no idea. My father'd kept her in the dark as well.

"I know," I said. "It's a shock."

"It's *impossible,*" she said finally.

"She faked her suicide."

Her hands flew to her cheeks. "Oh, my God!"

"I'm sorry I didn't tell you sooner, but I was afraid. I didn't know who to trust."

Jeannie sank onto my couch as though her legs had turned to liquid. "I just can't believe it," she said. "Your poor parents! Your poor *father*! All these years, he grieved and—"

"He knew," I said. "He helped her."

She stared at me and I saw the hurt work its way into her face. I knew how she felt. We'd both been duped. "How do you know?" she asked finally. "How was he involved?"

I started at the beginning, holding nothing back as I told her how my father and Tom Kyle had helped Lisa escape. How she'd changed her name to Jade and lived in San Diego and met Celia. I told her what I'd learned about her current life from Celia's e-mails and about their two children.

"This is . . ." She kept shaking her head. "It's just so crazy."

I sat next to her with my laptop and pulled up the Jasha Trace Web site. When the photograph of the band appeared on the screen, Jeannie gently touched the pendant at Lisa's throat.

"Unbelievable." She shook her head. "Just . . . extraordinary."

"Check this out, Jeannie," I said, clicking on the link to their tour schedule. I handed the computer to her, resting it on her lap. "They're coming to New Bern Saturday night."

Her eyes were huge blue marbles in the light from the computer screen. She looked at the schedule, then at me. "Why would they do that?" she asked. "Isn't it risky?"

"I'm sure they planned it so they could see Daddy," I said. "Lisa may not know he's dead." I went to the Google Web site, holding my laptop so she could see all the links that popped up for Jasha Trace. "I guess they're well-known in bluegrass circles."

"Wow." Jeannie looked at the list of links. She pointed to one of them.

"What's this page?" she asked.

"That's a site where you can share photographs, I think," I said, clicking on the link.

A page of tiny images popped up, and when I clicked on the first photo, I knew right away where the pictures had been taken: Lisa and Celia's December wedding.

"Oh, my," Jeannie said as we scrolled through the pictures. "I can't get over the fact that she's gay. I guess Matty was just an aberration. She looks so happy, doesn't she?"

She did. I wanted to be glad for Lisa as I scrolled through the pictures of her dancing with Celia, laughing with friends, hugging her son and daughter, but with every new photograph, I fought the gut-roiling sense of being forgotten.

"Oh, my *God*!" Jeannie said suddenly as a new image appeared on the screen. "Look!"

I saw what she was referring to even before she pointed to the top right-hand corner of the photograph: my father, sitting at a table, chatting with an elderly woman.

"He was *there*?" I sounded as though I was asking a question, although there was no doubt about it. Daddy had been at the wedding.

Jeannie scrolled through more images, leaning hungrily over my computer. My father was in a few of the photographs, usually off to the side talking with someone. In one picture, though, he laughed with Lisa. In another, he danced with a woman I was sure was Celia's mother, and in yet another, he was on the keyboard with the band, a wide grin on his face. I shook my head in hurt wonder over my father's secret life.

"When did you say they got married?" Jeannie asked.

"December twenty-ninth." I'd spent the week between Christmas and New Year's with Bryan at his parents' house in New Jersey, worrying the whole time that I'd deserted Danny and my father over the holidays. I usually divided my time in New Bern between the two of them, but I knew Danny didn't really care about Christmas and Daddy had encouraged me to go with Bryan. I'd still felt guilty and called every day. Sometimes my father didn't answer his phone and I pictured him napping to ward off depression over being alone for the holidays. Instead, he'd been in Seattle, dancing, chatting, and jamming with the band at his daughter's wedding.

"I suggested to him that we get away that week." Jeannie sounded equally stunned. "But he said he had a funeral to go to in Seattle. One of his close collector friends."

"He lied to you," I said. "There was no funeral." I was surprised by the anger I felt. It was one thing to protect Lisa by keeping me in the dark about what had actually happened to her. It was another thing entirely to be an active part of her family while leaving me behind.

Jeannie suddenly stood up, raising her arms in the air in a gesture of frustration.

"Why didn't he ever *tell* me, for heaven's sake?" she asked. "He knew he could trust me!"

I understood her pain completely. "I feel like"—I hunted for the words—"like Lisa and Daddy did everything they could to keep her existence—and their relationship—a secret from me." My voice locked up, and Jeannie looked down at me.

"I can't imagine what this is like for you," she said. "I feel so . . . *betrayed* myself. It's got to be a thousand times worse for you."

It was a *million* times worse, and I felt like I was going to crawl out of my skin. I set the laptop on the coffee table and stood up, needing to move. Needing to do something to erase the image of Daddy and Lisa laughing together, three thousand miles away from me. "I know this is irrational," I said, "but I feel almost as though they were laughing *at* me in those pictures."

Jeannie walked over to me and put her arm around my shoulders. "No, honey, now you know that's not true, don't you?" she asked.

"I don't know *what*'s true anymore," I said.

"You sit." She gave me a little shove toward the couch. "I smell coffee. I'm going to get us both a cup. Then we'll be able to think more clearly, all right?"

I nodded, flopping onto the couch again. I tried to empty my mind while I listened to Jeannie rooting around in the kitchen, but the images of my father at the wedding were burned into my brain and I couldn't get them out.

I spotted an e-mail notification on my laptop and clicked on it, surprised—and fearful—when I saw it was from Danny. I opened the mail.

Come over tonight. I have something to show you.

I stared at his message. This couldn't be good. Danny was much more sophisticated than I was when it came to using the Internet. If he believed Lisa was alive, who knew what he'd been able to find?

Jeannie was back in the room and she nearly missed the coaster as she set my mug on the coffee table in front of me. "She was terrified of prison, Riley," she said, lowering herself to the other end of the couch. "After the . . . you know, the shooting and everything, Deb would call me up, so worried. She'd say that Lisa couldn't sleep and she cried all the time. She felt so guilty that she'd taken a life, and she was afraid of being in prison with . . . you know . . . hardened criminals. If your father offered her a way out, she must have jumped at the chance. It was foolish of him, but I guess he was desperate to protect her. We have to forgive them both." She lifted her mug to her lips, but set it back on the table again without taking a sip. "Did Deb know, do you think?"

I held the warm mug between my palms. "I don't think she knew until just before she died," I said. "Lisa came here to see her." I told her about the brief e-mail from Celia telling my father that Lisa had made her plane, and then I began to cry. "I feel so *alone,* Jeannie," I said. "Totally alone. Dealing with all of Daddy's stuff." I waved my hand through the air of the living room. "And I feel responsible for Danny now. I worry about him all the time and I'm totally alone with that, too. Meanwhile, Lisa's surrounded by a happy, healthy, smiley family. Children and a partner and all those friends and Celia's family and I have no one!"

"Oh, sweetheart." She moved closer to me, taking the mug from my hands and setting it on the table. "I wish you could remember Lisa from when you were little. She doted on you. She adored you." She patted my hands where they rested limply on my lap. "You have to get in touch with her. You know that, right?"

I nodded. "I just don't know the best . . . the safest way to do it. And Danny can't know. He already thinks something's up, but if he knows for sure she's alive, he'll tell the police and that will be the end of her."

"He'd do that?"

"He really hates her. He blames her for everything that went wrong in our family."

"You could e-mail her," she said. "There's that contact information on the Web site."

"Who knows where that goes?" I said. "I have to be really careful. That e-mail probably goes to their band manager or something. I do have Celia's e-mail address from Daddy's computer, but I—"

"You need to tell Lisa you know she's alive," Jeannie said, "and that Frank passed away and that you'll find a way to meet up with her when she comes to New Bern."

I shook my head. "It can't be done by e-mail," I said.

"If she doesn't reply, I'd never know if she got my e-mail or if she just wanted nothing to do with me."

"You're right, you're right," she said quickly. "Somehow, you'll have to talk to her in person at that concert, then. I want to be there, too," she added. "I need to see her."

"Let me do this alone, all right?" I asked. "It's going to be hard enough with only myself to worry about."

She sighed, nodding reluctantly. "All right," she said. "I'll settle for just being there in the crowd." She broke into a wide smile. "I still can't believe this! When you talk to her, please tell her I'm relieved she's alive and well. That I'm glad she found the happiness she deserves and let her know that I love her."

I envied Jeannie for being able to see past the deception to feelings of warmth and love. The image of Lisa laughing and dancing, as though she didn't have a care in the world, would be with me for a long, long time. I didn't know what I would say when I was finally face-to-face with her. I was so afraid of seeing her. Of scaring her. She might turn away. Turn *me* away. But I remembered Celia's e-mail to my father, how she'd written that there would always be a place in Lisa's heart for me. She'd written those words years ago, but I'd hold on tight to them. I needed them to be the truth.

49.

At seven o'clock that evening, I drove through the dusky forest to Danny's clearing, determined to reveal nothing of what I'd learned. I wouldn't let him trip me up. I was only worried about what this thing was he wanted to show me . . . and I figured that out the moment he opened his trailer door to let me in.

The music on his laptop wasn't loud, but it was very familiar to me after listening to it nonstop for most of the day. Danny's computer was on the counter, and the Web site photograph of Jasha Trace was on the screen. The picture of Lisa and the group stared me in the face as I walked inside.

"Okay." I surrendered, standing with my back against the door. "What's going on?"

He sat down at the kitchen table. "Good ol' Verniece," he said. "She really wants the RV park."

I swallowed. *Damn it.* "What are you talking about?" I asked, lowering myself to the bench across the table from him.

"You can lose the innocent act," he said. "They couldn't talk you into turning over the park to them, so she tried to get it through me." He ran his hand over his short blond beard. "I didn't tell her that (a) I don't care about the park and (b) I don't have the legal authority to give it to her without your involvement . . . although I have to say I was surprised to learn that *you* had had no problem keeping me out of your dealings with her and Tom."

"Oh, Danny, I'm sorry." I felt my whole body sag in defeat. "I was desperate to find out what they knew."

"And what you didn't want me to know, right?"

"Do you blame me?" I asked. "You and I have different ideas of what should happen to Lisa. And how did you figure out about—" I pointed to the laptop, where Lisa was in the middle of a fiddle solo. "Jasha Trace? How could you . . . ?"

"I took a look inside our father's RV," he said. "Do you believe our old man?" He laughed, but there was nothing funny in the sound. "I always knew he worshiped her, but I'd really underestimated just how much. Anyway, I had to break the lock to get into the trailer. And I think you beat me to it, right?" He waited for me to answer, but I kept my expression stony and blank. "I found a newspaper ad on his table about the concert coming up," he said. "I saw there was a violinist in the group and she had on a necklace like the one Lisa used to wear. Daddy had all this bluegrass music there, but none of that band, which made me wonder . . ." He tilted his head, eyes on mine. "Did he have some of their CDs and you took them?"

I hesitated a moment, then nodded.

"I had to pay iTunes eight bucks for this CD."

"Danny . . ."

"Once I had her name, it was easy to find out everything else." He shook his head, and I recognized the hurt look on his face. It was the same expression I saw that morning in the mirror. "She's made one hell of a life for herself, hasn't she."

"Danny." I folded my hands on the table and leaned toward him. "I'm pleading with you. Please leave her alone."

"I wasn't sure how much you'd been able to find out on your own, but the way you've been avoiding me the last few days made me think you knew plenty," he said. "And when I opened the door a few minutes ago and you heard the music . . . Your face gave you away."

"Have you talked to Harry about it?" I'd lowered my hands to my lap and was anxiously rubbing them together.

"Not yet."

"What are you going to do?" I asked.

He didn't hesitate. "I'm going to tell Harry he can solve a cold case the night of that concert. He can be a hero, and Lisa will finally get what she has coming to her."

"Danny"—I was very close to crying—"she's not hurting anyone."

I might as well have been speaking Greek. "You don't seem to get it, Riley," he said. "Leaving aside all the crap she put our family through, she *killed* a man. If it was an accident—which I think is bullshit—she'll finally get to have her day in court. It'll be complicated by the fact that she ran off, of course, but still. And if you sincerely want to help her, you might line up a good criminal lawyer for her in Virginia."

"Damn it!" I pounded my fist on the table. "Can you leave it alone? Please! It's not only Lisa's life you're tampering with," I said. "It's her children's. It's her family's."

"*Most* criminals have families," he said. "That doesn't

give them a 'get out of jail free' card." He reached out to touch my fist, gently unfolding my curled fingers until they lay flat on the table. The gesture felt tender and it gave me hope. "What is it you want from her, Riles?" he asked quietly.

"I want to meet her," I said. "That's all I want. Just to meet her. What I *don't* want is to hurt her."

He withdrew his hand from mine with a sigh. "She killed someone," he said again, sounding tired. "That's the bottom line. She killed someone and she has to pay."

I stood up and walked to the door. "Will you promise me something?" I asked. "Just one thing?"

"What's that?"

"Think about this awhile longer before you talk to Harry."

"The concert's only a couple of days away," he reminded me.

"I know. But you can wait, can't you? What difference will it make if you tell him tonight or the day of the concert?" I opened the door. It was dark outside now, and when I turned to look at him, the trailer light illuminated the sharp angles of his face and the translucent blue of his eyes. "It's important that you think it through before you act," I said.

"I don't need to," he said. "I've done enough thinking."

I looked at his computer where it rested on the counter, the image of Jasha Trace a bright light in the dim trailer. Lisa stared at me from the life I was no part of.

I turned back to my brother. "There's something you don't know," I said quietly, using the only card I had left to play. "Something you couldn't have figured out, no matter how skillful you are at searching the Internet."

"What's that?" he asked

I swallowed hard. "Lisa's my mother," I said.

Two sharp lines creased the space between his eyebrows. "What the hell are you talking about?"

"It's the truth," I said. "Jeannie told me. Lisa's my mother. She had me when she was fifteen. Mom and Daddy adopted me."

"*Shit,*" he said, and his face softened, but only by a small degree.

I knew that wasn't going to be enough.

50.

When I left Danny's trailer, I drove straight to Jeannie's small, one-story white brick house in the DeGraffenried neighborhood. She was dressed in a blue robe when she opened the door, and it only took a glimpse of my face in the porch light to let her know something was very wrong.

She reached for my hand and drew me inside. "What is it?" she asked. "What's happened?"

"Danny knows everything."

"You *told* him?" She looked shocked, and I told her how he'd come to learn the truth about Lisa. I spoke so quickly that my words tumbled over one another.

"Will he go to the police?" she asked.

"He hasn't yet, but I know he plans to."

We were still standing by the front door, and now she motioned me into the room. "Come in," she said. "Let's calm down so we can think."

I walked into her softly lit living room and felt a jolt at seeing our old baby grand piano nestled in the bay window. I dropped onto an armless upholstered chair, my head tipped back to look at the ceiling. "I have to warn her," I said. "He plans to tell Harry Washington . . . do you know him?"

She nodded. "He's a good guy. Why Harry?"

"They're friends. He wants Harry to arrest her . . . or at least apprehend her at the New Bern concert. I'm not sure *what* Harry will do exactly, but if Danny tells him, I'm sure he'll have to do something."

"You have to e-mail Lisa, then," Jeanne said. "You really don't have much of a choice."

I looked out the window into the darkness. "Unless I could find a phone number for her," I said, "but she's probably unlisted. And she's on the road right now anyhow." My heartbeat sped up at the thought of calling her. Telling her who I was. I would scare her to death. What if she hung up on me? I was too chicken to risk a hostile response. Lisa had managed to fly under the radar for over twenty years until I started digging into her life.

Suddenly, I seized on an idea. "Her tour schedule!" I said. "It's on their Web site."

Jeannie stood up and walked toward the door to get her briefcase. "Let's look," she said, pulling her laptop from the case and carrying it to the couch. I moved from my chair to a seat next to her, and we were quiet as I guided her to the Jasha Trace Web site.

"There's the schedule," I said, pointing to the link.

She clicked on it and I quickly scanned the dates. Tonight they had off. Tomorrow night they'd be at Dulcimer, a little club I'd been to a couple of times in Chapel Hill, and the night after that was the New Bern concert. "I have to go to the one in Chapel Hill," I said. Chapel Hill was only a few hours from New Bern and right next to Durham. "I can spend the night in my apartment."

"What will you do?" Jeannie asked slowly, and I

guessed she was trying to imagine the scene, the same as I was. "What will you say to her?"

I sat back on the couch, gnawing my lip as I thought. "I'll tell her about Danny," I said. "That he knows. That he won't leave it alone and that his best friend's a cop. She'll have to decide what to do from there." I pressed my fingers to my temples, rubbing hard. "And I'll apologize," I said. "It's my fault she's in danger, Jeannie," I said. "I never should have tried to find her."

"You didn't know what you were getting into," she said. "You're hardly to blame."

I stared into space, unconvinced. I doubted Lisa would see it that way.

"Do you want me to come to Chapel Hill with you?" Jeannie asked.

I thought about it. It was strange that Jeannie was the person I felt safest with these days. "I should go alone," I said finally. I tried to imagine approaching Lisa at Dulcimer. I tried to imagine the look on her face. It wouldn't be welcoming. "I can't believe I'm going to do this," I said, my apprehension mixed with excitement.

"You need to."

"I'm nervous." I glanced at her. She was watching me intently. "I'm afraid she'll act like she doesn't know me. Turn me away. That would be the worst. Maybe she'll sic security on me."

Jeannie leaned forward to rest her laptop on the coffee table. "Come with me," she said, getting to her feet.

I followed her through the dining room to a small sunroom. A large desk stood at one end of the room, and a love seat and two chairs, upholstered with palm trees and monkeys, sat at the other. Beneath the windows along one wall was a row of white built-in cabinets, similar to those in my father's living room.

She turned on a floor lamp, then squatted in front of one of the cabinets. She rooted around for a moment, finally pulling out a small album. "Have a seat." She nodded in the direction of the love seat as she stood up again. I sat down on the love seat and she pulled one of the chairs close to me and opened the album.

"I used to be good about putting pictures in albums, before everything went digital," she said, holding the album so the floor lamp illuminated the pages. "Now I've gotten lazy." She gave a small laugh. "Anyway, these are mostly from a trip I took to California." She turned the pages without stopping to look closely at the photographs. "But I remember there are a couple from the year Lisa stayed with me, and there's one in particular I want you to see."

She turned a page and I spotted a picture of Lisa, her hair as pale as her skin, decorating a Christmas tree. She wore black leggings and an oversized blue sweater. I pulled the album closer to me. She was clearly pregnant.

"She was about six months there," Jeannie said.

"Oh," I whispered. Lisa smiled at the camera. It wasn't a full-blown smile of joy, but it was an expression that told me she was at ease with the photographer. With Jeannie.

"Unfortunately, that was the only picture I kept of her from when she was pregnant," Jeannie said. "She was camera shy then, for obvious reasons. But this is the one I wanted you to see." She turned the page and I saw Lisa in a hospital bed, the requisite blue and white hospital gown slipping off one shoulder, a dark-haired baby in her arms.

"That's you," Jeannie said.

Lisa's eyes were closed, her face at peace, her head

turned so that her cheek rested on my temple. The gesture spoke volumes. She'd loved me. She'd treasured me.

Jeannie lifted my chin with her fingertips until I was looking at her through my damp, blurry vision. "She's not going to turn you away, Riley," she said gently. "I am completely sure of that."

51.

I tried listening to an audiobook as I drove the two and a half hours to Chapel Hill the following day, but at least two thirds of the novel was lost on me. If Jeannie hadn't been with a client today, I would have called her to help steady my nerves. She told me to call tonight after I saw Lisa, no matter what time it was. "I'm not going to be able to sleep till I hear from you anyway," she said.

I couldn't believe it: tonight I would see Lisa. I'd gone over and over my plan in my mind, but it depended on so many things working to my advantage. Mostly, it depended on Lisa being willing to see *me,* and that was a huge unknown.

The traffic bogged down when I reached the Beltline around Raleigh. I passed the turnoff I used to take to go to Bryan's apartment, and for the first time since our breakup, the memory of him didn't tear me in two. I'd barely thought of him in days, I realized. The two years I'd spent waiting for him to officially end his marriage suddenly seemed like a colossal waste of my time.

A car on my right honked at something or someone, and I hoped it wasn't at me. I brought my attention back to the road. I was very early. I'd be in Chapel Hill by a little after five and the doors at Dulcimer wouldn't open until seven. I could spend the extra time finding someplace to have dinner, though the way I felt right now, I doubted I'd be able to eat. I'd sit in my car and wait, instead, thinking through every possible scenario that might come up as I waited to see Lisa.

The rush hour traffic clogged the streets of Chapel Hill, yet I managed to find a parking place only a block from Dulcimer. I turned off the ignition and wondered what to do next. It was five-twenty. My plan was to see the concert and then find Lisa backstage . . . but maybe I could track her down now, since I was so early? Bad idea, I thought. How could she perform after meeting up with me? Besides, I wasn't ready yet. I wondered if I would ever be ready. Once Lisa's world and mine collided, there'd be no going back.

With the air-conditioning off, my car quickly grew intolerably hot and I lowered all four windows. Chapel Hill was a college town and the sidewalk was filled with students, their chatter loud and lively as they passed by my car. They looked and sounded so much younger than me. In the last couple of months, I felt like I'd aged a decade.

In the distance, I saw some people in front of Dulcimer and suddenly wondered if the show might be sold out. Even though I'd never heard of Jasha Trace, it was clear from their Web site that they had quite a following. I began to perspire, from both the heat as well as from that new, unsettling thought. I raised my windows, then reached into the backseat for Violet's case. Bringing her along had been a last-minute impulse. I got out of the car, my purse over my shoulder and Violet in my arms as I headed in the direction of the club.

It was a little after six and the box office was open. I bought a ticket easily—so easily that I felt sort of hurt for Lisa that Jasha Trace wasn't going to have a sold-out performance after all. Stepping away from the box office, I looked up and down the street to determine my next move. There was a small music store a few shops away from where I stood and I ducked inside, hoping to find something to occupy my mind until the doors of the club opened.

I imagined Grady's record store had been something like this one, cramped and hot. I pictured Lisa working in that tight little space. She'd only been seventeen when she arrived in San Diego and I could only imagine how alone and frightened she must have felt. My own stomach was cramping from nerves right now, and I was twenty-five and not on the run from anyone or anything. How had she survived the fear? How had she survived the guilt of having killed someone?

I tried to get my bearings in the store, but was overwhelmed by the press of bodies and the eardrum-piercing music. I clutched Violet to my chest as I maneuvered my way through the narrow aisles toward the door. Outside once more, I walked a block to an empty bench on a patch of green lawn, and sat there, Violet on my lap, pulling my phone from my purse every few minutes to watch the time tick closer to seven.

By five after seven, I was inside Dulcimer, where rows of folding chairs faced the raised platform that served as a stage. The room was smaller than I remembered, and high redbrick walls made it feel even tinier. The occupancy sign on the wall read 150. Both of the concerts

I'd seen at the club had been general admission, and Bryan and I had stood shoulder to shoulder with other members of the audience, so I was surprised—and relieved—to see the chairs. I didn't think my legs would hold me up for the length of a concert tonight.

Standing near the concession booth, I looked toward the stage. The platform was elevated only a foot or so off the worn wooden floor of the club. A drum set and keyboard had been pushed against the back wall as if unneeded for this particular concert, but a couple of stools and a few microphones were near the front, along with a guitar on a stand. Seeing those props made everything real to me. In less than an hour, Lisa would be up there, only a few yards away from me. Finally.

I bought a beer and a paper container of nachos I'd have to force myself to eat, but I thought I'd better have something in my stomach to sop up the alcohol. People around me laughed and talked as they greeted one another. It was clearly a crowd of regulars and I was aware of being the odd man out. I looked toward the seats, which were starting to fill. Should I sit in the front row where I'd be way too visible or in the back where I could watch Lisa unnoticed? I compromised, picking a seat smack in the middle of the room, and I sat there feeling very alone as I chewed a tortilla chip that tasted like cardboard.

The building grew noisier as it filled up, voices bouncing off the brick walls. I noticed that many people wore T-shirts with the letters JT emblazoned on the back, and it took me a good ten minutes to realize that *JT* stood for Jasha Trace.

I felt conspicuous, alone in my center row clutching Violet between my knees, but as more and more people filed into the seats, it looked like there would be a decent crowd. The young guy sitting to my right read the back of a Jasha Trace CD, pointing to something on the case as he spoke to the woman he was with. The seat to my left was empty, and I was glad for that little bit of breathing room.

To the right of the platform was a door that appeared to be the only way to get backstage. I focused on it, picturing myself walking through it. I was still staring at the door when a burly young guy dressed in black jeans and a black T-shirt took his post in front of it. A yellow plastic badge hung around his neck. Security, I guessed. I would have to get past him to get to Lisa.

I'd finished my beer and half the nachos by the time the houselights dimmed, and I put the bottle and paper basket beneath my chair, knowing I'd never remember to toss them when it was time to leave. I had the feeling they would be the last thing on my mind.

A middle-aged woman with a sleeve tattoo and short, bright purple hair took the stage. She talked about the exits we should use in an emergency, told us to silence our cell phones, and then spoke endlessly about the up-coming concerts, and the audience grew restless. Or maybe it was just me. The beer and chips sloshed around in my stomach and I wondered how I'd get out of this row if I needed to be sick.

Jasha Trace came onstage with zero fanfare—the men with their banjo and guitar, Celia with her mando-lin and Lisa with her fiddle—and started right in on a fast-paced song I recognized from one of their CDs. My heart raced along with the music. I couldn't take my eyes off Lisa. Her hair—a natural-looking blond-streaked brown—hung a few inches past her shoulders, and it was loose and swingy as she played. Her features were sharper than I remembered from the pictures I'd seen of her, and under the harsh lights above the stage, I could see fine lines across her forehead even from where I sat. All four musicians wore jeans and T-shirts. I was pretty sure Shane was the guy with the beard and Travis the one with the shorter cropped blondish hair and glasses.

Celia no longer wore that short edgy hairstyle that was on their Web site and CD covers. Now her dark hair was in a sort of bob, the razor-cut ends radically layered and choppy. It was a very cool cut that made her look younger and hipper than Lisa, and my heart cracked a little. Lisa's life hadn't been easy. Not as a child under pressure to perform, or as a fifteen-year-old giving birth away from her family and friends, or as a seventeen-year-old on the run. Yet when the song was over and she lowered her fiddle, her smile softened her face and I saw the light inside her. The joy over what she was doing. Over the life she'd created for herself. She started playing again, the bounce of her hair like a symbol of the freedom she'd stolen for herself. I looked away from the stage, lowering my gaze to the back of the chair in front of me, suddenly wounded. She had a healthy family and I didn't. I wanted to be happy for her, but I couldn't help it. That hurt.

I must have stared at the back of the chair in front of me for a good five minutes before I looked at the stage again, and it was as though I was finally hearing the music for the first time. They were good musicians, all of them. Lisa sang harmony, but the vocals really belonged to Celia and Shane. The fiddle, however, was Lisa's alone, and when she took off on a solo riff, she had the audience on its feet. I stood up myself, but my knees shook and I had to clutch the back of the chair in front of me to stay upright.

They took a break about an hour in. Holding tight to

Violet, I waited in line to use the too-small and over-worked restroom. I wanted the numbness another beer would give me, but I couldn't afford the foggy brain that might come with it, so I bought a bottle of water for the second half of the show.

When they took the stage again, my anxiety intensified as I realized I had no idea what time the performance would end. As they played song after song and the minutes ticked by, I began to panic. What if they rushed out of the building afterward? Ran from the stage to a waiting car in the alley behind Dulcimer? What if this whole trip had been for nothing?

And why had I stupidly picked a seat in the middle of a row?

I waited until the end of the next song before getting to my feet. Mumbling "Excuse me" over and over again, I stepped on toes and forced people to stand as I slid past them, trying not to whack any of them with the violin case.

The burly guy dressed in black had been leaning against the brick wall, watching the concert, but when he saw me heading for the stage door, he took two steps forward to block my entry.

I gave him the warmest smile I could manage, and he leaned over so I could speak into his ear. I had to shout to be heard, the music was so loud this close to the stage.

"I need to see Jade after the show," I said. "I'm her sister and I have her old violin." I thought it would be best to go with *sister* rather than *daughter,* although I was certain either word would set off alarm bells when Lisa heard it. The guy frowned at me and I remembered reading Lisa's online biography: *the only child of a doctor and a nurse.* I hoped he'd never read her bio. I smiled at him again. "I wanted to surprise her with it," I said.

"Let me check it out," he shouted into my ear, and I followed him to a narrow shelf on the wall near the door. I couldn't blame him. For all he knew, I was carrying a weapon in the case. I worried that Lisa might see Violet as exactly that.

I rested the case on the shelf and opened it. He didn't try to remove the violin, but felt all around it with his fingertips. Then he shouted, "Come with me."

I closed the case and followed him through the door into a corridor painfully lit by bare fluorescent bulbs in the ceiling. A few closed doors were to my left, and an open door on my right led into an office. The woman with the purple hair sat at a desk, and she looked up when the guard and I appeared in the doorway.

"What's up?" she asked.

"This is one of the band's sister," the guard said.

"Jade's," I said to the woman. "I live nearby and I brought her old violin. I thought she'd like to have it. Can I see her after the show?"

I could tell the woman wasn't buying it. "She didn't say anything about anyone coming."

"No, I know. I didn't think I'd be in town, but I am, so I wanted to surprise her." I was speaking quickly. I sounded like I was making up my story on the spot. Which I was.

"I checked the case," the guard said. "It's a real violin." He glanced down the hall. "I've gotta get out there," he said. He left me standing in the doorway as he retreated back the way we'd come.

The woman looked at the digital clock on the wall. "I'll ask her when she's off the stage," she said, getting to her feet. "Sounds like they're wrapping up now." I could hear the applause, louder than before. "What's your name?" she asked.

I didn't want to tell her my name, but could see no way around it. "Riley," I said.

"Okay." She walked past me. "You take a seat in here." She pointed to one of the two chairs near her desk. "I'll let her know."

I sat down and watched her disappear into the hallway. I was breathing fast and hard, my hands sweaty on the violin case. This wasn't going to work. She'd tell Lisa and Lisa would panic and escape before I had the chance to see her. I sat there for a few minutes, Violet on my lap. The applause wound down and I heard the sound of chairs scraping the floor and the hum of a hundred voices. I pictured Lisa leaving the stage. The woman with the purple hair approaching her. And then I couldn't stand it any longer. I stood up and rushed into the hallway to find my mother.

52.

Jade

Celia dropped onto one of the fake antique dressing room chairs. "I'm getting too old for this," she said, but she was grinning.

"Remember Bonnie Raitt," Jade reminded her, as she did whenever they felt tired. Bonnie was one of their musical heroes and, at sixty-three, still touring. Jade and Celia were more than twenty years younger. It was true that they were wiped out after every performance, but they were also having the time of their lives. Jade had known from the age of five how it felt to perform in front of an appreciative audience. There was no drug in the world that could get her that high.

"I want to call the kids before we get something to eat." Celia reached for her backpack. "The guys said they'd wait."

"Good idea." Jade snapped her fiddle case shut and set it on the floor next to her chair.

Celia was pulling her phone from her backpack when the woman with the purple hair—her name was Kat, Jade remembered—poked her head into the room.

"Jade?" she said. "There's a girl out here who wants to talk to you."

Jade fought a groan. There was nearly always some aspiring musician who wanted to talk to them after a show, maybe to tell them how much he or she loved their music or to get tips on making it to their level. It was both a rewarding and tiring part of touring. She glanced at Celia, who gave a nearly imperceptible shake of her head.

"Please tell her sorry," Jade said. "She can e-mail me if she—"

"She says she's your sister."

A chill ran up her spine. Whether it was anticipation or stark terror, she couldn't have said. She glanced at Celia, whose eyes were wide with fear.

"I don't have a sister," she said to Kat.

"I have Violet with me!" A voice came from somewhere outside the room.

Kat quickly stepped back into the hallway, pulling the dressing room door closed behind her. "You can't go in there!" she shouted.

"Oh, my God!" Jade was on her feet, heading for the door.

Celia stood up to grab her arm. *"No,"* she said. "Don't!"

She brushed Celia's hand away and pulled the door open. "Let her in!" she shouted to Kat. She tried to see behind Kat to the girl in the hall.

Kat reluctantly stepped aside and a young woman walked toward her. She was only slightly familiar. Her wavy dark hair reached her shoulders. She wore no smile and her brown eyes were apprehensive.

Except for a brief glimpse from her mother's bedroom seven years earlier, Jade hadn't seen Riley since her eighth birthday in that Morehead City restaurant. The woman in front of her could be an imposter, although her gut told her differently. Those dark eyes, the long lashes, the shape of her mouth—yes, this was her daughter. She reached for her and saw the fear leave Riley's eyes as she stepped into Jade's arms. Riley's body shook beneath her hands and Jade knew she was crying. She pressed her cheek against her daughter's hair, only vaguely aware of Kat quietly retreating into the hallway, shutting the door behind her, and of Celia's hand where it rested on her back. She knew Celia was afraid—and that she should be as well—but the only emotion she felt at that moment was the pure relief of once again holding her baby girl in her arms.

"It's all right, it's all right," she whispered into Riley's hair, the way she had when her daughter was tiny.

They stood that way for at least a full minute, though Jade knew it could never be long enough. The pure emotion would give way to conversation at some point, and conversation was bound to lead in a direction she couldn't bear, so she held Riley as long as she could. Finally, Riley pulled away from her arms, wiping her eyes with her fingers. Jade felt Celia's gaze on her, trying to read her face. She couldn't find her voice. Her hand was still on Riley's arm, her fingertips unable to completely let go.

"I brought you something I thought you might like to have," Riley said.

She recognized the case the moment Riley held it out to her. The beautiful worn leather. The old tag with the colored-pencil drawing she'd made of a violet.

"Violet," she whispered, reaching for the violin, but Celia abruptly stepped between her and Riley.

"This isn't good, Jade." Celia looked at her, her face contorted with worry. "You're acting like this is no problem. What are you thinking?"

She knew it wasn't good. She knew only terrible things could come from this meeting, but right then, she didn't care. *Let me have this moment, Celia,* she thought. Still, Celia stood like a wall between Riley and herself.

"I know everything," Riley said to her, as if Celia wasn't there.

Celia spun around to face her. "You need to get out," she said.

Jade put her hands on Celia's shoulders. "Look, she's here," she said firmly. "We can't change that. She's here and I want to talk to her. Please."

Tears welled up in Celia's gray eyes. So rare, her tears. She wrapped her hands around Jade's wrists where she gripped her shoulders.

"It'll be okay," Jade said in an empty promise. She let go of Celia and turned back to Riley. "Come here," she said, guiding her to one of the chairs. "Sit down and tell me what you mean about knowing everything. How could you possibly . . . ?" Her voice trailed off. She hoped Riley *didn't* know everything. There were some things she never wanted her to know.

Riley glanced at Celia, and Jade realized she was afraid to speak in front of her.

"It's all right." She pulled a second chair close to Riley's and sat down on it, their knees almost touching. "There are no secrets here."

"Jeannie." Riley clutched the violin on her lap. "She told me."

Jeannie. Hearing her name alone was enough to make Jade miss the woman who had helped her through one of the toughest times of her life. "Oh, Riley," she said. "I'm so sorry you—"

"Daddy died about a month ago," she said. "I didn't know if you knew."

"I did," she said. "I sent him a postcard about our tour and when I didn't hear from him, I got worried. I found the obituary online." She'd cried for days. She owed him so much. He'd taken enormous risks to give her a life of freedom, and although he resolutely never spoke to her about Riley, he'd been her only link to her daughter. "I'm sorry," she said. "Were you really close to him? I know so little about you. He never let me know anything about—"

"What do you *want*?" Celia interrupted, her gaze riveted on Riley. She still stood near the door, and she sounded icy cold, the way she did when she was scared. "You two are chatting like you don't have a care in the world."

"Shh, it's all *right,* Celia," Jade said, then looked back at her daughter. "I've wanted to see you—to *be* with you—your whole life," she said. "I hope you understand—"

"Celia's right," Riley interrupted her. "Everything's *not* all right. I came here to warn you." Her knuckles were white on the violin case. "Danny knows everything," she said. "He blames you for so much. It's irrational, but that doesn't matter. He has a good friend who's a cop, and he plans to tell him who you are. I think the police will be waiting for you at the concert in New Bern."

There wasn't a sound in the room. Jade's blood turned to ice in her veins and her heart thumped hard in her ears. Standing out of her sight, Celia was so still Jade wouldn't have known she was there.

"I feel like it's my fault," Riley said. "I told Danny I thought you might be alive before I realized . . . everything, and once I did, I tried to keep him from discovering what I'd found out, but—"

"You *told* him?" Celia accused. "What, exactly? What did you tell him?"

"*Celia,*" Jade chided, but her whole body trembled. "Please."

The door suddenly opened and Shane stood in the hallway, Travis a step behind him.

"Did you talk to the kids yet?" Shane asked. "We're starving."

Jade looked at Celia. "You go. I need to talk to Riley."

"I'm not leaving you here," Celia said.

Travis looked from Riley to Jade and back again. He and Shane had to feel the tension in the air of the room. "What's going on?" he asked.

"Who are you?" Shane asked Riley.

"She's a friend." Jade stood up, her hands trembling as she picked up Celia's mandolin case and backpack and pressed them into her arms. "You all go eat. I'll get a cab to the hotel later."

"No." Celia shook her head. "I'm staying."

Jade gave her a pleading look. She knew Celia was as terrified as she was. She wanted to tell her she understood, but there was no time. She needed to talk to her daughter. Now. Alone.

"Please, Celia," she said.

Celia took a step toward the door, but stopped to look back at Riley. "I don't know what you've heard," she said, "but Jade's a good, good person." Jade saw those rare tears in Celia's eyes again as she left the dressing room. She probably felt as Jade did, that their whole life together had been heading toward this moment. Heading for an inevitable catastrophe.

She closed the door behind Celia and the men, then

turned to face Riley. "Should we go someplace?" she asked. "I don't know how long we'll be allowed to stay here."

Riley shook her head. "I don't want to talk in public," she said. "Let's stay here until they throw us out."

53.

Riley

"You're so beautiful," Lisa said.

Seeing her in front of me, seeing her humanness and feeling the love in her touch, made me feel incredibly guilty. "I'm afraid I'm ruining everything for you," I said.

"Let's not talk about that right now," she said firmly. "Right now, right this minute, I'm not in prison. I'm here with you, and I want to know everything there is to know about you." She sat forward in the chair. "I search for you on the Internet constantly, but it's like you don't exist," she said. "I check Facebook at least once a month. There are a bunch of Riley MacPhersons, but I can tell none of them are you. One of them has a nature picture as her profile instead of a picture of herself, though, and I always wonder, 'Is that her?'"

For the first time all day, I smiled. I felt a thrill, knowing that she'd searched for me. She'd guessed right: I was the Riley MacPherson with the photograph of a field of poppies as my cover picture and a spectacular rainbow as my profile shot. "That's me," I said. "I have to keep a low profile on social media. I'm a school counselor and the less the students I work with know about my personal life, the better."

"A counselor!" she said. "Oh, Riley, that's wonderful."

I thought of telling her that she became the inspiration for my career choice the day she took her own life, but I didn't want to talk about her deceit. I didn't want to talk about the choice she made to leave me.

"I love it," I said instead.

"That tells me so much about you," she said. "It tells me who you are, deep down inside. Daddy told me a little about Danny and how rough it's been for him, but he wouldn't ever tell me anything about you. I *do* know where you live, though," she said. "I found your address about a year ago. You're in Durham, right?" She rattled off my street address with startling ease.

I nodded. Some students had found my address, too. It wasn't hard to do. But I doubted that my students had it memorized and I felt both touched and unnerved that she did.

"I thought of writing to you a million times," she said. "I wanted to see you so badly, but there was no way to do that without risking everything. I would have sent myself—and Daddy—to prison." She swallowed hard, and I saw the effort it took for her to hold herself together at the thought of prison. "Now I guess it's going to happen anyway." She suddenly wore a faraway look. "At least they can't get to Daddy," she added. "Thank God for that."

"I'm so sorry I've stirred the pot," I said.

She shook her head as if clearing prison out of her mind. "Are you married?" she asked.

"No," I said. "I know you are, though. Jeannie and I

saw the photographs from your wedding. We saw Daddy there." I felt foolish saying the word *Daddy* in front of her when she knew better than anyone he was not my daddy at all.

"How could you possibly have seen the pictures?" Her eyes, the same clear blue as Danny's, were wide.

"They came up when I searched for Jasha Trace."

"Wow." She leaned back in her chair. "I never thought they'd be public like that. We weren't careful enough." She gave me a weak smile. "Having Daddy at the wedding was the most wonderful gift I could imagine, though, Riley," she said. "I hadn't seen him in so many years, and I could hardly believe he was there. We told everyone he was my uncle and he played along with it perfectly. He met our kids and they loved him." She looked at me quizzically. "Do you know I have children?"

I nodded, ignoring how much the question hurt.

"Alex and Zoe," she said. "I wish you could meet them. Daddy was so good with them at the wedding. I think he had a great time. He even jammed with the band. I hadn't seen that lighthearted side to him since I was a kid."

"I never got to see it." My voice trembled. My father's heart was already heavy by the time I was old enough to truly know him. Danny was right: Lisa and her fake suicide *had* destroyed our family.

Lisa bit her lip. "Oh," she said softly. "I'm sorry, Riley."

I drew in a breath, knowing I was about to make myself totally vulnerable. "When I saw those wedding pictures," I said, "I felt so left out."

She looked stunned. "Oh, *baby*." Her chair was close

enough that she could lean over and touch my hand. "Of course you did!" she said. "I'm so sorry."

I didn't want to cry. My mind scrambled to find a safer subject, but there were precious few. I thought of Matty. "After Jeannie told me you were my mother," I said, "I tried to call Matthew Harrison, but he's in Japan with a group of kids. Are you in touch with him at all?"

She looked puzzled. "Why would you call Matty?"

"He's my father, isn't he?"

She shook her head slowly. "Oh, no, honey," she said. "That was a boy I met in Italy. I'm embarrassed to admit that I didn't even know his name."

"Oh." I felt so disappointed. I'd wanted it to be Matthew. Someone I might have been able to meet. To know and to like. I sank lower into the chair, my hands still wrapped around Violet's case. Lisa didn't seem to know what to say any more than I did, and the silence filling the room was suffocating.

"Danny . . ." I said. "I never would have told him anything if I'd known he'd start digging for more information on you. I didn't realize there was so much to hide, and by the time I did, it was too late. He wants to see you pay. You have no idea how much he . . . hates you."

She tightened her lips when I said the word *hate*. "Please don't blame yourself," she said, but the look in her eyes was distant, and I knew she wasn't thinking about me at that moment. She let out a sigh. "I'll be back to looking over my shoulder every second, I guess," she said. "It's been a long time since I've had to do that." She shut her eyes as if collecting her emotions, and when she opened them again, her face was pained.

"This is so frustrating, Riley!" she said. "I want *time* with you and I don't know how to get it."

Her words lit a spark of anger in me—anger I hadn't even known was there.

"You could have had all the time in the world with me if you hadn't left." I tried to speak softly to take the sting out of my words, but she still looked hurt.

"I didn't want to be your mother from behind bars," she said.

"Maybe you wouldn't have had to serve that much time if you'd stayed for the trial," I said. "I know what happened was an accident."

"Please, Riley." She slowly shook her head. "Let's not waste our time together talking about this," she said. "Let's not talk about things that can't be changed."

"But if you'd had a good attorney, he—or she—could have defended you. They could have made the case it was an accident." I couldn't seem to let this go. I was suddenly so frustrated! I set Violet on the floor and stood up, pacing across the room. "Why didn't you stay?" My voice cracked. "Everything would have been so much better! You might have had to do some time, but I could have visited you. I could have *known* you. Danny would never have gone off the rails the way he did when he was a teenager. Maybe he never even would have gone to Iraq."

"Oh, Riley." She bit her lip again. "Maybe that's true," she said, "but I was too scared to take the risk. Daddy saw a way out for me. I trusted him to know what was best. And it ultimately turned out well for me. Until now."

"You mean until your daughter shows up and ruins everything." I sounded young and stubborn, like one of the adolescent kids I worked with, but I couldn't help myself.

"That's not what I—"

"Do you regret it?" I stood in front of her. "Running away?"

She hesitated long enough to tell me she didn't. "My life is far better than I deserve," she said, "but there's always been a huge hole in it. For you. For my family. I'm not just saying this because you're here. I thought I was doing the best thing for you. Giving you two loving parents. I didn't know Mom would die so young. I didn't know Danny would enlist and get hurt and suffer so much. I thought leaving was the best thing for you. The publicity . . . all the talk . . . it was already taking a toll on Danny. I didn't want it to take a toll on you, too."

"And you wanted to be free."

"Of course I wanted to be free!" she said, red splotches high on her cheekbones. "But not of you. Never of you. I love you."

I shook my head. "You got your freedom, Lisa, but Danny and I got a life sentence, living in a house full of lies."

She looked alarmed. "Call me *Jade*, Riley," she said as though she hadn't heard a word I'd said other than her name. "Please. You have to call me Jade."

I felt scolded. She could tell me she loved me all she wanted, but her actions said otherwise. They always had. Suddenly, I knew I had to escape that tight little dressing room. It hurt too much to be there with her.

I pulled the door open and charged out of the room before she could say anything else. I ran across the dark, deserted club floor and pushed through the double doors onto the sidewalk, gulping in the thick summer air. I started running toward my car as if I were afraid she might come after me, my feet pounding the sidewalk.

I was breathless by the time I reached my car, and I leaned against the warm metal door for a moment, my gaze riveted on the dark sidewalk as I watched for her to follow me, but she didn't.

Only then did I realize how much I wanted her to.

54.

Jade

She curled up in the chair in the corner of their hotel room while Celia paced the floor. Celia had held her when she got back to the hotel, letting her talk. Letting her cry. But now Celia was anxious to move on. She wanted to figure out their next step, while Jade's mind was still in that dressing room with Riley. She'd fantasized that one day, far in the future, she'd be able to talk to her daughter. In her fantasy, there was tenderness. Forgiveness and understanding. That had been unrealistic of her. She'd hurt Riley, and Riley was the last person in the world she'd ever wanted to hurt.

"Well, the first thing we have to do," Celia said, "is cancel that New Bern gig. We'll get a lot of flak for it, but we can't possibly—"

"No," Jade said.

Celia stopped pacing, looking at her like she'd lost her mind. "What do you mean, no?"

"What's the point, Celia? Danny hates me and he's friends with the police. He knows our schedule. He knows where we'll be. Even if we cancel the rest of the tour altogether, he knows how to find me now."

She scratched at a little stain on the arm of the chair. "It's over for me."

Celia sat down on the corner of the bed. "It's not just you this is affecting," she said. "It's me, too. Shane and Travis. Not to mention our kids."

She was right. Many years ago, Jade had spared herself and her family from a long-drawn-out trial and months—or years—of hurtful publicity, only to threaten her new family with something worse now. But you could only run so far from your mistakes.

"I know." Her voice came out as a whisper. "I'm so sorry. I know this messes things up for Jasha Trace."

"It *kills* Jasha Trace."

She cringed. Celia had been full of sympathy and comfort for the last hour. Now she was angry and Jade didn't blame her.

"I know it's going to be terrible for Alex and Zoe." Her voice broke on Zoe's name, but she kept talking. "There's just no way out." How would she ever explain it to their children? Would she be imprisoned in Virginia, thousands of miles from them? Her hand shook as she wiped tears from her eyes, and although she kept her own gaze on the arm of the chair, she felt Celia staring at her.

"There's got to be a way around this," Celia said.

"She's so hurt that I left her," Jade said. Those final moments with Riley were still on her mind. *I felt so left out,* Riley had said. She'd broken Jade's heart with those words. "She doesn't understand why I didn't stay so I could be involved in her life."

"Did you tell her the truth?"

Jade shook her head. *"Never,"* she said. She wondered how Celia could even ask.

"Maybe it would make a difference," Celia said. "Maybe she'd understand then. Right now, she's upset with you, and that's only going to make things worse for us."

"How can they be any worse for us?"

Celia didn't answer. She ran her hand over the puffy comforter on the bed, chewing her bottom lip. What could she say? Things were as bad as they could be.

"I have to try to talk to her tomorrow," Jade said. "I can't let things end on a sour note between us like they did tonight."

"Do you know where she is?"

"I have her address in my contacts." She looked into Celia's silvery eyes, so full of hurt. God, she was ruining everything for everybody she loved! "I hoped this would never happen." She shook her head. "I'm so sorry."

Celia stared at her for a long moment. Then she stood up and turned toward the window, looking out into the darkness. It was nearly two in the morning. Chapel Hill was asleep. So were Shane and Travis, in the room connected to theirs by a small living room. The men were blissfully unaware of how everything would change for them in the morning.

"We need to tell the guys," Jade said.

Celia didn't answer her. Instead, she lifted her backpack from the dresser and walked out of the bedroom into the living room. Was she going to tell Shane and Travis right now? Jade sat woodenly in the chair. She heard Celia moving things around in the living room for a few minutes, but she stayed where she was. Even when she heard the door to the hallway open and close, she didn't move . . . but she did breathe a sigh of relief. Celia wasn't going to tell them yet. Jade knew her well. Celia just needed time alone to think. She needed time to come to the conclusion Jade had already reached: it was over.

55.

Riley

After three weeks away from home, I felt like a stranger in my own apartment. When I got in, I lowered the air-conditioning and made my bed, moving on autopilot, trying not to think about the conversation with Lisa. I needed comfort food but my pantry was nearly empty and whatever I'd left in the refrigerator gave off a rank odor when I opened the door, so I made a cup of chamomile tea in the microwave, then forgot to take it out. Instead, I lay down on the couch and stared at the dark ceiling.

I kept picturing her face. The pale blue eyes. The sharp features. The lines across her forehead, especially when I'd gotten angry with her. I wasn't sure what I'd expected to happen during our meeting, but feeling anger toward her had been unexpected. Seeing her full life made the current emptiness of my own life stand out. That was hardly her fault, and I wished now that I hadn't acted like an obstinate adolescent, pushing her away before she could push me.

My phone rang and I pulled it from the pocket of my capris. *Jean Lyons,* the caller ID read. I'd wanted to talk to her but thought it was too late to call. I should have known she wouldn't be able to sleep, either. I was about to answer the call when a knock on my apartment door made me jump, and I sat up quickly. No one knew I was in town. No one except Lisa. And she knew where I lived.

The knock came again, much harder and more insistent this time.

I slipped my ringing phone back into my pocket and walked over to the door, leaning close to it.

"Who is it?" I asked.

"It's Celia, Riley. Please let me in."

I rested my hand on the dead bolt for a moment before turning the lock. Opening the door a few inches, I saw Celia alone in the hall light, looking pale and tired. I was sure I looked equally as bad.

"Why are you here?" I asked through the opening in the doorway.

"I need to talk to you," she said. "It's so important, Riley. Please let me in."

I hesitated. "Did Lisa send you?" I asked.

"No. I found your address in her contacts on her phone. I came on my own."

I knew she didn't like me and I was afraid of her reason for showing up at my door, but we both loved Lisa. We had that in common. I stepped back, opening the door.

"Come in," I said.

She walked into my small living room. She still wore her clothes from the concert, the T-shirt and jeans, but her hair jutted up as if she'd been running a hand roughly through it, and her face had lost every trace of the joy she'd exuded while she was onstage. I would hardly recognize her as the same woman.

"Can we sit?" she asked.

I nodded, lowering myself to the couch. Celia perched on the edge of one of the two Ikea chairs in the room, elbows on her knees as she leaned toward me.

"I'm sorry for how I treated you at the club," she said. "It's just that . . . I know you didn't mean to, but you've really messed up our lives."

I didn't know how to respond to that. It was the truth, but their lives had been dangling by a thread for years before I came along.

"I wanted to talk to you about your brother and his cop friend. Does he—Danny—care about you?"

"Of course he does," I said, "but it doesn't matter. Believe me, I can't fix this. If there was some way to do it, I would, but there isn't."

"Can you at least talk to him about it?"

"I *have* talked to him. It doesn't do any good."

"Maybe if Jade talked to him?"

I shook my head. That was a really bad idea.

Celia looked down at her hands. She twirled her wedding band around on her finger—a nervous-looking gesture—then raised her eyes to mine again. "I care about you, Riley, because you're Jade's daughter," she said. "I care about Jade more, though. I love her so much that I can't let you go on thinking she acted out of selfishness. No matter what happens to her or to Jasha Trace or to our family . . . no matter what happens, I can't let you feel that way about her. She was young. She thought she was doing the best thing for you by leaving you."

"I don't know how to get past that," I said honestly. "I don't know how to get past her walking away from me and then starting a whole new family for herself."

"Well . . ." She looked unsure of herself. "Maybe I can help you get past it," she said.

"How?"

She twirled her ring again, her gaze on the floor instead of me. Finally, she raised her eyes to mine.

"She was afraid of the trial," she said. "Afraid of what might come out."

My skin prickled and I said nothing, not sure I wanted to hear what she was going to say.

"Jade didn't ever want you to know any of this," Celia said. "She doesn't know I'm here and she'd be furious with me if she knew. But—"

"What are you talking about? She doesn't want me to know what?"

"Do you have a scar on your forehead?" she asked suddenly.

I nodded slowly. I lifted my bangs and leaned into the light from the table lamp.

Celia walked over to the couch and bent close to me, squinting. "It's barely visible, isn't it. That little scar."

I dropped my bangs over my forehead again, and she sat down on the other end of the couch. "What does my scar have to do with anything?" I asked.

"A lot, actually." She bit her lower lip, hesitating. Even when she opened her mouth, it was a moment before she spoke. "Steven Davis was your father," she said finally, the words coming out in a rush.

It took a few seconds for what she'd said to sink in. "Oh, no." I felt sick. "They were lovers?"

"No! God, no!" She looked horrified. "She had you when she was *fifteen,* Riley. He was forty. You could hardly call them lovers." Celia's cheeks were scarlet. "He *raped* her. She didn't think of it as rape back then. It took her years to realize that's what it was. Back then, she thought it was her fault. But he had total power over her. It happened when they were at a music festival in Italy."

She said something else, but her words were lost on me. I felt nauseous. All I'd eaten since breakfast were those nacho chips and a beer, and now the room began a slow dizzying spin around my head. I remembered the tape of the Italy trip. I remembered Steven Davis pointing his baton in Lisa's direction. How, at that small gesture, she stepped away from the group of students and performed for him.

"He asked her to come to his room to talk about a piece of music," Celia said. "Jade didn't want to go to his room alone and she got her friend Matty to go with her. But after they were in his room, Steven sent Matty on some errand and Jade was stuck alone with him."

The room spun wildly and I wasn't sure I could make it to the bathroom in time. "I feel sick," I said, getting to my feet, nearly stumbling as I crossed the living room. I shut myself inside the small hall bathroom, where I sat down on the closed toilet seat, my head lowered to my knees, hoping the nausea would pass.

I barely knew where I was. Durham? New Bern? My whole body felt strange, as though it no longer belonged to me. I was conceived during the rape of a barely fifteen-year-old girl by a man she'd trusted—a sick and repulsive man who was my father. How had Lisa felt every time she looked at me? Jeannie had said she'd cuddled me. She didn't want to part with me. Yet how could she not feel revulsion and anger each time her eyes rested on her "little sister"? I had to be a reminder of the worst time of her life.

"Are you okay?" Celia's voice came through the bathroom door.

"Yes." I sounded as weak as I felt. I stood up slowly. Splashing my face with cool water, I caught the briefest glimpse of my pale reflection in the mirror and looked away. I knew now where my dark hair and eyes came from and I didn't want to see them.

I opened the bathroom door. Celia touched my arm, tentatively, as if afraid I'd bat her hand away. "I'm so sorry," she said.

I wasn't sure I could walk all the way to the couch. Instead, I sat down on the carpeted hallway floor, my back against the wall. My phone cut into my hip bone and I pulled it out of my pocket and set it on the floor next to me. "Is that why she killed him?" I looked up at her. "Out of anger? It wasn't an accident?"

She sat down across from me. "What do you remember about that day?" she asked.

I shook my head slowly, afraid the dizziness would return. "Nothing," I said. "I was not even two, and I don't remember anything about it. Danny said I got the scar on my forehead that day, but I don't remember."

"I think it's good you don't," Celia wrapped her hands around her knees. "Jade said she was home alone with you, and Steven called to say he was coming over," she said. "He was the last person she wanted to see, of course. She hadn't been alone with him since . . . the day you were conceived."

I winced.

"She was terrified. She knew where your father kept the key to his gun case, so she got the gun, though she really had no plan to use it. It wasn't even loaded. She just wanted it close by in case he tried anything. Just to scare him. She left it in the den where she could get to it easily. Then she called Matty and asked him to come over, but Steven beat him there." She ran her fingertips over the short pile of my hallway carpet. "And do you know what Steven wanted?" she asked.

"Sex?" I asked weakly.

"No," she said. "He wanted his daughter. *You.* Somehow he figured out you were his child. His wife couldn't have kids, and he told Jade he planned to hire some high-powered attorney to get custody of you. He talked about how well he could provide for you and how he'd turn you into this great musician and on and on. She was so afraid, because whatever Steven wanted, he always got."

"So she killed him to stop him from trying to get custody of me?"

She shook her head. "No, Riley." She leaned forward, her hands flat on the carpet, her gaze on my face. "Ever since she was little," she said, "he'd abused her. Touched her. Fondled her. Whatever you want to call it." The angry scarlet color had returned to Celia's cheeks.

"Oh, no." I pressed my hand to my mouth as the dizziness returned. "Oh, how sick." I thought of the little girl with her tiny violin on the VHS tape. What price had she paid for her fame? That age-old question popped into my mind, *Why didn't she tell someone?* But I was a counselor, I knew the answer. He had complete power over her, like Celia had said. She'd been dependent on him for her lessons. For her future. He could ruin her with one phone call, which was exactly what he'd tried to do by keeping her out of Juilliard. My heart broke for the frightened and confused girl she must have been. I hated Steven Davis. I would never claim him as my father.

"So, they were in the living room and he was telling her how he was going to get custody of you," Celia said. "He convinced her he could do it, and she was so afraid she was going to lose you. I don't think she was rational at that point, Riley. She went into the den and got the gun, and then she decided to load it. She says she just wanted to scare him. Shoot out a window or something to let him know she was serious, but I think the point is, she was out of her mind right then with the fear of losing you. And when she went back into the living room, he was holding you on his lap."

I gasped. "I have no memory at all of this," I said.

She leaned forward to touch my knee with her fingertips. "I'm glad you don't," she said. "When Jade saw you on his lap and remembered the things he'd done to her when she was little, she snapped. She grabbed you and tossed you—that's the word she used when she told me what happened—she said she *tossed* you aside and then she shot the hell out of him."

I lifted my hands to my face, steepled together like I was praying. "So it wasn't an accident after all." My voice was a whisper. I felt numb with shock and sorrow. "And she still didn't tell anyone what he'd done to her?"

"She was afraid it would look like the motive," she said. "Her real motive, though, was protecting you."

For the first time, I could understand why Lisa had felt she had to run away. If the truth came out during the trial—that he'd abused her, that he'd raped her— well, she may have gained some sympathy from the jurors, but they would have known she'd had plenty of reason to kill him. She'd never be able to prove the shooting was accidental . . . because it wasn't.

"You hit your head on the coffee table when she pulled you off his lap," she said.

I touched my forehead and the small divot that had been with me all my life. When I lowered my hand, Celia rested her fingertips on my knee again. "I'm sorry to have to tell you all of this," she said. "I really am. But you needed to know. I couldn't let you think she'd ever willingly cast you aside."

I nodded. "Thank you for telling me," I whispered.

"Jade refuses to cancel New Bern," Celia said, resting her hands in her lap. "She'll take whatever Danny and his friend dish out. Even if it ruins her. And you know it will. She's being really brave, but she's going to be locked up for the rest of her life, and I'm so scared for her."

I pressed my fingers to my eyes and they came away wet. "I'll talk to Danny again," I said, hoping he hadn't already spoken to Harry. "But I don't think he'll bend."

She picked up my phone from the floor. "I'm putting my number in your contacts," she said, tapping the screen. "Call me after you talk to him, all right?"

"He's *driven*, Celia," I said. "All he cares about is hurting Lisa the way he thinks she hurt him. He's looking for justice."

She stood up. "I won't stop hoping." She leaned over, surprising me with a kiss on the top of my head. "And besides," she said, straightening up again, "justice comes in many forms."

56.

I didn't even consider going to bed after Celia left, although it was four in the morning. My body was exhausted, but my mind reeled. That image of Lisa pulling me off Steven Davis's lap and blowing him away in a fit of fury was never going to leave me.

I tried calling Danny, unsurprised when he didn't answer. I grabbed my duffel bag and locked my apartment door before heading down to the deserted garage. My phone rang as I got in my car. Jeannie again. I would call her from the road. Right now, I was anxious to get back to New Bern. I'd drive straight to Danny's trailer and wake him up. I had to tell him what I'd learned. I'd beg him not to talk to Harry . . . if he hadn't already.

The night was pitch-black and I had the road nearly to myself. I started to call Jeannie twice, but each time tears filled my eyes and I knew my voice would shut down on me, and I stopped the call before it could go through. I was nearly to Goldsboro by the time I thought I could talk without crying.

She sounded frantic when she answered the phone. "Are you all right?" Her voice surrounded me in the car. "I've been so worried. I had no idea what—"

"I'm alive," I said. "That's about the best I can tell you."

"What happened?" she asked.

My tears started again and I couldn't speak.

"Oh, honey," she said. "Tell me. Talk to me."

"Steven Davis was my father," I said.

She was silent and the dark air of my car filled with my sobs. I could hardly see the road in front of me.

"No," Jeannie said finally. "I don't believe it. I don't *want* to believe it!"

I told her everything Celia had said, my words nearly unintelligible. Jeannie had to ask me half a dozen times to repeat myself. By the time I'd choked out the story, her voice was thick as well.

"If only Lisa had told your parents what was going on!" she said. "They could have done something to help her."

"I know."

"She was such a gentle girl," Jeannie added. "I could never even picture her *holding* a gun, much less shooting one. Now it all makes sense. She would have done anything to protect you."

"And I was horrible to her, Jeannie!" I said. "I got so upset when I was talking to her."

"Did you tell her to stay away from New Bern?" Jeannie asked.

"She's coming anyway," I said. "I have to talk to Danny. I have to try to—"

A deer suddenly darted into the road in front of me, nothing more than a flash of tawny fur in my headlights. Reflexively, I yanked the wheel to the right as I let out a scream. My car went airborne, the steering wheel useless, the tires off the road, and I catapulted like a rocket, upside down, into the black night.

57.

Jade

Jade and Celia were quiet in the sterile breakfast room of the hotel in the morning. Across the table from them, Shane and Travis talked about the set list for that night's concert as they wolfed down their eggs and bacon, seemingly oblivious to the strain between the two women. Jade knew that Celia was upset with her, and who wouldn't be? She was upset with herself, but for different reasons. She wanted to see Riley again. She wanted to take a cab over to her apartment right that second, but fear held her back. The way Riley had left her the night before had been so decisive, as though she was washing her hands of Jade forever. If only she could have more time with her. She wanted to build the connection with Riley they'd never been able to have. The yearning was so all-consuming that it nearly overshadowed her fears about tonight's concert in New Bern. Had Danny already told his cop friend? Would she be led away in handcuffs once again? Her heart sped up at the thought of her hands bound together as they'd been so long ago. She didn't think she could take it. Twenty-three years ago, she'd been facing years in prison. That would seem like a walk in the park in comparison to what she'd be facing now. Not only had she killed someone, but she'd jumped bail and assumed a false identity and . . . oh, who knew what all the charges would be? At least Daddy wasn't alive to be charged as well. That would only have doubled her distress.

All she knew was that she would confess to everything. Every charge against her—she'd accept it without argument. There would be no trial. She was never going to let Riley learn that she'd had an abusive son of a bitch for a father.

She stared down at her plate with its untouched scrambled eggs and slice of bacon, and a small pathetic sound—a *whimper*—escaped from her throat.

"What's the matter?" Travis looked across the table at her, his fork in his hand. Travis was sweet. The caretaker of the rest of them, and the peacemaker, always. He hated any sort of conflict. But she couldn't say anything to put him at ease this morning. She could only stare at her plate.

Celia put her arm around Jade's shoulders. "It's all right," she said softly in her ear. "We'll work this out somehow."

"What are you talking about?" Shane asked. "What's going on? What do you need to work out?"

"No big deal," Celia said. "She'll be okay."

She wanted to tell the guys right now, over breakfast. They'd be caught completely off guard tonight and that seemed unfair, but Celia said they needed to "just sit with it" for a while. Jade didn't know what that meant, but she also didn't have the strength to argue with her about it. Celia had been gone a long time the night before and she was quiet when she returned, not wanting to talk. Jade hated the uneasiness between them. This could very well be their last few hours of freedom together, and they were destined to have a sour, miserable day leading up to . . . what? Would the police come for her before the concert or after? Would Riley be there or would she stay home, not wanting to watch the disaster she and Danny had set in motion?

"You really look like shit," Shane said to her.

"Shane," Celia chided. "That's not helpful."

Jade pushed her chair away from the table. "I'm going up to the room," she said, but she didn't stand up.

"You should lie down for a while," Travis said. "We don't have to be out of here till eleven."

She nodded, but couldn't seem to get to her feet. Her body felt rubbery, her bones like jelly. At eleven o'clock, all four of them would pile into the van they'd rented for this leg of their tour. She dreaded the two- or three-hour drive to New Bern, with Shane and Travis wondering what was wrong with her, and Celia's anger mounting. She would pretend to sleep.

Celia's cell phone rang. The ringtone was one of their original songs that was so perky and upbeat it made Jade cringe. Celia looked at the caller ID, then raised the phone to her ear.

"Hello?" she said, then, "Yes, I'm Celia."

Celia listened for a few seconds and Jade sensed a new tension in her as she got to her feet and walked away from their table. She watched her walk toward the windows, talking into the phone, but she couldn't hear a word from where she sat. For a moment, she wondered if Celia could be talking to Riley . . . but Riley couldn't possibly have her number.

Travis glanced over his shoulder toward Celia, then looked back at Jade. "Are you two all right or what?" he asked.

She looked at him. His face was boyish despite the

blond stubble of beard he always wore. She thought of a dozen responses, but none came out of her mouth. She watched Celia. She was still talking on the phone, but now she walked out the door of the breakfast room toward the hotel lobby. Where was she going? If Jade could have made herself stand up, she would have followed her.

"What's going on, Jade?" Shane asked.

She couldn't look at him. "Tell you later," she said.

Celia reappeared in the breakfast room. She was off the phone now, and her worried expression made Jade finally get to her feet.

"What is it?" she asked.

Celia clutched her forearm, probably harder than she meant to. "Okay," she said to the three of them, and her false-sounding calmness told Jade that something was terribly wrong. "Here's what we need to do." Celia looked down at the men, each of them with a coffee cup in his hand and confusion in his face. "Jade and I have to leave right away," she said. "I just called for a car."

A car? Jade frowned at her.

"You guys follow later," Celia said to them. "We'll all meet up at the hotel in New Bern, okay?"

"What the hell are you talking about?" Shane set down his cup. Jade wondered the same thing, but kept her mouth shut. She would find out soon enough. *An attorney,* she thought. Somehow, when Celia was out walking last night, she'd managed to reach a lawyer and they were going to see him or her. She didn't know if that was good news or bad.

"There's something we have to do and we'll explain it all later, but right now Jade and I need to pack." Celia tugged her arm. "Come on," she said.

"Hey!" Shane called after them as they walked toward the lobby. "I think you at least owe us an explanation." He was so loud, other diners turned to stare.

Celia ignored him, and Jade waited until they were in the elevator before she finally spoke. "What's going on?" she asked. "Who was on the phone?"

"A woman named Jeannie Lyons," Celia said.

"Jeannie!" she said. "Why would she be calling you? How could she have your number?"

The elevator doors opened and Celia took her arm again, walking her down the hallway toward their room, ignoring her question. It took Celia three tries to fit the key card into the lock and Jade's nerves were about to give out. She impatiently pushed the door open when the green light finally flashed.

"Tell me!" she said once they were inside.

"Listen to me," Celia said with forced calm. "Riley's been in an accident. She—"

"Oh, no!" Jade froze, her body unable to move a muscle. "Tell me she's okay," she pleaded. "*Please*. Where is she?"

"She's unconscious and she's in a hospital."

"Oh, God. Here? Can I go to her? How badly is she hurt?"

"Not here. A town called Goldsboro. Jeannie is there with her. It happened when she was driving back to New Bern last night . . . or I guess really early this morning. She was talking to Jeannie on the phone when it happened, and the hospital called her because her number was the last one dialed on Riley's phone."

"But how would Jeannie know to call you?"

Celia raked her hands through her hair and sat down on the edge of one of the chairs. "I can't help it if you're pissed at me," she said. "I know you will be, but I don't care. I had to do it."

"Do what?" She was scaring her.

"I went to see Riley last night."

"You . . . *where*? How did you find her?"

"I got her address off your phone."

She remembered hearing Celia rummaging around the living room of their suite last night before she left.

"Please tell me you didn't tell her."

Celia looked at her squarely. "I told her everything," she said.

Jade let out her breath, nearly doubling over as though Celia had hit her in the gut. She sat down on the corner of the bed.

"How could you *hurt* her like that?" she shouted. In a single blow, Celia had destroyed the protective wall she'd worked so hard to build around her daughter. "I spent my whole life preventing her from ever finding out. How could you do that to her? How could you do that to *me*?"

"I had to, Jade!"

Jade shook her head in disbelief. "I thought you were the one person I could trust with the truth," she said.

"I couldn't sit back and watch her destroy you. Destroy our family. I thought if I talked to her, if I—"

"Oh, my God." Jade interrupted her. "She must have felt so . . ." She could think of no word to describe the anguish Riley must have endured. "No wonder she had an accident. She had to be so upset."

"She *was* upset at first, but she was calmer when I left her." Celia twisted her wedding band on her finger. "Honestly. I thought she was all right or I wouldn't have—"

"What did she say when you told her?"

Celia bent over, her elbows on her knees, her head in

her hands, and she stayed that way for so long that Jade had to ask her again.

"Celia!" she said. "What did she say?"

"What you'd expect." Celia raised her face to Jade's. "She was horrified to learn everything you went through with Steven. And horrified to realize that he was her father."

"And horrified to know that killing him was no accident," Jade added angrily.

"She knows you did it because you were afraid for her," Celia said gently. "And before I left, she said she'd talk to your brother again. That's why she was going back to New Bern. Jeannie said—"

"So Jeannie knows, too?"

Celia nodded.

She'd never felt this sort of anger at Celia before. "If Riley's not all right, Celia, I'll never forgive you," she said.

"I didn't expect her to try to drive back in the middle of the night." Celia's voice broke. "I'm sorry," she said, "but I had to do it. I *had* to."

They packed in silence, and only when they got into the black Lincoln waiting for them in the parking lot did she speak to Celia again. "I want to talk to Jeannie," she said.

Celia nodded silently as she pulled her phone from her backpack. Jade copied Jeannie's number onto her own phone. It took her a couple of tries to get it right, the tips of her fingers suddenly big and clumsy.

Jeannie answered on the first ring. "Hello?"

Even after so many years, Jade recognized her voice and her heart swelled with love and gratitude. "Jeannie?" It felt strange to use her first name. She never had.

"Lisa? Oh, honey. Where are you?"

"Is Riley all right?" she asked.

"She's in and out of consciousness," Jeannie said. "We're just waiting to see, right now. She has a concussion and a couple of broken fingers, but they say she was extremely lucky. They had to cut her out of her car."

"Oh, God," she said, picturing the scene. "That's all that's wrong with her, though?"

Jeannie hesitated. "Physically, yes," she said.

"Oh, Jeannie." She squeezed the phone in her hand. "She called you after she spoke to Celia last night?"

"Yes. She called from the car and she was . . . well, I think she was in shock, really. So am I. Lisa, I can't believe it. Part of me wants to yell and scream at you for not telling the truth, and the other part completely understands. I only wish you'd told us what Steven was doing to you. We would have stopped it long before he was ever able to—"

"But then Riley never would have been born," Jade said. "I can't even bear to think about that."

"Oh, honey." Jeannie's voice was thick. "You know, she was afraid when she went to see you that you'd turn her away."

"Never!"

"I know that, but she felt like you'd abandoned her. When I saw that pendant around your neck in every picture of your band, though, I knew you hadn't. Not really."

"I didn't want her to know the truth, Jeannie," she said. "Ever. I didn't want *anyone* to know."

Celia rested her hand on Jade's knee. On the other end of the line, Jeannie was so quiet, Jade worried she'd lost the call. But then she spoke again.

"There's one more person who knows now," Jeannie said.

"Who?"

"Your brother."

"He knows the truth?" Next to her, she sensed the tension in Celia's body.

"He's here at the hospital. We drove from New Bern together. And yes, I told him. Lisa, he had to know."

"Has he talked to the police yet?" she asked.

Jeannie hesitated. "No, but I think he still . . . I don't know what he's planning to do. He's a hard person to read."

"Celia and I are on our way there," she said, looking out the car window as they passed a sixteen-wheeler. "I'm worried he'll have them arrest me at the hospital." She heard the tremor in her voice. "I want to have some time with Riley, Jeannie. Will he at least give that to me?"

"I'll talk to him," she said. "I'll do my best."

They hung up, and when Celia slipped her hand quietly into Jade's, Jade leaned her head against Celia's shoulder. She needed the support right now. All the pieces of her life that she'd spent years cobbling together were finally about to break apart.

58.

Riley

Through my closed eyelids, I was aware of a soft yellow glow, and even though I wasn't much of a believer, I thought, *Am I in heaven?* It wasn't the worst thought imaginable and I kept my eyes shut for a long time, even as I recognized Jeannie's voice coming from somewhere to my left.

"Riley?" she asked. "Are you awake?"

I remembered sailing through space in my car. The deer I hoped I'd missed. The horrible crunching, cracking sound of metal buckling around me. I remembered—or maybe dreamed?—the ambulance ride to an emergency room, strapped down so I couldn't move and not caring at all what happened to me. It had felt good to not care. To turn over control to other people. I'd floated along with whatever they did to me, slipping in and out of consciousness. I remembered the agonizingly bright lights in the emergency room. The exquisite pain in my head. Jeannie had been at my side. And Danny? Had he been there, too?

Now I opened my eyes partway, squinting against the light.

Jeannie sat on a chair next to my bed. She leaned

forward, holding my hand to her lips, and she smiled when I looked toward her. "There you are," she said tenderly. "There are those beautiful brown eyes. Are you feeling a little better now?"

I looked down at my swollen left hand and the splints on my index and middle fingers. My head throbbed. "I'm a mess," I said hoarsely.

She let go of my uninjured right hand to reach for the plastic tumbler on the nearby tray table.

"Water," she said, holding the straw to my lips.

I sipped. The water was lukewarm but felt soothing in my throat.

"Am I still in the ER?" I asked as she placed the tumbler back on the table.

"No, you're in a room. There's another bed in here, but at least for now, it's empty and you have the room to yourself."

I tried to turn my head to look at the other bed, but a searing pain on the top of my scalp told me that wasn't a good idea. Instead, I wiggled my toes. Stretched my legs. Took a deep breath. I needed to assess the damage I'd done to myself.

"I'm okay?" I'd meant it to come out as a statement, but it turned into a question.

"You're going to be fine," Jeannie said. "You broke two fingers and got a bump on your head. That's all."

I touched the bandage on the back of my head. "Stitches?" I asked. I couldn't remember. They'd either knocked me out or I'd been unconscious.

"Ten," she said. "You were unbelievably lucky, Riley. Your car, not so much."

I knew I'd wrecked my car. I knew it the moment the tires left the road. "Am I in New Bern?" I asked.

"No, Goldsboro. That's the closest town to where the accident happened, so they brought you here."

I remembered the flash of tawny fur in my headlights. "I hope I didn't hit the deer," I said.

"Ah, so that was what caused it. That's what they guessed."

I figured *they* meant the EMTs or whoever the first responders had been who found me. Although my aborted drive to New Bern was still a hazy memory, the conversation I'd had with Celia in my apartment was coming back to me more clearly by the second. I shut my eyes again. If only *that* had been a dream.

"Do you need to sleep some more?" Jeannie asked. "They said they'll wake you up every thirty minutes or so, but you can doze if you want."

I shook my head, grimacing at the pain. "Is Danny here?" I asked.

She nodded.

"I was on my way to talk to him," I said. "I have to tell him what Celia—"

"He knows," Jeannie said. "We drove here together from New Bern, and I told him."

"What did he say?"

"Not much." She gave a little shrug. I knew Danny perplexed her. "He was quiet," she said. "I don't know him very well, so I couldn't really tell what he was thinking. I do know he's worried about you, though. He's out in the waiting area right now. Are you up to seeing him?"

I started to nod, then caught myself. I wouldn't move my head any more than was absolutely necessary. "Yes," I said.

"And honey," she said, taking my hand again, squeezing it a little. "I called Celia to tell her about the accident."

"Celia? How did you . . ."

"Her number was in your phone. She and Lisa are on their way."

"They are?" My voice sounded like a child's. I felt an unexpected jolt of pure joy. In spite of the fact that Lisa was on a collision course with Danny, I wanted her here. I wanted her with me.

Jeannie started to get up, but I grabbed her wrist. "Call her Jade, Jeannie," I said. "We need to call her Jade."

I was alone in the room for a short time. I was able to reach the tumbler of water on my own and use the remote to raise the back of the bed until I was nearly sitting up, but every movement hurt. The hair around the bandage on the top of my head felt stiff—with blood, I guessed. I had the feeling I looked even worse than I felt.

The heavy door to the room opened and Danny walked toward me, shaking his head. "I'm so mad at you," he said, but I could tell he was more relieved than angry. He wouldn't talk to me that way if he thought I was going to die.

"I had to go see her," I said.

He stood at the side of my bed, his hands in his jeans pockets. "You had to go *warn* her, you mean."

"Yes."

"You didn't do a very good job of it," he said. "They haven't canceled the concert. At least not yet, and it's only a few hours away."

"Have you talked to Harry?" I held my breath.

"You asked me to wait, and I waited. I planned to see him this morning, but I haven't had the chance, since my little sister had an accident." His smile was small, but it reached his eyes and I felt his love. "I still plan to see him as soon as I get back to New Bern, though," he added.

I was sure he'd fantasized about tonight, watching Harry approach Lisa, either before or after—or, God forbid, *during*—the concert. Finally, after all these years, he'd see her get the punishment he thought she deserved.

"Danny . . ." I said, "I know Jeannie told you about . . ." My voice suddenly shut down and I couldn't finish the sentence.

"Yes, I know it all." He took his hands from his pockets and wrapped them around the safety rail of my bed, and I wondered if he was thinking about the fact that he wasn't my brother after all. "At least, I know the parts Lisa wants us to know," he said, "but—"

"She didn't *want* us to know any of it," I said quickly. "It was Celia who told me everything."

"And we know whose side Celia is on," he said bluntly.

I frowned. "Are you saying you don't believe her?" I asked. "What part of the story are you questioning?"

"It doesn't matter if I buy it or not," he said, his smile completely gone now. "The fact that the guy was a bastard isn't the issue. He was still a human being and she slaughtered him."

That was the undeniable truth. Maybe if it had been someone else's mother at risk here, I would have been among the first to say she should stand trial and serve her time. But this was *my* mother at the center of the storm. I couldn't let that happen.

"Please don't take her away from me, Danny," I pleaded.

He let go of the rail and walked over to the window. He looked outside for a moment, then turned to face me, his arms folded across his chest. "She never should have jumped bail," he said. "She should have stayed and—"

"Blame her jumping bail on Daddy, if you have to blame someone," I interrupted him. "She felt desperate, and she was so young."

The door opened with the slightest of squeaks, and a young, blond-haired nurse came into the room and walked over to my bed. Danny waited silently while she took my blood pressure, shined a flashlight in my eyes, and asked me if I knew where I was.

"You're doing awesome," she said when she'd finished. Then she nodded toward the door. "Your friend Jade is waiting out there to see you," she said. "Are you up for a little more company?"

I glanced at Danny. His face was like stone.

"Yes," I said. "Please let her come in."

59.

Jade

She shivered as she walked down the hall toward Riley's room, and not only because the air-conditioning in the hospital was set too low. Jeannie had said she'd be welcome in the room . . . by Riley at least. Jeannie hadn't been so sure about Danny, though, and he was the one who held her future in his hands. She felt like she was walking toward the executioner.

Jeannie had greeted her and Celia when they'd arrived at the hospital a short time earlier. If her life hadn't been in the midst of chaos, Jade would have been thrilled to see her. As it was, she'd felt close to tears when Jeannie hugged her. That hug told her that, at least in Jeannie's eyes, she was forgiven for everything she'd put her family through. For every lie she'd told.

Riley's nurse, a petite, perpetually smiling blond woman, had asked Jade if she was one of Riley's relatives.

"Jade's a family friend," Jeannie had answered for her. "Their families go way back."

Back as far as you can go, Jade thought now as she knocked lightly on the door. Pushing it open, she was relieved to see Riley nearly sitting upright in the bed.

Riley was pale and bruised, her smile uncertain, and Jade felt a rush of gratitude at seeing her alive and alert. At the other side of the room, Danny stood silhouetted in front of the windows. With the light behind him, Jade couldn't make out his features at all and felt instantly at a disadvantage. It was impossible, though, to miss the edgy tension that crackled in the room.

"Hi." She smiled at Riley as she walked toward the bed, trying to pretend this was a simple hospital visit rather than a reunion between three hurt, brittle, and wired-up people. "How are you feeling?" she asked.

"I'm all right," Riley reassured her.

Jade bent over to kiss her daughter's cheek. "I'm so relieved," she said. "I was terrified when I heard." She tore herself away from Riley and walked across the room, her body stiff with fear as she held out her hand to her brother. She'd never felt less sure of what to say in her life. There were no words to make up for the years apart.

"Danny," she said. He'd stepped away from the back-light of the window and she could see him now. He was so handsome, but the look in his eyes was ice-cold. He kept his hands buried in his pockets and Jade lowered hers to her side. "I'm sorry," she said. "For everything."

"Fine," he said, but she knew that nothing was fine. Nothing would ever be fine between them. Her father had told her that Danny was *troubled,* but now she saw for herself that *troubled* was too mild a word. Danny was a damaged soul. Those cold eyes and tight lips. What had happened to the happy, effervescent child he'd been? How much of the damage was her fault? She reached toward him again, this time to touch his arm, but he pulled away from her quickly.

"You killed our family, do you know that?" he asked.

"Danny," Riley said from the bed. Her voice was a plea.

Danny's hostile tone made Jade take a step backward until she stood next to the footboard of the second bed. She didn't know how to answer his question. She worried that he was right. "I never wanted that," she said. "I couldn't . . . foresee all the things that happened." She clutched the rim of the footboard. "When I think back to that time, it's just a gigantic mess in my memory." That was the truth. "I didn't know what to do," she said, "and when Daddy suggested—"

"Right," Danny said. "It was all his fault."

"I'm not saying that," she said. "I'm not trying to defend myself. I know I made terrible mistakes and I've had to live with what I did. The guilt. The separation from my fam—"

"And Riley and I had to live with two shitty parents in a house full of lies."

"Danny," Riley said, "I never felt that way."

"Well, lucky you!" he barked at her, and Jade had a sudden urge to slap him. *Don't talk to my daughter that way!* she wanted to shout, but she hardly had that right. She saw Riley shut her eyes and sink back into her pillow. *This is too much for her*, Jade thought, but she didn't know how to end it. They shouldn't be having this conversation here. Or now. Yet there was no time to have it later. Later, she could be locked up.

"Why the hell didn't you just tell the truth?" Danny asked. "Accept the consequences? You really fucked all of us over."

"I was afraid," she said. "I was frantic. I'd killed someone . . ." The day it happened, tucked so deep inside her memory, rushed back to her, and her voice cracked. "I relived that moment over and over and over and—I'm sorry, Danny," she said again. "Everything was such a mess, and I didn't know how to make it right. I was so screwed up."

"But did you ever, in the last twenty years when you were no longer 'so screwed up,' think of Riley and me and the disaster you left us? Did you ever, in the last twenty fucking years, think of coming back? Making things right?"

"Of *course* I thought about it," she said, "but Daddy would have paid if I ever told the truth."

"He paid anyway!" Danny pulled his hands from his pockets, raising them in the air to make his point. "We *all* paid. And it's about time you paid, too."

"Stop it!" Riley shouted. "I can't handle this any longer! Please stop it!"

It was as though they'd forgotten Riley was in the room, and they both turned to look at her. Her pale cheeks were tear streaked, and she'd pressed her hands, one of them bandaged, over her ears. Jade moved quickly to her side.

"Sweetheart." She sank onto the chair next to the bed, rubbing Riley's shoulder through the thin hospital gown. "I'm so sorry. I know this is the last thing you need right now."

"You two are tearing me apart." Riley looked from Jade to Danny. "I love you both," she said. "I *need* you both."

Jade looked across the room at her brother. His expression was hard to read, and she thought he was avoiding her eyes. She turned back to her daughter. "I'm here for you, Riley." Bracing herself, she waited for Danny to mock her words. How did she plan to be here for Riley when she was in prison? How had she been here for her over the last twenty-plus years? But Danny said nothing. Instead, he walked to the other side of Riley's bed, and for the first time, Jade noticed his limp. She remembered the note from their father: *Danny was seriously injured in a grenade attack.* She remembered being unable to sleep for days, and losing her baby as she grieved and worried and blamed herself for everything that had ever gone wrong in her family. She wanted to reach across Riley's bed to pull her wounded brother into an embrace, but that embrace would never be welcome. Her love for him would always be one-sided.

Danny bent low, pressing his lips to Riley's temple, and he stayed that way for a moment, whispering something to her that Jade couldn't hear.

He stood up, and without even a glance in her direction, headed for the door.

Jade panicked. She couldn't leave things with him like this, or the next person through that door would be carrying handcuffs. "Please forgive me, Danny," she begged, rising from her chair. *"Please."*

He turned to look at her, and again she was struck by the pain in his face. "Someday this is all going to catch up to you, Lisa," he said, making her catch her breath at the sound of her old name. "But it won't be because of me."

60.

Riley

The door shut behind Danny with a whisper, and Lisa looked at me. Her eyes were red rimmed and bloodshot, her face nearly white. She wrapped a hand around the safety rail, the way Danny had wrapped his a short time earlier.

"What does he mean?" she asked. "It won't be because of him?"

"He whispered that he won't tell Harry. The cop."

I saw the tension dissolve from Lisa's body and she lowered her head to her hands. For a moment she didn't speak. When she lifted her head again, she wore a sad smile. "I feel like I've been given a last-minute reprieve," she said.

"You have."

"I feel terrible for him," she said. "He's so hurt."

"I know." I nodded. "His life's been hard." I gingerly touched the spiky stiff hair on the top of my head again. I'd need to ask for more painkillers soon, but the last thing I wanted right now was to dull my thinking. "Is Celia with you?" I asked.

"She's giving us some time alone," she said. "I'm sorry she went to see you last night. I never wanted that."

"I'm glad she did," I said. "I needed to know the truth. Even though I'm not sure how I'm ever going to live with knowing he was my father . . . and everything that happened."

"Oh, Riley, I know!" She reached for my hand. She smoothed her fingers over my skin, and her touch felt like no other I'd ever known. I felt the love in it. "I was never an angry sort of person," she said, "but when I walked into our living room and saw you on Steven's lap, I lost it. I absolutely lost it." She squeezed my hand. "I still feel sick when I think about it. Everything about that day . . . everything that happened afterward . . . it's my nightmare."

I didn't want to hear any more about that day. I didn't think I'd ever want to know more details—the details my nearly two-year-old self had managed to block out. They could stay that way forever, as far as I was concerned.

"I'm sorry for getting so upset with you last night," I said. "Talking to Celia really helped. I don't know what I would have done if she hadn't come over."

"I'll thank her for that," she said, "if I ever get over being mad at her about it."

"Don't be," I said.

Lisa looked toward the window, a small, mystified smile on her face. "I can't believe this is happening," she said, turning her head toward me again. "I'm actually sitting here with my baby girl."

"I can't believe it, either," I said. "I wondered how different our lives would have been if you hadn't left. If we'd actually grown up in the same family, we probably would have moved in such different circles because of our ages. We never would have really gotten to know each other."

"Oh, I would have known you," she said. "I would have had my eye on you every waking minute."

A wave of pain ran through my head and it must have shown on my face. She tightened her hand on mine. "Want me to get the nurse?" she asked.

"Not yet," I said. "I don't want the interruption."

She nodded.

"I talked to a friend of yours," I said. "Grady."

She sat back in the chair, mouth open. "What? How could you have known about—"

"It's a long story," I said, not wanting to talk about Sondra Davis's blog at that moment. "I'll save it for another time. But he said to say hi if I ever found you."

She shook her head, a look of wonder on her face. "Flash from the past," she said.

"It must have been terrifying, leaving home like that without knowing a soul in San Diego. Starting your whole life over, knowing you'd never be able to see your family again."

Her eyes filled and I knew that I'd tapped a bottomless well of sorrow in her. She let go of my hand to press both of hers to her face. I touched her knee through her jeans, sorry I'd upset her. *This is my mother,* I thought. I couldn't believe she was right here. That I was actually touching her.

When she lowered her hands, her cheeks were red. "It was so hard," she said, "but I thought it was my only choice. I knew they'd tear apart every word I said in a trial. I was afraid I'd end up in prison forever."

"Daddy didn't know the truth?" I asked. "That Steven Davis was my . . ." I let the sentence trail away.

"God, no," she said. "I didn't want him to ever look at you differently. He thought it was Matty, like everyone else, even though I swore up and down it wasn't.

And Matty never had a clue what was going on. He was my best friend, but even he didn't know I'd had a baby."

I was relieved now that I hadn't been able to reach Matthew Harrison. I would have involved another person in the deception. He might have been the one to knock over the house of cards Lisa had so carefully constructed.

She gripped my hand again, more firmly this time. "Please, Riley," she said. "Don't think about it. Don't dwell on it. Your father was a nameless, faceless boy I met in Italy. It's better that way."

I nodded slowly. For now, at least, she was right. "I want to be in your life, Jade," I said, determined to use her chosen name.

She wore the first full, genuine smile I'd seen on her. "It makes me unbelievably happy to hear you say that," she said.

"Is it possible, though?" I asked. "Is there some way we can make it work?"

She looked thoughtful. "I think it's up to you," she said, after a minute. Then she tilted her head. "Are you willing to live a lie?"

I thought about the question, knowing it was an invitation to step into her world and leave mine behind. It was a world of deceit, but it had my mother in it, and that was all that mattered.

I nodded. "Whatever it takes," I said. And I meant it.

EPILOGUE

Riley

"Check this out," Jade says, opening the door to a walk-in closet. "It's bigger than the one I share with Celia."

"I don't have enough clothes to fill it," I say, peering inside, "but I absolutely love this apartment." What I love best about the apartment is that it's less than a mile from Jade and Celia's house, where I've been staying for the last two weeks. While I feel welcome there and I adore Alex and Zoe, their house is snug with a fifth person squeezed inside it. I will live nearby, as close as I can get. Now that I have a mother, I'm not letting her go.

I moved to Seattle at the end of the school year, and I've already had a couple of job interviews. I did well during those interviews, I think, although I hadn't been able to tell the interviewers one of the main reasons I think I've become a better counselor. During the year I've known Jade, my counseling has definitely changed. I no longer see the depressed sister from my imagination in every student I work with. I no longer lie awake at night, worrying about the kids who are struggling, afraid they might harm themselves. My emotional detachment from them makes me better able to help them.

I see their needs more clearly, unclouded by the haunting specter of the suicidal sister who never truly existed.

I know that the lies in our family hurt all of us, especially Danny and myself. Growing up in a household where something is terribly wrong, you feel the weight of that mysterious something even though it's unspoken. It eats at you. Confuses you. It leaves you wondering if your view of the world will ever make sense.

And the thing is, I'm now willingly perpetuating a new lie, though it has its roots in the truth. To Jade's and Celia's friends and family, I am Riley MacPherson, the daughter Jade relinquished for adoption when she was fifteen. My adoptive parents died and I searched for her, finally tracking her down. She's welcomed me, as have Celia and her family. We all feel fortunate to be together.

"This explains a whole lot about our Jade," Celia's mother, Ginger, said to me when I visited Jade over the Christmas holiday. She was showing me how to make ribbon candy, and she and I had thoroughly messed up the Linds' kitchen. "I've always felt there was something missing in her," she said. "Some sad place inside her. You've come along and filled it up."

How does Danny fit into the lives we're creating? He's not ready to come to Seattle, and I'm not sure he ever will be. He has no desire to leave his trailer in the forest. He's promised to respond to my e-mails and I'll go back East at least once a year to make sure he's doing okay. Jade and I don't talk about it, but I worry that Danny may always pose a threat to her. It's his love for me that will keep her safe and I'll nurture that love with everything I have in me.

In the apartment we're exploring, I open the door to a second bedroom and see that the window looks out on a park. I picture myself setting up my father's rolltop desk in that room. It's the one thing of his I've kept for myself. The desk will take up half the room, but it will be worth it.

When we're together, Jade and I don't talk about the past. We don't talk about the mistakes or the deception. We talk about what Alex and Zoe are doing in school. About the music Jade and Celia are writing. About my job search. We take the kids to the park and museums, and we laugh a lot. I see the joy in Jade's face and I'm happy to know that I'm part of the reason for it.

I walk from the bedroom that will become my office into the hall bathroom. The entire wall above the vanity is mirrored. My bangs are askew and I can see the small scar on my forehead. The bright lighting makes it stand out more vividly than I've seen it in years, and I lean forward for a good look.

Jade is in the doorway, and she watches me.

"Everybody has a scar, Riley," she says, touching my shoulder. "Maybe they've fought a terrible illness. Or they've lost a child, or been hurt by someone they love. Or maybe they've been unlucky enough to lose their family. But then again"—she smiles at me in the mirror, then reaches out to smooth my bangs over the mark—"maybe they've been lucky enough to find one."

ACKNOWLEDGMENTS

Whoever says editors don't edit these days does not have my editor! I'm enormously grateful to Jen Enderlin for her brilliant vision, her patience, and especially her passion. I thank you, Jen, and above all, Danny thanks you.

I don't know what I'd do without my amazing agent, Susan Ginsburg. Susan's a hands-on agent who treats my books as though they're her own babies, and she reads them with insight and wisdom. Thanks for your skill as an agent and for your warm friendship.

I'm also grateful to my agent in the United Kingdom, Angharad Kowal, as well as to all the folks at Pan Macmillan in the UK, especially publishing director Wayne Brookes (whose e-mail always makes me smile), Louise Buckley, and Becky Plunkett.

I'm in awe of the entire energetic and talented team at St. Martin's Press, including but definitely not limited to president Sally Richardson; my publicist, Katie Bassel; and the extraordinarily creative Olga Grlic, who I thank for this evocative cover. I'm so happy to be working with all of you.

Thank you to the two violinists who helped me bring Lisa and her music to life. Both Christina Wohlford and

Fiona Warren Hirsh graciously answered my endless questions.

Thank you to my brother, mystery writer Robert Lopresti, who unwittingly inspired this story with one of his own.

For their various contributions, thank you Kathy Williamson, Frank and Janine Palombo, Reggie McAllister, Donna Cohen, Patty and Ed Toth, and Tania and Philip Little.

As always, thank you John Pagliuca, for listening to me fret about people who exist only in my head. I don't know what I'd do without your patience and your out-of-the box brainstorming skills.

For the sort of support only other authors can provide, I thank the six other members of the Weymouth Seven: Mary Kay Andrews, Brynn Bonner, Margaret Maron, Katy Munger, Sarah Shaber, and Alexandra Sokoloff. I'm especially grateful to Brynn and Katy for reading a very early draft and not chortling with derision. Your comments were invaluable!

I'm indebted to my readers who join me on my Facebook page every day. I've turned to them for the names of characters and places, and they never fail to respond with enthusiasm and inventiveness. I owe Slick Alley, the Spoon and Stars Café, Verniece (my favorite!), and various and sundry other names to those creative readers. I'm grateful to them for getting into the writing spirit with me.

And to those of you who read and reread my books, thank you. Your e-mail and comments warm my heart and you are always on my mind as I write. I have the coolest job, getting to share my made-up worlds with people who care as deeply about them as I do. I look forward to sharing them with you for a long time to come.

Read on for an excerpt from the next book by
Diane Chamberlain

THE DREAM DAUGHTER

Available in October 2018 in hardcover from
St. Martin's Press

PROLOGUE

Chapel Hill, North Carolina

Carly

No one wanted to work with the man in the wheelchair.

"There's something strange about that guy," one of my fellow students warned me in the hall outside the PT ward. "If they try to assign you to him, say no."

I remembered his warning now as I stood in the doorway between my supervisor, Betty Connor, and the ward's director, Dr. Davies. Still, I was curious about the man who sat in the wheelchair by the window, a cast on his lower leg and foot. Crutches rested against the windowsill next to his chair. He was about a decade older than me, maybe thirty or so. He looked unkempt, his blond hair on the short side but tousled. His facial features were slack, his eyes half closed. I could see the shadow of stubble on his cheeks and chin.

"How about that patient for Caroline?" Betty asked Dr. Davies. "Broken ankle, is it?"

Dr. Davies nodded, light from the ward's windows bouncing off his glasses. "Displaced fracture of the lateral malleolus," he said, "followed by surgery."

Betty turned to me. "You haven't yet worked with a broken ankle, have you?" she asked, and I shook my head with some reluctance. I'd been a student intern in a private rehabilitation practice for the last two months, but this was my first time in the hospital ward and although I was excited to get started, my fellow student's warning echoed in my ears. *Say no.* Still, the man in the wheelchair looked harmless enough.

"I think it would be a good case for her," Betty said to Dr. Davies.

"I think not," he said. He was holding several manila folders in his hands and he tapped the top one with his knuckles. "The fellow's name is Hunter Poole," he said. "He sustained the broken ankle falling off a three story building, or so he says, but we think he intentionally jumped. He's alive only because some shrubbery broke his fall. He refuses to learn to use crutches. None of our PTs have been able to get him to talk, much less engage in any therapy. He's suffering from depression and—"

"Oh, I think I heard about him," Betty cut him off. "Didn't he say he was working on the roof and just slipped?"

"That's what he told the driver of the ambulance, but his explanation doesn't hold water." Dr. Davies tucked his free hand into his pants pocket. "It was nine o'clock at night, for starters, and there were no tools found on the roof or the ground, so you tell me if that sounds like he was working. We have him on suicide watch. Next stop for him is the psychiatric unit if he doesn't begin to come around today or tomorrow."

"Well, you're right that he wouldn't be a good patient for Caroline," Betty said. She looked at me. "You need to focus on building your skills right now," she said. "You don't need an unmotivated, clinically depressed suicide risk, for heaven's sake."

I nodded in agreement.

"There isn't anything you can do for someone who

won't cooperate," Dr. Davies said. "I plan to try to work with him myself today. Everyone else has given up."

The man raised his head slowly in our direction as if he knew we were talking about him and I felt his gaze lock onto mine. His eyes widened, brows lifting. Suddenly, he broke into a smile.

"You!" he nearly shouted, his voice so loud that several people in the room turned to look at me. "You're a physical therapist, right?" he asked. "I want to work with *you*." It was unnerving, the intensity of his gaze. The sudden disarming smile.

Oh, God, I thought. Just what I needed. A crazy man for a patient.

"Me?" I said, almost to myself.

"You!" he said again. Then in a calmer voice, "Yes, please. Please work with me."

"I didn't know he could smile," Dr. Davies said to us under his breath. He turned to me. "Are you willing?"

"Is he . . . dangerous?" I asked in a whisper. I was hungry to work, but not to be murdered in the middle of the PT ward.

"If you're asking if he's psychotic," Dr. Davies said, "we don't think so, though he's so closed off that it's been hard to evaluate him. You're the first person he's responded to. It would be wonderful if you could get him to open up."

"I don't know about this." Betty looked concerned.

"Hey," the man called across the room, his voice softer now. "I didn't mean to scare you." He actually chuckled. "I'll do whatever you say," he added. "I promise."

He sounded harmless enough. "I'll do it," I told Dr. Davies, holding my hand out for the man's chart.

Dr. Davies handed me the top folder. "Main priority

is getting him to use the crutches." He spoke quietly. "See what you can do."

"All right," I said, and I crossed the room toward the possibly suicidal man who was now grinning at me in a way that made me nervous. What did this guy want with me?

The large room had an almost electric atmosphere, very different from the somber private facility. WKIX played rock and roll over the loudspeaker and the Temptations sang 'My Girl' as I dragged a chair from against the wall and placed it in front of the man so I could sit facing him.

"I'm Caroline Grant," I said, lowering myself to the chair. "Most people call me Carly."

He nodded, almost as if my name was no surprise to him.

"Hunter Poole," he said.

"Why me?" I asked.

"You remind me of someone," he said. "Someone I knew briefly. Dark eyes and the exact same hair—long and blond, only she wore hers parted in the middle. It was nothing . . . romantic or intimate." He flashed that grin again. "Nothing like that, so don't freak out. Just . . . it feels good to see you." His accent was Northern. New Jersey or New York, maybe.

"I remind you of someone you liked, then."

"Yes." He chuckled again for no reason I could discern.

He *is* crazy, I thought. And hopefully harmless.

"I didn't know you . . . I mean *her* . . . well," he said, "but I—"

"You realize I'm not this person," I said firmly.

"Yes, of course. I'm not crazy. Though I know everyone here thinks I am."

"No, they don't." I tried to sound reassuring. "They just think you're depressed."

He nodded. "I am that," he said, suddenly very solemn.

"They have medication that might make you feel better," I said. "It could help lift your spirits."

"They have nothing that can help me," he said, "and the side effects of the medications are too great now."

This man was not suicidal. I doubted a suicidal person would care a lick about side effects.

"What do you mean, the side effects are too great *now*?"

He shook his head. "I don't know. Don't pay attention to anything I say."

"Is it your injury that has you so down?"

He looked away from me and I thought I saw the shine of tears in his eyes. "I lost someone I loved," he said.

"Oh," I sat back, surprised that he'd confided in me. "I'm sorry," I said. "Is that why you tried to . . . to hurt yourself?"

He turned to face me again. "Can we not talk about it?" he asked, dry-eyed, and I wondered if I'd imagined the tears. "It's too hard to explain the truth and I don't want to lie to you."

"Of course," I said, touched by that explanation.

"Tell me about you instead." He looked at my left hand. "You're engaged?"

I looked down at my ring. Joe promised me a bigger diamond someday, but I wanted this one. I wanted this one forever. We would both be graduating next month, me from the University of North Carolina, Joe from NC State, and our wedding would be the week after. Joe would graduate as a second lieutenant in the Army after being in ROTC for four years and we'd move to Ft. Eustis, Virginia where he'd be stationed. I hoped I could get a PT job up there.

"Yes," I said, "I'm marrying a wonderful man. But we're not talking about me. We need to talk about *you* and how we're going to get you well again."

He sighed. "I'm not very motivated," he admitted.

"I understand," I said. "But you said you like me. Or at least, you like the person I remind you of, right?"

He nodded. "Very much," he said.

"Then help me succeed," I said conspiratorially, wondering if that was a terrible ploy. I would never tell Betty Connor I'd used it. "You're my first patient in this rehabilitation ward," I said. "Make me look good to my supervisor, all right?"

He laughed and I saw a sparkle in his blue eyes. A few heads turned in our direction. *The new girl got the suicidal guy to laugh.*

"All right," he said. "It's a deal."

We got down to business then. I demonstrated how to use the crutches without putting weight on his ankle, and after a rough start, he got the hang of it. He was co-operative, doing everything I guided him to do as he practiced hobbling around the room. I led him to the ward entrance and taught him how to open and close the door while balancing on the crutches and his good right foot. Despite the discomfort he had to be experiencing, he remained cooperative, almost upbeat, and I felt excited, not only because I was doing what I'd trained to do but because I seemed to have magically brought him out of his shell when no one else had been able to. He actually sang along with a few songs on the radio as he practiced with the crutches, causing some of the people in the room to look at him, chuckling, and I smiled to myself as I walked next to him. He was probably a real charmer when he wasn't grieving.

He was getting winded from our circuits around the room, and I decided to let him have a rest before I taught him how to negotiate the stairs. As I helped him back to his wheelchair, the voice of the WKIX DJ, Tommy Walker, came over the loudspeaker.

"And here it is, as promised!" Tommy said. "The brand new Beatles' song! It's called 'Ticket to Ride'. Be sure to tell everybody where you heard it first. WKIX!" Tommy Walker had been talking about the new song all week as if WKIX was the only station in the world allowed to play it. My sister Patti was going crazy with anticipation and it seemed unfair that I would be able to hear the song before my Beatlemaniac sister. Patti was teaching her fourth grade class right now and had to keep a professional air about her, which I couldn't begin to picture, because even though Patti was twenty-four to my twenty-one, she was like a teenager when it came to the Beatles. She planned to drive directly from her school to the record store on Henderson Street to snap up the new forty-five.

To my surprise, Hunter began singing along with the song as I took the crutches from him, leaning them against the windowsill again. He knew every word as well as the melody, which simply wasn't possible, since 'Ticket to Ride' hadn't yet been played in the United States. He seemed oblivious to the fact that I was staring at him in awe as I took my seat across from him again.

"How can you possibly know this song?" I asked. "It's brand new, just released today. No one's even *heard* it yet, much less had the time to memorize it."

He looked briefly perplexed. "I have no idea," he said.

"Obviously I heard it somewhere. Maybe a different radio station?"

"That's impossible."

"Apparently not." He shrugged with a sheepish smile.

"You're not . . . you're not connected to the Beatles somehow, are you?"

He laughed. "I wish," he said.

"Have you been to England recently?" The song had probably been released in England first.

"Nope," he said.

"Are you a Beatles fan?"

"Isn't everyone?" he said, then added. "I own every one of their albums."

"But 'Ticket to Ride'?" I queried. "I just don't get it."

He shrugged again. "It's a great song and I guess I must have somehow heard it and subliminally picked up the lyrics."

"That's crazy," I said, but I was thinking about Patti. Wait until I told her about this guy!

I glanced toward the side of the room where there was a five-step staircase. "We should get back to work," I said, knowing my job was not to sit and talk about the Beatles with him. "Are you ready to try the stairs?"

"If you insist," he said. Turning around in the wheel-chair, he took the crutches from the windowsill and struggled to stand again.

"Have you been to a Beatles concert?" I asked as I walked next to him toward the stairs.

"I wish," he said again. "But alas, no."

"My sister took the train to New York to see them twice last year," I said. "August and September. And she's already saving up to go to their August concert this year."

"She should see them as much as she can," he said.

"You never know when they're going to just pack it in and say 'enough is enough'."

"She would die if they did that," I said.

I taught him how to ascend and descend the stairs using the crutches, but my mind wasn't on the task. Patti had recently stopped seeing a guy who was a boring stick-in-the-mud and now she was at loose ends. Would it be unethical to introduce her to Hunter? I didn't know. I tried to picture how I would broach the subject with her: "Hey Patti, I met this strange, really depressed guy with a broken ankle at work today and I think you'd make the perfect couple!" Joe would tell me not to meddle. *Patti will find her own guy when she's good and ready*, he'd say.

When we were done working together and Hunter was settled back in his wheelchair, he caught my hand. Looking into my eyes, his expression turned suddenly serious. "Thank you," he said. "This was a treat. You have no idea."

I was taken aback by the intensity in his eyes, the sincerity in his voice.

"You know," I said. "I'd really like you to meet my sister."

PART ONE

APRIL, 1970

1

National Institutes of Health
Bethesda, Maryland

As we sat in the stark basement waiting room in of one of the NIH buildings, I thought Patti was more anxious than I was. She cuddled one-year-old John Paul on her lap, her left foot jiggling. Sitting next to her, Hunter held her hand. The three of us had the room to ourselves and we seemed to have run out of small talk after the long drive from the Outer Banks.

A dark-haired woman appeared in the doorway. The name on her white coat read *S. Barron, RN.* "Caroline Sears?" she asked. She had a northern accent, I thought, much stronger than Hunters'. She'd barely pronounced the 'r' in my last name.

"Yes," I said, getting to my feet. "Can my sister and brother-in-law come in with me?"

"That would be fine," she said. "Follow me."

I walked ahead of Hunter and Patti as we followed the woman down a long bare corridor to a room nearly at the end. Inside the small room were six chairs arranged in a semi circle. The only other furnishings in the room were tall metal file cabinets that filled one wall.

"Have a seat," the woman said.

I sat next to Patti and John Paul, who was beginning to fuss. He'd been an angel during the long car trip, but I think now we were all getting stir crazy. Hunter took him from Patti's arms and began bouncing him gently on his knee.

"I'm Susan Barron," the woman said, settling into her own seat, a clipboard and file folder on her lap. Her gaze was on me. "I'm one of the designers of the study, though I won't be the person doing your examination," she said. "My role is to gather some information from you before-hand, all right?"

I nodded.

She opened the file on her lap and glanced at it. "You're twenty-six years old, correct?"

"Yes."

"We received the records from your obstetrician, a Dr. Michaels. You're about twenty-four or five weeks along at this point?"

"That's right."

"And your pregnancy has been uneventful until his last exam?"

"Well, last two exams," I said, shifting on the seat. I was tired of sitting. My legs ached. "Dr. Michaels told me a month ago that my baby's heartbeat was irregular, but he didn't think much of it. This last examination, though, he was more concerned."

"Right," she said. "And I don't know how much information you were given, but our study is actually full. We have all the patients we need at this time. However, your brother-in-law here"—she looked at Hunter—"is a puller of strings, I see, and he was able to get you in."

I smiled past Patti at Hunter. He sat there looking modest, but she was right. Hunter was a puller of strings. A fixer. I didn't think there was anything that he couldn't make right. Except for Joe. He couldn't fix what happened to Joe.

"So you need to understand that this study is in its very preliminary stage as we explore the uses and limitations of fetal ultrasound," she continued. "The technology is years away from being used on any regular basis and the images we can obtain are somewhat primitive. However, our previous study, as well as several recent studies elsewhere, have had very good results in terms of accuracy, but not in every case, and I need to be sure you understand the limitations."

I nodded.

"In other words," Susan continued, "let's say the ultrasound results appear to tell us there's something wrong with your baby's heart. They might be inaccurate. Conversely, they might give us the impression everything is fine when it isn't. I want to be sure you—"

"I understand," I said. Hunter had told me all of this. He'd explained the mechanism of the ultrasound. It was simply incredible to me that it was possible to visualize my baby while he—I felt certain it was a he, a miniature Joe—was still inside of me. Hunter said it wouldn't hurt at all. He'd read about it. He was the founder of his own company, Poole Technology Consulting, in Research Triangle Park—RTP—where he worked with enormous computers. He had access to all sorts of technology and material the rest of us couldn't imagine.

"Your baby's father," Susan said, looking at the folder on her lap. "Your brother-in-law told us he died recently?"

"Vietnam," I said. "Right after Thanksgiving."

"How difficult for you," she said. "I'm sorry."

"He didn't even know about the baby," I said. "He was only in Vietnam a couple of weeks."

Patti rested a hand on my arm. It wasn't a gesture of comfort so much as a warning for me to stop talking. Once I started talking about Joe, it was hard for me to stop. It was so unfair. Joe had been a structural engineer and we thought he'd be safe, away from the action. "I didn't discover I was pregnant until a few weeks after I learned he was killed," I said.

"Will you have help with your baby?" Susan asked, attempting to change the subject. I didn't hear her at first, my mind back on the day the captain and second lieutenant showed up on my doorstep with the news that literally brought me to my knees.

"Yes," Patti said when I didn't answer.

"Yes," Hunter agreed. "She has us."

"I live with them now," I said, coming back to the present.

"And where is that?"

"Nags Head," I said. "The Outer Banks." After Joe died, I'd moved from Fort Bragg into our old family beach cottage where Patti and Hunter had been living for the past couple of years. I'd expected the move to be temporary—just a few weeks off from my physical therapist job in a Raleigh hospital. But when I found out I was pregnant and my obstetrician told me I needed to take it easy, Patti and Hunter said I could stay with them as long as I wanted. Hunter worked three days a week at his consulting firm in Raleigh and I knew Patti welcomed my company when he was gone.

"Where are the Outer Banks?" Susan asked, confirming her northern accent. Anyone south of the Mason-Dixon line knew where the Outer Banks were.

"North Carolina," Hunter said before I could answer. "About six hours from here."

"You drove a long way for this," she said.

"I have to find out if my baby's okay." I folded my hands tightly together in my lap.

Susan nodded. "Fine," she said. She asked a few more questions about my general health, which had always been good. "And how about the rest of your family?" she asked. "Do you have other siblings?"

"Just Patti."

"And Patti?" Susan asked. "You're a biological sibling, right? Any health problems?"

"None," she said.

Susan turned back to me. "How about your parents? How is their health?"

"They died in a car accident when I was fourteen," I said.

"My." Susan made a note in the folder on her lap, then looked up at me. "You've had some difficult times."

I nodded, hoping this pregnancy wasn't going to be one of them.

"How about your late husband's parents? How is their health?"

"Good," I said, thinking of my robust, tennis-playing mother- and father-in-law. They lived in Texas and they didn't know about the baby. I'd been about to write them when Dr. Michaels told me something might be wrong. I was afraid to tell anyone after that until I knew the baby was okay.

Susan asked a few more questions about my pregnancy, which had been unremarkable, although the truth was, I'd been so distressed over losing Joe that I couldn't have separated my symptoms of grief from symptoms of pregnancy. I worried my grief had somehow led to a problem for my baby.

Finally, Susan got to her feet. "Follow me," she said to me. "You two?" She looked at Patti and Hunter. "You can wait here. Tight quarters in there."

I followed her into a tiny room with an examining table, a wooden chair, two rolling stools and a large machine bearing what looked like a small television screen. Susan handed me a pale blue gown.

"You can leave your bra on, but everything else off," she said. "Put this on so it opens in the front. I'll be back in a moment."

I undressed as she'd instructed and climbed onto the examining table. My baby gave a little tumble inside me. He'd been an acrobat for weeks now. I rested a reassuring hand on my belly. *There's nothing wrong with you*, I spoke silently to him. *You are perfect.*

Susan returned to the room followed by a very young-looking man with thick black hair, horn-rimmed glasses and a white coat.

"Good afternoon," he said to me. "I'm Dr. Halloway, one of the researchers, and I'll be doing your ultrasound. Nurse Barron explained everything to you?"

"I think so," I said. Susan had produced a stiff white sheet to spread across my lap and motioned for me to lie down.

"Is your husband here?" he asked.

"My husband died," I said as I lay back on the cool leather of the table. I wished he had checked my file first so I didn't have to say those terrible words again. I ran my fingers over the rings on my left hand.

"Oh," he said. "Sorry to hear that."

"Her sister and brother-in-law are her support," Susan said. "The brother-in-law—that Hunter Poole you spoke with?—they're both here."

"Ah, yes." He nodded. "You have an advocate in that

pushy brother-in-law of yours, don't you?" he said drily. I couldn't tell if he found Hunter's pushiness annoying or admirable.

"Yes," I said, grateful for Hunter and his advocacy.

Susan lowered the sheet to expose my big belly. It was hard to believe I had months yet to go in this pregnancy. Dr. Halloway squirted some cold gelatinous substance onto my stomach, then began running a smooth wand across my skin. Susan lowered the light in the room and indecipherable images appeared on the small screen. Both she and the doctor leaned forward, squinting at the picture. Their heads blocked my view, although every once in a while I had a clear view of the fuzzy moving image on the screen. If my baby was in that picture, I certainly couldn't see him. How the two of them could make head nor tail of what they were looking at was beyond me.

For at least two minutes, neither of them said a word as Dr. Halloway moved the wand this way and that, pressing it into my skin. *What do you see?* I wanted to ask, but I lay there quietly. In the light from the screen, I could see Dr. Halloway's frown. He pointed to something on the screen, speaking to Susan in muttered words I couldn't decipher. She also pointed to something and muttered her own response. My heart pounded in my chest. In my throat.

"Can you tell anything?" I asked finally.

They didn't seem to hear me. Instead, they continued pointing and mumbling to one another.

After what seemed like a very long time, Dr. Halloway lifted the wand from my belly and Susan used a white towel to clean the jelly-like substance from my skin.

"What did you see?" I raised myself to my elbows.

"Why don't you get dressed and I'll speak with you and your family about our findings," Dr. Halloway said. I turned my head from him to Susan and back again, trying to get either of them to look at me, but they seemed to be avoiding eye contact with me.

"But what are they?" I asked, beginning to panic. "Your findings? What did you see?"

"Get dressed and we'll talk," he said, the lighter tone he'd had before the exam gone from his voice. "I've taken some pictures and I'll show you then."

Dr. Halloway met with us back in that small room with the semicircle of chairs. I didn't know what had become of Susan. I sat between Patti and Hunter this time, and John Paul was nearly asleep in Patti's lap. I introduced the doctor, who focused his attention on Hunter instead of me when he began to speak.

"I'm afraid there's a serious problem with the baby's heart," he said, handing a couple of fuzzy black and white snapshots to Hunter.

"What do you mean?" I asked trying to pull the doctor's attention back to me. I was the one carrying this baby.

Hunter passed the photographs to me and Patti leaned over to see them. "How can you possibly tell anything like that from these . . . weird pictures?" she asked.

"Well, in many cases, we can't be sure what we're seeing because our images are still somewhat challenging to decipher," Dr. Halloway said. "But in your case"—he finally looked at me directly—"what we can make out is quite clear. I believe even you will be able to see the problem." He pulled his chair closer to us, scraping it on the floor. He pointed to a gray smudge on the image. "Your baby has severe stenosis of the aortic valve," he said, "which, I'm afraid, will inevitably lead to Hypoplastic Left Heart Syndrome."

"How serious is it?" Patti asked, as I searched the blotchy black and white images for my baby. I couldn't find him. I couldn't understand how anyone, no matter how brilliant and well trained, could find my baby in those pictures, much less my baby's heart.

"I'm afraid it's fatal," Dr. Halloway said.

My head jerked up. "*No*," I said. I felt Hunter's hand come to rest on my shoulder.

"Fatal!" Patti said.

"How can you possibly tell that from these pictures?" I argued, suddenly disliking this man intensely. "This is just a study. The nurse . . . whatever her names is . . . Susan . . . she said the machine—the ultrasound—could give false information. That it's just experimental and—"

"That's often true," Dr. Halloway said calmly. He was looking at Hunter again instead of me and I wanted to kick him to remind him this was *my* baby we were talking about. "But in this case," he continued, "we were able to get a remarkably clear picture of your baby's heart and I'm certain of my diagnosis. I'm very sorry."

For a long moment, none of us spoke. "When he's born, can he have surgery?" I asked finally.

"Your baby is a girl," he said, "and no. I'm afraid there's nothing that can be done for her."

A girl! That was nearly as much of a shock to me as the news about his . . . her . . . heart, and I instantly felt even more protective of my baby. I looked down at those stupid pictures on my lap. I wished we'd never come. I hated this doctor. Hated Susan Barron. At that moment, I was close to hating Hunter for insisting I come here.

"I can't lose this baby," I said. "He's—*she's*—all I have left of my husband."

"You have us, honey," Patti said, though her voice, thick with tears, told me she knew perfectly well that she and Hunter were not enough to erase this loss.

"What are our options?" Hunter said, as if we were all pregnant.

"You can try carrying the baby to term," Dr. Halloway said. "She'll most likely survive the rest of the pregnancy, but with HLHS, she will die very shortly after birth. Or you can abort," he added. "You live in North Carolina. You can have a legal abortion there due to a fetal anomaly, though it's not an easy procedure at twenty-four—"

"No," I said. "I can't do that. What if you're wrong?"

"I understand it's hard to accept," he said. "But you're holding the evidence in your hand." He nodded toward the fuzzy picture of my baby. I held the picture by the edges and I averted my gaze from it. If I didn't look at it, I could pretend I still had Joe's healthy baby inside of me. If I didn't look, I could pretend this last hour had never happened.

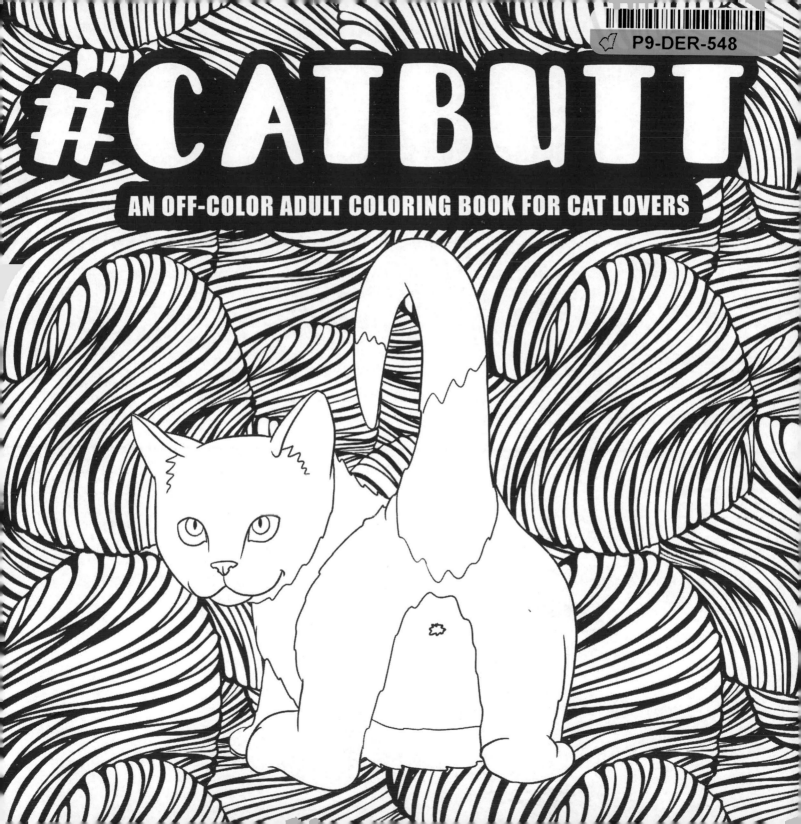

FREE DOWNLOAD!

WHAT the FORK?!

Shirt HAPPENS

Fork YEAH!

YOUR CODE: CAT4396

www.honeybadgercoloring.com/cat

BE SURE TO FOLLOW US
ON SOCIAL MEDIA FOR THE
LATEST GIVEAWAYS & DISCOUNTS

📷 @honeybadgercoloring

f Honey Badger Coloring

🐦 @badgercoloring

ADD YOURSELF TO OUR MONTHLY
NEWSLETTER FOR FREE DIGITAL
DOWNLOADS AND DISCOUNT CODES

www.honeybadgercoloring.com/newsletter

CHECK OUT OUR OTHER BOOKS!

www.honeybadgercoloring.com

CHECK OUT OUR OTHER BOOKS!

www.honeybadgercoloring.com

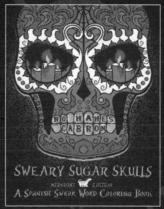

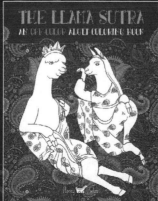

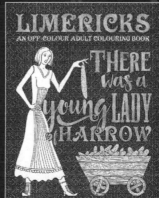

CHECK OUT OUR OTHER BOOKS!

www.honeybadgercoloring.com

Made in the USA
Columbia, SC
17 December 2018